Praise for White Horse Regression

White Horse Regressions is a mystery novel in the richest sense; it is delicately layered and immediately engrossing. As in Steve Lindahl's previous novel *Motherless Soul*, the setting and details are vivid, yet the story is built with deliberation. The characters, familiar and no, are both believable and dynamic. What sets this book apart from other mysteries I've read is the depth of the personal journey as well as the collective. It begins as what seems a simple murder that opens and expands, creating a cosmic enigma that remains on the reader's mind long after the story is complete, perhaps forever.
 –Jen Knox, author of *Musical Chairs* and *To Begin Again*

***

Across centuries and continents, through past lives regressions, intense relationships, and chilling evil, drawing on circuses, shadow puppets, and modern theater, *White Horse Regressions* is a powerful tale that keeps the reader riveted. Whether it is during the introduction of Buddhism into China, the stalking evil of Jack the Ripper, or modern murders and smuggling motivated by a terrifying search for power: the souls of Lindahl's characters are bound together until they can set themselves free. The key to their story is what they can recall from past lives. Can the protagonists remember? Can they learn how to ride the white horse of freedom?
 –Kenneth Weene, author of *Memoirs From the Asylum, Tales From the Dew Drop Inne*, and *Widow's Walk*

***

What begins as a murder mystery evolves into a hypnotic investigation that uncovers the centuries-old connections between a cast of characters fated to repeat the circumstances, intrigues and tragedies of their past lives. Through a series of sessions in which the participants regress to Victorian London and ancient China, stories within the story unfold, relationships are defined and rituals revealed, more questions raised than answered until a disturbing and seemingly unbreakable pattern emerges.

Mr. Lindahl's suspenseful novel moves backwards and forwards in a karmic dance that also twists and turns; a profound and poignant narrative about reincarnation as it relates to love and friendship, vulnerability and power, the myth of inevitability and the possibilities for better times to come.

–DM Denton, author of *A House Near Luccoli*, *A Friendship with Flowers*, and *The Snow White Gift*

***

The soul is eternal, and no more so than in Steve Lindahl's White Horse Regressions. It's the story of a group of individuals destined to share their lives with one another throughout time, be it in ancient China during the Han dynasty, in 19th century London during Jack the Ripper's reign of terror or in a small town rocked by murder in present-day Vermont.

It's been almost a year since Hannah Hersman's girlfriend was killed, and the police still have no leads, no suspects, and no one in custody. Undeterred and longing for closure, Hannah calls in Glen Wiley, a renowned hypnotist, as a last resort. Glen quickly discovers that in a past life Hannah was a prostitute in Victorian London named Rose and her girlfriend was Annie Chapman, a victim of Jack the Ripper. In fact, many of Hannah's friends and acquaintances were similarly connected to her, not just in then London but in multiple lives and multiple places throughout history. And, in all these incarnations, their existence is tied to a murderous plot that Hannah and Glen must uncover to ensure their future lives can avoid the pain and misery of losing their loved ones.

White Horse Regressions is a compelling supernatural thriller that drops you down the rabbit hole and spits you out into the filthy streets of a not-too-long-ago London, the palatial estates of a long-forgotten China and the seedy underbelly of small-town America. It's a gripping tale and an interesting read that held my interest long after I'd finished it.

–Patrick S. Lafferty, author of *Anno Domina, Thinking Out of the Box*, and *Miller Time*

***

Steve Lindahl brings us another in his series that deal with past life regressions. The search for the murderer of a popular actress results in a chain of events and deaths involving past lives of villains and victims from Victorian England to ancient China. The reader encounters a mix of relationships and complicated clues from regressions that threaten to pull the innocent into unknown dangers. White horses ride through history with mysterious consequences. Read at your own peril!

–Jean Rodenbough, author of *Tree, Bebe & Friends: Tails of Rescue*, and *Rachel's Children: Surviving the Second World War*

White Horse Regressions

Steve Lindahl

ALL THINGS
THAT MATTER
PRESS

White Horse Regressions

Copyright © 2014 by Steve Lindahl

All rights reserved. No part of this book may be reproduced or transmitted in any form or by any means without written permission of the author and publisher.

ISBN: 978-0-9894032-8-3

Library of Congress Control Number: 201433615

Cover design by All Things That Matter Press

Published in 2014 by All Things That Matter Press

For my family:
Toni, Nicole, and Erik

Acknowledgments

I would like to thank my family, to whom I have dedicated this novel. My wife Toni, my daughter Nicole, and my son Erik have spent countless hours reading my work, listening to my ideas, and encouraging me along the way. I am blessed to have them in my life.

I would also like to thank my publishers Deb and Phil Harris for the time they have spent on this project and for their belief in my work.

Thanks also to the members of my writing group, Joni Carter, Bob Shar, and Ray Morrison, for their wonderful suggestions, corrections, and inspiration and for sharing my love of writing fiction.

PROLOGUE

Stuart and Hannah sat in the audience of a small community theater in Springfield, Vermont, examining the set of *A Doll's House* while they waited for the performance to begin. Paige was cast as Nora.

"Isn't that picture odd?" Stuart whispered to Hannah, referring to the Asian-looking painting on the set. It did not belong to late-eighteen-hundreds Norway by any standard. "I'd like to have a closer look."

"If we stay after the show's over, there might be a chance we could go up on the stage. I'll ask Paige."

Stuart's wife, Jamie, was also an actress, and when rehearsal and performance schedules prevented Paige and Jamie from attending each other's shows, their significant others often went together. Jamie was currently in rehearsal for a production of *The Drowsy Chaperone,* so here they were.

The non-acting partners enjoyed their arrangement. Hannah had known Stuart and Jamie for years; before Paige, she'd been the tag-along friend, but had always felt welcome— more by Stuart than by Jamie.

The lights dimmed then slowly came up again. There was no curtain in this theater, so this was the signal that the performance was about to begin. Paige came out on stage, a dominant figure as always due to her red-orange hair. She set down the presents she was carrying and crossed to a Christmas tree on the far end of the stage. She started to add ornaments when Torvald Helmer, her character's husband, joined her on the set.

There was no doubt Paige was the star as she made Nora's transition from naïve to inured believable. Still Hannah could not stop thinking about the odd Asian painting, so out of place on the set.

When the play was over, while the cast was being congratulated by fans, Hannah asked her girlfriend if she and Stuart might look at the set up close. Paige took hold of Hannah's hand and led them both up onto the stage.

Hannah and Stuart went straight to the Asian painting, which was a watercolor depicting a scene that was, they thought, taking place in China. There were a number of people dressed in the types of robes associated with ancient times in that country who were watching what, at first glance, appeared to Hannah to be a film; a closer look revealed that behind the screen men were holding objects up to cast shadows It was a form of puppet theater.

"What is this?" Hannah asked Paige.

"It's been the talk of the cast. No one knows why it was included on the set, but you have to admit it's fascinating. I suppose it draws attention because it seems out of place, but I wouldn't want it taken away. There's something warm about it."

"Warm?" Stuart asked.

Paige shrugged. "Hard to say why. None of us saw it prior to tech week, so nobody was prepared. Some board member wanted it hung here. I heard he's a history buff. Anyway, he's got money so it's hard to say no. But enough about the set. Tell me what you thought of the show."

"I'm sorry," Hannah said, turning to Paige to hug her again. "You were fabulous. I can't say that enough."

"Were local models used for this?" Stuart asked, still focused on the painting. "Some of these people look familiar. This young girl in blue, for example, where'd they get her?"

Paige pulled away from Hannah, laughing a little and shaking her head. "I have no idea where or when that painting was done. I know what you mean, though. There's a man in it I thought might be someone I used to know. I think it's the way he's standing, with his shoulders hunched forward. I had a teacher who used to do that, but he wasn't Asian."

"Do you two want to go out for coffee?" Hannah offered.

Paige agreed, but Stuart begged off; he needed to pick up his daughter, Starr, from his parents.

***

Their happy mood turned gloomy as Paige was pulled for running a light almost as soon as they started to drive toward downtown Springfield.

"It's not fair," Paige said. "I swear someone's out to get me."

"It's just a ticket."

"No, it's more than that."

Hannah tried to convince Paige she was being paranoid, but later the words would seem prophetic.

***

The next night Paige's performance was as spectacular as it had been on opening night.

By the following weekend, the show was canceled. Paige was dead.

CHAPTER ONE

It had been ten months since her girlfriend was murdered; there was still no resolution. But the lack of progress wasn't what prompted Hannah Hersman to act. She wasn't worried about future victims. Nor was she concerned about retribution. The reason she had contacted a hypnotist and offered to pay for his help was that Paige's soul wouldn't leave her alone. Her dead lover came every night to haunt her dreams.

Hannah had read about Glen Wiley's ability to use events from past lives to solve crimes. His theory was that circumstances have a tendency to repeat when reincarnated souls return to similar situations, so if a similar crime had occurred in another time, there would, theoretically, be an abundance of additional clues to study. Her quick internet search revealed a good deal of ridicule concerning his ideas, but no one could argue with his history of success. And, she reminded herself, traditional methods were getting nowhere.

The murder had been gruesome and had made the national news. When Hannah called Mr. Wiley, he told her he'd already read about it online, but needed to be reminded about the details. She braced herself for what she had to do.

Hannah had known that she'd have to describe her lover's murder. She'd planned the words she would say, wrote them down, recited them dozens of times, to break their emotional hold over her.

"Paige was twenty-one and, according to the newspapers, an aspiring actress. Actually, she'd done quite well on the local stage. Her throat was sliced deep enough to cut her carotid artery. There was blood all over the motel room."

She tried to keep a soothing image in her mind as she shared the details. She thought of the constant flow of a gentle river. But while she was speaking, that turned to a river of blood and her voice cracked.

"All over the room?" he asked.

She thought she heard a quiver in his voice, as well, but that could have been her imagination. Hannah didn't want to tell Glen Wiley everything about her relationship with Paige. If he was a talented hypnotist, he would be able to find out things on his own. And that's what she was looking for: a professional who could reach into people's minds to discover their secrets. And if he was the real deal, she would do everything within her power to arrange for him to hypnotize Jamie Tilly. She'd love to know what was going on in *her* head.

She wondered what more to say. She'd shared that she was concerned about the lack of progress with the investigation. She'd used the term "girlfriend" when describing Paige, so their relationship was clear. She hadn't told him the specifics of the dreams she'd been experiencing since that horrific night, the dreams she thought might hold some clue, some explanation, some ... *something*, but she did describe the details of some of the most graphic ones, feeling that he had to know.

She spoke into the phone, still describing the murder scene. "One of the bedspreads was soaked with blood, as was a good portion of the carpet. Her blouse was torn open and a large X was cut into her chest. She was still wearing her jeans, socks, and sneakers. They said there were no signs she'd been sexually assaulted. I'm not sure I understand that. I mean, what other signs do they need?"

"They're saying she wasn't raped."

"This guy stuck his knife into her deep enough to kill, then kept doing it, long after she was dead. I think he enjoyed what he was doing. And I think there had to be other, more complicated, reasons behind this murder. And maybe, with your help, my dreams will tell us what those reasons were. But I do believe this crime was sexual, and, to me, that's rape even if Paige still had her pants on." Hannah was starting to cry. She hoped it didn't show in her voice.

"Fill me in on the rest of the details," Glen said.

Hannah continued, keeping her voice as even as possible. "Paige's body was discovered by Paul Trepanier," she said. "He's an antique furniture dealer who directed many of the plays Paige was in."

The details of the next part would be difficult to speak out loud. Hannah had prepared herself, but wasn't sure she could hold back her emotions. "They were about to have an afternoon meeting, assignation, whatever the hell you want to call it, at a motel in White River Junction."

Hannah felt guilty that her lover's betrayal at times hurt worse than her death.

"White River is a town about a half hour from Springfield. Paige made the arrangements. Paul told the newspapers it was the first time they had arranged to meet, even though they had known each other for years through their work in community theater. He said they had chosen a motel that was a distance away to avoid being seen. They didn't want anyone thinking Paige was trading sex for leading roles."

Hannah leaned back for a moment, sucked in a breath, and exhaled slowly. This was hard.

"Are you all right?"

"Yes. I just want to make sure I tell you everything the way it happened."

"I understand. She was your friend."

"Yes, she was."

Hannah got up from the couch and carried the phone into her bedroom. She stopped in front of the large mirror on her bureau and stared at her image. Her eyes were wet and puffy; her hair was disheveled. She was wearing a nightgown she had bought while shopping with Paige. It was two o'clock on a Sunday afternoon and she still hadn't changed out of the clothes she'd slept in.

She thought about the gown. Paige had bought one at the same time, black lace while Hannah's was pink cotton. At the time Paige smiled in a nervous way that seemed mischievous. She wouldn't say why she needed sexy lingerie instead of practical sleepwear; Hannah thought Paige was planning to look good for her. That was about a week before she was killed. It was now clear to Hannah that Paige had been preparing for her rendezvous with Paul.

"Paul was eating lunch at the McDonald's in Springfield when Paige called," Hannah continued, turning from the mirror to sit on her bed. "Half a dozen witnesses saw him there. He called 911 to report the murder thirty-nine minutes later. The police knew the exact time from the phone records. The timing was tight, but not impossible. Still, he's not considered a suspect. At least that's what they say in the papers. I don't know, but I can tell you he hasn't been in any of my dreams. And my dreams have been horrible."

"Given the nature of the murder," Glen told her, "I'm surprised everyone in your state isn't having trouble sleeping."

Hannah understood he was trying to exaggerate, but he had a point. There had been so much publicity. "It's peaceful up here," she said. "This type of tragedy is unusual. Everyone I know was talking about Paige's death for months, but they've moved on to other subjects. But *my* dreams won't stop."

"What are your dreams like?"

Hannah flopped back on her bed and stared at the ceiling. She'd known this would be hard, so she'd written down exactly what she wanted to say. "In one, I'm lying on a bed in a motel room, wearing a cotton gown." The same gown she had on at that moment, but she didn't tell him that.

"It's a different motel than the one where Paige was killed, but she's there beside me. She has all the wounds the newspapers described, but she's alive. She's leaning over me, stroking my hair, kissing my shoulder —and laughing. Her laughter is loud, but it doesn't sound fake. Then I hear applause. I turn to the side and see Jamie Tilly, sitting in a chair with a white horse standing next to her. There's a knife stuck in her chest, but it doesn't seem to bother her. She's watching us, smiling, and clapping as hard as she can. She's wearing a red dress, so it's hard to tell how much she's bleeding. The dress has a floor length skirt and a long sleeved top. She has on a bonnet that's tied in place with a ribbon. She looks as if she's come straight from a performance of a play set in nineteenth century

Europe, something like *Dracula*. She was in that show once, so it kind of makes sense. In that dream, and in the others, I always wake up before anyone speaks to me. If someone would say something, anything, maybe the dreams would make sense."

It felt to Hannah as if she'd said it all in one breath, although that would have been impossible. What she had not described was how she shook each time the dream was over and how her body was always so drenched with sweat that she'd have to change both her pajamas and her sheets.

She would tell all the dreams to Glen eventually, she knew. But first she wanted to come to terms with just this one.

The white horse confused her.

"Paige was an actress? Did they know each other, Paige and Jamie?" Glen asked

"Yes. They'd been in a number of plays together."

"This all sounds intriguing," he said. Then, after an awkward silence he added, "I'm coming up there."

CHAPTER TWO

It had been many years since Glen had been in Vermont; he was looking forward to going back. He liked the winding roads with their covered bridges, the historic homes—especially the Victorians—and the forested land on rolling hills. All of New England had recently become more interesting to him because his last case included two people who had spent nineteenth century childhoods in Maine. Glen loved the way they had described that region of the country. Hannah's need had been the perfect impetus for the trip.

Glen moved into a room in the Holiday Inn Express. While it was an acceptable accommodation, he didn't much like hotels. If it turned out he'd be staying more than a couple of weeks, he'd need to find another place to live.

***

Hannah knocked on Glen's door at precisely fifteen minutes to six, in keeping with their plan to meet for dinner. He didn't invite her in. Following her down to her Nissan Versa, he got in the passenger seat. Hannah was similar to how he'd pictured her while they were talking on the phone. She was a little overweight, but attractive, with light skin and long, copper-colored hair that he suspected was dyed. At five foot five, she was a couple of inches shorter than he, which he preferred, being less comfortable around taller women.

Hannah took Glen to an inexpensive restaurant where he ordered a burger with fries and she had a chicken sandwich.

"I can't say I know Jamie well," Hannah told him when he brought up the name. "I'm closer to her husband than I ever was to her, even though I met Jamie first. She does temp work to make some money without having the responsibility of a permanent job. She says she doesn't want anything to interfere with her acting. If you ask me, she's not half the actress Paige was. But she's pretty and talented, so who knows?

"I met her when she was assigned for a week to the Ford dealership where I work, to help with filing. She told me she and Stuart had been going through a rough period and she needed someone to talk to. I can be a good listener, so we got close. I learned pretty quickly that she and Stuart are always going through rough periods and it's Stuart, not Jamie, who needs the friend."

"But in your dream Jamie was the one with the knife in her chest, right?"

Hannah nodded.

CHAPTER THREE

At the auditions, Jamie could tell her only competition for the role of Miss Julie would be Frida Dellamo. Jamie was the right age for the part—early twenties—attractive and able to put on an aristocratic air without sounding overly theatrical. Frida was good, though too short and stocky for the role.

Jamie wanted to be certain Paul understood how important the role was for her, so she smoked a couple of cigarettes outside the studio and waited until all the other auditioners had left.

"That went well, don't you think?" she asked as Paul locked up. It was a chilly March night. He had on a white spring jacket and she was wearing a long coat that was as warm as a goose down blanket.

"I was pleased," Paul replied. "Things are starting out well."

"You could say *great*."

"We're a long way from great, but there is potential."

"Do you have a few minutes? I thought we might go over some ideas I have for the role, in case you decide to cast me."

Her suggestion was presumptuous, but Paul smiled. She was confident Frida wouldn't be coming back.

"Can we talk in my car?" He put his arm around her. "It's cold out here."

***

The first rehearsal was a read-through and some discussion of the play's significance in order to acquaint the actors with the script and get everyone thinking as a group about the message they were trying to communicate.

Jamie studied the other actors. Troy Allen was an attractive man, although not particularly striking, she decided. He had nice hair, thick and dark, and sideburns that he had let grow down to the level of his upper lip. He was about five foot nine, not short, but she would have preferred the role of Jean to be played by someone taller.

Allison Simpson, the third member of the cast, hadn't been in the business long. She had dark hair, darker than Jamie's but not as dark as Troy's. Her complexion was smooth, but she was not, in Jamie's opinion, very attractive because she was husky with a small double chin. She was glad Paul had chosen her. Allison would be easy to upstage.

Paul looked over his cast and told the actors to remember the importance that class and gender played during the nineteenth century. "At that time people were limited by birth more than they are today," he explained. "It must have been frustrating."

"Frustrating," Jamie repeated, with a touch of disbelief in her voice. "It's much more complicated than that, at least it is for Miss Julie. She says she wants to move among the lower class, but that isn't the entire story. She doesn't want to *stay* in their world. She wants to play there for a while then return without consequence. After her experiment with the 'little people', after her walk on the wild side, she wants to return to her normal life. Her problem comes after the game is over when she can't regain her stature. It's moving up that is the problem, not down."

"Neither move is easy," Paul told her. "Miss Julie can never be on Jean's level. That's why Kristin isn't jealous. She doesn't care what those two do because what happens between classes is meaningless. Today it's very different. We're all on the same playing field."

"There may not be titles and landed gentry, but there are still rich and poor," Jamie argued. "There are still people who rub the things they own in the faces of those of us who have to work for a living. To play this role all I need to do is to look around at the assholes of the world and the people who suffer because of them."

"Is that so?" Paul asked. "And where exactly would Miss Julie fit in our modern world?"

"She'd be the little rich girl with the snake tattoo hidden under her Neiman Marcus skirt. And if one day she let the wrong guy under that pricey skirt, you better believe she'd be planning her escape just like Miss Julie does. Times have not changed."

Jamie knew that directors were supposed to analyze the plays they work on and then translate that analysis into a unified message, but if Paul couldn't see Miss Julie in everyday people, in people alive today, then he was missing the human side. This was a great opportunity for her and she refused to lose it by allowing this production to sink into a stylized period piece. Miss Julie had to be able to feel and suffer or everything about this project would fail.

CHAPTER FOUR

"Dreams are complicated because they can be caused by many different things," Glen told Hannah when he was ready to regress her for the first time, on his second day in Springfield. He had spent his first full day exploring the town and thinking about Hannah's situation. He was happy to start the process with Hannah, but to achieve success she couldn't be the only person he would hypnotize. He hoped that if he could help her discover something interesting, she'd be able to convince her friends to give him a chance.

"Dreams are often a collection of old thoughts and memories arranged in strange, often random, ways," he continued. "There are people who say dreams can predict the future. I'm one of those people, but that's because I believe the future is often controlled by what's happened in the past.

Hannah lived on the top floor of a two-family house owned by the retired couple who lived on the first floor. Her apartment was fairly spacious with three bedrooms, a large kitchen, a living room, and a bathroom.

Glen decided to use the living room as the place for Hannah's first regression. She had a love seat, a wing back chair, and a couch that was too small to lie on without hanging over the edge. His decision meant putting her on the floor. Yet he still felt the living room was best. He'd found over the years that beds were bad for regressions. They had too many current memories associated with them, whether of sex or illness or sleepless nights, so that they inhibited the memories of past lives.

Glen took a green blanket from one of Hannah's loveseats and spread it on the carpeted floor. He instructed her to lie on it, which she did in an awkward fashion. She was dressed in a blue sweatshirt and sweatpants, having been instructed to wear clothing that was loose, comfortable, and as plain as possible to avoid anything that might distract her mind from possible memories of clothing of another era.

"For this session to work, you need to give yourself over to the process. The more doubt you allow during a regression, the harder it will be to succeed. The trick is to avoid fighting your skepticism. You should let it slip away, as if it were water in your hands. Put all your trust in me. Follow my words with your heart and you'll find your soul's memories."

Glen watched her for a moment. He concentrated on her breathing and tried to get his own rhythm to match hers.

He had asked her if she had a specific period of time she wanted to go back to. Her response was that all that mattered was justice for Paige. He decided that their best chance to find answers would be to focus on

Hannah's dream. He picked a specific detail: the bonnet Jamie had been wearing. It was black with a red ribbon while her dress had been red with black trim.

Before beginning, Glen asked Hannah to describe the bonnet to him one more time: a felt, flat-topped hat with a brim that was broad in front and narrow in back. The ribbon wrapped around and was tied in a bow on the right side with its ends hanging down about four or five inches.

Glen had a fairly good picture of it in his mind, but, more important, Hannah did as well.

"Stare at the ceiling," he told her. "Pick a spot to focus on then breathe deeply and relax. Think of the material the bonnet was made of. You said it was felt, so it had to be soft to the touch. Drift into it. Let go of what's around you and float back into the time of that hat."

Hannah squirmed as if she were finding it difficult to relax on the hard floor. Glen took a pillow from the couch. "Lift your head." He placed the pillow so she could be a little more comfortable. Hannah needed to relax entirely, although without slipping into sleep. It was always a tricky balance, especially the first time he regressed someone.

"Concentrate on the soft black color. Imagine yourself as a tiny being, floating in among the threads of that material. Let your mind drift. Become one with the felt."

For close to fifteen minutes, he softly coached her, watching the way her eyes twitched slightly under her closed lids. She seemed to fall asleep and he was concerned that the regression might not work. But he kept repeating over and over in his most gentle voice, "Drift back into the soft dark color. Drift back into the soft dark color."

**

Hannah knew she hadn't left the floor of her living room, but she felt as if she were traveling through a tunnel, spinning like a drill, a very slow drill. The tunnel was made of thick clouds the same black and red as Jamie's hat had been. The clouds were pulsing past her like the waves of a river. When she emerged, she was no longer in her home. She was in a different place and, more surprising, a different body. She knew she was Hannah, but she was also Rose, a young woman watching a man on a stage outside a circus tent. The man was a snake charmer. Two large boas were wrapped around his body.

**

The air was filled with the smell of canvas, straw, animals, and the people in attendance. Rose loved all those odors except the smell of people. She had spent too much time touching the bodies of unwashed men to feel anything except revulsion from the stench of body sweat. Fortunately, that day, the straw and canvas overpowered the scent from perspiration.

"Screw," a man yelled using slang Rose hated. Most days, she had to pretend she liked all the ways they called her a whore, had to laugh and act as if the men who used those terms were witty and fun. But today she wasn't working. She didn't turn. She wasn't certain he was shouting for her, but thought it likely. She was well known and pretty enough to be popular, especially among the sailors. She'd paid to see this and wasn't about to miss it. She moved deeper into the crowd, not looking back.

The show was the Bostick and Wombell Circus. Rose had skipped it the last time it had come through and had told Annie she wouldn't do that again. She loved the animal acts, especially the lion tamer, but would go to any show she could scrape up money to see. A few years earlier, before the laws had changed, she went to the freak shows regularly. She liked those, especially the Elephant Man. She'd paid to see that ugly creature more than once and could talk about him for hours.

Rose moved into the tent and took a seat in the bleachers. She had been to a circus before, of course, a number of times, actually, but the massive structures always impressed her. Those giant sheets of canvas suspended with ropes and large poles and raised up above her like a second sky had to weigh tons.

The admission price had left Rose without money. She'd have to prowl for a man to afford a place to sleep that night. But she wasn't worried. She could always stir up a few customers.

She took a bleacher seat a few sections away from the entrance. She wanted to sit alone, but the best she could do was a seat beside a woman who was with her husband and three children.

The act in the ring at that moment was a trained horse, a white horse. The elegant animal was trotting in a circle, guided by a man wearing a jacket with tails along with tight trousers, black boots, and a top hat. This animal trainer was directing the horse with a long whip. He never hit the animal, but each time he cracked the whip the horse would change pace or direction.

There was a woman standing on the horse's back, balancing on one foot, holding a parasol, and appearing as if she were floating on the powerful animal. The woman, who had the thin body of a dancer, was wearing a small yellow outfit with a short skirt and yellow tights, a color that had always meant joy and happiness to Rose.

About five minutes after the trained horse act was done, a woman in her early twenties came out wearing a red two piece outfit with long, tan frills and a black cape tied around her neck, accompanied by the same woman who had been standing on the horse. The trick rider lit a torch on a rack then handed the flaming stick to the woman in red, who tilted her head back and slipped the torch down her throat. It was amazing to watch. The fire had to be hot and painful, but she didn't flinch.

After the woman in red pulled the torch from her throat, the woman in yellow took it and held it up. While still holding the flame, she turned and stared directly at Rose. The look made Rose nervous. It wasn't as if this woman had picked a few people at random to connect with, as performers sometimes did. Rose was the only one with whom she made eye contact. If the woman had been a man … but Rose had never been with a woman. And *this* woman she would have remembered.

After Rose left the circus tent, Hannah—present but distant—wished she'd seek out the stables where the circus horses were kept to get a closer look at the white one and possibly the woman who had ridden it. But she couldn't control Rose's actions no matter how she tried. Although the things she did and the thoughts she considered all felt real, they were only memories. And Rose had decided to look for her friend, Annie Chapman.

Rose started walking toward the Old Bull tavern, where she thought Annie might be. The distance was long enough that she wished she could take the underground trains or the horse drawn trams, but she did not have any money. So she walked, keeping her eyes down to avoid stepping in puddles or horse manure.

Carriages wheeled by her at paces that weren't much faster than the speed she was walking. Their wheels were louder on the cobblestone roads than they were on the dirt ones, but Rose could easily accept the noise because of the way the stones kept mud to a minimum. She walked along both dirt and stone streets to get to her destination. The sun was setting when she arrived at the tavern.

Rose took a seat across from Annie, began to share drinks with her friend, and soon started to argue in a good-natured way. Annie told her what she had said to Eliza Cooper, a woman they had both known for years. Rose didn't like Eliza anymore than Annie did, but she didn't think it was a good idea to threaten the woman. Rose had pointed out that the real problem was that the man both Annie and Eliza considered their own, Edward Stanley, couldn't choose between them. *Couldn't or wouldn't*, Rose wondered.

Rose didn't tell Annie, but Stanley had flirted with her a few times as well. She didn't give in to him, though. She made him pay like all of her other men.

"I heard Madam Rentz's Female Minstrels is coming back to London next month. You'll go, won't you?" Rose asked Annie.

"Madam Rentz?"

"A minstrel show. I've heard they're fun."

"Oh, I'd like to see that when it comes," Annie said. "All ladies, you say? I wish I'd known when I was younger. I could've done it, right? I'm funny enough when I want to be. I could have painted my face and made the world laugh."

"Our bellies are full and we stay out of the workhouses most nights," Rose said. "We're doing all right,"

"Easy for you to say. You're the pretty one. For me the time ain't far off when the men won't no longer pay. What'll I do then? Where'll I go?"

"Tomorrow will take care of itself, Annie," Rose told her. She hated it when Annie went soft on her. "And if a drunken sailor'll pay for Eliza he'll pay for us—no matter how old we are. Have another gin."

"Didn't you spend all your brass?"

"I'm good for it," Rose bragged. "As soon as the street's dark I'll step out and be back with a shilling or two."

***

Glen pulled Hannah back. She'd gone into a life she'd spent as a London prostitute; that had to be a shock.

"That was astonishing," she said. She was still recovering. Her eyes were unfocused. She was breathing deeply as well as shaking slightly. He'd seen other clients react this way following a successful regression. A door to a part of herself Hannah had never known was now open.

"We can't control who we were in our past lives," he told her. "I'm sorry your first experience took you to a time when your soul was in someone who was down on her luck. It doesn't reflect on who you are now. We're all influenced by our past lives, but a person can be a saint in one life and a sinner in another. I see it all the time."

"You don't understand. The entire experience was breathtaking. It didn't provide any answers for my nightmares about Paige, but there was the white horse ... I *knew* that horse. It was the one I dreamed of. It was in the motel room with Paige, Jamie, and me."

CHAPTER FIVE

Glen had brought Hannah out of her trance sooner than he'd planned because he feared she would be displeased with the regression. Her reaction caused him to rethink his decision and he offered to put her under again.

"I can use specifics from the session you just experienced to send you back to the moment you left. I can't say if you'll learn anything about your dreams, but perhaps some more time as Rose might help."

"You think so?"

"I don't know. But I *do* know that if you go back you need to be prepared for what you might experience. The memories will be as strong as they were on the day Rose experienced them, just as they were during the previous regression. Remember, she needs money. Many of her customers will be drunk, possibly all of them. They'll probably be rough with her. They'll definitely smell bad and be filthy by today's standards. It won't be easy and it won't be fun."

"Do it," Hannah said, as she lay back on the blanket.

***

Rose and Annie were wearing similar dresses, with long sleeved tops and long skirts, the same dresses they'd worn for most of that week. Annie's dress was brown while Rose's was navy, but they were both dark enough for the women to walk relatively unnoticed through the streets of London. They wanted to attract customers, but they didn't want any trouble from the constables. Although *The Contagious Disease Act* had been repealed a couple of years earlier, there was still fear among all women walking the night.

"There should be Johns aplenty tonight," Annie said, huffing a bit as she struggled to keep pace with Rose. "There are two new ships in port and the air is as warm as my bloody ass. Did you notice there's almost no smell?"

"You mean the air or your ass?" Rose teased.

"Both."

It made Rose feel good to know she had such a close friend.

"The city never smells as bad when the wind's from the west."

"Look over there," Annie said, turning her gaze toward a group of three men. "Those sailors look like they might have a few shillings to spend."

Rose saw the men and started to walk toward them. They weren't wearing uniforms, but they were dressed in ways that proclaimed they were from the ships. They wore clothing suitable for working with the ropes on board: shirts with three quarter sleeves and loose pants. Rose knew how quickly a sailor could drop those loose pants when he wanted a poke.

Rose and Annie walked at a slow pace until they were about ten yards from the men. They pretended to be lingering to talk to each other, but they kept glancing at their potential customers. Both women hiked their skirts up their calves, a sign that the seamen should come close if they wanted to see more.

The shortest of the three started to approach. His broad smile told Rose he was interested. Rose also noticed he was walking a little wobbly. *Not such a bad thing. The sodden Johns are often the quick ones.*

Before the sailor was halfway across the street, Rose heard hoof beats from the south. She turned and was surprised to see the white horse from the circus that morning. The rider was a thin woman. Rose couldn't tell if it was the same person who'd been performing with the horse that morning, but she suspected it was. The horse turned right and disappeared up the dark alley where Rose had planned to take a sailor. The sound of the hoof beats was gone.

"Did you see the horse?" Rose asked her friend. "It was the same one I saw this morning."

"Men are more important than horses," Annie told her.

"Then you take this one. I need to find out where that woman went."

"You need the money, too, Rose."

Rose felt the sailor's eyes on her back as she turned and walked toward the alley, but she knew he wouldn't follow. Annie would have his attention—and his coins—before he could take another step.

The alley was dark, but Rose wasn't scared. She had used the doorways along this lane on many nights. They were places where she could raise her skirt while the men loosened their trousers. Those men were trouble, she knew. She was lucky she had never been hurt.

There were no horses in the alley, so Rose walked straight through to Whitechapel Road. She crossed the wide road, then turned away from the Thames to travel up one more block before stepping into a narrow lane. A number of stables lined the street, at least a dozen. It was possible the white horse had been left in one of them, but it would be difficult to know since the stable doors were all closed.

Rose wasn't certain what it was about the woman and the horse that attracted her interest. Perhaps seeing them twice in one day. In a city of over five million people that was quite a coincidence, enough to be considered a sign.

Rose believed in signs, although they sometimes led her in unexpected ways. When she was twelve years old she had been studying the clouds after dumping a copper of laundry water. Her mother took in washing and Rose always helped. That day, like many others, her mother had been drinking, which meant Rose was doing all the work. She'd taken a break to stare up at the sky and noticed a cloud that reminded her of a tree in the yard behind the British Museum. That place was special to her. It was quiet, peaceful, and away from her mother. On impulse Rose left the washing and started walking to the museum.

When she arrived she found a well-dressed man enjoying a stroll through the museum yard.

"You're a pretty one," he told her. Rose knew she was pretty, so she smiled and didn't say anything, not even thank you.

"You like this tree?" he asked.

"It feels nice here," Rose told him.

"You like to feel nice, do you?"

"I like to be here."

"The tree looks even prettier on the other side, away from the buildings," he said, reaching for her hand and leading her toward a place where they couldn't be seen.

He was the first man who paid Rose money to let him touch her. She was surprised by his offer, and not upset at all. It was only later that she started thinking there might be something wrong. A frightening image kept returning to her of the way the man's wide eyes had rolled as he had moved his hand up her leg. But the money was wonderful. She met him at the tree ten more times.

One day he didn't show. Rose never saw him again and never knew why. It took her almost a year to miss the money enough to look for another man.

These men became more important after her mother died. Because they were a part of her life, there was money for food, drink, shelter, and tickets to shows, the shows she needed because the tree was no longer her peaceful place.

Tonight, however, there was not enough money. Rose was broke and she'd missed her opportunity with the sailors. She went back to look for Annie.

"There you are," Rose heard her friend shout. Annie was standing on Whitechapel Road by the alley Rose had walked through earlier.

"You find the horse?" Annie asked.

"No. But the odd feeling about seeing it is still here. I wish I could afford to go back to the circus tomorrow, just to ask around."

"I can give you enough for a bed tonight and a show tomorrow," Annie told her. "It was a good night for me. I handled all three of those sailors."

"How could that be? It's been ten minutes since I left you, maybe fifteen."

Annie laughed. "Not a one of them was sober enough to finish what he started, but they all paid handsomely. Follow me back to The Old Bull and I'll buy you a gin."

***

Glen brought Hannah back again. He didn't want to push her too hard, especially on the first day.

"There was something special about that horse," Hannah told him after she had regained enough composure to sit up on the blanket.

Glen wasn't thinking about the horse. He was wondering if the sexual abuse might have passed from that existence into the current one. Powerful forces such as that often did. He would have preferred the focus of their conversation to be on that topic, but decided to follow her lead.

"Do you ride?" he asked.

"Horses?"

"Yes. Have you ever taken lessons or been on a trail ride?"

"My mother used to take me to a place up in Royalton years ago. I haven't been there in more than ten years."

Glen offered her a hand. She took it and he helped her up.

"We'll look tomorrow," Glen said. "If the stable is still there maybe we'll find a white horse as well."

"Make it Saturday. I have to work tomorrow, and in the evening I want to take you to meet Stuart."

CHAPTER SIX

Starr was eating applesauce and Frosted Flakes. Stuart had bought her a set of dishes decorated with pictures of Ariel, The Little Mermaid.

Stuart's task for the morning was to get Starr ready and then sit with her until the school bus picked her up for her kindergarten class. Jamie was scheduled to work at the community college, but wasn't due there until nine o'clock, so she was still asleep. Whenever she had a rehearsal scheduled for the evening she slept as late as possible.

Stuart, a maintenance worker at Milwood Leather, repaired the machines when they had problems and did carpentry, electrical, and plumbing work around the factory. He had to be at the plant by eight. That was company policy and Stuart's boss was a stickler for policy.

The phone rang. Stuart glanced at the screen. It was Hannah. While he generally took her calls even when he was rushed, it didn't take him long to regret the decision.

She started by apologizing for calling at such an early hour, but quickly turned the conversation to her regression. "I was hypnotized yesterday and it was an amazing experience," she said. "It was like another day in my life, only I was just along for the ride. I couldn't control anything. But the sensations were as clear as what I experience every day. I could see and smell things and feel whatever I touched just as if I was there. And 'there' was the city of London in the nineteenth century, so it was *not* something I know. I'd say it was bizarre, but it felt normal."

"Starr and I are rushing out the door," Stuart said. Hannah's idea of amazing wasn't always the same as his. "Does this have anything to do with the psychic you hired to look into your dreams?"

"The guy is fantastic. If anyone can figure out Paige's murder, he can. There's this connection between my dreams and these hidden memories. It has to mean something. I want him to hypnotize you, too."

"Why?"

"I could set it up. He wants to work with everyone I can think of who knew Paige."

"You know I'm not a suspect, right?"

"I'm not, either, and he did me. Besides, it's something I want to share with you."

"I've got to go." Stuart still needed to get Starr dressed, pack lunches for both of them, put together a bag of clothes for her since she was spending the night with his parents, and make sure she was ready for the bus. "Call me back tonight and we'll talk about it."

"Why don't I just bring him over? I'd like the two of you to meet. He traveled a long way to help us."

"Jamie's got a rehearsal."

"Who cares?"

"Nice, Hannah."

"You know what I mean. I want to share this with you, not your wife."

"Okay. Bring him over, but I'm not promising anything."

He regretted agreeing almost as soon as he'd done it, but their conversation ended before he had a chance to say more.

He wasn't looking forward to meeting this psychic of Hannah's. He didn't want anyone poking around in his mind, searching for some vague past life. He resolved to be as uncooperative as he could be.

"He traveled a long way to help us," Hannah had told him, but Stuart didn't understand why *"us"*. He didn't want help. Paige's murder was something the police needed to handle. At best, Hannah and her friend would just get in their way. Hopefully, that was all they'd do.

***

Alone, with still another hour before Hannah was due to bring the hypnotist over, Stuart decided to check his email for instructions from his contacts. It always scared him when a note came in, but he had to look. He had no choice.

It had started more than a year earlier, during the winter months when money was tight. Car payments and rent were both overdue and the price of heating oil was high and still rising. Although Stuart hadn't said anything to Jamie, the word eviction had been mentioned a couple of times in phone calls from their landlord. All he could think to do was ask his boss for an advance. He frowned as he remembered the exchange.

"You don't have family you can go to?"

"Family?"

"Yeah. Your father or maybe a rich uncle somewhere who still thinks you're worth the investment."

"No rich uncle, that's for sure. And my parents are retired. They have more than they can handle with their own expenses."

"Sorry to hear that," his boss, John Glodek, said. "I can't authorize an advance with work as slow as it's been lately, but I can swing a personal loan if you'd like. You can pay me back in the spring. With no interest. Things will be better then, for all of us."

Stuart asked for two thousand but, to his surprise, his boss doubled that amount. It would be hard to pay off four grand, but he couldn't worry about the future when it was so hard just to get through each day.

When spring arrived they were still living paycheck to paycheck.

Jamie was involved in two separate productions, neither with pay. Stuart couldn't remember either of those shows, but he couldn't forget how Jamie had cut back on her temp work to make time for them. He was left with the entire responsibility for their bills.

Stuart saw John every day when he reported for work. He kept his eyes down, trying his best to be invisible, convinced that if he admitted to his boss that he could not pay his debt, he would lose his job. He had a mental image of Jamie and Starr sleeping in his Taurus.

"Stuart," John said one morning after the workers had finished a meeting, "I need to talk to you. Please wait around."

This was it, the conversation Stuart had been dreading.

"You've been avoiding me. I have to assume it has something to do with the money you owe me."

"I'm sorry," Stuart said, looking down to avoid eye contact, feeling like a child caught misbehaving. "The money you lent me is gone and I'm still behind. I need more time."

"It doesn't sound as if time is going to help. But I might have a solution. Someone asked me if any of the guys who work here might want to make a few extra bucks. I thought of you."

"I'm interested." This was the first hint of hope he'd had in months.

"His name is Victor Wood," John said. "He lives outside of Concord, but he's looking for someone in this area. He told me the work wouldn't be very demanding, and it pays well. I don't know, but you might want to look into it. I told you before I don't care about interest, but you need to pay back the base. This idea isn't so you and Jamie can have some pocket cash. If it works out, we'll set up a payment schedule. You understand that, right?"

CHAPTER SEVEN

Victor Wood lived in a two story Victorian home on a wooded tract of land in a wealthy area southwest of Concord. Although the style of the building was old, it had obviously been renovated recently. Stuart smiled. The condition of the building was a sign that Mr. Wood had some bucks.

Stuart left his car in the drive by the side of the house and walked along the curved concrete path leading to the front door. A man was on his knees digging in the dirt, planting what looked like begonias in the garden bordering the home. Stuart was surprised he was working in such chilly weather. The ground had to be hard.

The man, who was wearing jeans and a blue coat over a light red flannel shirt, rose as Stuart approached. He was about five-nine, of average build, but he stood tall as if he was convinced he had a more impressive stature. He had thinning hair, but his smooth skin indicated that he was no more than forty-five. To Stuart, who was twenty-five, that was old enough to deserve his respect.

"John Glodek sent me," Stuart said, offering his hand to shake. Victor Wood was wearing work gloves, so he just held them up and shrugged. Stuart pulled his hand back.

"Who?"

"John Glodek. He owns Milwood Leather. He's my boss. He sent me to talk to you about doing some part time work. Are you Victor Wood?"

"Yes. I know who you're talking about. Let's go inside. I'll fix you a cup of hot chocolate if you'd like one. I need something to warm me from inside."

Instead of going up the front steps, they walked toward the back of the house. When they reached the back door, Mr. Wood held it open as Stuart entered an enormous kitchen that held two stoves and three refrigerators and a vast expanse of counter space. Victor Wood clearly has money, Stuart thought. And the desire to show it off.

"Some people I know might have an opportunity for you," Victor told him as he filled a stainless steel saucepan with milk and put it on one of the burners

"What opportunity?"

"They need a courier."

"I can do that as long as the hours don't interfere with my other job."

"Most anyone can carry packages from one place to another, but the man they're looking for needs a few special requirements. Do you have references?"

"I'm honest. John can testify to that."

"John?"

"Yes. My boss, remember?"

"Of course I remember. Do you want marshmallows?" Victor pulled out two brown ceramic cups along with a container of Nestle cocoa.

"No thank you."

"They're looking for someone who can work at night, so the hours shouldn't conflict with your day job. It's simple. You'll receive two addresses. You'll pick up a package at one and drop it off at the other. There will be no contacts at either. If you see people, you should avoid them. You'll know the packages by a symbol of a horse that will be stamped on the outside with white ink. It will show up against the brown cardboard."

"And these people that I'm to avoid?"

"It'll be late at night, so most of the time you just need to be as quiet as possible. I think you're beginning to understand why I say they're looking for someone special. They don't want any publicity concerning these packages, so if you agree to work for them you'll need to keep your arrangement a secret. You understand that, right?"

Stuart nodded.

"And you're still interested?"

He nodded again.

Stuart's instructions were to come in anonymous emails. His responsibility would always be the same: pick up a package at the first address and deliver it to the second. And after he had read the emails, he was to delete them.

***

Stuart left home at one o'clock in the morning on a Thursday, a week and two days after he had accepted the secret task. It was a cold, April night and would get colder as dawn approached. His destination was deep in Windsor County. It wasn't an easy drive. The dirt roads were deeply rutted, causing his car to bounce around like the sled he had when he was young, the one he used to ride on the hills near Killington Peak.

He was to find the package at Paper Birch Farm, a small horse stable that provided boarding, training, and riding lessons. He'd been instructed to enter the barn and look for a box in one of the stalls, then take the box to a home construction site in Ludlow. The home was just a shell so there would be no one inside. He was to leave the box leaning against the back door.

Stuart was wearing his winter coat, which was hooded, insulated, and black. There couldn't have been a better jacket for sneaking around on a cold night. He wasn't wearing gloves, so he kept his hands in the hand warmer pockets, another good feature of his coat. But his face was exposed, so he was still chilly when he parked his car and walked up the drive onto the property.

The drive opened to a large gravel parking area near a riding ring. The farmhouse was a small, one story building. There didn't seem to be any activity. There were no lights on either inside or out.

Stuart saw the stable on the other side of the ring. It was open as his instructions had said it would be. In fact, it had no doors. He walked as quickly as he could around the ring, entered the barn, and flipped on the small flashlight he had brought with him. He needed to get the package and get back to his car.

There were no horses and no sign that animals of any kind had been in the thirty-yard-long barn recently. It was good he had brought his flashlight, he realized. If the place was abandoned the electricity was probably cut off.

Stuart zigzagged down the wide center aisle, glancing into the stalls that lined either side until he found the box leaning against the far wall, a white horse stamped clearly on its surface. Stuart took the box and hurried back to his car.

***

It was close to three-thirty when Stuart made it to the drop-off house in Ludlow. Time was tight, so he parked right in the drive and carried the package around to the back where he leaned the package against the door as instructed. Job finished.

He still had to get back in at home without disturbing Jamie or Starr, but he was fairly confident he could manage, although Jamie usually slept in the living room. She claimed it was because his snoring kept her awake, but he knew the reasons were more complicated than that.

***

The hardest part of Stuart's new "job" was keeping it a secret from his wife. Sneaking out late at night was only one part of it. He still had to put in his hours at the leather company, and find the time and energy to take care of Starr—with very little help from Jamie.

It took him just a little more than a half a year to pay John Glodek back. Stuart received his money in envelopes taped to the packages he delivered. His employers were generous, but he didn't know who they were. He imagined a number of reasons for their need to remain anonymous, none of which were good. So when his immediate need for cash ended, Stuart resolved to quit.

CHAPTER EIGHT

When Stuart walked up to the large home, the changes in the garden were the first things he noticed. The plants Victor Wood had been placing around the house were gone. Perhaps those small shrubs were seasonal or perhaps they hadn't done well in the shade. He would ask about them if he needed some small talk before he brought up his decision to quit delivering the packages.

"May I help you?" the woman asked after she opened the front door. She had dark red hair, dyed. He guessed she was in her late sixties or early seventies. She was wearing a pretty blue blouse along with darker blue slacks and a necklace and earrings with blue stones that matched her outfit. Her clothing seemed formal for a Saturday afternoon at home; he wondered if she was preparing to go out.

"Is Victor home?"

"Victor? No one by that name lives here."

"I mean to say Mr. Wood."

"I'm sorry?"

"He's about so tall," Stuart told her, holding his hand up to indicate someone an inch or so smaller than his own height, "maybe mid-forties."

"You have the wrong house."

"That's impossible."

The woman shook her head and began to close the door.

"I was here last March," Stuart said, taking a step back to be less intimidating. "Victor Wood was working right there, in the garden. He took me into the kitchen to talk."

The woman opened the door a little wider, but stayed inside and kept her hand on the knob.

"We did have some landscaping done last spring."

"A man did the work?"

"Yes. His name might have been Victor. His card said his company was called Evergreen, but I don't believe there was a real business. He knocked on our door and said he would work for cheap. He told the truth about that, but most of the shrubs he planted died. Of course it was March, too early for planting. We didn't think about that at the time and he didn't bring it up. You say he let you into our home? I don't see how that's possible."

"You have a kitchen that's big enough for a restaurant. The cabinets have a stained wood surface and even the refrigerators have the same façade. There are three of those and two stoves. You must entertain a great many people."

"We do, which also means that our kitchen is no secret."

"You think I'm lying? Why would I do that?"

"I don't know. But it doesn't make much difference. We already know we were foolish to hire a stranger."

"He made me a cup of hot cocoa."

"As I said, it doesn't make much difference now. I've told you everything I know about that man. I hope you find him."

***

Since Stuart couldn't contact his employers through Victor Wood, he tried to send an email. He did so by replying to the last message they had sent to him. It bounced back just seconds after he sent it. He had been told to delete all messages after he read them, but a few were still in his trash folder. He tried those as well. Each one showed a different address, but they all produced the same result.

He considered asking John Glodek to contact Victor Wood, but decided it might be best not to bring the subject up again. There was something suspicious about the way the packages had to be moved that Victor Wood's disappearance confirmed, and Stuart didn't want his boss knowing he'd been involved in something illegal. And if his boss already knew because he was a part of whatever was going on, Stuart would be in a worse position. He couldn't afford to lose his job at Milwood Leather, so he kept quiet.

After a great deal of thought, he decided that when the next email arrived he would ignore it. *What harm could that cause?* He did, after all, have a right to quit. So Stuart skipped an assignment. His *what harm* question was answered almost immediately.

The evening after the night when Stuart did not sneak out to transfer a package, he received another email with instructions for his next assignment. The text in the message included the warning: "Don't miss this one!" It also had two attachments, both pictures. The first was of Jamie leaving the studio where she rehearsed. It was dark and she was alone. The second was of Starr. Stuart's daughter was on the green in front of their apartment. He was probably nearby since he never left her alone for more than a minute, but the picture's message was clear: Starr was every bit as vulnerable as her mother.

***

Stuart's next assignment was to take a box from the porch of a suburban home to a place beside a dumpster behind one of the oldest apartments in Springfield.

CHAPTER NINE

"Do you have a minute to look at something in my car?" Troy asked Jamie as they walked out of the rehearsal hall.

"Stuart's waiting up for me," she said. She knew her words sounded like an excuse since rehearsal had ended early.

"I think you'll be pleased," he told her. She was wary, and hoped she hadn't been flirting too much. Earlier that evening they had been rehearsing the scene where Jean kisses Miss Julie's foot. When they took a break she suggested that it might be fun if he moved his lips up a bit.

"Your knee?" he had suggested.

"Whatever," she'd responded as she shrugged her shoulders. Then they'd both laughed. Someday Jamie hoped to make audiences laugh that hard.

Troy got into his gray Volvo while Jamie poked her head through the passenger window. He reached under the driver's seat and pulled out a bottle of Grey Goose. He flashed it at Jamie. It was the yellow label, with a hint of lemon. She immediately opened the door and sat beside him.

There were times when Jamie could resist a bottle, but as the quality of that liquor grew, her power to do so weakened. Troy had picked her favorite vodka. She didn't know if he had asked around or simply made a lucky choice. But the sight of that expensive bottle immediately reminded her of the kick of a swig. She loved that sensation.

Stuart called her names such as boozer, drunk, and lush during their arguments, but she didn't believe she was an alcoholic. She could stop if she wanted to. She'd only had a couple of drinks the entire time she was pregnant, not counting before the plus sign showed up on the pregnancy test. In any case, Starr was born healthy and if she wanted to party that was her own business.

Stuart had also told her that she'd never be a great actress if she continued to drink. That was ridiculous. Drinking eased her nerves and helped her concentrate. Besides, he drank—just not as much as she did. But wanting more of life was part of her nature. It wasn't just the alcohol. It was in everything she did and it made her a better actress.

"I have two bottles," Troy said. "We can sneak back into the rehearsal hall. Paul hasn't locked it yet. We can hide in the costume room. He won't know we're there."

"And do what? Spend the night here?" She glanced down at the Grey Goose and thought about how a taste or two would put that wonderful swirl back in her head and make everything in her life fun for a time. *What the hell. One night can't hurt.*

***

Hannah pleaded with Stuart to let Glen do a regression.

"Jamie's at a rehearsal and Starr's at her grandparents, we have the place to ourselves. It's the perfect time for you to try something new."

"I suppose."

Glen was increasingly intrigued by the relationships Stuart and Hannah had with Jamie. He looked forward to meeting her himself.

"You're dressed right," he told Stuart, who was wearing loose jeans and a green sweater, no shoes, just white athletic socks. "The first rule is to avoid clothes that would be a distraction, like tight things that might pinch. A regression is a journey into your own memories. When and if you get there, you'll be wearing whatever you had on in that previous life."

Glen told Stuart to lie on the couch face up and to find a spot on the ceiling that he could use as a focal point. That wouldn't be hard. The room hadn't been painted in years and there were chips in the spackle.

"Breathe deeply and evenly. Imagine you're walking on a path through a forest. The path is covered with a thick canopy of tree branches. It's a hot summer day, but it is comfortable in the shade of the woods. You've been walking for a long time, but you're not tired. Each step you take sends you deeper into your own history. You are headed toward something important, something in your past that is always part of your subconscious, something that affects every decision you make. Count the trees as you pass them. Each one represents years. You're going further and further back, past many lifetimes."

Stuart sat up. "I did something like this with Jamie once," he said. "When we were first married she was showing me her acting exercises. She had me trying to be a tree rather than counting them but it had the same feel as this. You know, weird."

"Please try, Stuart," Hannah said. She put her hand on his shoulder and gently tried to push him back down, but he resisted. Glen didn't know why, but it was clear Stuart was going to be uncooperative. He doubted there would be a regression that night.

CHAPTER TEN

Jamie's tongue felt fat, her throat pasty, and she could taste vomit. Her head hurt and her stomach was queasy, as if she might puke whatever was left if she made any sudden movements. It wasn't the first time she'd felt this way, so she knew it would pass. She was lying on the floor face down, so she rolled over and sat up, only to realize that she was wearing her *Miss Julie* costume.

She was in the rehearsal room. It was a large room with tall ceilings and a few small windows up at the top of one wall. Still, there was enough light to see. She climbed to her feet and looked around. Troy wasn't there. That was good, but the clothes she'd been wearing weren't there, either. Other than the chairs and old tables set up to simulate the set for the play they'd been rehearsing, the only things in the room were the chair and table where Paul sat while he was directing, jotting notes in his script as he watched. But now the table held only a small model horse about the size of her fist mostly white with some gray on its legs and head. Perhaps it was a prop from a past production. She went to put it in a pocket in her dress, but it had none. She decided to hold onto it anyway.

Jamie tried to recall how she'd ended up alone in the rehearsal room. The last thing she could remember was drinking from Troy's bottle. They'd hidden out in the makeshift dressing room with the flimsy curtain that didn't reach the floor. It was a silly place to hide. If Paul had checked the area before he left he would have seen their feet. But he hadn't come into the room.

After they heard Paul leave the building, Troy pulled out the bottles. He took a couple of swallows from the first one, but made Jamie kiss him twice before he let her have any. That wasn't so bad, even when he stuck his tongue in her mouth. She'd been an actress long enough to be quite skilled at kissing men who didn't interest her. Still, when she finally got her hands on the bottle she was a little irritated with the way he had been teasing her. She decided she'd chug as much as she could. Vodka flowing down her throat was the last thing she remembered.

Jamie heard a noise coming from outside the rehearsal room. Marisa, a volunteer who normally arrived about nine o'clock in the morning three days a week, including Saturday, to answer the phone and take reservations. She'd been involved with theater people long enough to ignore odd behavior. If they were backstage during a show, Jamie could have walked by her naked without attracting notice. But this was different. She wasn't supposed to wear her costume and she was definitely not supposed to spend the night in the studio.

Her clothes were probably in the costume shop on the other side of the building. She could try to sneak by the community theater office where Marisa would be sitting or she could shoot for the closest exit and drive home wearing the dress, and then explain to both her costumer and her director why she took it home. Jamie sighed. She didn't have a lot of options. Maybe she could sneak the dress back before anyone noticed it was gone.

She looked down at the small plastic horse she was still holding. She knew she should put it back on Paul's table so he could fidget with it during rehearsals or whatever else it was he did with the toy. Then she thought it might be fun to steal it. She whispered, "It looks like it's just you and me, buddy, and we have to make a break for it."

***

"Is that you?" Stuart yelled as the door opened. Jamie stepped into their apartment, a dismayed look on her face. This wasn't the first time Jamie had stayed out all night. But what she didn't know was that Stuart had spent the night pacing, waiting for her. She also didn't know that Stuart had good reason to be scared.

"This is the dress I'm going to wear as Miss Julie," Jamie told him. "I wanted you to see it. I stayed after the rehearsal to sew the trim. Do you like it? Sorry about the time. I lost track."

Her story was ridiculous. She was sewing? And that's why she was more than twelve hours late? But the why of Jamie staying out all night didn't matter. That she was alive and home was what counted.

Stuart spoke slowly. "You look beautiful," he said. And it was true, she did look good in the nineteenth century dress she was wearing, despite the tale her face told of a very rough night. Her costume seemed to pull him to a place that was somehow home. He didn't understand why he had the sensation, but he knew what he felt.

He took her hand and pulled her toward him. Then he put his arms around her and kissed her.

CHAPTER ELEVEN

On the night of Stuart's failed regression, Hannah was too tired to drive, so Glen dropped her off at her home before heading back to the Holiday Inn in her car.

Hannah let herself in, hung her coat on the standing rack, and went to the bedroom. She took off all her clothes except for her panties, dropped everything on the floor, and pulled on a pair of red flannel pajamas.

She went down the hall to use the bathroom, but was too exhausted to even brush her teeth. She returned to her bedroom, flipped off the lights, pulled the covers back, and crawled into bed.

Feeling so tired that she could have curled up for the night on the porch outside her door, Hannah was unable to sleep, her thoughts swirling. She counted backwards from a thousand, a trick her father had taught her when she was in high school. When she reached somewhere in the upper eight hundreds, she finally fell asleep.

***

Paige and Jamie were riding double on the white horse. Paige was in the saddle and Jamie was sitting behind her with her arms around Paige's waist. They were wearing identical black nightgowns, exactly like the one Paige had bought the day she went shopping with Hannah. To sit astride the horse they had to pull their gowns up, so their naked legs were exposed. There was blood everywhere. It ran over their bodies and down their bare legs. It covered the white hair of the horse. It came from the black-handled broadsword that skewered both women, entering through Jamie's back and exiting through Paige's stomach.

***

Hannah jolted awake. She looked at the clock. It was only thirty minutes since she had gone to bed. She knew she wouldn't be able to go back to sleep. The fear generated by her nightmare had flooded her body with adrenaline. She got up, intending to drink a glass of warm milk, but when she reached her kitchen, she grabbed the phone and dialed Glen's hotel instead.

***

Glen was awake. He had been unable to get Stuart's failed regression out of his mind. He knew Stuart had been resisting, but he didn't understand why. It seemed more than just skepticism. His behavior had signs of fear rather than doubt.

"Hello." He wasn't surprised when Hannah was on the other end of the line. There wasn't anyone else he knew in Springfield.

"I can't sleep," she told him. "Paige was in my dreams again, along with Jamie. They were both ...." Her voice was shaky and weak. It faded before she finished what she had to say.

"I'll come over," he said. "I've got your car."

"No. I just need someone to talk to."

"I can be dressed and over there in twenty minutes. You sound like you need a friend."

"You don't mind?"

"Of course not."

It took Glen only slightly longer to get to Hannah's than he'd thought it would.

"Thanks for coming," Hannah said when she opened the door. Her hair was disheveled, her feet bare, and she was wearing a pair of red flannel pajamas with a snowman pattern. Glen was surprised she hadn't changed when she knew he was coming over. Perhaps she was too upset to think of her appearance.

Hannah's front door opened into her living room. The TV was on and turned to CNN, but the sound was turned low. He noticed she had been sitting on her couch drinking something out of a mug. *Warm milk? Or herbal tea?* He didn't think it was anything stronger. She didn't seem the type.

"Are you okay?" he asked as he hung his coat next to hers.

"I'm exhausted," she admitted, "but when I try to lie down, my mind races."

"Well, we'll see if we can do something about that. But first tell me about your dream."

He offered no comment after she recounted the details. Instead, he led her back to her bedroom, had her get into bed and lie on her back. He wasn't planning to hypnotize her this time, but the effort to help her sleep would be similar. He turned off the lamp on her end table, leaving the hall as the only source of light. Then he sat beside her and spoke in a soft, monotone voice, telling her not to fight her thoughts, just to let them drift.

After a little less than a half an hour Hannah rolled to her side and curled up with one hand tucked under her head, breathing evenly.

He decided he'd spend the night on her couch, but sat beside her a while longer, worried that if he got up she might wake.

As he watched her, he felt a wave of loneliness that surprised him. Hannah had to trust him to put herself in such a vulnerable position and he felt complimented by that trust. But for some reason, he felt empty rather than fulfilled. His emotions confused him.

Glen's life had no room for a woman, a fact that seldom bothered him. He traveled a great deal to find and work with people who had the best potential for communicating with their past lives. When he wasn't traveling around the world he was concentrating on his writing or conducting lectures.

This was one of those rare times that he felt dissatisfied with his life. Sitting close to Hannah and watching her sleep was a level of intimacy he wasn't accustomed to sharing with anyone.

He had to be careful not to fool himself about what her trust meant.

CHAPTER TWELVE

When Hannah woke, she remembered that Glen had been with her when she fell asleep, but she didn't know he'd spent the night. She got up and walked down the hall toward her living room without bothering to change out of her pajamas and found him asleep on her couch, still wearing the clothes he'd had on the night before

"Good morning," she said. He jumped, startled, and lifted himself up on one arm. He looked around the room and finally at Hannah in her red snowman pajamas. He appeared confused as well as a bit disheveled.

She thought how comfortable she felt with Glen in her house and how silly it was for him to stay in the hotel when she had a perfectly adequate guest room. She would suggest he move in with her sometime soon, when the time was right.

"You suggested we'd drive out to the horse farm this morning," she said, "to look for a white horse. It sounds like a wild goose chase to me, but I'm up for the trip if you are."

"You'd be surprised how many times I've worked with people who've found answers to their problems just by opening their eyes. The white horse is meaningful to you; that means it's woven into your life somehow. We just don't know how yet."

***

There were no white horses at Fowler Farm. Most of them were bays, although there were a couple that were black, and there was one buckskin. When Hannah had ridden there, it had been called Grassy Creek Farms, but now it had a new name and apparently new owners. All of the horses she remembered were gone.

Hannah tried explaining why they had driven all the way up from Springfield.

"I used to ride here when I was a child," she said. "I'd like to show my friend around, share some of the memories."

"Just stay out of the stalls and don't mess with the tack," they were told. "Oh, and we don't own the land where the trails used to be, so use your own discretion about the woods. Most of the trails are overgrown by now anyway."

"I still don't think this is the way to learn more about my dreams," Hannah said when she and Glen were alone, leaning on a split rail fence and watching the horses in the field.

"It isn't as crazy as it seems. A connection between your past lives and your present one can come out in your day-to-day activities. I've seen it before."

"But I haven't been here for almost twelve years. It isn't part of my day-to-day life."

"I know, and maybe we *are* wasting our time out here. But there's that horse in your dreams and your regression. How else are you connected to horses?"

"But the horse isn't the only thing that keeps showing up in my dreams. What about Jamie? She could be a clue. I think we need to regress her."

One of the horses, a black mare, suddenly stopped grazing alongside the others. She tossed her head and jumped forward, then galloped in a circle, found another patch of thick grass, and started to graze again. Hannah thought how the horse was like them, trying to move somewhere but not getting very far.

Hannah turned toward Glen, who was still watching the horses. On impulse she said, "We're wasting money on your hotel. I've got an empty guest room and I'd like it if you were closer." When the words came Hannah felt a little winded, as if she'd just climbed a large set of stairs. She hadn't been interested in a man since she'd met Paige.

"Good idea," Glen answered with some emotion in his voice, but he quickly shifted back to a business like tone. "I'll bring my things over later today. And I think you're right about Jamie. The question is how do we convince her to let us have a session with her."

Hannah was glad that they, unlike the horse, were moving forward. "I've got an idea," she told him. "Let me talk to her director."

CHAPTER THIRTEEN

"Glen's an expert on past lives," Hannah told Paul. "He's been written up in *Time* and *Newsweek*. He even worked with Shirley MacLaine once." Actually, Glen had told Hannah that he had worked with some guy who knew MacLaine, not the actress and spiritual leader herself, but Hannah stretched the truth a bit because she wanted Paul to take notice.

Hannah told him that Glen wanted to regress all the people in the cast of *Miss Julie*. "He thinks the project would make a great article for the *Rutland Herald*."

"Does he?"

"That's right," she said. Paul could provide an opportunity for Glen to regress a few more people in Paige's circle. "Glen might even be able to place something in a national news outlet. He's written hundreds of articles about past lives and been on lecture tours about the subject. He's got connections."

"He was in both *Time* and *Newsweek*?"

"He knows publicity."

"I guess he does."

"He just wants some time with your cast members. If he finds something it might sell your show beyond anything you've ever dreamed of."

"I don't suppose there's any harm in this friend of yours speaking to the cast. Would you both like to come to the rehearsal tonight?"

***

Jamie brought her dress back to the studio that night. "I was looking at it after yesterday's rehearsal," she told the costumer. "I pulled it off the rack to hold it up and spilled coffee on it. That was so stupid. Then I had to do something to keep it from staining, so I took the dress home and soaked it over night. I washed it this morning and you can't even see the spot. I was hoping you hadn't noticed it was gone."

"I came in this afternoon to finish the trim and it wasn't here," the woman said, clearly irritated. "I was going crazy, literally. You don't ever take costumes home without letting me know. You've been involved in enough shows to know that."

"I'm sorry. I was upset."

"So was I."

Jamie had managed to wiggle her way out of another situation. There was still the problem of her street clothes, though. They didn't appear to be in the costume shop.

After the dress was safely put away, Jamie walked toward the rehearsal room. Facing Troy was her next challenge.

When Jamie entered she found Troy and Paul talking to a man she had never met, and, of all people, Hannah Hersman. At first she assumed they were discussing the play, but when she got close enough to hear she discovered the discussion had nothing to do with theater. They were talking about hypnotism. They stopped speaking when she approached.

"I have something of yours," Troy told Jamie. He put his arm around her shoulders and pulled her away from the others so he could speak to her in private.

"I figured you did," she responded with a little irritation in her voice. Troy led her toward the side of the room where a paper bag sat on a chair. Her clothes.

Paul sat down at the director's table and started leafing through the script, while Hannah kept talking to the stranger. Jamie felt free to talk to Troy without being overheard.

"What you did wasn't funny," she said.

"I'm sorry for everything that happened. It wasn't a joke, really." Jamie studied him to see if she could see a hint of a smile. She had expected him to mock her, like a frat boy might laugh at a party girl. She'd even planned out a few retorts, but it didn't appear they would be necessary.

She felt that his apology sounded empty. "What were you thinking?" she asked. She couldn't remember much of what had happened the night before. She hated when she had a blackout.

"I wasn't in any condition to think," Troy told her.

"You took my clothes and left. You could think well enough to plan that."

"You asked me to take your stuff. Don't you remember?"

"Why the hell would I do that?" As soon as she asked that question she wished she hadn't. The knowledge that she couldn't remember anything gave him the upper hand.

"You got sick on your jeans. You wanted me to clean them."

"My jeans?"

"That's right. Then you gave me everything you were wearing and said I might as well clean it all. I did what you asked. I even washed your sneakers." He paused for a moment. "I'm sorry I left you. I wouldn't have done that if I wasn't so out of it."

Jamie wasn't sure she believed him, but decided to accept him at his word. "Don't say anything about last night to anyone, okay?" she said.

"Of course not," he told her. "I can be discreet."

Could he? Jamie wondered.

CHAPTER FOURTEEN

Stuart was napping on the couch while Starr watched her *Happy Feet* DVD for what seemed like the hundredth time. He was tired because he was still being forced to move packages late at night. He'd become quite good at sneaking around, particularly at the places where he picked up the boxes. Although the spots kept changing, most were horse stables. He had no idea if he would ever lead a normal life again.

"Time for bed," Stuart told his daughter.

Starr had a few favorite phrases. "I don't want to" was one of them.

"Come on," Stuart said. "It's bedtime for both of us. And you get to sleep with the toy of your choice. Let's look in your toy box so you can pick one."

"I want Cow," she said. She sounded more agreeable now.

True to his word, Stuart let Starr look through her toy box. He held the lid up while she rummaged through the contents. He was expecting her to pull out the Asian doll she called Cow or a stuffed animal like Hotdog, the red dachshund she had worn holes in over a year of cuddling. But instead she picked out one he hadn't seen before, a white model horse.

He looked closer. He didn't want to tell her to pick a different toy, but he would if the hard plastic animal appeared dangerous to sleep with. It was a new toy. He didn't know where it had come from, but it looked familiar. Suddenly he realized where he had seen it before. The realization took his breath away. John Glodek had a model horse exactly like it on the bookcase in his office.

CHAPTER FIFTEEN

At first Jamie wasn't enamored with the idea of being hypnotized by Hannah's friend, but she was also savvy about marketing. The man was a world-renowned expert in his field, however crazy that field might be. She knew that if they could get him to announce that someone from the cast of *Miss Julie* had once actually lived in the nineteenth century, news outlets would pick up the story. Combine that publicity with her intent to work her part until it was absolute perfection, and she had a golden opportunity to earn her big break.

Paul said he didn't want the regressions to interfere with the evening rehearsals, so he had each actor arrange a time to meet with Glen when nothing else was scheduled. He told the cast that the options were before rehearsal, after rehearsal, or on a weekend. He let Hannah have a key to open the studio after Jamie swore to her trustworthiness.

Jamie was the first to schedule a session. She didn't have any temp jobs cutting into her daytime hours, so she requested an afternoon time. She knew Glen was free all day. But although Glen was available, Hannah was not. And he wanted her to be there.

Hannah had brought up the possibility that the cast might object to being watched. "Regressions," she said, "are personal. I wanted privacy when you regressed me. I imagine they will, too."

But Glen argued for her presence. "Isn't it the nature of an actor to want an audience?"

They decided on six o'clock on Tuesday night.

***

Glen had moved a few racks of out-of-date men's suits in the costume room, then he had positioned an old couch from the prop room in the makeshift space, providing a comfortable spot for the regression.

When Jamie met Glen and Hannah at the studio she was looking forward to the hypnotism, hoping to find a connection with the time when August Strindberg had written *Miss Julie*. She wanted the publicity, and was excited to try a new experience.

If he can't reach the nineteenth century, perhaps he can get me to the night I spent with Troy. I'd like to know what really happened then. I wonder if this guy could pull out a memory from when I was drunk. Of course, even if he could, I wouldn't want to share it with Hannah, for sure.

Jamie sat on the couch then dropped back to her back and lifted her legs up in one motion. She picked out the intersection of two drop ceiling panels as a focal point before Glen had a chance to tell her to do so, and was staring at it while listening to him talk about traveling back to nineteenth century London.

He told her to imagine that she was floating through a large, gray fog. She was able to capture the mental picture he painted for her so well that she soon lost the sensation that she was lying on a couch in the costume room. He started describing a scene that was hidden in the recesses of her soul. "The streets are so narrow that if carriages try to travel in opposite directions they have to have their wheels up on the stone sidewalks before they can pass."

She was quickly where he had been leading her, and took over the description of what she saw. "Two Broughams are facing each other. The horses seem wary and a bit confused. Both drivers are having a rough time keeping their animals under control. Most of the buildings along this street are three stories tall, with shops on the lower level and apartments above them. The roofs are slate, so there's an expensive feel, although all the buildings I can see are in need of some repair. There are shopkeepers working in their stores. One of those shops is a florist; the air is filled with the smell of cut flowers. People are leaning out the windows of their apartments to talk to their friends on the street below. There is a sense of community in this section of the city, but I don't feel that I belong here. My clothes are shabby and dirty compared with what these people are wearing. They look at me with disgust, and most of them cross the street to avoid getting too close. I hate these people."

***

Annie was walking through this wealthy section of town because she wasn't familiar with it and was concerned that she wouldn't be able to find her way around after dark. She worried that the people who could see her in the sunlight would remember what she looked like. It would be hard for them to forget someone who was as out of place as a clay cup on a silver tray. There was nothing she could do about it, though. She kept her eyes down as she moved forward.

She turned down a side street where the stables were located, looking for a sign outside one of the carriage houses. Walter Sickert had told her to look for a white horse painted on wood. He said she would know it when she saw it.

There had to be hundreds of signs like that in London, and even on this street the chances were the sign she was searching for wouldn't be the only one.

Annie walked the street twice and found a few signs that fit Sickert's description, but he had said she would know it and none of those seemed to stand out.

Then Annie noticed a sign with a woman on it. The woman seemed to be an artist working on a painting of the white horse. Sickert was an artist, so there was a connection. This stable had to be the one she was looking for. She would come back that night to meet the man whose name Walter had given her.

***

"Move forward in time," Glen spoke in a soft voice. "It is night now. You are back on the street in front of the stable with the sign you identified this afternoon. There is a man waiting for you inside. You know you are at the right place, so you don't waste time. You go straight to the door."

"Yes. I go to the door, but it is a carriage door. I look around for another entrance. There doesn't seem to be one on this side of the building, so I approach the large wooden door. I pull on the handle. The door is latched, so I knock as loudly as I can."

***

The door opens slightly and a man peers out. "Who be you?" he asks in a weak voice.

"Walter Sickert sent me," Annie tells him.

"Are you his screw?"

"Sometimes I'm with Walter, if that is what you mean. But I don't belong to anyone."

The door opens wide enough for Annie to walk in, so she does. The man is short and very thin, wearing a baggy cotton shirt with loose trousers held up with suspenders. He has on boots.

The man seems young because he's so small, but his face is weathered and he has lost most of the hair from the top of his head. The lamp he carries is the only light in the barn.

"He's waiting for you upstairs."

"You're not the man I'm here to see?"

He shakes his head and laughs.

"How do I get up there?"

"Go over there." The man points to the last stall on the left, then turns away, dismissing her. She sucks in a breath and moves away. When she rounds the last stall, she sees a stairway heading up into darkness. The oak stairs are worn from use, as are the walls at the height of her hands on either side of the stairway. It is a narrow passage, so thin that if she meets someone coming down while she is going up, one of them will have to squeeze against a wall to let the other pass.

There is less light upstairs than there had been below, but Annie can see a bright glow from a room two doors to the left of the stair top. She walks toward the light. Like a moth toward a flame, she thinks.

As she enters, she sees there are four lamps, all lit and positioned evenly around the man standing in the center of the space. He is tall, with gray hair and a bushy white beard, and is working on a painting resting on an easel. A bridle and saddle are positioned on a table near him. He is painting a picture of tack.

"It would have been nice if you had one of those lamps in the hall," she tells him.

"I'm looking for someone who knows her way in darkness."

Annie laughs nervously. "I'd say you've found her."

"Perhaps. Do you need money, Annie? You *are* Annie, right?"

"I am."

There is silence until she realizes he is waiting for her to answer his first question. "I have ways of earning my keep, but I can always use an extra shilling or two."

Annie tries to look the man in the eye, but he continues to concentrate on his painting.

"I'm looking for a model," he says. "Walter said you would be perfect. Can you hold a pose?"

"I'm perfect? Did he say why?"

"You have a hard look about you. He said I would find your appearance interesting."

There is something about that answer that unnerves Annie. She takes pride in being hard when it is what she has to be, but she isn't sure she likes being described with the word by others.

"What's your name?" she asks.

"Albert."

He doesn't offer a last name. But, then, in her line of work, they seldom do.

"So, Albert, you need a model. Is that all you need?" There has to be a reason for the secrecy. She had assumed she was there for sex, since it was Walter who had given her name to Albert. But perhaps this artist just wanted to look and draw.

"There is something else, Annie, but we'll get to that later. For now just sit over there. I'd like to sketch your face."

***

It took Jamie a moment to catch her breath after Glen brought her back, but as soon as she did she started comparing her regression with acting. "I've had roles where I became one with my character to such an extent that I found myself speaking in her voice when I was nowhere near the stage. This was more intense than that. I *was* Annie Chapman. I was thinking her thoughts and experiencing her emotions."

Jamie was experiencing an epiphany. She'd always believed that everyone went around once and that was it. The session with Glen had convinced her there was more. It would take her a while to figure out what her new-found knowledge meant, and her mind was racing down countless unfamiliar paths. Had Stuart been with her in all her lives? Would she remember anything about who she was in this existence?

Her life had changed forever.

CHAPTER SIXTEEN

"Would you wait for a minute?" Glen asked. "We need to talk."

They were sitting in Hannah's Versa. She had the keys in the ignition and was about to start the engine. Jamie's regression had left her with a great many questions. "All right," she said. She'd hope to be able to ask her questions in some place a little more comfortable, but he was clearly not going to wait.

"The regressions, yours and Jamie's, have revealed a connection to the serial murderer known as Jack the Ripper. I've been thinking about it since yours, but I wasn't convinced. Connections to historic figures are rarer than people imagine. In your case, the murders could be what ties the souls together. Understand, though, the connection isn't definite. Yes, a woman named Rose Mylett was found dead shortly after the Ripper murders. Your name was Rose, but that was a common name back then. Even if you were the Mylett woman in your past life, the connection to Jack the Ripper wouldn't be proven. Most of the London investigators thought she'd strangled herself. They said it was either an accident while she was drunk or suicide. I haven't seen anything in your current—"

"You're supposed to tell me these things as soon as you think of them," Hannah interrupted. "That's why you're here."

"I didn't want to worry you."

"I'm not a child," she snapped. "I thought of the Ripper connection on my own, you know. I've heard of Annie Chapman."

"I wasn't treating you like ...."

She reached for the keys again but he put his hand on hers to stop her. "Most events that occurred in our past lives have no effect on our present. That's why I look for continuity and something I call circularity, a pattern that persists through multiple lives. I didn't want to clutter the discussion. But then Jamie's regression—"

"How did she change things?"

"History is clear about Annie. She was the Ripper's second known victim. Given the way Paige was killed, it isn't much of a leap to assume that there is a pattern here and that Jamie is at risk."

Hannah leaned back in her seat and turned her eyes toward the ceiling of her car. She paused, exhaled slowly, then drew in a deep breath.

"I contacted you hoping you might help solve Paige's murder," she told him. "Please don't get distracted by Jamie."

"Distracted?" Glen was surprised by her comment. "It's not that at all," he said. "Everything is tied together. Helping Jamie helps us get to the bottom of what happened to Paige."

"You think I'm heartless, don't you?"

"I didn't say that. But you need to remember that I can't bring Paige back. Jamie is still alive. If we work together we have a shot at saving her from the same fate."

"Do you have any idea what Jamie puts her family through on a daily basis? There may be a marriage license filed away somewhere, but it's meaningless when it comes to responsibility. Stuart's raising their little girl with no help at all. Look at him the next time you get a chance. Every day he's more exhausted. I know I sound bitter but off stage Jamie's drunk more than she's sober. Paige deserves justice while Jamie deserves nothing, not even the miserable life she's chosen for herself." Hannah's voice cracked. She knew how she must sound.

"Didn't you say she is your friend?"

"Poor choice of words, I guess."

"There's something else, isn't there?"

"What are you suggesting?"

"There has to be something you're not telling me."

Hannah didn't know how to respond. "Even if we could convince Jamie she was in trouble, she wouldn't accept help from me."

"Is it Stuart?"

"Do you think I have feelings for him?"

"I'm just asking."

"I don't like to see Stuart treated the way Jamie treats him, but that's because he's my friend. That's all there is to it."

"Then why do you care so much what happens to Jamie?"

"I said I *don't* care what happens to her."

"We've talked about Jamie before and you never acted this way. Something about her regression bothered you."

"It's nothing."

"Then there *is* something. Tell me what it is."

Hannah turned away from him, put both hands on the steering wheel, and stared down at the floor mat. "You're going to think I'm an idiot."

"What I'm going to think is that you're an intelligent woman who's been through a terrible experience. Your lover died. Now you're trying your best to deal with that loss and with the horrible way it happened."

"You said you couldn't bring Paige back, but I thought you'd done just that."

"I don't understand."

Hannah had backed herself into a corner. She knew she had to try to explain what she was feeling even if putting words around her thoughts might ruin them.

"When you sent me back to my past life with Annie, I recognized the warmth I felt in her friendship—*and* the name Annie Chapman. Paige and Annie were killed in the same way. I suppose I put two and two together and came up with five. In any case, I was certain I'd discovered a part of Paige I hadn't known existed. I thought there was an entire lifetime of experiences tucked in the back of my memory, and that with your help I could pull them out and relive them. But Annie didn't have Paige's soul, she had *Jamie's*."

CHAPTER SEVENTEEN

Jamie seldom had trouble sleeping, but this night was different. Rehearsal worries were keeping her awake. It was Allison's fault. She wasn't putting in enough time. She wasn't off book yet and when she read the lines she sounded illiterate. Jamie couldn't understand how Allison got the role. Better actresses had auditioned for the part. And Paul, damn him, was trying to *coax* her into performing. He was kissing ass when he should have been kicking it.

Jamie rolled to her back and flopped her arms down like a child throwing a temper tantrum. Then she raised her left hand out to touch Stuart, to wake him so she could complain about that night's rehearsal. But his side of the bed was empty. *Where the hell is Stuart?*

She wondered if he had been restless and moved to the couch in the living room where she normally slept, although he'd never done that before—unless she'd told him to. She turned on the lamp on the end table beside the bed and saw that the door to the bathroom was open, but he wasn't there. Maybe he was using the one off the hall to avoid waking her. She tossed the covers back and got out of the bed, straightening her oversize *Rent* tee as she went in search of her husband.

She glanced into the hall bathroom as she passed by. The door was open, the light was off, and Stuart wasn't there. Once in the living room, she flipped on the light. No Stuart. That meant he had to be in his office or Starr's room. Office first, she decided.

The office door was ajar. The only light was the dim glow of his screensaver. She stepped inside. No Stuart there, either, so she went to their daughter's bedroom, the last place she could think of to look.

Jamie turned the knob on Starr's door as quietly as she could then tiptoed in. She left the door open so that some light would spill into the room, but it still took time for her eyes to adjust. Starr was asleep.

Jamie glanced around. Stuart wasn't in that room, which meant he wasn't in the house—at least not in any of the obvious places. She decided to check in the closets and behind the shower curtain in the hall bathroom. The situation was strange, scary strange.

Stuart wasn't anywhere she could think to look. After she'd rechecked the entire house, she concluded he had to be outside, although she couldn't imagine why. She went back to their bedroom, dug under a couple of pairs of sneakers and found a shoebox where she had hidden a pint of Gordon's Gin. She took a few sips then went back to the living room to wait, only leaving her post for occasional visits to the shoebox.

***

"This is a switch," Stuart said as he walked in the house. "I'm usually the one sitting right there waiting up for you."

"Where have you been?" She was in no mood to listen to his smartass comments.

Stuart was exhausted, and he only had a short time before he had to start his day. He was also aggravated by the smell of alcohol wafting from her mouth. "I've been working this schedule for more than a year," he said, "and this is the first time you've noticed? Don't pretend like you care."

"Working this schedule? What the hell does that mean?"

"You've been drinking, haven't you?"

"Don't try to turn this back on me. Just tell me what you're talking about."

"I'm not trying to turn anything. It's just that there's a lot to tell and I could use a drink myself at the moment."

Jamie stared at him, wide-eyed. He hadn't had a taste of anything stronger than beer or wine in more than a year. "Okay," she said. "But you wait here. I don't want you to know where I keep it."

***

"You've never looked in any of the packages?" Her question made sense, but he hadn't expected her to ask it.

"The cardboard's always glued. There's no way I could get inside one of them without leaving a sign that I had. If I contact the police they might X-ray it or have some other way to see what's inside, but I've been too scared to do that. When Paige was killed, all I could think of was that it could have been you."

"Or Starr," she said.

"Yes. So I kept doing what I was told to do."

"And all the packages are the same size?"

"I didn't say that. They're all shapes and sizes."

"You think it's drugs?"

"I don't know. What I do know is I can get into a lot of trouble from both sides, but I don't see that I have much choice."

"There's always a way to fight back. We just have to figure out what it is."

Stuart sighed. He should have known her first inclination would be to fight back. His was to protect his family.

CHAPTER EIGHTEEN

Troy had told Hannah he was eager to be regressed, that Jamie had said her session had been a wonderful experience. That was good, Hannah had thought wryly, since Glen would most likely want to regress her again. They scheduled his session with Glen to take place immediately following the next night's rehearsal, in order not to conflict with his day job. Hannah and Glen were in the costume room and ready to get started when he arrived a few minutes after ten.

"I take it this is the place where the journey begins," Troy said.

Hannah jumped. She hadn't heard him approach.

"Journey is not a bad description," Glen told him. "But it's a little inaccurate. All I can do is help you pull out memories. Your journey has already taken place. It might have happened years or even centuries ago. You can't change anything I'll show you, but it can be an interesting experience."

"He makes it sound clinical," Hannah said.

"It *is* clinical," Glen argued.

"It's also a ride, and if you enjoy your ride half as much as I enjoyed mine, you'll find it one of the most exciting experiences of your life."

"So what do I do?"

Glen instructed Troy to lie down on the couch, pick out a spot on the ceiling, and relax.

"That's all there is to it?"

"Pretty much. After that you just listen. I'll walk you back through time and together we'll see what's there."

Hannah took a seat on a folding chair near the couch. This was the third time she was watching Glen at work, if she counted the less-than-stellar results with Stuart's regression. She'd learned from Glen that she was part of a family of souls that moved through life after life together. Discovering that Jamie had shared a past life with her indicated that Jamie's soul was also in that family. Hopefully, Troy would belong as well. The more connected souls they could identify, the easier it would be to see the big picture.

***

Troy fought the urge to close his eyes, wanting to keep his focus on the spot on the ceiling, but his head was whirling and his vision grew more blurry from moment to moment. He felt as if he were spinning through space, that his mind was somehow slipping into the consciousness of a person whose name was Peter Arkwright. He knew the name because he *was* that person.

***

Peter Arkwright had a wet rag in his hand and was scrubbing his master's carriage. Sometimes, only to himself, he thought of it as his own carriage. He was, after all, the only one allowed to drive the beautiful black Brougham. He took pride in that fact and in the careful way he cared for the coach.

He was down on one knee working on the right front wheel when the woman returned from her session with Mr. Moss. It bothered him that such a worthy gentleman sent for a common whore.

"Albert gave me something to deliver," Annie told Peter. "I'm to ask you to take me to Hosier Lane. You're to leave me there."

"You call Mr. Moss Albert?"

"He told me to."

"Did he?"

"You're to harness the horse and drive me in Albert's coach. That's what he said."

"Did he say which horse?"

"The white one."

Peter grumbled, but had no choice. In a few minutes the carriage he had worked so hard to clean would be back on the muddy streets, and inside it, sitting on one of the fine fabric seats, would be this cheap, fat whore in her greasy rag of a dress.

Milky was the horse Mr. Moss wanted him to use, although she was actually closer in color to gray than white. She was a beautiful mare who stood a proud fifteen hands high. She'd learned to work the harness early and was excellent at her job, responding to the slightest shift in the reins. He had never used a whip on her and was certain he would never have to.

Mr. Moss had been impressed when he first saw Milky, the only horse ever to be born in his stable. He called her an omen. Peter had no idea what she was a sign of, but he was glad she got to stay. She made a beautiful picture when she was pulling the carriage.

After Peter had Milky strapped in position he held the door for Annie to take her place in the carriage. She was carrying a package that she wouldn't let out of her hands even when she was stepping up to her seat. She obviously took her responsibility seriously.

The city was dark and quiet. Very few people were about. Peter wanted to get back as quickly as possible. He didn't enjoy transporting a whore, and the London air was heavy with a fog that smelled like dead fish.

When he reached Hosier Lane, Peter pulled back on the reins to stop Milky and let his rider out. He didn't get down from the driver's seat as he would have if he had been carrying a person of some importance. The screw waited a while before finally realizing she would have to open the door for herself. Peter smiled. Morality wasn't the only thing this whore was lacking; she didn't seem too smart, either.

He glanced back briefly as he was leaving and saw that she was approaching a sailor, a large man wearing a type of rimmed hat that looked to Peter to be distinctly French. He was curious enough to watch as she spoke with the man briefly before handing him the package.

He snapped the reins gently. Milky responded and Peter steered the carriage back across the river.

CHAPTER NINETEEN

"They want me to go up by Alburgh and cross the border from there," Stuart said to Jamie. "I'll be gone overnight."

He was glad he had finally told her about his second job. He was tired of carrying the burden himself, worried about what he was being forced to do and scared that there was apparently no way out.

"What am I going to do with Starr?" Jamie asked him. "These aren't just any rehearsals. We open in two weeks and Allison isn't close to being ready. We need to spend as much time as we can working with her."

"My parents will keep Starr. You won't have to miss one minute of one rehearsal." He tried not to let his voice reflect the bitterness he felt at her ever-present self-absorption.

She frowned. "What about you?"

"I'll be there for your show. I haven't missed one yet."

"That isn't what I'm asking. I'm worried about you."

"So am I. I have no idea what's in those boxes and I'll have a hell of a time explaining that to the border police. But I don't have a choice. Remember those pictures of you and Starr. And I don't think these guys make empty threats."

"I just thought of something," Jamie said. "Hannah and this friend of hers are doing some publicity for the play. I don't know if you saw the article in the *Herald*. I left a copy on the kitchen table."

"I didn't read it, but Hannah introduced me to that Glen guy. He's a little weird. And, truthfully, she hasn't been herself lately, either."

Her expression was animated, the way she often appeared when she was acting. "They hypnotized some of the cast and found out that Troy and I shared a past life in nineteenth century London."

"You believe this stuff?"

"There's no way they could have faked it. What I experienced felt totally real. Troy said the same thing."

"Okay. So?"

"I was a whore."

"This gets better all the time." Was she just saying these outlandish things to get attention?

"Listen to me, all right? I was a whore and this guy hired me, but not for sex. He wanted me because I knew most of the sailors around the London wharf and he needed someone to carry boxes to certain ones. And like you just said, I had no idea what was in the boxes."

"So what are you saying?"

"I think you need to talk to Glen."

Stuart shook his head.

"You can't pretend nothing's going on. Things are just going to get worse. And what if something goes wrong on one of your jobs and they kill you? You're like one of those thugs who thinks he's leading the high life—until his body's found floating in a river."

"I don't think I'm leading the high life. I think I'm screwed."

"Please talk to Glen."

"All right, all right. If it'll make you feel better, I'll talk to him. But on Saturday I'm going to Canada."

CHAPTER TWENTY

The wait to cross into Canada was a few minutes over an hour. Stuart knew he had nothing to fear from the Canadian officers since he wasn't bringing anything illegal across the border. It was the American side that made him nervous.

The border guard who dealt with Stuart was a stocky, purse-lipped woman who wore a black uniform of slacks and a short sleeved shirt with large patches on the sleeves and identifying pins on the front. She also wore a revolver holstered on her right hip.

After examining his ID, she launched into the series of questions he had expected. Where he was going, social or business, how long he was staying; questions from a script that he was able to answer with ease. She signaled for him to drive on without asking him to open his trunk. He prayed the Americans would be as lax when he returned.

It took ten minutes to drive from the border to the little town of Noyan, Quebec. Stuart wasn't hopeful that he'd be able to find a small hotel; his web search hadn't yielded any results. And he didn't want to stay in a bed and breakfast for fear of being too noticed. He might try to nap in his car a bit, if his nerves would let him, but his intention was to just keep moving until it was time to look for the package.

Stuart came up with a plan after a little reconnaissance. He'd leave his car along a road near the border and carry the box by hand through the woods into the U.S. Once he hid it in the woods of Vermont, he'd hike back to Canada for his car, and drive through the official border crossing without anything to declare. It was thin, but it was the only plan he had. But first, he had to retrieve the package.

Stuart turned onto a small side road, parked, and walked up to the gray bungalow situated along the banks of the Richelieu River at a point where the water was so wide it seemed more lake than river. He stopped in the yard for a moment to make sure he was alone. The box was supposed to be under the porch on the river side.

There were no vehicles in the drive, and he couldn't see any activity around the building. At this point he could pass as a lost American tourist.

This assignment wasn't simple burglary, as the others had been. International smuggling was a serious crime. He could end up in prison for a year or more.

He was foolishly driving his own car with his own license plates. He hadn't thought of that. Thoughts of all the things that could go wrong swirled through his tired mind until he gave himself a mental shake. He wasn't accomplishing his goal by having an argument with himself in the middle of someone's front yard, but he certainly was increasing his chances of getting caught.

His instructions were that he would find the box under the front porch, but the structure was built low to the ground. There was only one step from the deck to the lawn. Stuart did not think someone could fit a hand under the wood much less a box comparable to the ones he'd been moving about Vermont. He kept circling the building until he reached the far side. The land sloped off somewhat in back allowing for a larger space.

He dropped to his knees to look under the porch. There was something there. It was difficult to see it well since the only light he had was from the moon and stars, but the object appeared to be what he was after. He lay down on his stomach and slid his head and shoulders into the tight space. He could feel the cardboard, but it was difficult to get a grip on the box.

The only way he could get the box out from the space where it was wedged was by placing one hand on top and one underneath, then shifting to the right a little, and then to the left, kind of shimmying it out a tedious fraction of an inch at a time. It took close to fifteen minutes before the box had moved enough for him to get a decent grip on it and slide it free. Of all the boxes he'd transported, this one was the largest. It wasn't particularly heavy, but its size would make carrying it awkward. It was large enough, three feet by four feet, although only roughly six inches thick, that he'd have to put the back seat down in order to fit it in his trunk.

It was after three in the morning when Stuart was finally back on the road, driving to where he planned to leave his car, a patch of woods about halfway between the highway and the river. There were a few farms in that rural area about a mile north of the border, and plenty of undeveloped land along the side of the roads with plenty of room to pull over. He figured he had about three hours until sunrise, which should be enough time to carry the box into Vermont, hide it, and make his way back before anyone noticed the car—if nothing went wrong.

It took him about twenty minutes to find a place deserted enough to leave his car. He should have scoped the area out when he first crossed the border instead of heading directly up to Noyan, he realized. He'd be lucky if that was the worst mistake he made this night.

He left the car far to the side of a dirt drive that faced a vine covered gate that looked as if it hadn't been opened in years. He grabbed the box, then checked the latitudinal and longitudinal coordinates on his portable GPS and jotted them down on a small pad he'd brought along. He slipped his backpack on and squared his shoulders, setting himself for the task ahead.

The vines on the gate had sister plants all along the perimeter of the forest. He had put the box down in order to break his way through, hoping it wasn't poison ivy.

Once Stuart was beyond the fringe of the forest, the canopy provided by the leafless trees was sparse enough to allow the light of the moon to show him the way. Of course, the moonlight alone wasn't enough to show him the *correct* way. He needed the GPS for that.

The box was not heavy, but it soon felt as if it were. It was awkward to carry and he was forced to keep shifting its position. Stuart was growing exhausted from the effort. He had brought some rope along as part of his emergency supplies. He pulled out the coil and tied a length around the box, fashioning a handle of sorts which made lugging the package easier.

The Vermont border with Canada may be one of the least protected areas of entry into the United States, he knew, but that doesn't mean it isn't watched. Stuart knew he wasn't alone when he came across a couple of lawn chairs near what looked like a bike path running east to west. The official border patrol wouldn't waste their time in the thick, mostly deserted forests, but vigilantes might. There was a northern group that was similar to the armed collection of radicals who had patrolled the Mexican border in Arizona. Stuart was still in Canada, but it wasn't unheard of that they'd set up watch points on both sides.

If it were vigilantes and they noticed Stuart, he believed they'd limit themselves to following him while they contacted the police via cell phones, so he didn't think he'd be in immediate danger. If they were armed, he was fairly certain they wouldn't use their guns. The fact that the chairs were empty suggested to him it was a daytime operation. Nevertheless, he was as quiet as he could be while he walked past.

He walked along the bike path for a hundred yards or so before he reentered the woods. A good tracker would find his entry point no matter how careful he was, but he hoped his tactic would delay anyone looking for him even if it wouldn't stop them. *Better safe than sorry.*

Once Stuart was back in the woods he needed to use the GPS to reorient himself. He twisted the device around in his hand before returning it to his backpack. His thoughts returned to a conversation he'd had with Jamie after her session with Hannah's hypnotist. She talked about her ambition in a way he'd never heard her speak before.

***

"I focus too much on becoming a star," Jamie told Stuart. "When I think about the importance of theater in my life there's more to it than that."

"I know," Stuart replied. "You're an artist. Your body's your instrument and the stage is your canvas. You've told me this before."

"That's not what I'm trying to say, not this time. I think my love for theater has a lot to do with the way the stage offers me a chance to lead another life. I hope that doesn't sound bad. I don't mean that my life with you and Starr isn't enough. It's just that sometimes I need to be someone other than the person I am."

"Is that why you drink?"

"Maybe. I'm not sure. But I know that when Glen Wiley hypnotized me he showed me how I once *was* someone other than the person I am today. And that person was flawed in ways that go way beyond the failings I have now."

"It's how you deal with failings that's important. Everyone has them."

"Exactly. And I've been dealing with them in ways that are wrong. I think I'm addicted and I don't just mean to alcohol. I need to step away from acting for a while. I need to spend more time with my family."

She had finally admitted they belonged together.

CHAPTER TWENTY-ONE

There was a road at the edge of the woods. He knew from his planning that this was Line Road, the boundary between Canada and the USA. Yet there were no customs officials here, just a chain link fence on the other side that he thought wouldn't be hard to climb. He wasn't certain where the actual border was. If it ran down the middle of the road, he would be in his home country before he encountered the fence.

When he reached the fence, he leaned the box against it, tossed his backpack to the other side, and started to climb. The fencing came above the top crossbar, but the cut ends of the wire had been bent over. Stuart placed his right foot carefully and jumped to the other side. Less than a minute later, he was in the cover of trees again—this time, thankfully, in an American forest.

Stuart checked his watch. The sun would be up in less than an hour. The hike had taken him longer than he had expected.

It took him a while to find what he thought would be a perfect hiding place, but he finally tucked the box between two large rocks, snapped a picture, checked the GPS, and jotted down the coordinates. Then he turned north and started retracing his steps.

Crossing the fence the second time, his luck turned: a car drove by while he was still on the fence. Stuart ducked his head to hide his face, hopped down, and darted across the road. He was back in Canada now, but had to get into the woods in case someone started chasing him.

Stuart had been weaving through the woods and climbing over fallen trees for about twenty minutes when he began to hear the sounds of others in the forest. It was hard to tell where the sounds were coming from but he thought they were ahead of, rather than behind, him. And now the sun was coming up. He no longer had the advantage of darkness.

Stuart came across the bike path after ten more minutes of hiking. Either he had wandered further north than he had planned or the path had dipped south. The ease of traveling along a clear trail was tempting but he knew he would be foolish to take it for long. If people were looking for him, he needed to be as inconspicuous as possible, *and* do everything he could to misdirect their search. He decided to repeat the technique he had used earlier and ran along the trail for close to a hundred yards before turning back into the woods and heading southeast.

When Stuart reached the eastern border of the forest he paused for a few minutes. The road looked quiet, but he wanted to be certain. Within seconds, an aged Toyota passed by, very slowly. Stuart ducked out of sight. They *had* to be looking for him.

It was not safe. He moved back into the woods and surveyed his surroundings carefully, finally choosing to sit on the ground between two large trees that had fallen side by side. If all went well, he'd be safely hidden until nightfall, when he could sneak out and make his escape.

Stuart was close enough to the road to hear passing cars, but there was very little traffic. The temperature was above freezing, but not by a great deal, so some of the leaves on the ground were crisp with a thin layer of ice while others had thawed and were limp. There was a slight smell from the decaying leaves, but it wasn't as strong as it would be later in the day when the temperature rose.

Stuart wondered about the people who he believed were searching for him. He had crossed the border back into Canada rather than the other way around, so they were likely to be Canadian border patrol. He was glad he no longer had the box with him and that there was nothing in his backpack that could be considered contraband.

It took less than an hour before boredom caused Stuart's fears to fade and his thoughts to turn away from his predicament. He lay back and stared up at the tree tops swaying in the wind. It was too cold to lie down for long but at that moment his need to stretch outweighed the discomfort of the near freezing ground against the length of his body. He wiggled about before sitting back up. He was moving more than he should, but he was confident he wouldn't be discovered, hidden by the broad trunks of the fallen trees.

Stuart sat on the cold ground all day, shifting position frequently to keep his muscles from getting too sore. Occasionally he heard someone, or something, in the woods nearby. He thought about the situation that had forced him to hide behind a tree like a frightened rabbit and he convinced himself that Jamie was right: this couldn't continue.

When darkness finally fell, Stuart got up, stretching his stiff legs until he could move comfortably. When he was confident he was alone, he began the trek out.

He was relieved to find his car undisturbed. Once he was certain no one was watching, he was quickly on his way.

Stuart drove across the border without incident. Now all that remained to do was retrieve the box. He checked the GPS and was surprised at how close to a street he had hidden the package. He found it easily. Tomorrow night, he would drop it off, finally putting an end to his mission.

CHAPTER TWENTY-TWO

Miss Julie opened on a Friday night. Glen was surprised that the attendance in the eighty-seat facility was so low, but Hannah explained it wasn't uncommon, that some people felt it was like charging to attend a final dress rehearsal.

Paul had told Glen to stop the regressions of the cast members after only Jamie and Troy, claiming that certain theater board members thought the article in *The Herald* was embarrassing. Glen hadn't had a chance to work with Paul and harbored a suspicion that the director might have had his own reasons for wanting the sessions to stop.

Sitting next to Hannah in the third row, with Stuart on her other side, Glen realized that something felt wrong to him. The feeling had nothing to do with Hannah or with Stuart. There was something odd about the show they were set to watch.

"The painting's back," Hannah whispered to Stuart.

Glen looked at the watercolor hanging on one of the upstage flats. It had a distinct Asian feel about it, a look that did not belong in Sweden in the late eighteen hundreds.

"What do you mean *back*?"

Hannah leaned in to answer, "It was on the set of *A Doll's House*. Stuart and I were so surprised by it that I had Paige walk us up on the stage to look at it closely. It's a painting of a puppet theater in China. Paige told us there's a wealthy board member who owns it and likes to show it off."

Troy Allen and Allison Simpson were the first to occupy the stage. In the opening scene their characters were talking about Miss Julie, preparing the audience for Jamie's grand entrance. Troy had on a three piece suit with a jacket that had tails. He looked like a butler, which Glen assumed was because his character, Jean, was a servant of Miss Julie's.

Allison was wearing a yellow dress with vertical stripes of darker yellow, long sleeves, a long skirt, and a high neckline with ruffles. Glen knew enough about the nineteenth century to realize that her outfit was typical for a servant from that period.

When Jamie came on stage Glen's gaze was drawn to her. It was her presence rather than her costume, which was every bit as modest as the one worn by Allison. It was gray with red trim and a loose top with blousy sleeves. Glen was glad the director hadn't given her a low neckline. Some Victorian gowns were low cut, of course, but most were designed for practical, everyday wear.

After Jamie's entrance Glen started to lose himself in the performance. She could speak in what he heard as a soft, coquettish voice but what was in reality a voice loud enough to project throughout the theater. She also seemed to upstage the other two actors physically—without trying. The actress disappeared as Jamie Tilly became Miss Julie. Hannah had told him that Jamie considered this role to be a stepping stone for her. He could understand why she would think that, but he doubted any talent agents would see a show this far from Manhattan.

Glen had regressed many people to the nineteenth century and had studied the reactions of all of them, but this play gave him a very different view of what life was like in that period of history. August Strindberg, the man who'd written it, had lived in that time and was trying to comment about its hypocrisy. According to a note in the program, Strindberg was the son of a servant who married an aristocrat. Miss Julie is a woman of high class who steps down to have an affair with a servant. There were certainly autobiographical elements in the work.

About the time Jean and Julie left the kitchen to have their off-stage affair, Glen started feeling that there was an odd relationship between this show and his work. The past lives he had explored so far were all from the period in which *Miss Julie* was set. Was it a coincidence, he wondered, or were the actors familiar on some level with the time and for that reason drawn to this particular revival. Hannah, who was neither acting or working backstage, was emotionally involved. Stuart was her best friend and his wife was the star. Glen decided he needed to look deeper.

"Who picks the plays they do in this theater?" Glen asked Hannah when they were driving home.

"A governing board makes the final decisions. People who aren't on the committee have to speak to them if they have a particular favorite they want produced."

"Did Jamie argue for this one?"

"I don't know. A couple of years ago she convinced them to do *Three Penny Opera*."

"I don't know that one."

"It's a musical. The song *Mack the Knife* is from it. You've heard of that, right?"

"Sure. Bobby Darin sang it in the fifties."

"You should have heard our Macheath. What a voice! The guy drove from New Hampshire an hour each way for the role. I wish I remembered his name. Anyway, the play's about a marriage that angers the bride's father, another version of *Romeo and Juliet*, I suppose. It's set in Victorian England."

"In the nineteenth century? Like *Miss Julie*? And Jamie argued for it?"

"Yes, yes, and yes."

Glen grew pensive. Maybe the Victorian pattern was a coincidence—but maybe it wasn't.

CHAPTER TWENTY-THREE

At Glen's insistence, Hannah convinced Jamie to invite her and Glen to the cast party; they were never closed events, and she had attended occasionally in the past. "You're the hypnotist, aren't you?" Allison asked Glen less than a minute after Hannah and he stepped into the room. Hannah slid a little closer to him. Allison's eyes were focused on Glen and she did not want to be left out of the conversation.

"Jamie and Troy both said the experience was awesome. When's my turn?"

"Sorry," Glen told her. "Plans have changed. I thought Paul would have told you."

"He didn't."

"Would you still like to try it? You should have time now that rehearsals are over."

Hannah looked at Glen, who was smiling pleasantly, before turning her gaze back to Allison, trying to decide if the woman was simply making conversation, and hoping not. They'd been lucky with the other two cast members, so Allison was the next logical step.

"It sounds like fun," Allison said. "Tell me when and where."

Hannah was about to suggest a time for Allison to come by her place when she noticed Stuart lurking behind the young woman. It was clear he'd been eavesdropping. That he showed any interest in regressions was a surprise. What wasn't was that Jamie was not with him. She's probably getting her drink refilled for the zillionth time, Hannah thought.

"Pick a day," Glen told Allison.

"Tuesday, if that's all right."

Hannah and Stuart's eyes met for a moment. He glanced away then turned and started to leave the room. "Excuse me," Hannah said to Glen and Allison, and followed Stuart out to the foyer where there was a staircase leading up to what she imagined were some fairly fancy bedrooms. He started to climb the stairs. She was curious and didn't know if he had noticed she was trailing him.

She could see four open doors at the top of the stairs. No one was in the single room on the left. She could, however, see a bed with a pile of coats, with her own white one on top. She turned the opposite way and went down the long hall. Stuart had to be in one of those rooms.

The first room was set up to be a study, housing a desk, a bookcase, and a couch with a matching chair, all in shades of brown. But no Stuart.

She moved on to the next room and found Stuart sitting on the bed with his back toward the door. It wasn't until she was through the door that she noticed Jamie sitting next to him. Their faces were close and his hand was resting softly on Jamie's leg. Their body language showed an intimacy she hadn't seen between them for years.

"Hannah," Jamie said, sounding surprised. "I'm glad you made it. Where's Glen?"

"Talking to Allison."

"Allison?"

"Yes. She asked him to regress her. Apparently she heard how good the experience was."

"I told her that."

"You and Troy both did."

"Do you think he might have time for me?" Stuart interjected. "I think I might be a better subject if he is willing to try again."

"I'll tell him."

Hannah turned to leave the room, but not before noticing that the drink Jamie was holding was a bottle of water.

CHAPTER TWENTY-FOUR

Jamie knew where she wanted the conversation to go, but she had to be careful how she got there. Stuart sometimes had a stubborn streak. So she reminisced about the time they had snuck out at night and lay on the grass in Stuart's backyard counting the stars, and about the tent village they had built out of a pile of her mother's old blankets strung up on a clothesline. They had raced through the tunnel of tents on their hands and knees.

She also had talked about the "telephone" they had made from two Beefaroni cans and some string and how she had tried to speak over it, promising Stuart they would be best friends forever. But he hadn't understood what she had been saying and later she had been too embarrassed to tell.

Finally, she moved the conversation to the regression session she'd had with Glen, a step closer to what she needed to say. "I've changed ever since I learned I've had multiple lives. There's more to us than just our day to day 'this life' stuff. I can see possibilities where I couldn't before."

"What possibilities?" He sounded interested, which she took as a good sign.

"When I was regressed I discovered things that had always been hidden. That made me wonder about other concepts I'd brushed off because there was no proof. There are powerful forces that are part of our lives. I'm sure of that now."

"Are you talking about God?"

"Putting a name to it doesn't do it justice, even if the name is God."

"Okay. Call what you're feeling a possibility. I can understand that. It sounds like something you want to explore."

"It is."

"How?"

Stuart's question made sense, Jamie was surprised by it. She was feeling rather than thinking, which was the way she generally dealt with complex issues. She had no actual plan; however, she wanted one.

"Any suggestions?" she asked Stuart, touching his arm as she spoke.

"Hannah's been trying to get us to go to church with her for years."

Jamie didn't want a bunch of stodgy old people telling her what she had to believe. "I don't think so," she said. "I want to explore these thoughts on my own. What I've been through is entirely mine. I want to draw my own conclusions about it."

"Hannah says they let you do that in *her* church."

"Do they?"

"I'm not saying they won't quote Jesus and all that, but Hannah says they listen to your doubts and your theories no matter how outrageous. She says they're very nice people. It's been a while since she brought her church up. She would be way beyond surprised if we told her we wanted to go with her."

"The regression left me thinking about something else," Jamie stood up and turned to face him. The time was finally right to say what was actually on her mind. "There's no other way to say this. I'm scared—for you."

His head jerked slightly.

"The woman I was in the eighteen hundreds was living her entire life on the edge. She existed one day at a time, prowling the streets each night to find enough cash to pay for a place to sleep. She had sex with men of every type imaginable, some of them extremely brutal." Jamie stopped speaking to study Stuart's expression. When she was certain she still had his attention she continued. "But most of that was just a part of her daily routine. It was the man who asked her to deliver his package who truly scared her. There was an aura of power about him. He was polished and sophisticated. He didn't hurt Annie, didn't even touch her. Yet she was under his control." Jamie touched Stuart's leg, then leaned in toward him.

"I'm still scared, but not for Annie. Her life is only memories. You're the one I'm worried about. History is repeating itself. You're being forced to retrieve and deliver packages just like Annie was. This has to stop."

Jamie could feel the tension in Stuart's body. His voice quivered as he said softly, "Stopping is what's dangerous. They know you and they know Starr. If I even think about refusing to do what they ask, something horrible will happen."

"The longer we wait, the harder it'll be. It's like you're stuck in quicksand. You worry that trying to save yourself will cause you to sink faster, but if you do nothing, you'll still go down eventually."

"Not as long as I cooperate and I'm careful."

"What would have happened if the border patrol caught you? You don't even know what was in the box. Starr and I want you around. If you keep this up eventually you won't be."

She took a deep breath. "I was Annie Chapman, who was the one moving packages back then. According to nineteenth century history she was one of Jack the Ripper's victims, murdered in a ritualistic act of violence very much like the way Paige was killed. There's a lot going on here that I don't understand, a lot of similarities with what's going on today. It's scary."

Stuart put his arms around her and pulled her close. "I don't understand this stuff either, but, my God, it's horrible. There's so much more to this than I imagined. We'll talk to Glen and get him to help us understand the relationships between your past life and what's been happening to me. If it means telling him about the smuggling, well, we'll just have to hope you're right. There are too many coincidences. We can't figure it out by ourselves."

Stuart hadn't agreed to stop delivering the packages, but Jamie was satisfied. They were starting to fight back.

CHAPTER TWENTY-FIVE

Stuart and Glen were currently the only two men in Hannah's life she thought of as more than acquaintances. As soon as Stuart became a less available friend due to the apparent change in his relationship with his wife, she began to look at Glen differently. He was eighteen years older than she was. He dressed a little dorky with his dark rimmed glasses and baggy clothes. But he was intelligent, exciting, and had filled a little of the void left by Paige's death. If she was to be honest with herself, she would have to admit that she hadn't asked Glen to move into her guest room for purely economic reasons. She didn't like being alone.

"I want to regress you again," Glen told Hannah.

"Now?" They hadn't stayed at the party until the end, but it was still close to eleven.

"There has to be a reason Dr. Saffell was terse with me. It may have nothing to do with either your past life or with Paige's death, but then again it might. I'd like us to take another look at nineteenth century London. We hadn't met the doctor before your last regression, so we didn't have any reason to look for someone who might be similar to him. Now we do."

"I'll go change." While she searched for something suitable to wear, she replayed the last few moments of the cast party.

***

She'd come downstairs to find a small group of people clustered around the piano in the great room, singing Broadway songs as Allison played with reasonable skill. Glenn had taken the opportunity to approach Dr. Saffell, hoping, he'd told her later, to gain some insight into the process involved in choosing the plays for the season.

"Dr. Saffell," Glen said, "you have a lovely house. I wanted to thank you for hosting this party. We're friends of Jamie."

The doctor reached out to shake Glen's hand. "Nice to meet you."

The conversation faltered. Clearly, Glen felt uneasy. She held her hand out to Dr. Saffell. He shook it.

"I believe we've met before," he said. "You were Paige Stackman's friend, weren't you?"

People rarely mentioned Paige to Hannah and when they did, it was always with an implied sense of sorrow. Dr. Saffell's tone sounded more like he was speaking about someone who'd suffered some minor sickness rather than a woman who had been murdered in an extremely brutal way.

Hannah was also surprised that the doctor said they had met. She couldn't remember that ever happening. She was about to ask him where when he changed the subject.

"Have either of you seen Jamie Tilly? I want to tell her how amazing her performance was."

Hannah and Glen both shook their heads negatively. Hannah hated to lie, but she didn't want to reveal that Jamie and Stuart had been exploring the upstairs rooms of his home.

Dr. Saffell left to look for Jamie, leaving Hannah alone with Glen.

"He didn't act like he wanted to talk to us," Hannah commented. "He was almost rude. And I'd swear I've never met him before."

**

Glen already had the green blanket spread out on the floor. Hannah got down on her back as gracefully as she could.

She picked out a focal point, the same spot on the ceiling she had chosen the last time Glen regressed her. She tried to concentrate on the spot rather than on Glen. Even though she wasn't looking in his direction, she could feel him approaching her. She knew that he was holding out his right hand. Perhaps she had caught a glimpse of him with her peripheral vision, a glimpse brief enough not to register in her consciousness. Or maybe she had some mystical connection with Glen that kept her in touch with where he was and what he was doing.

Glen's hand came to rest on Hannah's left shoulder. His touch wasn't intimate. It had the feel of a brother's hand, strong and kind. Hannah was surprised at the disappointment she felt.

"What's wrong?" he asked.

"Nothing."

"I can see in your expression that something's bothering you. Don't lie to me, please."

Hannah sat up and pulled the blanket around her shoulders.

"Does it have something to do with Stuart?"

"It's not your concern."

"Whatever you're going through is serious enough to interfere with our work. When that happens it becomes my concern."

"I'm sorry I disturbed your session. I'll lie back down and start to count backwards. Would that help?" she asked sarcastically.

Hannah leaned back, but Glen reached out and kept her from lying down.

"It isn't just the work. You've become a friend. Tell me what's bothering you."

"I don't need a friend. You want to help? Don't talk."

Glen shook his head and pulled his hand away. "This isn't like you, Hannah."

Hannah was silent for a few moments. "I miss Paige. I know I can't bring her back, so I keep looking for something else—someone else. I thought I had what I needed when you began to help me find answers and that's still true. Paige deserves the truth. I still want to give it to her. I just feel so alone.

"It helped when you moved in. I can't begin to tell you how much I hated the emptiness of my home before you shared it with me, but I miss holding someone in my arms. I miss the smell of someone else's hair. I miss knowing someone cares about me more than anyone else in the world."

Glen stood up and walked back to the couch. He sat down, leaned back then said, "I'm sorry. Forget about the regression for tonight. If we want to solve this murder I need to know more about the victim. Tell me how the two of you fell in love."

"I never said I was in love with her."

"Yes, you did."

***

Five years earlier, Hannah had considered returning to college. She had attended The University of Vermont after high school, with the intention of majoring in accounting. But in the middle of her second semester she started feeling lethargic. Whether from depression or some undiagnosed physical malady, she felt unable to study and her grades plummeted. She decided her transcript would look better if she was a dropout rather than a failure. Three years later she felt ready to try again.

The University of Vermont did not want her back.

After she opened the rejection letter she didn't want to be alone, even if her only other option was to be with strangers. She put on a dress and drove to a karaoke bar she'd heard about in Brattleboro.

Hannah noticed the karaoke singer with the red-orange hair as soon as she walked in. And the woman's outfit could have been cut from the same roll of green paisley fabric as Hannah's. But their dresses were stitched together in very different ways. While Hannah's was cute with short sleeves and a skirt that was just above her knees, the singer's was sexy. It had a low neckline, a drawn-in waist, and a skirt that stopped mid thigh. The comparison made Hannah feel like an ugly sister.

The girl was singing *China Girl* and swaying in a way that made it impossible to look elsewhere. It was an odd song for any woman to sing, but she did it justice. Apparently, the lady in the matching dress was talented as well as sexy. Hannah's day couldn't have been worse. She considered driving straight back to Springfield, but wasn't ready to face another fifty minute drive. Instead, she ordered a Long Island Iced Tea from the bar then found a table and sat down alone. She hoped some guy might pick her up. If one did, she knew she'd go anywhere he suggested. She needed a warm body to hold.

The bartender, a woman wearing jeans and a Tom Brady football jersey, brought Hannah's drink to her table. The staff were the most casually dressed people in the room.

"Hi, there, lady in my dress."

Hannah looked up from her drink to see that the singer had put down the karaoke mic and had come to her table.

"You've got good taste," the singer said with a slow smile. "Mind if I join you?"

"Have a seat," Hannah told her, nodding toward the chair on her right. The woman kept standing. "And, actually, our dresses aren't alike at all. Yours shows you off. Mine covers me up."

"But, look, they're exactly the same pattern." The girl moved so close to Hannah they were almost touching. She picked up the hem of her skirt and held it next to Hannah's. The skirt was so short when she lifted it she came close to showing off the pattern of her underwear rather than her dress.

"It's amazing," the girl said. "Where did you buy yours?"

"Some place in Chester. I forget the name."

"Speaking of names, I'm Paige. And you are?"

"Depressed and likely to remain that way until I get more alcohol in my system."

"That's a shame, but I was asking for your name. You alone?"

"It's Hannah. And I am alone. How about you?"

"I'm with that group over there." Paige nodded at a table across the bar. "But they won't miss me if I sit here for a while."

"I've had an awful day," Hannah told her, not waiting to be asked. "I was rejected from UVM. I dropped out a while back, but always thought I could go back. I guess I was wrong."

"I see," Paige said, her voice taking on a soft tone. "Rejection feels bad, but maybe school isn't for you. There's lots of other ways to learn. What did you want to study?"

"Accounting"

"Oh, Lord. It sounds like you caught a break. Excuse my reaction, but I can't think of anything more boring."

"I suppose I could study another drink," Hannah quipped. She caught the eye of the bartender and pointed to her empty glass.

"If you really want to, there are other ways you can do it. You could pick a different school, maybe sign up for one of those Internet degrees.

Or you could take a class or two. If you prove yourself you'd likely get into the degree program eventually. I've seen that happen before."

"Have you?"

"I've got an idea that'll make you feel better. You can sing, can't you? I mean, isn't that why you're here?"

"I came to listen."

"You could do *Everybody Hurts*. It's in the selection book. I always sing it when I want to get over something. Nothing feels better than your own voice. It's empowering."

The bartender brought Hannah a fresh drink. Hannah handed her a ten and told her to keep the change.

"This," Hannah said holding the drink up, "feels better."

"It won't in the morning."

"To hell with the morning."

Hannah downed half her drink, then sat back in her chair and appreciated the rush that came with the alcohol.

"Maybe I *will* try a song or two," she conceded. But she got up too fast and felt dizzy. She had to lean on the table.

Paige jumped up and put her arm around Hannah to keep her from falling.

"I'll do a duet with you. In these dresses it'll look like we planned it. Do you know *Defying Gravity*?"

"No, but defying gravity sounds like something I can do." Hannah started to laugh. "Watch me fly!"

"Oh, you're flying all right. Everyone can see that."

Hannah laughed. She was ready to laugh at everything.

***

"The walk up to the karaoke mic was the last thing I remember about that night," Hannah told Glen. "I woke up on a couch in an apartment Paige shared with the three people she was with at the bar. Turned out they were just roommates. I had the worst headache ever and my stomach was just as bad. Every time I sat up I felt like puking. My dress was wrinkled and I had spilled something purple on it. I kept the dress, but I never got the stain out."

"Paige wouldn't let you drive home," Glen said. "That was nice of her."

"Saved my life, I guess. I was worried about work, but she convinced me to call in sick. It didn't take much convincing. I knew I couldn't drive, so I stayed there all that day. We hit it off and kept in touch afterwards. We started going to movies and plays together. We tried about anything we could think of that was fun. We played pool, went bowling, and even raced go-carts one time. She became my best friend."

"You said you missed holding someone in your arms?"

"Did I?"

Glen nodded.

"Sometimes Paige and I would hold on to each other for hours because it felt right. It's good to have someone who cares. You can call that whatever you choose. But remember, when Paige was murdered she was in a motel waiting for Paul Trepanier, who happens to be a man. And she was the first woman I'd ever been with. Until then, all my relationships had been with men."

Hannah worried that laying out the whole truth might ruin her memories of Paige, so she didn't add the more personal details.

CHAPTER TWENTY-SIX

Hannah had been at work when Jamie called to ask if Stuart could have a session with Glen. She was pleased that Stuart had changed his mind, even if he wasn't coming alone.

Jamie and Stuart had been sitting in Hannah's living room for only a minute or two when Jamie began explaining Stuart's situation. He didn't add anything to what she said and didn't correct any of her details. It was clear to Hannah that he was ashamed of the hole he'd dug, but she quickly decided he was not at fault. She knew Stuart had been trying to do right by his family.

"I wanted to go to the police," Jamie said. "But Stuart's afraid the word could get out. But we have to talk to somebody about this."

"If I could find out who's sending the instructions things would be different," Stuart said, sounding defensive.

"How can we help?" Hannah asked.

"I'm not sure you can," Jamie told her. Then she turned and addressed Glen. "But *you* might be able to, if you're willing."

"Are you coming to me because you see a connection between the packages Stuart's being forced to carry and the ones you carried when you were Annie Chapman?"

"Yes."

Glen had told Hannah how souls that impact each others' lives often return to repeat their actions in other incarnations. It made sense that Stuart was a part of what had happened to Rose and Annie.

Hannah was impressed by Glen's poker face; she knew how much he wanted this regression.

Glen said, "I can bring out your memories, if that's what you want. And it might help."

Hannah tried to read Stuart's expression. He seemed slightly relieved, but he wasn't speaking much. Coming to them had probably been Jamie's idea, she decided.

Glen continued, "It isn't unusual for events in one life to tie over to another, especially if the events are traumatic." He turned to Jamie. "But it would make more sense if you were the one being forced to smuggle items across the Canadian border since you were Annie in your past life."

"All the more reason to regress Stuart," Jamie insisted. "If he was with us in that time, we need to find out something about him."

***

Stuart watched as Hannah took the green blanket off of her couch and spread it on the floor. Glen had not given him any instructions, but the blanket was a good indication that they expected him to lie on it. He got down on his back.

Glen started to explain what he was about to do as he looked down at Stuart. "Souls often travel together from incarnation to incarnation, especially if there is a powerful event that links them together. Hannah and Jamie are a part of one of those spiritual families, and chances are you are, too. I think it's safe to assume you were with them in England during the 1800s, so I'm going to steer you toward those memories."

Glen had used the image of walking in a forest when he had tried to regress Stuart the previous time, but realized that scene wouldn't work because of Stuart's experience in Canada. This time he used floating through a cloud to provide a mental picture in which Stuart was surrounded by an environment that was peaceful and could have existed in any period of time.

"You're drifting back to nineteenth century London. The city is a thriving metropolis, filled with people from all over the world. Most of them are in London looking for work. There are poor and homeless, from Africa, Asia, and often the Americas."

Stuart knew quickly that Glen had been right. He *had* been a part of the life Jamie remembered. However, he had no sense of Hannah. But Hannah and Jamie had said they were both there. He could feel his knowledge of Jamie blending with a knowledge he was remembering of Annie, as well as himself blending with the person he had once been.

Stuart looked down at his hands to see brown skin. He was not English. He was Ratinam Pillai, a yoga master brought from Tamil Nadu in southern India by a wealthy man with the given name of Lucius.

***

Ratinam was standing in Carter Lane near St. Paul's Cathedral. He was waiting for the courier to bring him the next package. He didn't know who the courier would be, but he was hoping for Annie, the woman who had delivered the last two boxes. Ratinam didn't usually take an interest in the people he worked with, but this time was different. He felt a connection with her that made him suspect he had known her in another life.

He knew she was a drunk and a prostitute; he could see in her eyes that her life had been hard. Her problems with spirits and low status were similar to issues he had dealt with in his own life. He had found solace through Vedanta Yoga and wished he could share that with her. But Lucius had spelled out a specific purpose for Ratinam and would not like it if Ratinam strayed from the goal he'd given him.

Ratinam smiled when he saw it was Annie who approached him. "What have you brought me today?"

"I have no idea," she retorted. These words were becoming their normal banter.

She pulled a wooden box, about as wide as her forearm, half again as long and thick as her hand, from under her cape. The cape looked expensive. He wondered how much they were paying her to carry the packages through the city.

"The stone we're after could be in there."

"Stone?"

As soon as she spoke, Ratinam realized he'd said too much. He was not supposed to give her even the most obscure hint.

"Do you have a place to stay tonight?" he asked, changing the subject. The last time he had seen her she mentioned that she needed money for the lodging house.

"Yes, and it's getting late. I need to go there."

Annie was always rushing away. When Ratinam had arrived in England he'd been naïve enough to believe that leaving the caste system behind would mean fewer class problems. He was wrong. Even Annie acted superior most of the time, like any other white woman when face to face with a brown man. With her, however, there were signs that she felt opposite from the way she acted. When she was close enough to hand him the package, her hands shook slightly. Yet he knew she wasn't afraid to be on the streets after dark. She also averted her gaze, as if she were shy, when he knew shyness wasn't a problem for her. Yoga was the way to get beyond Annie's feeling of inferiority. Ratinam needed to find a way to bring it to her.

"Do you want to know what's in the box?" he offered, shattering the rule of secrecy. He knew it was crazy. If Lucius found out there was no telling what he would do. Ratinam would certainly lose his confidence and the gold that came with it. He might even lose his life. Lucius's thugs were also Indian, but that wouldn't stop them from killing him if that's what they were paid to do.

"You're saying you might tell me?"

"I'll let you see," he whispered, "but you must follow me inside. I cannot open it out here."

Ratinam saw Annie's eyes dart to the only other person on the street at that late hour, a drunk who was sleeping with the rats near a pile of day old, rotting garbage that hadn't made it to the river.

He turned, walked up the stoop of the nearest row house, and opened the door. He held it for Annie, who stepped past him and into the building.

Ratinam led Annie into a room on the first floor at the back of the house. There was a fireplace with a brown mantel and surround, and an ornate sideboard, brown as the fireplace, with a large mirror behind it. He lit an oil lamp, and she could see that in the center of the room was a round table, also brown but a lighter shade. There were two large windows, both covered with long, off-white drapes. The room smelled of a combination of coal smoke from the furnace and oil from the lamp. There was also a familiar mildew odor that would have allowed Ratinam to recognize the room with his eyes shut.

Ratinam studied his companion. Scattered around the room on various surfaces as well as the floor were oriental artifacts. He wondered if she would react.

Annie walked around the room. She reached out to touch a small jade statue of a long-haired man riding a dragon. She picked it up, causing Ratinam to twitch slightly. But a feeling of trust kept him from taking it away from her. *Why do I trust her?*

"These are pretty," Annie said, "and I suppose they are worth a great deal. Are they stolen?"

"Not in this century," he said, not expecting such a question.

"There has to be a purpose for the secrecy. Why does Albert pay me to deliver them when he could just bring them himself?"

Instead of answering her question, Ratinam placed the box beside some tools on the table then picked up a chisel and started to pry it open.

"Don't you do this if it will cause trouble for you."

"This piece is important," Ratinam said. He brushed aside some straw and pulled out a stone tablet with characters chiseled on its surface. He knew she wouldn't be able to read the words, but he held it up for her to see anyway. "This is written in a language called Sanskrit. To us, it's worth more than all the others combined."

"Why are you telling me this? You don't know if I'm a bloody thief. You have no idea what I'm capable of doing."

"The tablet would be worthless to you."

"Some of the statues are gold, aren't they? Those wouldn't be worthless."

"I know I can trust you."

"What do the words say?" Annie asked, switching subjects.

"They aren't words, exactly. They are sounds to be used in chants."

"That's bloody strange."

He flinched at her language. "The sounds, when used properly, can connect mind, body, and spirit in a way that opens new worlds. Someday I would like to teach you."

***

Hannah watched Jamie as Glen called Stuart out of his hypnotic trance using a soft voice. Stuart had spent the entire session with Annie, Jamie's life in that period. He spoke about a connection Ratinam had with Annie, a connection that was buried in their memories, as if what they shared was a form of timeless love.

Hannah thought about the concept of spiritual families and wondered if during the current life and the one from the nineteenth century those two souls got together while in other lives they didn't. Or perhaps they were always together and her own soul was always the third wheel.

Jamie stepped toward Stuart and offered him a hand to help him up. When he was on his feet she hugged him. Hannah wondered what she was thinking. The connection between Ratinam and Annie was beautiful, but if life was repeating itself there was a lot to fear. Annie Chapman wasn't just some woman who lived in the nineteenth century. She was a prostitute who had been murdered, and in as brutal a manner as Paige had.

"Do lives repeat themselves?" Hannah asked Glen. Jamie moved away from Stuart to turn to look at Glen. Hannah guessed the same question had been on her mind.

"Sometimes," Glen told her.

"With changes?"

"Of course. There are far too many factors in the equation of life for it to be any other way."

"You weren't surprised when Ratinam started talking about delving into people's memories?"

"I didn't say that."

"Seems as if he should have been one of *your* past lives, not one of Stuart's."

"You're right. It doesn't make much sense."

Hannah was surprised by the phrase *much sense*. "We're in an entirely different world here," she said. "*Sense* doesn't even apply. Is hypnotism a talent that moves from soul to soul as if it's contagious?"

"Ratinam wasn't a hypnotist. He used yoga. There are many paths into our memories."

"Is that supposed to make everything clear?"

"I can't make it clear. I'm as confused as you are."

***

Jamie was irritated with the way Hannah and Glen were throwing around irrelevant theories while she and Stuart were dealing with real problems. Couldn't they understand the need for urgency?

"What do we do about Stuart's situation? We don't know who these guys are. He gets his instructions through anonymous emails."

Stuart was looking at the floor. "They've also sent threats against Jamie and Starr. If I knew who they were, I'd go after them, but as it is I'm helpless. That's why we're here. We're scared to go to the police and we need to talk to someone. We have no idea what to do."

Hannah told him, "You'll end up in jail if you don't stop. Do you think the threats are real? What would they gain by hurting Starr or Jamie? They couldn't force you to deliver the packages after they did something like that and they know it."

Jamie wasn't as certain. She considered what had happened to Annie in her past life. What if history was repeating itself? She had hoped Glen would tell them what to do based on something he learned from Stuart's memory. Instead Hannah was the one doling out the advice.

Jamie had to use all her acting skills to keep her expression from revealing the fear she was feeling. "Hannah's right," Jamie told her husband. "We've got to end this now."

CHAPTER TWENTY-SEVEN

"If the packages Stuart has been forced to deliver have similar contents to the ones Annie delivered, then something truly bizarre is going on," Glen told Hannah after Jamie and Stuart were gone. "Stuart needs to stop what he's doing, but if we lose his association with the smugglers we're going to lose the best potential lead in Paige's murder we've had since I arrived."

"Stuart's safety is more important."

"I'm not sure cutting off his activities is going to help him stay alive."

"If that's how you feel, why didn't you say anything?"

"I didn't know what to tell them. Events from past lives don't always reappear, but sometimes they do. You were right when you said that the status quo was unacceptable, but I'm not sure what's going to happen. Remember, Jamie has Annie Chapman's soul."

"Are you scared?"

"For them? Yes."

Hannah wished Glen wasn't so confused. She said, "We'll talk in the morning. I think I'll call in sick."

**

Hannah lay in her bed, her mind racing. She stared into the darkness, unable to sleep. She was worried something would go wrong, but, more than that, she was feeling guilty. After half an hour of tossing and turning she got up, stepped into the hall without turning on a light and knocked on Glen's door.

"Are you awake? I need to talk."

"Come in."

He was sitting up, leaning against the headboard of his bed. There was enough light coming through the open door for her to see. She walked to his bed and sat beside him.

"I was certain I was giving Stuart the right advice, but now I'm not so sure."

"They know your answers aren't perfect," Glen said. "They needed to hear what someone else thought so they can consider all their options."

The lump in Hannah's throat kept her from speaking for a moment. She held her breath then tried to force the words out, but as she spoke tears began to flow and she started to shake. Glen reached out and drew her close. He slid down in the bed. She curled up next to him and rested her head on his chest.

"For a long time I've thought Stuart got a raw deal with Jamie." Her voice cracked. "She always came first in their marriage. It didn't seem fair." She shifted her arm across Glen's stomach and hugged him. "I told them to do what was good for Stuart, not for Jamie. I wasn't even thinking about her."

"It's all right. You helped them by talking it through. It's their decision, not yours or mine. They know that."

"Kiss me, Glen. Please kiss me."

***

Glen hadn't had his arms around a woman in years. But the smell of her hair and the soft feel of her skin were as familiar as if he'd been with Hannah hundreds of times. Was he touching a memory from one of his own past lives? He didn't think so.

With little effort, he bent slightly to touch her lips with his. It was as if Hannah was breathing life into him.

Despite the fact that she had brought Glen to a point where it was almost impossible to think, he still recognized there was something wrong with what was happening. Hannah was kissing him because she was upset. He just happened to be there when she needed someone to hold. His feelings for her were emotional and spiritual, but at that moment they were being overwhelmed by the physical.

Hannah pulled back and he thought the moment was over. For an instant he grabbed her so she couldn't move away. But that was wrong and he knew it. If she didn't care enough to keep kissing him, he wanted her to go.

She didn't leave the bed as he'd expected. Instead she moved on top of him, straddling him, sitting as straight as if she were riding the white horse from out of her past life. Hannah pulled her pajama top up and over her head, then tossed it aside and leaned forward to kiss him again. Glen put his hands on her shoulders. He held her for a moment as he stared at her. He was a memory expert and this was a memory he wanted to keep forever. He pulled her close and kissed her again as all his worries about what was in her heart vanished.

***

Hannah woke up in the middle of the night and glanced at the clock on the bureau. It was after two. Glen was sleeping beside her, but he wasn't snuggled up next to her. She slid out of bed as quietly as she could. She found her pajama top easily, but the bottoms were tangled up with what Glen had been wearing. She found them and slipped out of the bedroom without waking him. The morning would be awkward enough without spending the entire night in his bed.

She was feeling that she might have pushed Glen too fast. He was as serious and focused a man as she had ever met, so she imagined he would have some second thoughts in the morning. She needed to keep him occupied. She would call in sick, but it wouldn't be to stay home to talk. Before Jamie and Stuart came over the plan had been to regress her. Hannah would convince him to return to that plan.

She closed the bedroom door before she flicked on the light. She had started to straighten out her pajamas so she could put them back on when she caught a glimpse of herself in her mirror behind her bureau. She stared, thinking how there didn't seem to be anything different about her after sex with Glen. So much for afterglow.

She thought she was too fat to be pretty, although Paige used to tell her that skinny girls didn't look as good with their clothes off. Paige had thought of herself as too thin, but she wasn't.

She studied her pillowy body and decided it was fortunate there hadn't been much light in Glen's room.

He was the first person she'd been with since Paige, and it had been a big step. She turned her back on her image, grabbed her pajamas, and dressed. She turned off the light and crawled into bed.

Hannah lay on her back for a while, thinking about Stuart and Jamie. She wanted Stuart to be happy, but she couldn't deny the fear that she'd no longer have his friendship now that Jamie seemed to have changed. A few tears came to her eyes as the wish that was in her heart turned to a prayer. She prayed that things wouldn't go *too* well for her friends. It was the most selfish prayer Hannah had ever said.

***

Glen reached for Hannah only to discover her side of the bed was empty. He thought for an instant he might have been dreaming until he realized he was naked. He wondered if she'd just gotten out of bed and was in the kitchen fixing breakfast, but immediately doubted that since there was no smell of coffee brewing.

If Hannah wasn't cooking he'd start the meal. There were eggs, Swiss cheese, and some green peppers in the refrigerator, so he could make omelets.

The coffee was brewed and the eggs almost done when Hannah came into the kitchen. She was wearing black slacks and a gold sweater. Glen wondered if she'd changed her mind about staying home.

"Good morning," Hannah said. "I have to call in to work first thing. It won't take but a minute."

"Go right ahead." Glen used a spatula to move Hannah's omelet to the buttered toast he'd put on her plate. When he turned back to her she was starting to dial the phone. "I missed you this morning," he said. He hoped there wasn't too much emotion in his voice.

"Sorry. I sleep better in my room." She held up a finger then spoke into the phone. "Hi, Laura. It's me, Hannah. I think I may be getting a bit of a stomach virus, so I'm staying home. Tell Dan for me, would you? Thanks. I'll probably see you tomorrow."

"I was hoping you might regress me today," Hannah said after she hung up. "We never got to that with all the stuff that happened."

"Stuff?"

"You know what I mean. Stuff like Stuart and Jamie coming over and telling us what they're going through. Rose was a friend of Annie's. Maybe she knew Ratinam. If you regress me we might find out and be able to help."

She clearly didn't want to discuss what had happened the night before.

"You said you wanted to stay home to talk."

"I have a feeling Rose could give us a little more to talk about."

"You don't think we have enough now?"

"This is about last night, isn't it?"

"Is that wrong?"

She appeared to collect her thoughts before speaking. "Sometimes putting words to things can make them seem less magical. I don't want to do that to us. I *will* say this. You were exactly what I needed. But no matter what happened, or what happens in the future, you can't stop being the man I hired to find Paige's killers. There's too much at stake here."

It wasn't her argument that won Glen over. It was the way she said *I don't want to do that to us* and in the process acknowledged that there actually was an *us*.

CHAPTER TWENTY-EIGHT

Jamie and Stuart had agreed to stop keeping secrets from each other. He told her the password to the email account he'd set up to receive his instructions. When she checked for messages, she found the next note. Stuart was to carry another package across the US/Canadian border. This time he was to find a box at an apple farm in Hemmingford, Quebec. Jamie read the message, then tagged it. Their resistance had begun.

Later that morning, Troy called.

"They're doing *Noises Off* in Concord. If you're going to the auditions I thought you might like to carpool."

"Concord is far," Jamie said. "You plan to drive there every night?"

"I've done it before. And I've got friends who'll let us crash at their place if rehearsals run too late. You'd make a great Brooke."

Troy's words brought a wide smile to Jamie's face. She loved it when someone told her she'd be good in a role and Brooke was a double compliment. For any actress to play Brooke well she had to have a good body. The role required spending a great deal of time on stage in her underwear, something she'd enjoy.

"I love that play," Jamie said.

"You'll go nuts when *Miss Julie* is over," Troy told her. "You're way too good for the homemaker role."

"When are the auditions?"

"The week after next on Monday and Tuesday nights. I plan to go Tuesday."

"I'll think it over and call you."

CHAPTER TWENTY-NINE

After breakfast Hannah put on one of her green University of Vermont T-shirts and the gray sweatpants Glen liked her to wear for the regressions.

In the living room, Glen had spread the usual blanket on the floor. She took her place and stared at the spot on the ceiling as Glen spoke softly, almost chanting the words that had the power to send her swirling. She slipped into another hidden memory.

***

It had been over two weeks since the circus had moved on. Rose was sure she wouldn't see the white horse until the performers came back. Just as well. She had no idea why she felt connected to the woman who rode that horse. She had always admired strong women and the rider looked strong, but they hadn't even spoken.

Rose gradually went back to picking up men for money and was able to earn enough to cover her nights in the lodging house. She even had enough shillings to buy rounds at the Old Bull a few times and to pay Annie back everything she'd borrowed. Annie had disappeared, both from the pub and the streets. Finally, Rose saw her one night in East London and was able to talk to her.

"I've got another source for money," Annie told Rose. "Can't tell you who it is, but I'm doing well."

Rose assumed her friend had a regular who didn't want his name revealed. She'd had a few of those herself over the years. The only regular Rose had now was an Irishman who wasn't concerned about secrecy, but did want privacy.

"I don't care who knows I pay for your favors," he told her, "but nobody has the right to watch us." Since doorways in dark alleys were where Rose accommodated most of her customers, the only solution she'd thought of had been to lead him down those alleys until they found a stable with an open door.

This time they slipped into a stable they'd never used before. They walked into the building and lit a kerosene lamp they found on a table. But before they settled in a place where Rose could hike her skirt she discovered something that set her mind awhirl: two tickets and a pamphlet from the circus on a small shelf outside a stall that housed a white horse.

"She's been here," Rose said. When she realized her companion had no idea what she was talking about she added, "There's a woman owns a horse like this one. I've been trying to find her for weeks."

"Why," he asked.

He sounded a little gruff, but Rose answered anyway. "She was a performer in the circus. When I saw her I felt like I'd known her before, but I couldn't remember when or where. Then I saw her again riding near this stable, so I tried to follow. I lost her—at least until now."

"I'm the one paying, not her."

"You can have your money back. This is more important."

"When I'm with you, you don't tell me what's important. You understand?"

"I need to find her."

He grabbed her arm and pulled her close. His grip was tight enough to hurt. "All you *need* to do is concentrate on me."

Rose was scared he'd make enough noise to chase the woman away—if she happened to be somewhere in the building. She had to get rid of him with as little disturbance as possible.

He pushed her against a stall wall, indicating he wanted her from the front this time. She wished he had chosen a less intimate position, but she lifted her skirt anyway. He grabbed her thighs and raised her off the floor. She put her arms around his neck to keep from falling to one side. She'd been with him many times before, so she didn't feel angry or humiliated that he was forcing her. She just wished he'd hurry, so she could get busy looking around the stable for clues.

He was finished quickly, which probably meant he'd been aroused by being rough with her. It was the first time he'd ever shown a violent side, but she knew from painful experience that violent patterns get worse. She'd have to think about making this the last time for him.

Once he left the stable, she started looking for clues.

The dirt floor outside the white horse's stall was the first place she checked. The circus brochure had been on the shelf there; there might have been something else with it that had fallen. She studied the ground, but without success. There were too many shadows for her to be certain she hadn't missed something small, so she got down on her knees and brushed the dirt with her hands.

The only thing her search unearthed was a page of newsprint under a carriage near the back of the stable. The news was old and Rose was convinced the paper was unimportant. Since it was greasy and smelled of fish, it had probably been the wrapper for someone's lunch.

She tossed the paper back to the ground, then returned to the stall. The horse was at her, but didn't appear to be nervous. If this was the circus horse, it was used to strangers. Rose opened the stall door and peeked in. Although the straw that covered the floor of the stall was partially wet, overall the area was clean. The soiled bedding must have been picked out and disposed of no more than a few hours earlier. The horse had fresh water and hay.

The white horse came over to Rose and nuzzled her arm. Rose stroked its neck and scratched its ears, wishing she had some small treat, a piece of apple or some such to offer. The horse lost interest and went back to eating from the hay rack when Rose stepped out of the stall.

She went to a large wooden cabinet that appeared to be an old wardrobe that was now doing duty front of the empty stall where saddles were kept.

It wasn't locked, so she opened it to find bridles and reins hanging inside, along with brushes and hoof picks. There was something on a waist-high shelf. At first Rose couldn't figure out what it was. But then she realized she'd seen it at the circus. It was a special saddle girth that had two fixed handrails. It was what the performers put on the horses to help them with their hand stands and other trick riding. She was in the right place.

Rose knew there were floors above the stable, since most of the buildings in that part of London were three or four stories tall. She needed to find the stairs. Perhaps the woman she was looking for might be living above. She looked carefully, but could not find the stairway. There had to be another entrance to the building from outside. She hurried out to see if she could find it.

Just as she had suspected, there was a second entrance, a smaller door that led to the stairs. It, too, was unlocked, so she climbed up to the second floor hall. There were two wall sconce lights burning, so she could see thick doors that she knew led to flats. She had no way of knowing if the woman was behind one of those. She couldn't knock, especially not at this late hour. She considered making her way up to the next floor but decided instead to leave the building. If Rose kept her eyes open, perhaps she could find the woman she sought.

***

Glen's voice pulled Hannah into the twenty-first century. She stayed on her back and continued to stare up at the ceiling as she reoriented.

"Are you all right?"

"Why did you bring me back?"

He raised his hand to his temple. "I came close to ending the session earlier, when that man was threatening you."

"But I think Rose is on to something."

"I think so, too. I'll send you back again, but not today."

Hannah shook her head. "We need to do something to find Paige's killers. I don't want to stop until we know."

"You have issues when it comes to Paige. Issues that go way beyond wanting to solve this case."

"So what if I do?" She turned away.

He touched her arm. "Have you ever really said your goodbyes?"

"Of course not. One day Paige was here and the next day her insides were splattered across a motel room floor. It seemed stupid to say goodbye."

"You still need to say it. Get your coat, Hannah. We're going to the cemetery."

CHAPTER THIRTY

Hannah noticed that Glen was breathing heavily by the time they reached the place where Paige's grave was located. The walk had challenged her as well, but not nearly as much. She was used to climbing Vermont hills.

"Do you know where she is?"

"No. We'll have to look."

"Then we'll split up. I'll start at the far end and you start here."

The cemetery was outside a Baptist church. Hannah was a Jew turned Unitarian, about as far from Baptist as a Christian could be. Paige had grown up in this church, but hadn't attended any church after her parents had moved to Utah. Hannah had tried, without success, to get Paige to come to a service at the Unitarian Universalist Church. Neither had ever suggested attending here for many reasons, not the least of which being the Baptist position on homosexuality. When Paige died, her parents arranged for her to be buried in their family plot. She probably would have objected if she could have, Hannah mused.

The church was a little white building with a steeple. The cemetery was on a hill above it. Mourners could stand by the graves of their loved ones and look down on the place where they worshiped. Hannah was surprised by how peaceful and comfortable she felt as she moved from headstone to headstone looking for her friend's name.

"Here she is," Glen shouted.

The stone had a two layer base that made Hannah think of a wedding cake. The top section was flat and about six inches thick. Engraved on the front, along with Paige's name and the years of her birth and death were the words "In His will is our peace."

Paige would have been furious if she had known what words her parents would put on her grave, Hannah knew. She'd complained often that her parents were constantly trying to get her to live a more traditional life. Hannah'd never met them, because Paige knew how they would react, but it wasn't just Paige's sexuality they objected to. They hated her choice to be an actress. "Prancing around on stage" was how they described her art. The quote they'd chosen made Hannah suspect they were saying that God had to kill Paige to bring *them* peace.

"I'll leave you alone," he said, then turned and walked back to the church where they'd left her car.

Hannah stood facing Paige's grave for a few minutes before she got up the courage to speak. "I'm sorry I didn't come before." Her voice shook and was barely above a whisper. But Hannah knew Paige could hear her.

"Glen says I need to tell you goodbye and I'm not sure I can do that. I'm certain you're out there somewhere, listening to what's in my heart.

"Stuart's got himself mixed up with something dangerous. We think it may be the people who killed you. Glen and I are trying to figure it out. I know it's silly, but I need to know that what I'm doing respects your memory. Help me make the right decisions.

"Oh, about Glen. He's a hypnotist and he's very good. He's been helping us look back into the memories of past lives we've led. He thinks there may be connections between what's happened here and what happened back then. I think he's right. We've discovered a nineteenth century smuggling operation that was bringing architectural artifacts into England. It's got to be related to everything that's gone wrong. We're trying to find out how."

Hannah dropped down to her knees and put her hand on Paige's tombstone. She took a moment to catch her breath and to try to stop shaking. It had been such a long time since Paige had died. She'd been in Hannah's dreams, but Hannah hadn't tried to speak with her—until now.

"I don't know if it's right to pray to a person, but that's what I'm doing. Glen thinks I'm here to say goodbye, but I'm not. You're not gone. I know that because souls don't die. So I'm asking you to help us, Paige. Help us find out who killed you and help us bring whoever did it to justice."

CHAPTER THIRTY-ONE

Stuart was home alone when the police arrived at his door. Starr was with her grandparents and he had no idea where Jamie was. When he saw who was ringing his bell, his mind whirled and, for an instant, he stopped breathing.

One of the officers was a sturdy, blonde woman in her mid to late thirties. The other was a man with short, dark hair and a thin mustache. The man was smaller than the woman and appeared to be about ten years younger. They were both dressed in blue uniforms. The man had a baseball style cap with the word "POLICE" on it. He was holding his hat with both his hands in front of his body in a gesture that appeared to be respectful. The potential meaning behind his humble stance terrified Stuart.

"What is it?" Stuart cried. "Is it my daughter?"

"No," the woman answered. "We're here about your wife."

"What? Tell me."

"We're sorry. Your wife is dead. Her body was found this morning in an inn in Chester."

Stuart was having trouble standing. He stepped back into his apartment and was barely able to make it to a chair in his living room.

The police followed him in.

"Can I get you a glass of water or something out of your fridge?" the male officer asked. He sounded as if he'd never had to deliver news like this. An angel of death in training, Stuart thought.

Stuart shouldn't have listened to Jamie. He should have kept delivering the packages.

"What inn?" Stuart asked, as if that made a difference.

"The Fullerton," the woman told him.

He thought how he'd always wanted to stay there. "What was Jamie doing there?"

"We don't know," she said, then added, "We need you to come with us."

He took a deep breath and acknowledged her instructions with a nod.

"If you need some time to get ready we can wait."

"Will this take long?" He had to let his parents know when he planned to pick his daughter up.

"Three, maybe four hours," the man told him.

The call could wait until he got home.

Stuart had watched enough crime shows to know what was going to happen and that it wasn't going to be easy. They needed someone to identify the body. After that they would take him to the station for questioning. He'd lost someone he loved, so they would treat him with respect, but if reality was anything like TV, family members were the first suspects.

Stuart had been with his parents the night before. They'd taken him and Starr out to eat, and he'd stayed at their house for a few hours after Starr went to bed. For at least part of the night, he had an alibi.

He shut his eyes and cursed his self-centered thoughts. Jamie deserved better.

***

Just under five hours later, Stuart walked through his front door. It had been worse than anything he could have imagined.

They had taken him to the hospital, just as he'd thought they would. Jamie was in one of those stainless steel drawers, covered with a sheet. The orderly pulled it back so Stuart could see her face. Yes, it was her.

***

At the police station, the officers had asked questions rather than answering them. The two officers who had come by his apartment were still with him. When he told them he'd been with his parents the night before, they made a call to send a patrol car out to see them. Apparently his alibi was confirmed because they eventually began to tell him some of the details of the murder.

"The body was half naked," the male officer said. "Troy Allen discovered her."

"Did I hear you right?" Stuart reacted. "The Troy who was in the play with her? Is that supposed to be a joke?"

"We don't joke about murder," the woman told him.

"Why was Troy there?"

"He claims he was about to have an affair with her," the man told Stuart.

"What about my daughter?" Stuart asked. "What about Starr?"

"Is there a reason you're worried? Do we need to look into something else?"

"No, I'm just concerned."

"We had an officer talk with your parents. Starr was fine when he was there," the woman told him.

"Jamie wasn't having an affair," Stuart said. It had suddenly become important to say that out loud. "She wasn't always the perfect wife, but all of that had changed. We were on the right path, all three of us."

The officers nodded in fake agreement.

***

His first inclination was to follow Troy, but he couldn't picture Troy as anything other than a fall guy. There were smart and powerful people involved in this somehow. He knew that from what Glen and Hannah had discovered through the regressions, as well as his own experience.

A regression was the answer Stuart was looking for. He couldn't talk to Jamie anymore. He couldn't find out what was on her mind. But Jamie had been Annie Chapman and the world that woman had lived in was still an open book for him.

Stuart needed to convince Glen to regress him again. He would call Glen and Hannah in the morning.

He went to his room, stripped down to his boxers, flopped back on the bed that was now his alone, and cried.

***

When the phone rang, Hannah and Glen were sitting in the kitchen in the clothes they'd slept in, eating crumb cake and sipping coffee. Hannah picked it up.

"Thank God you're there." The words came fast and the speaker sounded out of breath.

"Is that you, Stuart?"

"She's gone ... Jamie is ...."

Hannah didn't understand. "She left you?"

"No. I'm trying to tell you. She's dead. Jamie's been killed."

"That's impossible!" Hannah was stunned.

"She told me to ignore the emails. I didn't want to, but she insisted. I saw her body. The way she was killed looked just like what was done to Paige. It had to be the same person."

"But you were here talking about this just two days ago. How long could you have ignored the emails?"

"They must be watching us. They must know what I'm thinking."

"Maybe the emails have nothing to do with this. Maybe it's just a coincidence."

"I doubt that. Troy found Jamie the way Paul found Paige. She was in a motel, sliced up, blood all over the room. They're saying she was waiting for him. But that doesn't make sense. Things were getting better. You know that. God, I miss her. I don't know what to do or who to talk to. And I'm scared for Starr. She doesn't know anything yet. I have to tell her and I have to protect her. I haven't mentioned the smuggling to the police. I'm worried I'll go to jail if I do. What would happen to Starr then?"

"Breathe deeply and try to get yourself under control. Starr will be all right. I'll do what I can to help you, and your parents are always there. But you're right not to tell anyone anything. You need to think first. Glen and I will be right over. You have to be strong."

Stuart paused for a moment, then said, "Troy told the police they were about to have an affair. Jamie wouldn't have done this to us. Two months ago maybe, but not since that regression she went through. She was changed. She said she learned a lot from her life as Annie and the experience made her appreciate her family more. Now she's been killed the way she was in that past life."

"Hold on. We're on our way."

Stuart hung up without answering.

***

"I should have said something," Glen told Hannah as they drove to Stuart's apartment. "I wasn't sure, so I didn't speak up. This case is strange in many ways." But even as he spoke, he knew the problem wasn't with the unexpected. Jamie had apparently been butchered after she was killed, just as Annie had been. Every book on Jack the Ripper told Annie's story, organs pulled from her body and tossed around.

"No need to beat yourself up. Jamie knew what happened to Annie. She didn't have to be a regression therapist to understand what that meant."

Some of the tension left Glen's shoulders, but he still felt terrible.

"How is the case strange?" Hannah asked.

"There are generally well-defined connections between souls and roles. Say the soul of your mother from a past life is now your best friend. If your mother did something important that affected you—for good or bad—your best friend is the one most likely to repeat the action. Yet in this case that isn't always true. Look at Stuart. Before I regressed him he was a skeptic, but in the past life he was helping people discover their other selves. Those behaviors are polar opposites. And what about the smuggling? Ratinam was working with artifacts that had regression secrets carved into them. If the stones were needed to pull memories, he couldn't look into past lives until he had them. And since the stones were hidden in a past life, he couldn't find them without the memories.

"There seem to be odd aspects to Jamie's murder as well. It's true that a violent act can repeat in one life after another. But this sounds as if it has as many similarities to the killing of Paige as it does to Annie's murder."

Neither of them spoke. The counterpoint of the steady sound of the car engine with the uneven beat of the tires was as hypnotic as any technique Glen had ever used. He took a deep breath. Hannah wasn't wearing perfume, but he could smell the soap she'd used.

CHAPTER THIRTY-TWO

Stuart was in the kitchen when the doorbell rang, staring blankly at the empty glass and cordless phone in front of him. He had let his family down in a way that was inexcusable and had resulted in the worst tragedy they had ever known. He'd brought crazy, ruthless people into their lives and his worst fears had been realized.

Hannah rushed through the door as soon as Stuart opened it. She grabbed him and wrapped around him as if she were using her body to build him a shelter.

"I'm so scared for you." Hannah's voice was slightly muffled by Stuart's neck.

Glen stepped around them and said, "Tell us what happened."

Stuart was relieved. That was much easier than trying to deal with the comfort Hannah was offering.

Stuart pulled away from her and said, "It's like I told you on the phone, Jamie's dead. She was killed in a motel and mutilated the way Paige was and the way Annie Chapman was in Victorian London. I can't believe this happened to her. And it's my fault. I shouldn't have listened to her. I should have kept on delivering those boxes for as long as they wanted me to."

Hannah reached out again, this time taking his hand, but Stuart pulled away once more. "The police said Jamie was about to have an affair with Troy Allen, but I think she was set up."

"Why do you think that?" Glen asked.

"Things were getting better." Stuart looked at the floor as he spoke. "I think maybe Paige was set up, too."

"I don't know about Jamie," Hannah told Stuart, "but I'm convinced Paige had planned to meet Paul."

"Are you going to help me?" Stuart asked Hannah.

"That's why we're here."

"Then you have to believe me. Jamie was *not* in that room waiting for Troy. I don't know whether they killed her before or after, but somebody took her to that motel. I'm certain of it."

"What difference does it make what we believe?" Glen asked.

"Because I want you to regress me."

"Why now?"

"If what happened to Jamie was a repeat of what happened to Annie, maybe we can learn from the past. My soul was in someone associated with Annie. Maybe I can discover something about her murder that will change the way people are thinking about Jamie."

"That might help, but I'm not sure I'll be able to regress you so soon after you've lost someone you loved. A regression isn't something you do just because you want to. You have to be psychologically ready. You need to relax completely and free your mind from the worries of your current life. But I have a different idea. This morning our plan was to regress Hannah, at least until you phoned. I'm thinking we should do that. The reason I was going to send Hannah into her memories of Rose was because it felt as if she was about to make a breakthrough. If you're right about Jamie being set up, then her death could be connected somehow to Paige's. Anything we can do to shed light on Annie Chapman's murder will help us with the others."

Stuart said, "I want to find out if the thugs I was working for are responsible for Jamie's death. If you think this will help, I need you to do it."

"Just find me a place to lie down," Hannah said.

***

Rose had already paid for her night's shelter, a straw bed at the lodging house, so she made her way up to the second floor, found her place, stripped down to her chemise, and fell asleep under the blanket.

Rose slept until close to noon. She planned to spend the day looking for the rider. She decided to get something to eat at one of fish and chips stalls near where she'd been the night before, since the greasy newsprint in the stable made her believe someone who had been there had bought a meal from one of those places.

Rose found The Fish Shop just a block from the stable, in a brick building that had some tenement apartments above it. Rose had never eaten there, but she'd bought many a meal from places like it. She preferred fried food.

She moved across the street and stood to eat. Her food had come wrapped in a sheet of newsprint just like the one she'd found at the stable. The paper was a practical plate. By keeping it in a funnel shape she was able to reach in with her fingers to pull out potatoes or pieces of fish. She kept watch for the rider, but didn't see her. When she was done with her meal Rose tossed the paper away and moved toward the stable, keeping her head up and her eyes open as she walked.

She passed a furniture shop, glancing inside the open door to see a craftsman leaning over his work. In the next building there was a shoe repair shop and a hat shop. She reached the stable without any sign of her quarry. She turned around and started back to the place where she'd bought her meal.

Rose paused for a moment as she passed the furniture shop. She didn't care much to watch the man at work, but she needed to collect her thoughts and plan her next search route. While she was standing in the doorway she felt a hand on her shoulder and spun around, finding herself face to face with the woman she was looking for.

"Do you know Annie Chapman?" the woman asked with an American accent Rose placed immediately.

"I do," Rose answered. She immediately realized that she shouldn't have said anything until she knew what this woman wanted from Annie. She'd been too surprised to think.

"Your friend is mixed up in something more dangerous than she realizes. I'd like to talk to you about Annie, if you have a few minutes. Let's go back to the stable. We can be alone there."

Rose did not know anything about this woman. Following her to a private place was foolish, but she made her living taking strangers out of sight, so she shrugged her agreement.

"You were in the circus," Rose said as they walked side by side.

"That's right, and I'm with it again."

"It's back in London?"

"Yes. There were scheduling problems, so the circus returned. I never left England."

"When I saw you, you stared at me like you knew me."

"Did I?"

"Yes. And later I saw you riding the white horse. It was late at night. You were riding toward your stable. I followed, but I couldn't keep up." Rose remembered that Annie was with her that night, but she didn't want to mention her friend's name again, unless the woman did.

"Who are you?" Rose asked.

"That's complicated. I'll explain more when we get to the stable."

"At least tell me your name."

"I'm Molly. You don't have to tell me yours. I already know it's Rose."

Rose wondered what that knowledge meant. Molly must have been spying on her. That's how she knew of her friendship with Annie. They walked in silence for a few moments until they reached the stable. Once they were inside, Molly was the first to speak.

"You were here last night, with an Irishman."

So Molly had been there while Rose had been searching for her. Rose cringed a bit at the revelation that Molly had been watching when she gave the favor she'd been paid for.

"I have an easier way for you to make money," Molly told her.

"What I do isn't as bad as people say. Women like me get put down because proper ladies don't like the way we get their men. Who cares about the society mouths? Yeah, it can be dangerous at times, but I think it's safer than standing on the back of a horse."

"I joined the circus because it's an easy way to move around Europe."

"So money had nothing to do with it?"

"Not in my case. Circus owners get rich, not performers."

"I believe that."

"I have a talent for recognizing people who are important to the cause I believe in. I think you're one of those people. I thought so when I first saw you."

"And Annie?" Rose brought her friend's name up even though she had promised herself she wouldn't.

"Someone else got to Annie."

The tone in Molly's voice made Rose think there could be some problems between Molly and the people Annie was mixed up with. She didn't want to agree to something that might hurt her friend.

Molly kept talking. "The man who approached Annie likes to work with vulnerable people he can control. You must admit that prostitutes are in that category."

Clearly Molly hadn't accepted Rose's defense of her occupation.

"Aren't you doing the same?" Rose asked.

"I haven't chosen you because I think I can control you. I've chosen you because you're someone *he* might choose, especially since you know Annie. That's why it is so important we talk."

"I'm here and we're alone. If it's important, start talking."

Rose didn't intend to be snippy, but the irritation she felt caused her words to come out that way. She resented Molly's statement that people like her were vulnerable and easily controlled. She had always earned her own way and she didn't give up her soul the way some married women did.

Molly was near the shelf where Rose had found the circus tickets the night before. She leaned against it as she started to speak. "There are a number of people who bring items into this country without following the required laws."

"Smugglers," Rose said, nodding in agreement. She knew many sailors who made money bringing brandy, tobacco, or tea into London illegally. They spent some of their money on her. "Are they the ones Annie is involved with?"

"I believe so. The people I am looking for are moving priceless art around London, mostly items from the Far East. In some ways these items are much more valuable than the wares of common smugglers, but what is most odd is that they are also easily identifiable, and, for that reason, difficult to sell."

"Then why are they going to all this trouble?"

"I don't know. My employer hired me to discover the answer to that question. So far I've had limited success."

"Who do you work for?"

"Someone in New York who cares about ancient art."

Rose was hoping for more specifics. Molly was saying that Annie made a mistake by agreeing to work for a man she didn't know, but at the same time she was offering Rose a job without revealing much about her own background.

"Annie is putting her life at risk by working with these men," Molly told her. "They are dangerous. I need you to watch out for her."

"Men are predictable. Annie can handle them." But you do not seem at all predictable, Rose thought, and that scares me.

She decided she needed to speak with Annie before she agreed to anything.

"Can I think about it?"

"Certainly. We can meet here at eleven o'clock tomorrow night."

Molly must have known she'd want to talk to Annie, but didn't say anything about keeping their conversation a secret. Was the thin circus performer in contact with Annie as well?

CHAPTER THIRTY-THREE

"Come back to us," Glen's voice called out in a steady, easy tone. Hannah heard him and drifted back into the reality of her modern life.

When Hannah was caught up in Rose's memories she looked through the mind of the woman she had been in an earlier life, but kept her own identity as well. She didn't forget the problems of her current life. But the grief from Jamie's death had been pushed aside by Rose's concerns; when Hannah returned from the past that pain returned, washing over her like an ocean wave.

"Are you all right?" Glen asked.

"Just give me a minute." Hannah slowly swung her legs around so she could sit up, but didn't try to stand. "I'll be fine. I just need to catch my breath."

Stuart was sitting in a wingback chair and staring in her direction, but she could tell he wasn't seeing her. He was too focused on his own pain.

Hannah could empathize. She remembered how time seemed to slow down and how she had been filled with an eerie, numbing sensation after Paige died. When she couldn't process the level of grief she was experiencing, she shut down.

Perhaps Glen's idea to regress her rather than Stuart had not been a good one. She'd wanted to help and hoped that going back into Rose's memories was one way she could do that. But Stuart's past life memories had something to add as well. And at this point in time he needed to be doing something constructive.

"We shouldn't stop now," Hannah told Glen.

"You know how I feel about that. It would be too much of a physical strain for you to be regressed multiple times in a single day. I already let you stay under longer than I should have. You saw how much time it took for you to get your bearings back."

"I'm not talking about me. I'm saying you should regress Stuart."

"Yes," Stuart said. "Please."

"I'm sorry, Stuart. You've been through too much to risk the strain of a regression. You've lost your wife. You need to take time."

"I didn't *lose* my wife," Stuart told him, anger in his voice. "Jamie was *ripped* away. Mourning her won't make me better. The only thing that will help is to find out who killed her and why. You've convinced me the answer is in the past. Now you've got to help me find it."

"Sometimes," Hannah said to Glen, "doing nothing is the most stressful thing you can do."

Glen turned and took a couple of steps as if he were trying to move away from them both. He stopped, shook his head slightly, then turned back to face Stuart.

"You've got a friend here," Glen told him, nodding in Hannah's direction.

"She's the best."

"I'm not sure this will work. Will you be able to concentrate?"

"Try me."

"All right then, we'll try. But I'm pulling you back if I see any sign that the process is putting too much strain on you."

***

"This is different from any form of meditation I know," Ratinam told the man he was with. Stuart knew everything Ratinam knew and Ratinam knew the man's name was Lucius. They were alone in a room with no furniture, but with a number of stone items scattered about. They were sitting on small throw rugs positioned side by side, and they were facing a candle in a silver candlestick holder. The silver was probably worth more than everything Lucius was paying him, but Ratinam wasn't tempted to steal it. Practicing yoga gave him an inner peace that wasn't worth risking with a foolish theft.

"The use of a burning wick as a focal point is called Trataka or Yogic gaze. It's a common technique, but adding other items brings the process into an entirely different world. I can't promise it will take you where you wish to go."

"Don't give me excuses. Make it work."

"So much of meditation has to do with state of mind. If you are angry it will not succeed."

"I can push my anger out of the way and allow the memories to fill the void. But when I want the anger back it will return. My emotions serve my needs more than you can imagine. So don't try to use that argument. It will fall flat."

"Take off your clothes," Ratinam instructed Lucius.

The wealthy man did not seem to object to the command from his Indian servant. He immediately removed his coat and began to work on his boots. He was clearly having problems with them, so Ratinam helped his employer. Boots were out of style; Ratinam wondered why Lucius still wore them.

After the boots were off he stood to remove his collars, cuffs, and cotton shirt, carefully folding the shirt and laying it out on the floor beside his rug. He removed his front flap trousers and most of his undergarments until he was wearing only a pair of silk drawers, a sign of a wealthy man. He took them off then sat again on his rug without any hint of shame that he should be in such a state in front of his servant.

"Give me the artifacts," Lucius commanded.

"Lie on your stomach. It will be difficult to hold all these pieces in place at once. This one touches the Mooladhara, which is your root place, between your legs at the point where they reach your torso. It is relatively thin, so you should be able to keep it in place by squeezing your thighs together. The other ones need to rest on your spinal column. The Svadhistana should be the lowest, by your tailbone. The Manipura is the next one up, slightly above the small of your back. After that comes the Anahata, which should rest on your back at the level of the center of your chest. The last three move up your spine and over your head, starting at the base of your neck, then the back of your head, and finally the crown. I call these Vishudh, Ajna, and Sahasrara. The stones are not actually named with the words I've given them. But the words correspond to the places on your body I have mentioned, so we will use them."

"I'll lie down while you arrange the stones as they should be." Lucius moved as he spoke.

Ratinam knew it would be best if he placed the icons, but he also knew that touching a white man was something that could get a servant killed. He'd had to wait until Lucius gave the order. Now it would be fine.

"You'll need to balance the Ajna and the Sahasrara; those are the ones on your head."

Lucius was flat on his stomach with his arms straight at each side. He reacted to Ratinam's instructions by moving his hands to his head as the stones were positioned. He used his left to hold the one on the back of his head and his right to hold the one on his crown. The smallest of the icons was about the size of his fist. The others were various sizes with the largest being at least four times the size of the smallest. Some of them were heavy, but if Lucius squirmed under their weight they would fall off.

"Although the stones run up your back, you should think of their essence as passing straight through to the front of your body," Ratinam told him.

"And this will help pull my memories of past lives?"

"I've studied the texts that are chiseled in some of the other artifacts and followed what they say as well as I can. The body stones are placed on your energy centers while others are positioned around the room. I've set up everything the way it needs to be, but the effort to reach back into your head has to flow from you. You need to be relaxed. You are a rope to the distant events, flexible but strong."

"Albert Moss picked me because I understand what you're saying. You don't have to repeat it. I know more than you can imagine."

Ratinam had heard about Moss before the man had forced him to come to England. Although he believed what he had heard, he didn't understand why God had chosen to give so great a gift to such a selfish man.

"Don't speak," he told Lucius, refusing to be intimidated. "It's important that you relax, that you become one with the stones on your body."

Albert Moss claimed to be like the Dalai Lama, but Ratinam knew he was not the incarnation of a deity. He was a soul whose memories left a door cracked from past lives. Not a god, at least not yet, but a man whose gift came with the possibility of unlimited power. Lucius, however, was simply a test subject.

"This is your mantra for today. Prama-purusartha. It means the supreme goal of life. Repeat it slowly. Let your mind drift into its essence. Allow all other thoughts to float away and concentrate on this one sound. Look for the path you were on in your other lives. Find it and move forward."

"I'm ascending, floating through a spiraling cloud."

"Don't tell me anything, just absorb the experience. Prama-purusartha. Prama-purusartha. Say it softly, but let it persist. Prama-purusartha."

Lucius chanted softly. Ratinam watched as his body seemed to rise from the floor ever so slightly.

"Prama-purusartha. Prama-purusartha."

CHAPTER THIRTY-FOUR

"Absolutely amazing," Glen exclaimed as he brought Stuart out of the trance. "What they said about Moss changes everything."

His excitement caused his voice to shake slightly. Moss's soul was somewhere out there, a soul that maintains the memories of its past existences.

"It doesn't change the fact that Jamie's dead." Stuart's monotone voice revealed an emotion exactly opposite from Glen's enthusiasm.

"I'm sorry. That was disrespectful. But I've never experienced anything like this. Sometimes individuals can remember bits and pieces, but I never heard of a soul that remembers consistently from one incarnation to the next."

"Are you all right?" Hannah asked Stuart.

"Yes. I'm a little weak, but I should be fine. Why did you bring me back?"

"The regression you were describing wasn't like the ones I've guided you through. Lucius was using a mantra. And I'm still hesitant about putting too much strain on you after all you've been through."

"That's what you say, but you don't seem to be concerned about what happened to Jamie."

"Take it easy, Stuart," Hannah said. "He's got your best interest at heart."

Stuart looked away from Glen and down at the floor.

Glen touched his shoulder. "What you just told us about Lucius is important. It can't help Jamie, but maybe it will help Starr."

Although Glen was committed to helping them uncover the truth about the murders, he was thrilled to be on the verge of a breakthrough in the study of past life memories. He wasn't ashamed of that reaction since he had spent years studying the subject, but he would have to be careful that he didn't appear unsympathetic.

Hannah suggested they take a break, and offered to put on a pot of coffee.

"Is Starr still with your parents?" Hannah asked Stuart as they sat around his kitchen table, sipping coffee and eating the bagels Hannah had found in Stuart's bread drawer.

"Yes. I asked them not to tell her about Jamie, so she doesn't know."

"Is there anything we can do to help you?"

"No. I want to put it off as long as I can."

"But you're planning to tell her when she gets home?"

"I'm picking her up. We'll have the talk in the car, I suppose."

"Do you want us to stay?"

"No. But please come back."

"Of course we will."

"No, I mean I want you to come back this afternoon. I don't think I can get through another night alone." Stuart turned to look at Glen. "I'd prefer Hannah came alone."

"I don't think that's a good idea," Glen said.

Stuart didn't speak.

"You need to be careful. If Hannah spends the night with you so soon after Jamie was killed, it will appear as if you wanted your wife dead."

"I've got Starr to consider."

"That's *why* you need to be careful."

"Starr knows Hannah. Having you here might scare her."

"We'll go back to Hannah's. She can leave me there and pack a few things, *if* that's what she wants."

Glen looked at Hannah and saw surprise—and anger—in her expression. He realized that he should have let her speak for herself. There were times when he could be so stupid.

CHAPTER THIRTY-FIVE

"I'm sorry I slept with you," Hannah told Glen as she drove back to her apartment. She knew he wasn't happy about her staying with Stuart, but she was mad. "Clearly, it complicated things."

Glen didn't answer.

"When we get to my place I want you to regress me again. That's what you're here for."

She glanced away from the road to look at him when he said, "I should have let you speak for yourself. I'm sorry."

She could tell by his eyes that he was sincere. She looked back at the road as a pickup truck approached going in the opposite direction.

"So am I. Stuart needs me and I intend to be there for him. But that's *my* decision to make."

"I understand. And I trust you."

Hannah tightened her grip on the steering wheel. "I don't need you to trust me. I need you to find out about Paige. There's no other commitment between us."

"I won't let anything interfere with this case. It's too important. And you don't have to choose between me and him. You didn't promise me anything."

Other than one night, she completed his sentence in her head.

***

Stuart wasn't ready to hear his parents' condolences, especially with his daughter in the room, although they both tried, hugging him as soon as he walked inside.

"Not here," Stuart told them in a whisper. "Not now." He knew it was cruel to push them away, but if Starr saw their grief she'd be scared. He had to think of his daughter first. "I'll call you later, after I've had a chance to talk to her."

"Hi, honey," Stuart said as he turned toward his daughter.

She looked up. "Hi, Daddy."

He picked her up, shifted her to his left arm and reached for the bag of her clothes that his father was holding. Stuarts' father shook his head; he'd help them to the car. Before leaving, Stuart hugged his father one more time.

"Don't forget to call as soon as you can. Your mother's very upset and we're both worried about you. Are you sure you can drive?"

"I'll be careful," Stuart told him. "I won't let anything happen to Starr."

Stuart turned up the radio as they drove home, hoping his daughter wouldn't notice how upset he was. He tried to be strong, but found it almost impossible not to cry.

When they reached home he brought her to the living room and sat beside her on the couch.

"I need to tell you something important. Mommy's gone away."

"Is Mommy in a play?"

"She's gone to another place, to heaven." He didn't believe in heaven, but he couldn't think of anything else to say. "She wants to be with us with all her heart, but she can't. Remember, you'll never be alone. I'll always be with you and so will Grandma and Grandpa. I know Mommy is glad about that."

He wanted to tell her about someone Jamie would be with, but there wasn't anyone else Starr knew who had died. Both sets of grandparents were alive, although Jamie's parents were just names to her. They hadn't been to Vermont since the week Starr was born. Starr's world was now him, his own parents—and Hannah.

Starr started crying, but in a quiet way, as if she was imitating him.

"You're crying because you're going to miss Mommy," Stuart said. "So am I. But she'll have friends where she's going and we'll still have friends here. Aunt Hannah's coming over in a little while. It will be good to see her. Remember, we will always love you and so will Mommy, even if she can't be with us."

***

Hannah decided to pack before the regression. She didn't know how long she'd be staying with Stuart, but she decided to pack for three days, since she could fit that much in a single suitcase. Glen would be staying in her home, alone. But the regressions had to move forward. They were more important now than ever.

"I'm ready when you are," Hannah told Glen as she put her case down by the front door.

"I've got a different plan," he told her.

"Please don't make this complicated."

"Give me a chance to explain."

"All right." Hannah didn't want to cut him off, but she was wary of what he might say.

"You and I have a relationship."

Here we go.

"Maybe it doesn't mean much to you, but it does to me. And I believe it must have existed in our past lives as well. I think you should regress me rather than the other way around. If I was a part of Rose's life, we can learn as much from my memories as we have from yours."

What in hell are you talking about? "I don't know how."

"You've watched me enough to know what to say. And I've been through so many sessions, I should be the world's best subject."

"Should be? You've never been regressed before?"

"I never had anyone I trusted enough."

His statement sucked all the arguing out of her. He was right. They *did* have a relationship. Regressing him might be a way she could find out if anything about that relationship made sense. It could also be another step forward in their attempt to find out who killed Paige and Jamie.

"What do I do?"

"The same things you've seen me do. I lie down on the floor and stare at the ceiling. You talk to me in the most soothing voice you can muster. You tell me to relax, to envision clouds or a long tunnel of tall trees or some other soothing image. Then I want you to tell me about things you saw when you were Rose. The goal is to guide me back to where you were before."

He spread the blanket on the floor and positioned his body for maximum comfort, then nodded.

"Relax," she said, imitating the tone she had heard him use. "Drift back in time. Imagine you're floating through water you can breathe."

Hannah hadn't come up with the water imagery on her own. She'd read a couple of books on past life regressions when she first considered contacting Glen and learned that water was an image used by many regression therapists because of its connection to life in the womb. She hadn't mentioned the books she'd studied because her research paled in comparison to Glen's. He'd studied the subject for decades. But this session gave her a chance to show him she knew something.

She continued, "You're letting the current carry you back. It's swirling around and you're spinning into another place. You're in London, near the Thames."

She kept talking to him gently, guiding him into his memories, hoping he was going where she wanted him to go. "There is a woman named Rose in your life. You can see her. You want to talk to her."

Finally, Hannah's effort paid off and Glen spoke. His voice was soft and even. "I'm in the head of another person," he said, "a woman named Molly."

"You changed genders?"

"I know Rose, but, more important, Rose knows Annie. Rose has left the stable and gone back to the street. She wants to think before she gives me an answer. If she doesn't accept my offer, I'll need to think of another way to get close to Annie. Annie's the key. The others are out of my reach. But that is tomorrow's worry. Now I have to saddle Baraka. I need to ride out of London."

"Baraka? That's a pretty name. What does it mean?"

"White."

***

Molly grabbed Baraka's bit and bridle off the peg outside of her stall, opened the gate and slipped the tack on her horse. After leading Baraka out to the central area of the stable Molly began to saddle her. While she was tightening Baraka's girth, she heard a voice behind her.

"I've thought about it enough."

Rose had returned. "Then will you help us?" Molly asked, certain such a quick decision meant refusal.

"I know what Annie would say if I spoke to her."

"Are you sure?"

"Yes. But I don't know if she's right. Annie can be self destructive at times."

"Can't we all?"

"I'm willing to work with you, but if I ever think what you're doing isn't in Annie's best interest, I'll be done."

"Fair enough."

"Do you still want me to meet you here at eleven tomorrow night?"

Molly wasn't sure how to answer. If she gave Rose time to think, she might change her mind again.

"I think I'll switch Baraka to a carriage," she said. "Would you help me do that?"

There was a Spindle-Back Runabout at the rear of the stable, light enough for the two women to handle. Rose pulled it away from the wall while Molly removed Baraka's saddle and brought her horse into position in front of the buggy.

"Would you hold her?" Molly asked. When Rose agreed, Molly positioned the harness over Baraka, switched to a bridle with long reins, arranged the shafts of the carriage on either side of the horse, and fastened them in place.

Baraka was an extensively trained circus horse and was so good at following commands she felt like an extension of Molly's body. Molly had taught her using a great deal of discipline and love. Their relationship was almost like that of mother and child.

Molly could have easily put her horse in harness without a second pair of hands, but she wanted Rose to bond with Baraka. Her plan appeared to be working. Rose didn't simply stand in front of Baraka, holding her in place. She stroked the horse's neck and ears while Molly work with the buggy.

"I'd like you to go with us," Molly said, choosing her words carefully. It was a request not a command.

"Where would you take me?"

"The man Annie's working for is dealing in stolen art from some of the oldest temples in the world. I'd like you to see a few of the items I've recovered."

"Why?"

"Seeing the ones we've taken back will help you recognize others."

"Is that so? I thought you needed me to contact Annie."

"Yes, I want you to contact her. I also want you to stay with her long enough for me to find her boss."

"When were you planning on telling me all this?"

"I'll tell you more while we ride over to see the artifacts."

Rose paused, as if she expected Molly to offer more instructions. But when there were none she got up in the carriage. This recruitment was taking the turns Molly had hoped it would. All Molly had to do to make her come along was to make her curious.

CHAPTER THIRTY-SIX

"Come back to me," Hannah said, once again using her most gentle tone. She was kneeling on the blanket, watching Glen wake up. "Slowly open your eyes. You are back in the twenty-first century. You're name is Glen Wiley. Come back, but remember everything you have experienced."

Glen opened his eyes, shook his head, and took a couple of deep breaths. Hannah reached down to touch his hand.

"Are you all right?"

"Yes. I'm just a little groggy."

"I did it, didn't I? I sent you back into a past life like I'd been hypnotizing people for years."

Glen sat up. "I was Molly?"

Hannah wasn't sure how to react. He was the one who had been detailing the events of his past life.

"Apparently," she told him, since she had to say something. "You told me people can change genders. Are you embarrassed?"

Hannah didn't see how she could have done anything wrong. The memories seemed real enough.

"It's just that Molly seems so different from me."

"There's nothing wrong with being a woman," she told him, trying not to smile. "Get in touch with your feminine side, Glen. This is the twenty-first century, you know."

Hannah laughed. He had often talked about people who were shocked when they discovered they were a different gender in another life, but Glen was supposed to be the one who had seen it all.

She took a deep breath. "I suppose I should have a little more sympathy."

"It isn't just the gender thing. It's that Molly was a circus performer and I've always been a klutz."

She had to admit that it was cute, the way he was trying to hang onto his masculinity while being a little self deprecating. She wondered if he was trying to impress her. He was still sitting on the blanket and she was still on her knees. She twisted around to get next to him.

"You're not a klutz," she told him, putting her hand on his knee. She knew he'd been fishing for a compliment. "In fact, you seem rather agile, to me. For an old guy, that is." She laughed again, but he didn't react.

"She could stand on the back of a circling horse and she was good at it. That difference alone is enough to confuse me."

"But the memories were in your head."

"Of course they were. I know what I saw. It just seems odd, that's all."

"Maybe you're focusing on the wrong things. Molly was searching for people who were smuggling artifacts. Given what we learned from Stuart, you're doing something similar."

Glen's face brightened slightly. "You're right. Molly was much more than a circus performer."

"There are other similarities. I was Rose and Rose sought out Molly. In this life I was the one who found you and brought you here to look into Paige's murder."

Hannah's voice trailed off as she spoke. She'd never previously considered the possibility that she'd known Glen in a past life, but it was clear that she had. Perhaps there was something to their one night. She needed to find out more about Molly and Rose.

"Are you going back to Stuart's now?" Glen's question interrupted her thoughts.

"He needs me," Hannah told him.

"Yes, I suppose he does."

CHAPTER THIRTY-SEVEN

When Allison Simpson had told Dr. Saffell how impressed she was with his home, he had laughed and said he'd bought it to impress people like her, people who were thinking about working for him.

"I'm already impressed," she had said.

"Then it must be working."

She knew it was his mind, not his wealth, that brought her to his side. But if he wanted an excuse to surround himself with luxury, he was entitled. After all, he'd been around enough times to develop an appreciation for fine things.

"Come in," Dr. Saffell said when he opened the door, his voice commanding, rather than inviting. Allison obeyed quickly.

"You can leave your coat on that chair," he told her, pointing to an upholstered bench. "We'll go to the den."

She pulled off her blue ski jacket and laid it down. She was wearing black slacks with a pink V-neck sweater over a white shirt. She was dressed well enough to attend a social function, but she was fairly certain he hadn't invited her over for wine and finger food—not this time.

She followed him into a room where a set of two couches and two matching chairs were positioned in a horseshoe shape around a broad coffee table. He took a seat on one of the couches and indicated that she should sit across from him on the other. There was a flat screen television in the room, but it wasn't turned on.

"Do you need me to take a role in another play?" Allison asked. She had enjoyed playing Kristin in *Miss Julie* and was hoping he would ask her to do something similar.

"Not this time, Allison. This will be a real life drama. You heard what happened to Jamie?"

"Yes. How horrible. Who would do a thing like that?"

"She had a child."

"I know. Starr. Jamie used to talk about her after the rehearsals—when she wasn't criticizing my acting."

"Do you know Stuart?"

"I met him a couple of times."

"He isn't good for that little girl."

"He isn't?"

***

Allison believed the world has a natural rhythm and that problems occur when there is a disruption in that rhythm, problems from paper cuts and pimples to war and genocide. Before she met Dr. Saffell six months earlier, she'd believed that the disturbances in the world's rhythm were unavoidable.

Caught up in her own low self-esteem, she'd expressed her insecurities by wearing old, baggy clothing that made her feel as if she were hiding in a tent. Allison believed she was too fat to be pretty, so she tried to pretend she didn't care that no one wanted to spend time with her. That's why she was shocked when Dr. Saffell approached her outside the Shaw's store on Chester Road.

"I'd like you to be in a play," he had told her.

"Me?"

"Yes. It's *Miss Julie*, the August Strindberg classic. I'm not directing it, but I'm influential. There will be open auditions, but if I say the word you'll be chosen."

"I've never done any acting."

"I'll work with you."

Dr. Saffell's offer sounded suspiciously like a proposition. But there was a chance that he was being honest about the play he spoke of and that he saw something in her she didn't know was there. At first she didn't want to complicate her life, but then she realized her life was not complicated *enough*.

"Acting seems kind of scary," Allison told him. "Suppose I work with you for a couple of nights then I tell you if I think I can do it. Would that be all right?"

"Here's my card. Come by my house tonight around eight thirty."

***

Allison took her groceries home then went out shopping again, this time for new clothes. She bought a light blue, scoop neck sweater and a pair of white polyester pants at Peebles. In the intimates department she found a pair of boyshort panties she liked and a matching demi bra that would work with the sweater. She bought those in white so the underwear wouldn't show through her new pants. The last item she bought was a pair of silver pumps. The two inch heels would look nice without being too showy.

At seven thirty she was dressed and leaning in toward her bathroom mirror, applying makeup from a bag she hadn't unzipped in months. She used her eyeliner to draw thin, copper lines above and below her brown eyes then leaned back to study her chubby face. *He'll think I'm a joke*. She picked up her lipstick, a light pink that complemented her skin tone, and applied it to finish her look.

Dr. Saffell answered the door and ushered her into the same den he would lead her to six months later. He smiled and started asking questions.

"What point are you at in your life?"

Allison wasn't certain how to respond. She had hoped he'd notice how she looked and perhaps even pay her a compliment. But she was also prepared for him to be all business and talk about nothing other than the play he had mentioned. Instead he had chosen a third path, asking a question that confused her.

"Point in my life?"

"Yes. More specifically I would like to know if you are trying to create something with your life or if you are just coasting through it."

"I thought we were going to talk about acting."

"We are. Life is acting."

She thought about his statement for a moment and decided it was bull shit, but she tried to answer it anyway.

"All right then. My life has been a series of lows and I'm at the bottom of one of those. You gave me a little hope earlier, when you mentioned my being in a play. It's something I've always thought of doing. For a moment I imagined I'd been *discovered*, like the women you read about in the tabloids."

She chuckled at her last comment, but Dr. Saffell didn't even smile.

"You need to *discover yourself*. I can help you with that."

Allison looked around the room, found a wing back chair, and sat down. "Can you?"

"I can help. But if you want your life to change you have to be the force behind that change. You've already taken a couple of steps in the right direction. This is the first time you've taken pride in your appearance. You look nice."

Allison started to speak, but Dr. Saffell held up his hand. "Yes, I've been watching you for a while. But the other step you've taken is the most important. Do you know what that is?"

"Please, tell me."

"You've come to me."

Allison felt a shiver flash up her spine. There was something in his voice that scared her and intrigued her at the same time. She felt the way she had years earlier when she was at a carnival on a ride called The Zipper. She'd felt like screaming, but didn't want the ride to end.

She took a deep breath and said, "Can we talk about the play?"

"I'd like to keep our focus on you. Is that all right?"

Allison nodded.

"How important is it for you to do something about the life you've been living?"

"The life I'm living?"

"If you want to find a better way, you need to be honest with yourself. Honesty is the most valuable trait a soul can possess. It is life's goal. There is only one other that is more critical: trust. You will work on trust when we are ready to move on."

"I don't understand what you're talking about," Allison said. "But I'm ready to do something about my life. So if this is the lesson you have for me, rather than that play you talked about, I'm all right with that."

"Don't you worry, Allison Simpson," he said. "You will be playing Kristin in *Miss Julie*, but you will also be playing a new role in your real life. Good things are about to happen."

***

In the months that followed good things *did* happen. Her confidence grew, but so did her opinion of Dr. Saffell. It became apparent to her that he was not just talented and brilliant; he was also superior in a way that would have seemed impossible to her just one year earlier.

Dr. Saffell could remember things, not just things from his own life but things from other times. He'd explained that the memories were foggy, but that he had a plan to correct that. When he'd called her unexpectedly, she'd thought he needed help with that plan. She was willing to give him anything he asked for. She would sacrifice her own life if that was what he required.

Instead, he'd started talking about Stuart and Starr.

"We need to protect the young girl."

"How can I help you do that?" She phrased her words in a way she was certain he would like. Her first impulse had been to ask why, but she'd learned that while Dr. Saffell loved questions about philosophy, he did not appreciate questions about his instructions. *Ours not to reason why….*

"I want you to get to know Starr. Call Stuart. Offer to babysit."

"I have no experience with children."

Dr. Saffell shook his head. "Haven't I taught you that you can accomplish anything you try?"

She felt ashamed that she had expressed doubt over a task that teenagers do.

"I'll call him tonight." She turned from Dr. Saffell slightly because she knew she was blushing.

"Good. Troy is going to help with that call."

"Troy? I didn't realize you knew him, other than seeing him in the play of course."

"Like you, Troy is a student of mine. He's helped me a few times."

"I'd help you, too, if you asked." Allison regretted speaking quickly.

She was always eager to do whatever Dr. Saffell wanted, but she sounded like a school girl.

"Troy's outside in his car. I've asked him to follow you home and to stay there until you've made the call."

His words hit her like a fist. He had just told her he didn't trust her. She felt tears welling up, but struggled to contain them, hoping he hadn't noticed.

"Don't take this wrong. If Troy had a call to make, I'd send you."

Allison knew she hadn't yet proven her value. That time would come, if she followed instructions.

CHAPTER THIRTY-EIGHT

Glen augmented his income with the articles and books he wrote, as well as the time he spent on the lecture circuit. The current case and the one he'd worked on down in North Carolina had kept him busy for almost a year. In that time, he'd grown accustomed to having other people in his life. His feelings were further complicated by the fact that Hannah was someone he wanted to have a closer relationship with.

He'd imagined the new living arrangements—him alone, her at Stuart's—would give him the time he needed to write. Instead, he couldn't concentrate.

Maybe it will come. This is still Day One.

Since he couldn't work on his writing, he'd use the time in another way. It had been a double breakthrough to learn he had once been Molly. Of the past lives he had uncovered over the years, this was the first one of his own. To learn that he had not only been a woman but such an *athletic* woman was almost unfathomable. And Molly was a key to understanding what was going on in that lifetime. He had to get back into his memories to discover more about her.

Hannah had been Glen's guide into his other existence. He considered calling her to set up a time for another regression and laughed at the idea of such a role reversal before deciding not to pick up the phone. She wanted to be with Stuart and he had to accept that.

He decided to try self-hypnosis, although he'd always been skeptical when one of his clients got excited about trying it. But, because he had years of experience regressing others and knew specifically which memories he wanted to draw out, it might work in his case.

There was a mirror on the inside of one of Hannah's bedroom closets. If he opened that closet door and slid the bed over to create a little extra space, he could sit on the floor in front of it. He could imagine his image changing from its own puffy-cheeked, nerdy look to the graceful, athletic appearance of Molly.

Glen always told his clients to wear loose clothing, but he didn't have anything appropriate. The sweats Hannah had worn when he regressed her were probably in her bureau. He was small and she was a little husky, so they would fit him well enough. He would have to dig through her personal things and he wasn't sure how she would feel about that, but if he was careful, she would never know.

He went into Hannah's room, stepped to her bureau, and opened the top left drawer. It was filled with white, athletic socks. He had no idea why she needed so many pairs. He closed that drawer and opened the one next to it. Her underwear drawer.

Her bras and panties were in a single drawer on opposite sides, folded neatly. He closed the drawer quickly, guilty at invading her privacy. But the guilt wasn't enough to stop him from moving to the next drawer, where he discovered her tops. They were also folded neatly. He pulled one of the piles out to see if her sweatshirt was there. It wasn't, but the thought of it reminded him of the day she'd worn it while sitting on the floor wrapped in the blanket, telling him about her history with Paige. Her honesty that day, along with his careful listening, had brought them closer than he had ever been with a client, close enough to lead to their one night together. That thought led him to thoughts of Hannah with Stuart. He shook his head and took a deep breath to get past those images.

In the next drawer he found the gray sweatpants and blue sweatshirt together. He pulled them out, unfolded them, and laid them on her bed. He pulled off his own clothes, dropping them on the floor, and put on Hannah's sweats. He felt a sense of intimacy with Hannah that was nice but also strange enough to make him want to shake off the sensation.

Glen went straight to the spot in front of Hannah's mirror and sat on the floor, cross-legged. He held his back as straight as he could and began to recite Molly's name as if it were a mantra. He tried to visualize her long black hair and dark eyes instead of his own, to imagine the shape and feel of her woman's body under the sweats. Gradually, his reflection began to blur slightly and he tried to refocus it as a picture of Molly. He thought he was about to succeed when his own visage returned, storming back like an unruly child.

Glen stood up and stretched. He was sore from sitting on the floor too long and he hadn't made any progress. But he got back down in the same position.

This time he tried a different mantra. He recited *Om*. It was a common choice, used often because of its power, but perfect for him because of its meaning of immortality. Instead of forcing pictures of Molly, he tried to let all his thoughts slip away. Before he could reach into his memories, he came tumbling back into his current reality.

Glen tried a third time and a fourth. He tried again and again, until he had to admit defeat. *I need Hannah. Her presence is what draws me back to the other life we shared.*

***

Starr fell asleep on the couch after she ate a few bites of the peanut butter and jelly sandwich Hannah made her. Stuart finished his lunch and went to take a shower. Hannah was left watching the sleeping child.

Hannah ran through the ways she might explain death to a child, but she couldn't think of anything that would ease the pain.

A terrible thought struck her. *What if Starr wakes up while he's in the shower and thinks her father's gone to the same place her mother has?*

Before she lost Paige, Hannah had been sheltered from death. Her grandparents on both her father's side and her mother's had died when she was so young she couldn't remember them. And her parents were both alive and healthy. The thought reminded her that she hadn't seen them since the summer because they lived so far away. She resolved to take a trip out to Michigan after the mystery of Paige and Jamie's deaths was solved.

Experiencing her own past life had changed Hannah's view of death. She had always believed that souls were eternal, but now she had proof. Paige would come back someday, and, if what Glen said about souls traveling together through time was true, they would meet again in the next life.

Hannah wished she could use her new knowledge to reassure Starr, but she was sure the idea was too complex for a child's view of the world. It could scare her, or, worse than that, leave her with false hope. Hannah didn't want to do that.

Suddenly the room was filled with the music of The Indigo Girls. *We get to be a ripple in the water. We get to be a rock that's thrown.* Hannah reached for her purse as quickly as she could. It was her cell phone, ringing at the worst time possible. Turning it off while Starr slept hadn't occurred to her; she didn't get many calls. She pulled it out and glanced at the screen. When she saw that the call was from Glen she pressed the key to send it to voicemail.

Too late. Starr was awake.

"Daddy," Starr called in a groggy, high voice. She sat up and started to cry, her bare legs splayed out awkwardly as if they didn't belong to her.

Hannah tossed the phone back into her open purse and went to Starr. She sat beside her on the couch, but the toddler pulled away and cried louder. Hannah wasn't sure what to do. She thought she should put her arms around the child and comfort her, but touching her seemed to make things worse.

"Easy, girl," she said, sounding as if she were talking to a dog. "Your dad's in the shower. He'll be right out."

"No! I want Mommy!"

"I'm sorry."

Starr screamed louder.

"Your dad will be right out, I promise. He's in the bathroom."

Hannah stood up and backed away a couple of small steps to give the child some space. Starr stopped screaming, but continued to cry.

Hannah had known Starr for a long time, but hadn't spent enough time with the child to fill in for her mom. Of course, Jamie hadn't spent much time with her, either, but she had lived in the same house and maybe when Stuart wasn't around she played the role of a mother better than Hannah'd thought.

Stuart came out of the bathroom shirtless and barefoot, his wet hair slicked back. He tossed down the towel he was carrying, sat beside his child, and hugged her.

Hannah listened to her voicemail.

"We're close," Glen's voice said. "Rose and Molly are keys to what happened to Paige and now to Jamie. I need you to help me discover what was going on back then. If we don't keep looking someone else might be killed. I couldn't live with myself if the next victim turned out to be you."

Hannah dialed Glen's number. "I'll come home after supper tonight," she told him after he repeated his concern. He obviously wanted to talk more, but she didn't. She said goodbye and hung up.

"I thought you were staying here tonight." Stuart was holding his daughter and rocking her.

"I'll come back to spend the night. Glen's trying to find out what happened to Paige and ... you know what I mean."

"This isn't a good time to talk." He looked down at Starr again. "But what you're saying is bull. I'm disappointed in you. I need a friend right now. I thought you were that friend."

"But I *am* your friend. I'm your best friend."

"Just go."

CHAPTER THIRTY-NINE

Glen could tell by Hannah's expression and body language that she wasn't sure she should have come home. He offered to let her choose which one of them was to be regressed, hoping that the decision making process would help get her mind off Stuart. She couldn't work if she was depressed.

"We can learn from both Molly and Rose. I have no idea which one of the two can teach us more."

"You really don't care?"

"It's your call."

"Then you go back first, but I get my chance, too. I'll go change now so as soon as I bring you back I'll be ready."

Glen felt his stomach tighten as she stepped down the hall and into her bedroom. He didn't hear her close the door. He couldn't see her opening her bureau because he was standing in the living room, but he knew that was what she was doing.

He had folded the sweats carefully and put them back in her drawer. She'd never said he shouldn't go into her bedroom, but the fact that he felt the need to cover his tracks underlined his feeling that doing so had been inappropriate. He wanted to apologize before she said anything, even though he knew that would be foolish.

Hannah came back into the living room, tying the drawstring on her sweatpants as she walked. She wasn't wearing the blue sweatshirt this time; instead she had chosen a white Cape Cod Tee.

He thought he could feel tension in the room. He wondered if she did, too. She gave no indication that anything was amiss.

Glen got down on the floor and lay on his back. As soon as he was in position Hannah began to speak. She had learned the process quite well and in a very short time Glen was once again living his experience as Molly.

***

Molly drove the cart for a little more than an hour. She wondered if Rose would be trying to memorize the way; that was what she herself would do in a similar situation. But the roads twisted about, and the moon and stars kept disappearing behind clouds that blew across the sky, so there wasn't enough light for her passenger to see clearly. Molly was relieved; she would need to work with Rose for quite a while before she could trust her.

They arrived at the country home where Molly had been staying. The fact that it was a working farm, although tended by others, gave the place an innocent appearance and made it safer to leave while she was on the road with the circus. Molly drove the buggy straight to the barn, which was shared by Baraka and the cattle.

Molly put a rope around Baraka's neck and led the mare away from the buggy. She tied her to a post in the center of the barn and started to brush her. Molly would have been sponging the horse if the weather had been warmer, but Baraka hadn't worked up a sweat. She'd be fine with a good brushing.

When Molly was done she led her horse to a stall and left her there. Then she led Rose out of the barn and toward the house.

The floors inside the cottage were broad planks of oak. The pine furniture was all simple. There were two small tables, four straight backed chairs, and a rocking chair.

"What I want to show you is in here," Molly said as Rose followed her into a side room where there was another table and two more chairs.

"These?" Rose looked at the two small stone statues on the table. They were about the size of her fists. One was a horse with an enormous saddle. The other was a Buddha with his arms raised above his head.

"We haven't recovered many items. We hope our luck will change now that you will be helping us."

"I thought my role was to protect Annie."

Molly paused before saying, "It is. But in the process we hope to retrieve a few more stolen items."

Rose shook her head. "It was a long way out here just to see a toy horse and a fat man doll."

"When I first began my work we didn't know where the smugglers were. All we knew was that priceless objects were showing up in the collections of some very wealthy people, people who had no qualms about buying from thieves. Those artifacts, which are similar to these, have been identified as originating in China about two thousand years ago.

"I was told there was a position being held for me in the Bostick and Wombell Circus. I was instructed to buy a horse and learn to ride it while standing on its back. That was tricky, but I was willing to try."

"And you're great at it."

"Thank you. But let me continue."

Rose nodded and sat down.

"The only criterion they gave me was that the horse should be white. I thought that odd, but it's worked out. Many of the stolen items have a connection to *The White Horse Temple*, the first Buddhist temple in China. The criminals use white horses as symbols of their association, so Baraka was chosen to attract their attention. I was lucky. She turned out to be a magnificent animal.

"This horse," Molly continued, holding up the stone sculpture, "is also magnificent in her own way. She went missing more than a thousand years ago and here she is today, in nearly perfect condition."

"How do you know what happened so long ago?"

"Are you asking if this could be a fake?"

Rose shrugged.

Molly didn't know how much she should reveal. "It's not. You'll have to take my word."

The people Molly worked for had what seemed like an endless supply of money. They used those funds to hire experts in New York to study the recovered artifacts. Sometimes there were records, even drawings, to refer to. Over time, a pattern had been established. Molly knew that the Buddha and horse both fit that pattern.

"You leave these items you call priceless lying about in this house for days, even weeks?"

"No one knows they're here. That's the best security anyone can have."

"I know they're here—now."

"Are you saying I have to worry after today?"

Rose stood up, walked to the table, and picked up the horse. She twisted the little statue around in the small amount of light that came through the room's single window. "It's nice, but not as magnificent as Baraka."

"Few things in this world are."

"All right." Rose set the statue back on the table then returned to the chair. "Tell me what you want me to do."

CHAPTER FORTY

"Come back, Glen. Come back to me."

Glen felt the world around Molly start to fade away. He was spinning back to the twenty-first century and to the floor of Hannah's living room. He wasn't ready to give up Molly's world, but he was drawn to Hannah's voice. She had said *Come back to me*. As he returned to his own time, the reason for his desire to have a relationship with Hannah grew clear.

"Are you okay? Did I do it right?" Hannah asked, kneeling beside him and grabbing his hand as she spoke.

"Yes, of course. Are you ready to go? Is that why you brought me back so quickly?"

"I didn't want to hurt you. I guess I'm not as confident in what I'm doing as I thought I was."

"You were perfect. Now let's switch positions."

Hannah was already dressed in the sweats so she was ready. Glen was wearing jeans and a long-sleeved blue shirt. He hadn't even thought about his own clothes, but they hadn't affected his regression at all. As Molly, he had been wearing a dark dress with long sleeves and a full length skirt, an outfit as distant from his current attire as he could imagine.

"I'm ready," Hannah said.

"Go back," he told her softly. "You are with Annie. You are scared for her. You believe what Molly has told you about the people she is working with. You want to tell her what you know, to protect her, but you know she won't believe you. Why should she? The only reason you believe Molly is because you have a sense about her that she is honest and good."

"It's not working. I can't force all those thoughts into my head. Most of them are there already, I suppose, but I have to think of them myself, don't I?"

"I'm sorry. I don't know why I said all that. I'll start over." He paused, then began again. "Ease into those distant memories. You are Rose. Molly brought you back into London and now it is at least a day later, a day you are with your friend Annie. Go back. Look at Annie's face. She is your friend, the best friend you have in the world."

***

Annie was a little drunk, as she was most every night. They were joking about a time more than a year earlier when they took two men for three shillings and left them in an alley with their trousers down. The men were mad, but too drunk to do any harm.

Annie laughed. "Remember how the little one tried to run after us. He fell flat on his face and the other one tripped on him."

"I'm glad we never ran into them again."

"Me, too."

Annie and Rose had been through a great deal together. They'd had five abortions between them, and had both been beaten many times when they were foolish enough to choose violent men. Living through times such as those was when good friends were needed the most.

A man came into the tavern and signaled to Annie from across the room.

"That's Peter," Annie told Rose. "Albert must need me. I have to go."

"Lord, Annie, you make this Albert sound like he's your lover."

"I wish he was."

"I thought you said he was too old."

"I told you he has gray hair, but up close anyone can see he's younger than I am. We'll talk about this later." Annie got up and walked toward the door.

The man who had signaled her stayed in the room. Rose was surprised at first, but then thought it might be the people around Annie he was supposed to watch. She got up, and, just as she'd expected, the man Annie had called Peter followed her out the door. Rose knew the streets, especially at night. She had no trouble evading him and catching Annie in time to follow her.

A minute later Annie was met by a dark-skinned man. Rose couldn't see his features because there was so little light. Rose trailed them from a distance.

Annie had talked about a gray haired man with a white beard, but this person was not that man. He was also not one of her johns. She walked with her customers in an entirely different way. This time she was walking side by side with the man, similar to the way she would walk with a friend but with a different intimacy.

Then Rose saw it. Annie was holding the man's hand, like a school girl with her first crush.

Annie had joked about wanting Albert to be her lover. Now Rose could see the insincerity in her humor. She already had a lover and this young man was the one she had chosen. *Why hasn't she told me?*

She followed until the pair entered a building on Whitechapel High Street. Rose couldn't go inside without being discovered, but she'd found a building she could study during the day, something she could tell Molly, something that would help her earn her keep. Rose turned to retrace her steps.

She'd walked a little more than two blocks when Peter came into view, walking with someone who fit the description Annie'd given her of Albert. His hair shimmered in the dim moonlight.

Rose got a little too close before she recognized them, and turned around abruptly, which was a mistake, as it drew their attention to her, and they started towards her. She began to run as quickly as she could, but she knew she wouldn't be able to outdistance them. She'd have to outwit them instead.

Rose didn't know the Whitechapel area as well as she knew other sections of London, but all alleys have things in common. She turned down one and was out of sight for a moment. She found a pile of garbage beside one of the buildings, mostly a mixture of old straw and manure from the stables, but there was also wood from broken barrels and some iron from old cart wheels. Rose could tell from the smell that the far side had been used as a privy. She jumped behind the pile and lay face down in the muck, praying that Albert and Peter would not stop to look for her.

The men ran past her hiding place as she had hoped, but she stayed hidden, waiting to make sure they didn't double back. When she finally stood, she looked at her dress in dismay. It would be difficult to walk the streets in her condition without being noticed, even this late at night. She needed to find a change of clothes.

There was a gate between two houses across the street from the garbage pile where Rose was standing. She jogged over to it and found it unlocked. She was able to go through the space that separated the buildings to the back where women often left their laundry hanging. There was a clothesline with what appeared to be dresses on it three buildings down from where she was.

One was a yellow gingham dress that looked like something an American would wear. It also looked as if it would fit her, so Rose put it on. She cleaned her hands and face as well as she could on a pair of men's long johns then went back to the street. She dropped the clothes she had been wearing in a pile. No one would know who they belonged to.

Rose felt comfortable walking at a slow pace as she went toward the Old Bull Tavern. Even if Albert and Peter noticed her, her new outfit made her confident they would not realize she was the same woman they'd chased.

As Rose walked along the deserted street she thought about what Molly had told her about the people Annie was working with. Rose had agreed to work with Molly, but at this point she hadn't revealed anything the woman didn't already know. That would change if she told her about the building on Whitechapel High Street. The choice seemed easier now that Molly's accusations appeared to be true. Why would Albert and Peter have chased her unless something was wrong.

***

Hannah heard Glen's voice calling to her from a distant place. "Wake up," the voice said. "Leave your memories of Rose behind and come back to the present time. Open your eyes slowly. That's right. You are Hannah Hersman again. You are in the living room of your own home."

Glen slowly came into focus as Hannah realized where she was. She tried to sit up, but felt a little dizzy, so she lay still, looking at her friend. He was on one knee bending over her like a father checking on his child. Impulsively she reached up to pull his head down to hers and kissed him.

CHAPTER FORTY-ONE

Allison called Stuart to express her condolences as she'd been instructed, although she wasn't comfortable with the grief process. But Dr. Saffell had told her to make the call, and to convince Stuart to let her help him with Starr.

Dr. Saffell's purpose was not always clear to Allison, but she believed he had wisdom that was far greater than hers, wisdom from thousands of years of living. She was certain that following his instructions would prove to be the best course of action for everyone, even if what he had suggested could send her to jail for the rest of her life.

"I was so sorry to hear about Jamie," Allison told Stuart. Her voice was shaking, but she wasn't concerned. Her trembling could have been from emotions rather than nervousness. "She was a talented woman."

"I always thought so."

Allison was disappointed by the abruptness of Stuart's reply. She didn't want him to hang up, so she said, "If there's anything I can do to help, let me know."

"Thank you."

Her offer had sounded clichéd, and she knew it.

"I mean what I say. I'm not just making the offer. How are you doing for meals?"

"Our refrigerator is full."

"I got to know Jamie during the rehearsals, you know. We didn't always get along, but I'm really sorry about what happened, and I truly want to help her family. I can wash dishes or vacuum or even clean your bathroom." She paused for a moment then added, "I sound desperate, don't I?"

"Not desperate, but a little guilty."

"Like I said, I didn't always get along with Jamie."

"Jamie was outspoken. There were a lot of people who didn't get along with her. Maybe the person who killed her was one of them."

"I wouldn't do anything like that," she said quickly, voice shaky again. "I wouldn't even *think* of anything like that."

"I didn't say it was you. There's more to all this than you could possibly know."

"I just called to say I was sorry for your loss. That's all."

"I guess I *could* use a little help watching Starr until she's ready to go back to daycare. She's been through so much. I'm not going out anywhere, of course, but I don't like leaving her alone even for the time it takes me to take a shower. The woman I thought I could depend on let me down. Maybe you can step in for her."

"I'd like that."

"Starr needs a woman to help her through her grief, especially at night. It's worse at night, for both of us."

"I'm sorry to hear that."

***

Allison reported her progress to Dr. Saffell after she made her arrangements with Stuart.

"Who is this other woman he spoke of?" he wanted to know.

"He didn't say, but I think it's Hannah Hersman. She's a friend of Stuart and Jamie's."

"I know Hannah. I met her at the cast party. You need to take Starr tonight, if you can, before Hannah is involved again."

"That soon?"

"Yes. Wait until he leaves you alone with her then bring her out to the parking lot. Troy will be nearby. Call him and he'll pick you up."

"And if Stuart doesn't leave us alone?" Hannah's voice was shaking worse than it had earlier—this time from fear.

"Be strong, Allison," Dr. Saffell told her. "What you're about to do is important. You have to trust me."

***

Hannah and Glen were sitting at her kitchen table finishing dinner, a simple meal of pasta and salad. Hannah had suggested they open a bottle of Chianti, but Glen was concerned the alcohol might affect a regression if they decided to try again.

"I should get back to Stuart," Hannah told him. "He was disappointed when I came over here."

"I know he's grieving, but of all the people in this town Stuart has the most to gain from our regressions."

"You're right. This is as much about Jamie as it is about Paige."

"I think we're close to learning something critical again. I'd like to go back into Molly's thoughts."

"Molly? Not Rose?"

"I don't think you're ready for another regression yet."

"And you are?"

"I wasn't under as long as you were." He wanted to add that she had been too dizzy to stand at first, but that wasn't exactly true. She had pulled him down and had started kissing him. His lack of response to her advances had seemed to irritate her, although she'd said nothing about it since.

"If you want to go first, that's fine with me. Just don't make excuses."

"Let's do it." Glen suspected any other answer he gave would lead to an argument. "I want to jump forward in time. We know Annie was killed because we know the history. Try to lead me back to the first conversation Molly had with Rose after the murder."

CHAPTER FORTY-TWO

Molly hadn't heard from Rose for the few days before she read about Annie's murder in the London Gazette. The news hit her hard; the practical impact was a major setback in her attempts to track the activities of Mr. Moss and his gang.

Molly had to ensure that Rose's grief didn't cripple the gains they'd made, but at the same time she needed to ease her new friend's pain. Performing in the circus had given her a great deal of strength, but it had also exposed her to many people who lived with more pain than she could imagine. The empathy she'd developed as a performer added to the strength she needed to work as a detective.

Molly was in the Old Bull now. She felt as out of place among the drunks and prostitutes who patronized the place as she had among the freaks at the circus.

"Have you seen Rose recently?" she asked the bartender. He shook his head but didn't speak. She was sure he would have responded the same way whether he had seen Rose or not. She ordered an India Ale and took a seat at a corner table.

Rose came in when Molly was about halfway through her second glass. She ordered a gin, brought it to Molly's table, and sat down.

"I'm glad to see you," Rose said. "Do you want to know why?"

Molly raised her eyebrows, but didn't speak.

"Somebody who knows who you are is going to see the two of us together and I'll end up like Annie. It's what I deserve."

"I told you Annie was mixed up with some bad people."

"You bloody well did. But a dog doesn't fight when it's alone in the ring."

"You're blaming this on me?"

"It was my decision to work with you, so I'm the one who deserves the blame." Rose looked up from the table and shouted, "You hear that, all of you? I'm the reason Annie's dead."

"Easy, Rose," Molly said, holding both her hands out, palms down. "It's not your fault and it's not mine. Annie was a dead woman as soon as she started to deal with the smugglers."

"How in bloody hell do I know that stuff is actually stolen? All I have is your word. For that matter, how in the hell do *you* know?"

"We shouldn't be talking about this here."

"Then why did you come?"

"Because I care about you."

Rose took in a deep breath and looked down. Molly understood her confusion. Their relationship had been entirely business. Rose had provided a few clues about Albert Moss, and some of them had turned out to be quite significant. But there had been no overtures of friendship.

"If I can't even believe you've been honest with me, how am I supposed to believe that?"

"There are things I want to talk to you about that I don't feel comfortable saying here. Let's go for a walk."

The streets of the east end were not safe, yet Molly understood that Rose had dealt with the danger long enough to be numb to it. And as for herself, she'd been in worse situations. They walked slowly, avoiding the alleys and smaller streets.

"Tell me what you know about Annie's murder," Molly said.

"All I know is what I read in the papers, but I know she was cut up. The men in the Old Bull have been telling stories since it happened. The chance of any truth in those tales is about as likely as clean water in the Thames."

"Then you have no idea why her body was violated that way?"

"No."

"It appears to have been a ritual," Molly told her, "and I have reason to believe it was a powerful one. It has to do with a secret important enough for someone to spend countless lifetimes searching it out."

Molly stopped walking, turned to Rose and looked directly in her eyes. She had admitted that smuggling wasn't her main concern. The rest might as well come out.

"The ritual is somehow connected to the effort to retrieve that secret. Albert Moss is the latest incarnation of that relentless soul. The theory is he needed Annie for the ritual because the process requires human sacrifice and Annie was someone he thought he could butcher without anyone else caring—or even noticing."

Rose pulled away. Her eyes filled with tears as she spoke through clenched teeth. "None of this makes sense. If what this man wanted was to get Annie alone long enough to kill her, he didn't need to have her carrying packages around London. For a shilling she'd have gone anywhere he asked."

"The artifacts are important, too. Some of the pieces are extremely valuable and have been sold illegally. I've traced it back to Albert Moss. I know he's the one who sold them. That's where he gets his money. The art comes from Buddhist temples in China and Tibet. It went missing hundreds of years ago."

Rose started walking again. Molly turned quickly and went with her.

"What did you mean when you said he's spent 'countless lifetimes searching'?" Rose asked.

"Have you ever heard of the Dalai Lama?"

"No."

"He's a religious leader from the far east, a Buddhist. Over the centuries, each time this man has died his followers have searched for and found his soul within another. It's a system that's provided continuity even greater than what the Popes have provided to the Catholic Church. They say the Tibetan Buddhists have only had one leader through their entire history. Some even say the Dalai Lama has memories from his past."

"You're saying Albert Moss is the Dalai Lama?"

"Every force has an opposite."

The two women stepped to either side of a muddy hole where street cobblestones were missing.

"You're confusing me. What does this have to do with the stolen art?"

"All of the pieces we've recovered went missing centuries ago. They could only be showing up now if someone knew where they were hidden."

"And from this you've determined that Moss shares a soul with the man who stole the art?"

Molly heard the doubt in Rose's voice and knew she had to explain further.

"There's an Indian named Ratinam Pillai who's been working with Albert Moss. It's said he can recover past lives."

"Recover?"

"He can help people discover memories. Annie knew him."

"Is he the man she met on Whitechapel High Street?"

Molly nodded. "He's one of the main reasons we needed to know what Annie was up to."

"They seemed close. They were holding hands."

"That's what you told me." Referring to the first time Rose had reported what she'd seen when she followed her friend might have been a mistake since Rose now saw her actions as a betrayal. Molly tried to refocus by adding, "Moss's association with Ratinam gives legitimacy to our theory."

"But why would Albert Moss need to remember his past lives? I thought you said he was born with that ability."

"We hope to find the answer to that question soon."

They turned a corner onto a narrower street, but Molly took Rose's arm to move her in the opposite direction, away from a couple of men who were standing halfway down that block.

"Is Ratinam an expert with rituals?" Rose asked.

"I've been told there are rituals involved in his process. He's a yoga master."

"Rituals that involve cutting a person open?"

Molly silently walked alongside Rose for another half a minute before saying, "No matter how you feel about what happened to your friend, you must not try to do anything on your own. Getting yourself killed won't bring Annie back. Remember that."

***

"God bless Molly," Glen said, his voice shaking slightly. He was still lying on his back.

Hannah smiled, thinking how he was blessing a different version of himself. She had called him out of his trance, then watched him ease his way back from nineteenth century London.

Glen sat up. "What Molly told us explains why we have more questions than answers. The man we're after knows things from the past, things *we* don't know."

Hannah shrugged. "Criminals always know things the people chasing them don't know. Wouldn't that be the case even if we weren't dealing with past lives?"

He stood and brushed some lint off his pants. "We don't even know where to look. We're like people with amnesia trying to reconstruct our history by watching a collection of home movies."

"We're not just limited to the next film in a pile," Hannah said. "We can think about what we've learned and *pick* the next place to look. You've been doing that all along."

Hannah was surprised by the way Glen reacted to her comment. His eyes opened wide and he was almost grinning. "You're right," he told her. "We're looking in the wrong place."

"That isn't what I said."

"Yes, it is, and it's also what Molly implied."

"I don't understand."

"The artifacts Rose was carrying across London originated in ancient China. Whatever was in the boxes Stuart brought across the Canadian border probably did as well. We need to go back thousands of years before Paige, Jamie, and even Annie died."

CHAPTER FORTY-THREE

Allison walked back and forth between her closet and bed, pulling outfits off their hangers and spreading them out. Each time, after she laid a set of clothes where she could see them, she shook her head and paced around the room. Sometimes she wished she could go back to when her clothing was a wall to hide behind rather than a tool to impress. Dr. Saffell had helped her more than she had thought possible, but he'd also brought complicated choices into her life.

She pulled on a gray knit dress with a black belt and turned toward the mirror. It would have been fine for an office interview, but it was too dressy for a babysitting job. She pulled the dress over her head and tossed it back on the bed. This time she chose a pair of light blue jeans. Her weight was still down, so they were easy to snap. They were, however, too long. She had intended to wear them with high-heel boots, but had never bought the boots.

Allison added a gray sweater, rolled up the cuffs of her pants then put on white socks and a pair of Reeboks. This time when she looked at her image she was pleased. She hoped she could live up to Dr. Saffell's expectations when she dealt with Starr.

She left the clothes she had rejected spread out on her bed and made her way down the hall to her kitchen. She pulled a container of leftover macaroni and cheese out of her refrigerator, dumped it and a leftover chicken leg onto a plate, and microwaved her dinner. It wasn't much, but it was enough. She was a nicer person when she wasn't hungry, and being sweet would be more important this night than any other time in her life.

When Allison was done eating, she pulled on her coat and walked out to her car. She sat in the driver's seat for a moment before starting the engine. Dr. Saffell had told her to remember she was a strong woman, capable of anything she set out to do. He had also told her that Starr needed to be taken from her father for her own good. It was Allison's responsibility to help that little girl. She would not let Dr. Saffell down.

After Stuart welcomed Allison into his apartment and hung her coat on the coat tree by the front door, he led her to the kitchen. Starr was still finishing her dinner, so Allison took a seat across the table from the little girl.

Allison tilted her head down slightly, but kept her eyes focused on his. "I'm here now and I want to help, so tell me what I can do."

"Yes. You're here and we're grateful for that. Aren't we Starr?"

"I could start by washing the dishes, if you'd like."

"The dishes can wait. We both need someone to talk to."

Allison wasn't used to conversations with kids, so she wasn't sure what to say. Talking to either of them about Jamie's death would be hard. This was what she was afraid would happen. But she knew it was necessary if she was to begin to win their trust.

"I was ten when my grandmother died," she said as if she were speaking to Starr, but with words she intended for Stuart. "My parents didn't believe in bringing children to funerals, so I didn't get a chance to say goodbye. It was something that bothered me for years, until a very good friend explained that dying is a change rather than an end. The fact that I couldn't see her or hold her didn't mean that she no longer loved me. She was in a place where she couldn't communicate with me, though. Does that make sense?"

Starr looked away.

The truth was that Allison had never met any of her grandparents. Still, what she was telling Starr wasn't a lie. Dr. Saffell was living proof that people go on after they die, just in another form. A little story to make Starr feel better was a good thing and it served her purpose.

Stuart said, "I don't know what to do about a memorial service. Jamie wasn't the religious type, so having something in a church doesn't seem right. I've still got a little time to make my decisions, because the police aren't through with her body. I think I'm going to have her cremated."

Allison couldn't believe Stuart had just said all of that in front of his daughter. She didn't believe in hiding facts from children, but she did think he could have been more considerate of the child's feelings. No wonder Dr. Saffell had determined Starr shouldn't remain with her father.

"Should we go into the other room to watch some TV?" It appeared that Starr would never finish her lima beans.

"Do you have a favorite show?" Allison asked Starr the question but Stuart answered for her.

"Starr loves *Finding Nemo*. We could watch that if she hasn't worn out the DVD."

"Do you have anything else?" It had been years since Allison had seen the movie, but she remembered that it was about a fish who loses his son after his wife dies. Even though it was set in an ocean, it was still a little too close to reality.

"We've got *Fly Away Home*."

That one was about a young girl who has trouble adjusting to losing her mother. If there could be a worse choice than *Finding Nemo*, Allison thought, Stuart had just named it.

"Why don't we just watch whatever's on," Allison suggested.

"Starr and I like the Game Show Network. Is that okay with you?"

She couldn't picture Starr liking or even understanding TV games, but it sounded like a choice that wouldn't do any harm.

"Let's go," she said. She stood up, but waited as Stuart picked up Starr.

A rerun of *Deal or No Deal* was on, complete with lots of shouting. Apparently Allison had been wrong about Starr. She was watching the show as if the contestants were making deals for her stuffed animals.

"It's the constant noise," Stuart said, nodding at the TV. "It gets her mind off bad things. I know because it works the same way for me. I appreciate you coming over," Stuart said. "It seems so empty when it's just the two of us here. I suppose it's weird to feel that way so soon after losing someone."

"I don't think there are any rules about what you're supposed to feel."

"I thought Hannah would help me get through this, but she's with that hypnotist friend of hers. Did you meet him?"

"Briefly."

"Really? I thought he scheduled regression sessions with everyone in the cast."

"He skipped me." Actually, although she had asked Glen to regress her when they had met at the cast party, she hadn't shown up for the appointment. She had been scared by the idea of someone roaming around in her mind.

"Jamie loved the experience. When Hannah suggested that Glen send me back, I agreed."

"You did?"

"I was an Indian living in Victorian London, a yoga master. I knew Jamie's other self and had a relationship with her. He pulled my memories from a time when I was meeting her, so I don't know how close we became. She was murdered in that life just as she was in this one. She was famous, Annie Chapman, one of the victims of Jack the Ripper."

"That's horrible."

"True. But to me it means we'll be back together someday. My thinking is that if we've had past lives, we'll have future ones as well. Maybe that's optimistic, but it's something I can hang on to when everything else seems to be falling apart."

How could Allison console Stuart when she knew more trouble was coming his way? Tears threatened. She shook her head and tried to steel herself.

"What was the regression like?" Allison hoped to turn the talk back to his past life.

"It was vivid."

"Vivid?"

"Glen claimed that he helped me recall ancient memories and that's all he did. But it wasn't like I was remembering. It was more like I was living a whole new life. It was so intense I now have memories of the memories, if that makes sense."

Allison nodded as if she understood, but she didn't.

"Like I said, I was from India. I was forced to go to England to work with a man who lived in London. He was trying to retrieve hidden memories and I was his expert. But we didn't do it the way Glen did it with me. There was a physical aspect to the way I worked and there were ancient stones that I used in a ritual."

"How strange. Did the ritual work?"

"I came out of the regression too soon to know for sure. To be honest, I don't even know if any of that experience was real. Like I said, it was so vivid it's hard to think of it as something other than an actual memory. I never gave a second thought to past lives before Glen showed up and yet there I was, back in one of my memories, helping someone else go back into one of his. I'd probably shrug the entire thing off as hocus pocus if it wasn't for Jamie."

Stuart sat up and seemed to stiffen. "Glen says there's a connection between what happened in our past lives and what has happened to us now. People in both centuries have wanted something so much they've been willing to kill for it. Maybe these murderers are the same souls or maybe they're not. I don't know, but I hope Glen can figure it out."

If anyone could defeat the forces Stuart was talking about, Dr. Saffell could. Allison wished she could share the truth about him with Stuart. She hoped Stuart wouldn't hate her forever.

Starr started to snore lightly.

"I guess she's ready for bed," Allison said.

"We could let her lie there a little longer. It won't hurt her to sleep on the couch for a few minutes."

"I could put her to bed while you get some rest."

"I appreciate the offer, but she needs to be carried to her room and dressed for bed. Just wait here. It shouldn't take me more than a few minutes."

After Stuart carried his daughter out of the living room, Allison looked for the remote. *Family Feud* was next in the lineup, which meant more yelling. She turned it off and sat on the couch.

She thought about Dr. Saffell and wondered why he had decided that Starr needed to be taken from Stuart. Allison spoke under her breath. "I must keep total faith in whatever Dr. Saffell asks of me." She took a deep breath then repeated the words *total faith* a couple of times as if they were a mantra.

When Stuart returned to the living room he brought a half empty bottle of Gordon's gin with him. He sat on the couch beside her and took a drink.

Allison was startled by the sight of the liquor. The doctor's concern had proven right. She shouldn't have felt any doubt.

"Would you like some?"

"No, thank you."

"This was one of Jamie's. She had issues." After he spoke, he lifted the bottle to his lips again.

"I should have been able to make her life better."

"Happiness had nothing to do with her death."

Stuart took another drink of gin then shook his head and stared at the floor. "I'm not talking about her death. I'm talking about her life. She deserved better."

As the alcohol began to take hold, he revealed more and more about his life with Jamie. "Her life was not the one she planned, but in the last couple of months she came to realize that her days would have been empty without Starr. She told me our family was important. She said she wanted to spend more time with us. She was also supportive of what I was going through. People think I was the stable one and Jamie was more of a second child than a wife and a mother. They didn't know her."

Stuart's speech gradually became slurred until his conversation consisted of repeating "Jamie was beautiful" and "Did I ever tell you how beautiful she was?"

He twisted around on the couch and brought his face up close to Allison's. She wondered how she should react if he tried to kiss her, but he didn't. He took a deep breath then spoke as if he were making an important point. He said, "Jamie loved Starr," with emphasis on each word. He seemed more concerned about her love for their daughter than her love for him.

Stuart twisted about again then lay down and positioned his head on Allison's lap. She wasn't sure if moving away from him would be the best thing to do or if stroking his hair and comforting him made more sense. She ended up sitting stiffly at the end of the couch and waiting until he fell asleep. Given the amount of liquor he'd consumed, it probably made no difference how she reacted to his strange advance.

When Stuart started snoring, Allison gently lifted his head and slipped out from under him. He had drooled on her lap. She stood beside him, looking down at his limp body and poked him in the shoulder a couple of times. He didn't stir.

It was time to take Starr.

***

Allison had to struggle to pull her phone out of her pocket while holding Starr with her left arm and balancing the gym bag she'd filled with clothes and some stuffed animals on her shoulder. She was jostling Starr like the girl was a bag of groceries.

Troy answered before the first ring was complete.

"We're in the parking lot," Allison told him.

"Be right there." She could hear Troy turn his engine on as he spoke. Allison had done what Dr. Saffell had asked her to do.

Troy pulled into the lot and stopped his gray Volvo in front of her. She watched him reach over to open the passenger door. It had taken him less than a minute to get to them from where he'd been parked. She slid into the car, still holding Stuart's little girl in her arms.

CHAPTER FORTY-FOUR

"Try not to focus on Rose," Glen told Hannah. "You want to relax past the memories of the Victorian era so you can go further back. You need to go to a life you led thousands of years ago. Listen to me. I'll tell you things I know of ordinary life in ancient China. I'll guide you back there."

"If I was there, we'll find it." Hannah was nervous. She'd grown accustomed to her life as Rose and now was about to step into a completely different world. Would she be a man or a woman? Would she be healthy or sick? And, most importantly, would the life she had led back then be one she could be proud of today?

Glen had insisted they wait until after dinner to conduct the regression, so that Hannah would be completely rested. He was sending her back rather than going himself because he wasn't certain he had a presence during that time. In this life and in Molly's his roles had been to search for the criminals who stole, smuggled, and even committed murder to get their hands on a select group of ancient artifacts. If Hannah found her way into the life where the thefts began, there might not be anyone there to investigate the crimes.

Once again Hannah took her place on the blanket on the floor in her living room, and once again Glen spoke gently, asking her to drift back through the mist of time to another life in another place. She slipped into Rose's existence out of habit, but Glen recognized she'd done so and prompted her to keep drifting back.

"You're looking for a memory that has been hidden for almost two thousand years. Try to look for the signs. In the place where you were living, most of the people worked from morning to night tending their land, growing wheat or perhaps rice. If you were a woman you probably worked side by side with your husband and any children who were old enough. Other members of your family might have had land next to yours, cousins or brothers and sisters. Some of your land was dedicated to taxes, but you would have worked that land as hard as the rest. You would dress in a tunic every day, a long one that reached the ground. You probably wore it with a belt. You might have had a few tunics so you could change when one was too dirty to wear, but if you weren't rich you wouldn't have many. Keep going back further into the recesses of your thoughts. The name of the land where you lived would have sounded something like Ts'i, Sung, Ch'en, or Wei. Try to recognize the sound when the thoughts come spiraling into your head. A white horse may be the clue you are looking for."

Steve Lindahl

***

Sometimes Kao Si was jealous of Kao Hui because her daughter was too young to work. What a life, she thought, sleeping all day while her mother carries her on her back. Kao Si would never admit her feelings to her husband. He would call her lazy. Everyone woke at sunrise and worked outside until it was dark. That's just the way it was. Unless there was rain. It was nice when there was rain.

There was none that day, but there was something else that stopped their work. Shortly before the noon break, two men arrived. They were riding on white horses with many tablets and small statues tied behind the saddles of the animals. They both had dark skin and wide eyes so they must have come from a faraway place where people looked different.

Kao Si's husband, Kao Jin, put down his hoe and approached the men.

"Welcome. We rarely get visitors out this far in the country. What brings you our way?"

"This is She Moteng," the taller one said. "And I am Zhu Falan. We are on a long journey, bringing sacred texts to Emperor Ming of Luoyang."

"Are you hungry? We can't let travelers pass without offering a meal. My family was about to stop for our noon break. This is my wife, Kao Si, with our daughter who is called Kao Hui."

Kao Si bowed as low as she could. She wanted to say welcome, but she didn't speak because she did not want to seem too forward. The men were dressed in patched robes that had been dyed yellow-orange. Their clothing, along with the way they had spoken of sacred texts, told her they had to be religious men. They dressed as if they were poor, but the horses they rode were magnificent and the statues she could see strapped to those horses' backs were beautiful. Perhaps they had taken a vow of poverty, but they were now working for the emperor who had taken no such vow.

Kao Jin turned to his wife. "Prepare some rice and millet wine for these fine men."

Although millet wine was not an expensive drink, Kao Si was surprised that her husband had offered the men more than simple bowls of rice. It seemed to her that he was trying to impress them for his own advantage. That was a wise move. Perhaps he was more ambitious than she had thought.

Inside the one room hut they called their home, Jin and Si had a simple wooden table and two benches, their only furniture, as they slept on mats. Jin had made the table and benches himself and Si believed he had done a good job with the work. They didn't have many material things to take pride in, but she liked the table. They offered the seats to the travelers. Jin and Si sat on their bed mats while they ate.

"The statues we carry are protected by the Emperor," She Moteng said when they were done. "No one would dare touch them without our permission."

"I know," Kao Jin replied.

"They're statues of the Buddha. You are welcome to look at them if you wish."

"I'd like that."

"Come. I'll show them to you. Some of the smaller ones are made of pure gold."

She Moteng stood up and bowed to Kao Si. He and Kao Jin stepped out of the small home, leaving Kao Si alone with Zhu Falan.

"Your husband seems interested in our statues."

"My husband is no fool. The emperor's protection is enough to temper his interest."

Kao Hui began to cry, so Si picked her daughter up and cradled her.

"Perhaps she is hungry?" Zhu Falan said.

"I fed her outside before you arrived."

"I see. And you know your daughter well enough to know it isn't time for her to be hungry again. You are an amazing woman."

"It is not unusual for a mother to know her child."

"That is true, but there is more to my words than you know at this time."

"Then you must be the one who is amazing."

"Perhaps I am, in certain ways," Falan told her, then changed the subject. "Would you prepare some tea?"

"I have none to offer you."

"We have come from India and I have brought a great deal of tea with me. If I give you some, would you prepare it? And share it?"

"Is it the emperor's tea?"

"Yes. But there are times when the emperor is generous. I know he will not mind you having some of his tea. And perhaps he wouldn't mind your husband having a gold statue, if the circumstances were right."

"A gold statue? Even the smallest one must be worth a fortune."

For Kao Si a dream of wealth had always been as likely as that she might sprout wings and fly. She was overwhelmed by the idea that her family might be allowed to keep one of the statues. The money would bring choices they never thought they could have. They might buy more land and have tenant farmers pay to work it. Kao Hui might not have to lead a life of constant hard work as her mother had. It was amazing to think about, yet she wondered about the right circumstances Zhu Falan spoke of.

"Your words sound very generous. How can you be certain this is something the emperor would be willing to do?"

"The emperor wanted us to come this way. He knows something about you and would be happy to share many things."

Kao Si was dumbstruck. What the monk was saying was that it was *she* they were here to speak with. How could that be? She had spent her entire life in this small community. Her parents had arranged her marriage to Kao Jin, a simple farmer. There was nothing in her life worth crossing a plot of land. Yet these two religious men had traveled great distances to see her.

"Did you delay your appointment with Emperor Ming to visit our humble home?"

"Our visit is part of our appointment with the emperor. We cannot be late while we are here."

Kao Jin came back into the house with She Moteng. Jin was carrying one of the gold statues, a figure of a man sitting cross-legged on a pedestal. The sculpture was about the size of Jin's fist.

"Why do you have that?" Kao Si asked her husband.

"Holding it will bring us luck."

"It would only bring us luck if we were to keep it."

Kao Jin stiffened and turned to the two monks. "Forgive my wife. We would never do such a thing. We are farmers, content to work the land from the day we are strong enough to hold a hoe to the day we die." He turned back to Kao Si. "Do not talk in such a way, Si. These men work for Emperor Ming. The wrong words could cost us our lives."

"Forgive me, my husband. I was only repeating the words of Zhu Falan."

The monk nodded in agreement. Kao Jin looked at his guest with amazement in his eyes. Then his gaze drifted down to the gold in his hands. He could not stop looking at the small statue of the sitting man.

The situation was confusing to Kao Si and somewhat frightening. Few people in even the nearby villages knew her name, so how had these men from many thousand li away come to know of her existence? They were religious men. Perhaps her ancestors had guided them to this place. If that was so, they were indeed important to her.

"The statue is of Siddhartha Gautama Buddha, the most respected man ever to live. We call ourselves Buddhists in his honor. As we said, the statue belongs to Emperor Ming. It is not a gift to either of you, but we do have other gifts to share. And perhaps, as I mentioned to Kao Si, the circumstances will be such that we can leave it with you."

"What other gifts?" Kao Jin asked.

"We brought a dress for Kao Si," She Moteng said. "It is still in a package tied to my horse."

"You must be tired from your journey," Jin said. "You are welcome to stay with us for as long as you need to rest. You may also unburden your animals so they can rest as well."

She Moteng and Zhu Falan looked at each other and smiled. "I will get the dress," She Moteng said as he stood up to leave the small hut.

"Do you have a gift for Kao Jin as well?" Kao Si asked.

Zhu Falan told her. "The emperor is interested in you."

No one spoke as She Moteng left to get the dress. Kao Hui began to cry again and Kao Si knew that this time her daughter was hungry. She picked her child up and held her.

Kao Si breast fed her daughter outside most every day without a thought of privacy. It was common practice for all mothers. But the two monks made her uncomfortable and for that reason she did not want to feed Kao Hui while they were near. It was an intimate act she did not want to share with them.

When She Moteng came back in the hut, he presented Kao Si with the most beautiful dress she had ever seen. It was silk with a long burgundy skirt and a gray top with full sleeves that would reach down over her elbows if she put it on.

"I'm dirty from my work in the field. I will go down to the creek and bathe so that I can wear this gift. Thank you very much. I will take Kao Hui with me and feed her while I am down there. Please do not worry about us while we are gone. My husband will see that you are comfortable."

"We will be fine," Zhu Falan told her.

Kao Jin nodded, still clutching the statue as if he had found a tiny lover.

The creek was in a wooded area beyond the land of three other families. When she reached it there might be other women bathing, but most of her neighbors should be working their land. That was good. She didn't want to put on such a dress in front of others. It would seem as if she were showing off.

***

"Come back just a bit," Glen said softly. "Not all the way, just enough to listen to what I have to say."

Hannah started to open her eyes, but stopped as she began to comprehend the words he was saying. She kept her breath even.

"I recognize the names of the monks. They're important people. Pay attention to what they do and say. I think you've hit the right memories."

Hannah drifted back into the memories of her life as Kao Si.

CHAPTER FORTY-FIVE

Kao Si felt clean from her dip in the creek and beautiful in the dress the monks had brought her. She had never known silk before, and now her body was wrapped in it. The way the sleek material rubbed across her bottom and her thighs as she walked, gave her a sexual sensation that was more intense than anything she'd ever felt with Kao Jin. She wondered if there might be a spell on the dress, one that would draw her to She Moteng and Zhu Falan in ways she was never drawn to Kao Jin. But even if someone had told her a spell existed, she would not have been able to give up the dress.

Kao Si stepped back into the hut carrying her daughter, but aware that everyone in the room was staring at her. Kao Jin looked up from his gold statue. They had been married for more than two years now, but he still had no knowledge of the way she would look if they had money.

"You make that dress wonderful," She Moteng told her.

"I'm certain it is the dress that changes me."

"It does you justice in a way that the simple tunic you wore could not."

"That is unfortunate. Simple tunics are all I own."

"Perhaps that once was true, but your situation has changed."

"Are you saying I can keep the dress?"

"It is yours along with three others we have with us that are of equal value. Those are what you must wear on your journey. Your old tunics would be inappropriate."

"Journey?" She turned to look at her husband. Kao Jin continued to grasp the gold statue. It suddenly became clear to Kao Si that she had been sold.

Kao Si hugged her daughter. The monks had given her the dress so she would leave the house, allowing them to plan her life when she wasn't there. *But what were their plans for Kao Hui?*

"If the dresses you offer me are of the same silk used in this one," Kao Si said, "they are a fine quality." Kao Si struggled to keep her voice from shaking, but she was not strong. "What will Kao Hui wear on the journey?"

"Su Liu is still nursing her own child," Kao Jin told her. "I am a wealthy man now. I can afford to hire her to take care of Kao Hui."

The room seemed to swirl, but she managed to keep her balance. She wanted to tell her husband that she would not leave her child in the care of their neighbor for any amount of money, but the words would not leave her tight throat.

"There is no need to worry about your duty. My daughter will be fine."

"Your daughter?" Kao Si screamed. "You spit on the ground when you learned she was a girl."

Kao Jin turned to the two monks. "Forgive my wife. She can be headstrong at times, but she will go with you."

Zhu Falan spoke to her in a gentle tone. "You are to be one of Emperor Ming's consorts. You will be one of the most powerful women in the world."

"I will die before I leave her! I had nothing of any value until Kao Hui was born. I will not walk away from her even if the emperor commands me to."

"We did not expect this reaction," She Moteng said.

"You cannot back out of your deal now." Kao Jin wrapped his arms around the statue.

"May we take your daughter with us as well?"

He shook his head. "If Kao Si is to be a powerful woman her daughter will command a great deal of respect. I cannot allow her to go for nothing."

"Then take another statue."

"One of my own choosing?"

"Yes."

Kao Jin nodded in agreement, then bowed to both the monks.

"Realize that the statues are not just a source of gold," She Moteng told him. "They are images of the wisest man ever to live. If you turn to them for guidance, your life will go in good directions. If you see them only as a source of wealth, your life will get worse rather than better."

"Perhaps your idea of worse is different than mine. I have not chosen to be a monk."

"No, you have not."

She Moteng turned to Kao Si and asked her, "Will you come with us now that you can bring your child?"

"I am happy to serve the emperor, but I don't know either of you well. How can I be sure I can trust you?"

Zhu Falan stepped forward to speak to her. "We are Buddhists. It is our *belief* that we are bringing to Emperor Ming. Buddha has said, 'On life's journey faith is nourishment, virtuous deeds are a shelter, wisdom is the light by day and right mindfulness is the protection by night. If a man lives a pure life nothing can destroy him; if he has conquered greed nothing can limit his freedom.' We live by those words and we will treat you honorably. You can choose to stay here if you do not believe what I say."

Kao Jin stomped his foot causing everyone to turn toward him. "We have made a bargain. The statues are mine even if Kao Si decides to stay with me."

Kao Si said to the monks, "My only request is that we leave right away. I don't want to spend another minute in the house of a man who would sell his wife and his child."

***

"Leave your memories, Hannah" Glen called to her. "Come back to our time."

Hannah felt herself spinning as she slipped through the years and back to the blanket on her living room where the journey had begun.

"We need to study what we've learned," Glen said.

It took a few minutes for Hannah to collect her thoughts. She pulled herself up to a sitting position. "This past life was every bit as vivid as the one in England. How many of my soul's experiences are trapped in there?"

Glen smiled. "All of them, but this is the one we've got to concentrate on. Can I use your laptop?"

"It's in the kitchen."

Glen spun around and rushed down the hall. Hannah struggled to her feet to follow.

Glen was already typing on the laptop when she joined him. "Look at this," he said. "I knew I'd heard those names before. Zhu Falan and She Moteng were the monks who brought Buddhism to China. At that time Tao was the primary religion, but Emperor Ming had taken an interest in what was going on in India. He arranged for the two men to bring statues and copies of Buddhist scriptures or sutras. This was one of the most important events in the history of the world and you were part of it. At least, Kao Si was."

"Was she mentioned in any of the articles?"

"I didn't find anything about her or her daughter. But that doesn't mean your memories are wrong. It means the written accounts of that time are incomplete."

Hannah hadn't studied the beginning of Buddhism in China, but she understood how important an event it was. Being there was akin to traveling into the wilderness with Lewis and Clark or circling the world with Magellan, only instead of discovering something that was already present, these monks were bringing something new. But why did they want Kao Si?

When Hannah finally spoke she said, "I have to call Stuart."

"Then do it."

Hannah's phone was in her purse in the living room. She left Glen to do more research. Stuart's number was preset on her phone, so she quickly made the call. His phone rang about six times then went to voicemail. "Hi. It's Hannah. I'm checking on you. I'm sorry I'm not with you tonight, but Glen and I made some good progress. I'll talk to you tomorrow."

Hannah tucked her phone away and went back to the kitchen. Glen was still intent on the computer screen.

"More progress?" she asked.

"Not really. It's one of those historic events that's mentioned on lots of websites, but all with the same level of detail."

"Which is limited, I'm guessing."

"Exactly. Historians don't know anymore about the actual experiences of Zhu Falan and She Moteng than they know of Mary and Joseph's journey to Bethlehem. They know where they came from, where they went to, and what they were riding. That's about it."

"In both those cases, the historians also know why they were traveling," Hannah suggested.

"That's right. The monks were bringing icons and religious texts to Emperor Ming. That's recorded history."

"And that purpose was in my memories as well." Hannah was bothered by the concept of Kao Si joining the monks on their journey, so she added, "But wasn't it odd that a woman and her baby could travel with two men back then? My impression of China's civilization two thousand years ago was that mixing genders wasn't acceptable."

"I think the answer lies in her poverty. Kao Si worked in the fields along with her husband every day. She was used to living her life along side of a man. She was also used to a lack of privacy. As for the monks, they were concerned with something that overrode any conventions they might have otherwise adhered to."

Hannah wanted to learn more about Kao Si, but knew Glen would never regress her so soon. She suggested the next best option: sending Glen back to that same era.

"I'm ready when you are," he said as he closed out the website he'd been studying.

Glen and Hannah went back to the living room. This time he took the position on the blanket and she sat in a chair next to him. She started guiding his regression and in a few minutes he seemed to be drifting back into his memories. But after a while he sat up.

"I tried to go toward your voice, but when I let my memories drift in that direction I found I couldn't quite reach the goal. I kept trying to focus on the monks and on ancient China in general, but nothing related to those thoughts seemed to be in my head. Perhaps your existence as Kao Si was prior to any lives we shared."

"Do you want to send *me* back again?"

"You need time between sessions to let both your mind and your body recover. Here's what I think we should do instead. I want you to send me to Molly and Rose's time. We've got more to learn from them."

"But Kao Si's life can tell us what the killers are after."

"Tomorrow you'll be ready to go back to that era, but right now I need to go to Victorian England."

Hannah agreed, so Glen lay back down on the blanket and closed his eyes while she began to guide him back into a life they knew he had led.

CHAPTER FORTY-SIX

The morning after Rose left her in the street, Molly showed up at the lodging house where Rose spent each night. Rose wasn't there, and Molly concluded that the only reason Rose would be out at seven-thirty in the morning would be to avoid *her*. The logical next assumption was that Rose had gone after Albert Moss.

That was as foolish an act as Molly could imagine, but she was afraid it was what Rose had in mind. Annie was dead, and, given the friendship between the two prostitutes, Rose was sure to seek revenge. That meant she was either on her way to the stable where Annie had first met Albert Moss or to the house on Whitechapel High Street where Rose had said she'd gone with Ratinam. Since Molly had no idea where the stable was located, her options were limited.

Molly walked to Whitechapel. Unless she was extremely lucky, she'd have to return for a number of days before she'd have a chance of finding Rose—unless she happened to be standing outside.

Suddenly, she had an idea: the building where Rose had seen Annie and Ratinam. Maybe, just maybe ….

The sun had set, so the street was dark save for some dim gas street lights. She could stay in the shadows, minimizing any risk that Mr. Moss might look out a window and see her lurking on the street.

Molly walked up and down the street a couple of times, looking for some sign of activity in the building. Finally, there was a bright, flickering light in a second story window; a gas lamp. Rose could be in that room, but there was an equal possibility that Moss's thugs were up there.

Molly was about to head back to The Pavilion when a thin dark-skinned man walked up the other side of the street and entered the building. While he certainly appeared Indian, she couldn't be certain he was Annie's Ratinam.

Molly walked toward the building. She'd been with the circus long enough to know the only people who got anywhere were the ones who took risks. As she reached for the door it opened and the man she'd been following stepped out. He was carrying a leather satchel.

"What are you doing here?"

Molly stumbled backwards. She'd warned Rose about Ratinam for good reason. "Are you Annie's friend?" Molly answered his question with one of her own, her voice stammering a bit.

He stepped past her. "Follow me. Move quickly, before someone sees you."

They turned up Whitechapel High Street with him a couple of steps ahead of her. "I'm looking for Rose." He hadn't acknowledged Molly's question, but, feeling braver, she kept speaking. "I'm worried about her."

"You should be. You have no idea what you're dealing with."

"Everyone in London knows Annie was murdered."

He turned left when they reached Cambridge Road and stopped.

"Are you Ratinam?"

"How do you know my name?"

"Annie talked to Rose before she was killed."

"Death is not permanent."

"Is that how you rationalize killing people?"

"I had no part in her death."

"She didn't just die. She was cut up and her guts were tossed around the street. But you know that, don't you?"

He moved off without responding. They walked until they reached the corner of Green, where Bethnal House was located. Molly was worried that Ratinam might enter that lunatic asylum and expect her to follow. To her relief, he kept walking and turned into a building at the end of that block.

"Where are you taking me?"

"Rose is in here."

Entering what seemed to be an abandoned building would be foolish. Still, Rose needed her.

Ratinam held the door for her as Molly stepped into the dark building. He followed and shut the door.

It took a while for Molly's eyes to adjust, but there was light coming in from a number of windows along Green Street. When she could see, she realized she was standing in a large empty room; the only visible objects were the pillars holding up the next floor.

"Where's Rose?"

"Have patience."

"Don't tell me about patience. Rose is my friend."

"Your friend?"

Molly turned around to see Rose standing by a door to a back room. Molly ran to her.

"I thought I was just one of the links in your connection to Moss and his cohorts."

"I was worried about you," Molly said. Nodding toward Ratinam, she added, "I thought *he* was one of the cohorts."

"Did you get the stones?" Rose asked the Indian man.

"They're in the bag."

"Then there's no need to worry," she said to Molly. She turned back to Ratinam. "Did you bring her here for a reason?"

"If I didn't bring her, she'd probably be dead. She was looking for you."

"Come along, both of you," Rose said. "Let's get started."

Rose turned and entered the room she'd come out of. Molly and Ratinam followed. There was a blanket spread out on the floor, surrounded by lit candles.

"Are you sure this will work?" Rose asked Ratinam.

"No. But since you and Annie were close, there's a good chance for success. She died recently. Her spirit is most likely still near to us."

"This is a séance?" Molly asked.

"I don't like that word," Rose told her. "There are too many frauds who use it to steal money and hope from people in mourning. Ratinam promises that isn't the case here."

Ratinam spoke up. "You've been tracking Mr. Moss for some time now," he said. "I probably know as much about you as you know about him. You've taken some of the artifacts."

"They were stolen. I was hired to restore them to a place where the world can appreciate them."

"I'm not sure that *stolen* is the right word for what those items were before your people took them, but it certainly fits now. How art should be appreciated is a matter of opinion. Mr. Moss acquired the art hundreds of years ago; some of the pieces were probably stolen but most were traded for. He hid the work and waited long enough for it to reach a great value. Gradually he's been selling some to raise money to live on while accruing new work to sell to future generations of collectors. It's a simple system, if you have the ability to remember."

Molly was ecstatic. Ratinam had just confirmed her theory about Moss's abilities. "Like the Dalai Lama."

"That's a bad comparison. He's anything but a living god."

"An evil Dalai Lama?"

"Even *that* gives him more credit than he deserves."

"Are you two going to talk all night?" Rose asked.

"Sorry," Molly said.

"What should I do now?" Rose asked Ratinam.

"Take off your clothes. Your spirit has to be free."

Molly wondered if Ratinam might have a selfish motivation that had nothing to do with Annie. She looked at Rose who was already in the process of removing her clothing.

Molly couldn't help but compare Rose's body with her own. Rose was a little heavier. She had a bit more of a pot belly than Molly had expected and her breasts sagged a little. Molly's own body was trimmer and tauter, but Rose was very beautiful. Molly was surprised that the hard lifestyle hadn't taken more of a toll.

"Should I lie down?" Rose asked.

"On your stomach," Ratinam told her. "I need to place the stones on your body. Concentrate on the way the smooth surfaces feel, then allow yourself to drift off. You'll be in among spirits, surrounded by souls that haven't found their way back to the physical world. Annie should be one of them. Reach out to her. Call her. Let her find you."

***

"Why did you bring me back?" Glen asked as he sat up on the blanket in Hannah's living room.

"Ratinam was working with Rose, not Molly. I want you to send me back to the session they were having. I can learn far more than what you can as an observer."

"You should concentrate on the time of Kao Si, since my soul wasn't part of that incarnation. While you work on China, I can study London. But neither of us should do another session today."

"What about Stuart?"

"What about him?"

"His soul was Ratinam's. He can tell us more about the session in the warehouse than either of us."

CHAPTER FORTY-SEVEN

Stuart woke to a headache and a slightly queasy stomach. Obviously, he'd consumed too much of Jamie's stash. That girl from the play had been drinking with him. Where was she—Allison, that was her name—now? Maybe she was taking care of Starr.

Stuart stood up, took a moment to be sure he had his balance, then started towards the kitchen for tomato juice. The front door was open. Could Allison have left? He hoped to hell he hadn't done anything to chase her away.

Stuart closed the door, turned the dead bolt, and continued to the kitchen. The door to Starr's room was open, too. He glanced in to check on his daughter.

The hangover was slowing down Stuart's responses; it took him a moment to realize there was something wrong. Starr wasn't in the bed. She wasn't asleep on the floor. She didn't appear to be anywhere in the room.

Stuart ran for the kitchen. Maybe Allison had his daughter up and was feeding her breakfast. No such luck. His head was swirling, and this time it wasn't from last night's drinks. He was scared. He started looking in odd places, under the table and in all the cabinets. Starr didn't play tricks like that, but if there was a place where she might be hiding, he checked it.

He ran back to the guest bedroom where Allison had been supposed to spend the night. She was gone. Starr wasn't there, either. Maybe Allison had taken Starr outside. That would explain the open door.

Still, he was going to give her a bit of a lecture when they came back. She hadn't even left a note.

Or had she? He ran to the kitchen, which seemed the most logical place to leave it. No paper other than a stack of bills he had to pay soon. He rushed back to the living room and looked where he'd been sleeping. It made sense that she'd leave a note where he'd find it when he first woke up. Nothing. He even got down on his knees and looked underneath all the furniture.

He ran back to Starr's bedroom, but again nothing. It was in the last room, his bedroom, that he found the note.

"Don't call the police."

"What the hell should I do?" Stuart yelled. He crumpled the note and tossed it on the floor then kicked at the bed Starr had been sleeping in. Pacing anxiously, he almost dialed 911 twice, but each time he knew in his heart that if he did, the police wouldn't find his daughter until after she was dead.

"I need to talk to somebody," he said in a too-loud voice. He dialed Hannah's number.

"Stuart?" Hannah said. She sounded groggy.

"Pu-put Glen on," he told her, stuttering.

"Are you all right? You never call this early."

"Starr's gone."

"What do you mean *gone*?"

"I woke up this morning and she was gone. Allison took her."

"Allison? From the play?"

"I need to talk to Glen."

"Just a minute." Stuart could hear Hannah telling Glen that Stuart wanted to talk to him and why.

"Stuart?"

"She left a note that said I shouldn't call the police. These have to be the people who killed Jamie. If I don't follow their instructions they'll hurt her."

"Don't do anything. We'll get dressed and be over there in less than ten minutes. We'll talk about it when we get there."

Stuart hung up his phone. He sat on the couch and stared at the bottle of gin. It was almost empty, just a couple of swallows left.

***

"I don't understand what Allison was doing here," Hannah said to Stuart.

"Have you tried to call Allison?" Glen said almost simultaneously.

"Her phone rolls to voicemail every time."

"We could go to her house."

"I don't know where she lives. I tried to look up an address for her. It must be unlisted. I thought about calling a private investigator, just to track her down. But hiring a detective could piss off whoever's behind this worse than calling the police. I don't want to make the wrong move. I have trouble believing Allison acted alone."

"You're right to be cautious," Glen said.

"So what should I do?"

"The answer is in the past. We need to keep looking there."

"We're talking about my child here. She's all I've got left. Swear to me this stuff is real. Tell me we won't be just playing games when we should be out looking in the real world."

"We can't look for her, because we have no idea *where* to look," Hannah told him. "Allison wouldn't take Starr unless she had a reason. Hanging tight is the best way to learn what it is. Someone will contact you."

"I don't think I can stand waiting," Stuart said.

Glen said, "We'll do a regression while we're waiting. We'll be here if they call, but at least we won't be sitting around doing nothing."

Hannah wasn't sure she'd be a good subject. She was too upset. "I can try, but I think both Stuart and I are too nervous to clear our thoughts."

"I can do it," Glen said. "Molly has a lot more to tell us."

***

Ratinam's ritualistic treatment of Rose was the most mysterious event Molly had ever witnessed, and also the most erotic. He put the stones on her naked body, even positioning a long thin one between her legs, instructing her to squeeze her thighs to hold it in place. Ratinam called out the names of the stones as he reached for each one: Mooladhara, Svadhistana, Manipura, Anahata. He touched Rose's skin gently when he placed the stones and even massaged her back with his hand balled up in a fist.

"You are drifting back. You are entering the spirit world. While there you will locate Annie and drift into her consciousness. Gradually you will learn what it was like to feel what Annie felt and to think the thoughts that were important to her. You will become one with her."

Ratinam stood at Rose's head, holding the Sahasrara stone in place on her crown. He seemed to touch her with a great tenderness, causing Molly to have trouble understanding the man's relationship with Annie and her killers.

Rose began to speak softly, describing what she was experiencing as she began her search for Annie's spirit. "I'm walking, but very slowly as if I'm moving through water. People who are no longer living surround me. My father is one of them. I hated that man for the hard way he treated me. His fists would fly out without warning. It wasn't to teach me or punish me or help me in any way. My father did it because he enjoyed it, as if he experienced a sense of power from inflicting pain on his child. But now there is a gentleness that pervades his spirit. He floats through me and I experience his sincere apology.

"My mother passes by as well. At first I'm upset because she's near my father. If there were ever two people who did not belong together, they were them. But once again things are different in this spirit world. For one thing, my mother is sober, but beyond that there is the sense that she has somehow reconciled the inner turmoil that had caused her to hide from life. I'm glad for her. No one deserves the level of pain she experienced when she was alive.

"Finally Annie comes out of the crowd. I recognize her although her appearance is different from the woman I knew when she was alive. She floats through me the way my father did, but with Annie I feel more than a simple apology. I understand her life. I feel the anger she had and the humiliation she experienced from the men she serviced. My own experience wasn't that different from hers, but I accepted what I had to do. In life I hadn't known how angry Annie was.

"Annie's bitterness was focused on the way Mr. Moss cut her open and spread her guts around the street. Yet, as with my father and mother, Annie is now experiencing peace.

"Annie had love within her that she never understood until she met Ratinam."

CHAPTER FORTY-EIGHT

The ringing sound of a cell phone pulled Glen back from Molly's memories. The scene of a naked Rose lying on the floor as part of Ratinam's ritual faded out of his mind, replaced by the realization that he was lying on a blanket in Stuart's living room. He shook his head and sat up.

Stuart was shouting into the phone. "Where the hell are you?" There was a pause.

"I understand what you're saying ... of course ... I'll do whatever it takes." There was another pause as he listened to the reply.

"I'll follow your instructions."

After Stuart hung up, he explained, "They said I was right to keep the police out of this."

"Of course they did," Hannah told him.

"They said she was fine and that Allison was taking care of her."

"So Allison wasn't on the phone?" Glen asked.

"No. It was a man's voice. I didn't recognize him."

"What do they want you to do?"

"It's like I suspected. These are the same people who had me smuggling boxes. They said they'll contact me by email and let me know what I need to do. They told me not to talk to anyone about this."

"Then they don't know about us?" Hannah asked.

"I guess not. I didn't ask them. "I think you better go home," Stuart said.

"We want to be here for you," Hannah pleaded.

"I don't know how these people will react if they find out I've talked to you, so I'm asking you to stay away. I intend to do whatever it takes to keep Starr alive. You can't help me now."

That word, *now*, was hurtful. Glen looked at Hannah and saw that she had tears in her eyes. But it wasn't just Hannah's emotions that concerned him. He was convinced that Stuart was making a bad choice. His decision to submit to all demands had not kept Jamie alive and there was no reason to believe the results this time would be any different. But he also knew bringing that subject up would likely cause more harm than good, so he took Hannah's hand and walked to the door.

***

Stuart left his home that evening to go to Paper Birch Farm, the riding stable where he'd picked up the first box he'd been asked to smuggle. The email had said he was to meet someone in the barn. He assumed it would be Allison, if only because anyone else would give him another face to identify.

Once again Stuart parked near the riding ring and walked to the barn. This time he was less concerned when he passed the farmhouse. The kidnappers wouldn't have sent him here if there was someone inside he wasn't supposed to meet. They also had him show up earlier in the evening than the last time he'd been there, another indication that there was less chance he'd be caught where he didn't belong.

Stuart walked straight into the barn and looked for Allison. He wasn't sure what he'd do to her when he saw her, but he knew he had to be careful. She was the key to getting Starr back.

"Allison?" Stuart called as he walked down the aisle between the stalls. "I know you're here. Come out where I can talk to you."

He remembered where he'd found the box the first time: in a stall toward the back of the barn. He walked directly there, but it was empty. There were still no horses in the barn, so there wasn't any straw on the ground. Stuart wondered if this was some elaborate joke, or maybe a test of his willingness to show up alone.

He turned around and saw a person standing at the entrance to the barn. It wasn't Allison. It was Troy, the actor who had found Jamie's body.

"Troy?" He was surprised to see someone other than Allison, especially someone he recognized. "Where's Starr?"

"Your daughter is safe."

"She'd *better* be safe."

"I'm just the messenger."

"If anything happens to her, you're dead. You have my word on that."

"You're to get back in your car and follow me."

"Where to?"

"Back to your apartment, but you can't go inside. You'll park then I'll drive you where you need to go."

"And where is that?"

"I can't tell you."

"Will Starr be there?"

"I don't know."

"You don't know much of anything, do you?"

"Like I said, I'm just a messenger. I'm supposed to tell you that things will happen if you don't do as you're told."

Troy didn't say *what* things would happen. He let Stuart's imagination say it for him.

After Stuart left his car, Troy had him lie in the back seat while he drove. The only things Stuart could see were the tops of trees. When they arrived at a mobile home tucked in a wooded area, he had no idea where they were.

Stuart followed Troy up a small wooden porch, through the front door, and into a great room that combined living room, dining room, and a kitchen area. Victor Wood, the man who'd first hired him to move packages, was sitting at a table. He stood up when they entered. There were some oddly shaped stones positioned around the table.

"I knew you'd be behind this," Stuart said.

Victor smiled then said, "Take a seat."

Stuart did as he was instructed.

"I want you to look at these and tell me what you think."

Victor had a stack of photographs. He handed one to Stuart.

It was a picture of two women in a living room. The furniture was of an old style and the dresses the women were wearing had to be from at least a hundred years ago.

"I've seen this before. It's a scene from *A Doll's House*."

Victor handed him another photo. There were two people in this picture as well, but one was a man. The woman was on the floor and the man appeared ready to strike her.

"It's a picture of Paige Stackman. Why are you showing this to me?"

"Focus on the time frame. Here, look at the rest of these."

Victor handed Stuart the entire stack of photos. Every shot was a scene from that play and Paige was in them all.

"Concentrate on how she looks. Think for a moment that this is your own living room and Paige is there, talking to you. Tell me about her. Describe her with as much detail as you can."

Stuart was there to cooperate, so he pushed his anger to the back of his mind, looked at the picture, and began talking about Paige's costume.

"She's wearing a long dress with a high collar and billowy sleeves. It looks heavy, like it might be wool. I don't know for sure. It's pink, which seems to clash with her red-orange hair."

Victor turned to Troy. "Wait for me out in your car. We'll be all right in here." He sounded irritated.

"Did I do something wrong?" Stuart asked as Troy walked toward the door.

"You knew Paige well, didn't you?"

He was wary about the direction this was going.

"She was Hannah's friend and I know Hannah."

"She was more than that, wasn't she?"

"Yes, she was Hannah's partner."

"She was more than that to you."

So Victor knew.

"We were only together a few times. I was mad at Jamie and Paige just wanted to be with a man, but we didn't intend to hurt Hannah. I didn't think anyone knew about us."

"Look at the first picture again. This is your living room. You're sitting there with these two women. It's the latter part of the nineteenth century and the one in the pink dress is a Victorian version of Paige. There are no cell phones or DVRs or microwaves. There's just you, Paige, and this other woman. Describe Paige to me."

"Why did she have to die?"

"It's about the nineteenth century. You performed regressions back then and damn near hit the goal we gave you. Now describe Paige to me."

"If you want a regression, talk to Hannah's friend."

"You were the best ever, far beyond what Glen Wiley could ever be. Now put yourself back in the 1800s and tell me about the woman in the pink dress. Make everything up if you like, but it better sound real."

"We're not alone. Her friend is there, sitting on a love seat, knitting."

"Is she Annie?"

"I don't know Annie."

"Yes, you do. Go on."

"Paige could be wild at times, but never hurtful."

Could was the wrong word to use. He needed to pretend she was alive when he told his story. This was one of the hardest things Stuart had ever done. Paige didn't belong in the nineteenth century, but, just like Jamie, she didn't belong in the present, either. But he had to make up some life story for her that would work well enough to satisfy Victor Wood.

"She's a talented pianist and loves to sing while she plays. She knows *Long, Long Ago* by heart and can sing a half dozen others as well. I've spent hours listening to her perform in her parlor. Of course, her husband was always there as well."

This seemed to be a direction that suited Paige, since she was a good karaoke singer. He wasn't certain how the song title came to him, but he knew it was right for the time. He'd always been good with historical trivia, especially with the Victorian period. This was the first time that talent had ever done him any good.

"You told me she could be wild," Victor said.

"I also said she tried not to hurt anyone she cared for. Appearances were important in the nineteenth century."

"I don't want to hear what you think you're supposed to say. I want to hear a story from the depths of your soul."

I don't have a story. But he had to say something close to what was expected.

"Paige was—"

"Call her Mary Ann. Think of her as Paige, but use her name from that time."

Her name? Wood was asking him to talk about someone real? This was impossible.

"I didn't know the woman."

"Yes, you did. The memories are in your head and you have the ability to pull them out."

"If Glen was here, maybe."

"You don't need him. Look at the picture and start with that. Mary Ann was a whore and a drunk but also your friend. You knew her before you knew Annie."

"Glen sent me back once. I was called Ratinam and I was a Hindu."

"That's right. Look at this picture." Victor handed Stuart a photo from another stack. It was Jamie in a scene from *Miss Julie*. She was wearing the costume that had affected him so dramatically the night she wore it home. *Was that a past life memory?*

"Does this bring back anything?"

"Jamie was my wife," Stuart said, his voice cracking. "You must know that." He took a deep breath. Starr was the only one he could help now and to do that he needed to appease these people. He kept staring at the photograph as he tried to control his emotions.

"Was there ever a sense of déjà vu when she was in this role?" Victor asked. "The purpose of these pictures is to help you crack the door open slightly. You were Ratinam, but do you remember anything more than your name? Look back at the pictures of Paige and tell me if the name Mary Ann Nichols has any meaning to you."

Stuart's head was swirling. He'd been there for Starr since she was born. He'd never tired even when Jamie left almost all the responsibilities to him. But this made all the other things he'd done for his daughter pale. If he couldn't get this right, who knew what these lunatics would do. They had killed Paige. They had killed Jamie.

Mary Ann Nichols. He let the name spin around in his mind. What had Glen told him to do? Relax. How could he do that now? Victor had said he was once better than Glen at this stuff. The memories were up there. If he just concentrated hard enough he should be able to get into his own head.

"I'm starting to remember," Stuart said. "I knew Mary Ann through Mr. Moss. He could remember parts of his past life better than anyone I had ever met, without any help from me or anyone else. There was something about a consort he had known. He was looking for her soul in the prostitutes in London. He never told me why, but Mary was the first one he went after. She didn't work out."

"Why didn't she work out?"

"I'm not sure. I regressed her. I remember that."

"Do you remember how?"

"Yes," Stuart said as he reached over and picked up one of the stones Victor had placed on the table. He held it up and examined it closely. "Things are coming back, but they aren't all clear. Ratinam used these stones when he regressed Lucius and Mary Ann. How did you get them?"

"The stones were hidden hundreds of years ago to be brought out when they were needed. They were in some of the boxes you moved for us."

Stuart wondered what the penalty was for smuggling artifacts. The punishment probably would have had something to do with the value of those stones.

"Tell me more about Mary Ann," Victor commanded.

The memories were there without hypnotism and without ritual. He concentrated harder.

"Everything isn't clear, but I have the feeling that she was brought to Ratinam to use for practice regressions. I believe she was the first woman he worked with in England. There might have been others in India, but what he did there isn't coming back to me. Most of the white people weren't comfortable around me, but Mary Ann was an exception."

"You said *me*. That's good."

"I'm not certain if her comfort came naturally to her or if making her living from men of all types had hardened her over the years to things as trivial as skin color and country of origin. Either way, she was able to put herself at ease enough for me to regress her. But perhaps a relaxed state is not as critical as I once thought. You've brought back old memories and I'm as far from relaxed as I can be. Of course, the memories that are coming now are not as clear as a regression. They're more like everyday memories."

Victor didn't appear to be interested in Stuart's analysis of the process. "Where did Mary Ann go when you regressed her?"

"She was a Buddhist monk who was connected to the court of a Chinese emperor. She was a man during that incarnation. Switching genders is not unusual."

"Tell me more about Mary Ann's other life," Victor said, again leading him back to his memories.

"I had assumed she had many lives over such a long time span, but when I regressed Mary Ann she always went back to the same existence. Something important must have happened during that time."

"How about Annie? You regressed her, didn't you?"

Stuart understood that he had to do whatever Victor asked him to do, but he wasn't looking forward to discussing Annie. Annie and Jamie were one, and he had just lost Jamie. The still-present pain of his loss reminded him that he could not live through losing Starr. He closed his eyes and began to talk about Annie.

"I tried, but Annie and I had a relationship that interfered with my ability to work with her."

"I don't understand."

"She had a small income from her ex-husband and did some crochet work as well, but most of her money came from prostitution. She wasn't comfortable with my reaction to the time she spent with other men."

Victor Wood stood up and leaned in toward Stuart. "You're telling me you didn't look into Annie's past lives?"

"I talked to some of Annie's friends about her."

"You wouldn't lie to me about this, would you?"

"I've been as honest as I can be." Stuart was surprised by Victor's reaction and felt the need to reassure him. "I know what you're capable of and that cannot happen to Starr."

"You know much less than you think you know, although I'm surprised how well this session has worked. During your life as Ratinam you remembered a great deal from the lives you led before that one. Some of your ability is coming back to you now, although you're nowhere near where you need to be. Still, I'm pleased and I know others will be as well."

"Can I see my daughter?"

Victor shook his head.

"I've done everything you asked."

"I know you have and that's good, but there's much more we need to accomplish before you are ready. She's in good hands. Allison is with her."

"That doesn't make me feel any better."

"Next time I'll bring proof that she's alive and well."

"Next time?"

"You didn't think this was all I wanted from you, did you?"

165

CHAPTER FORTY-NINE

"It does no good to cry."

Glen was showing very little compassion despite knowing that Stuart had been Hannah's best friend for years.

"I know it's hard. You want to be there for him and you can't, at least not in the normal way. But you've got something to offer that is more important than a shoulder to cry on. You've got your life as Kao Si."

Before they learned about Starr's kidnapping, Hannah had been looking forward to being regressed again. Now she couldn't stop berating herself for letting her friend down.

He was right. She needed to go back into her memories again.

***

She Moteng had become Kao Si's friend. She met with him often, generally in her quarters where they could be alone. They got away with their rendezvous because She Moteng was a religious man and one of Emperor Ming's favorites. Although it was improper for a consort of the emperor to be alone with another man, no one was brave enough to gossip about them.

There was nothing sexual about Kao Si's relationship with She Moteng. He came to her on a regular basis to tell her about Kao Hui. Kao Si was living in a level of comfort she had never imagined possible, but she still regretted coming to the palace. Kao Hui had been taken from her within days of their arrival. They had been at court for over fourteen years. Soon her child would be of an age to marry.

"Marriage is not Kao Hui's destiny," She Moteng said when she mentioned the word. "You must know by this time the truth of our trip to your farm on the day when we first met. We were not there by chance."

"I've long suspected that was the case. It was Kao Hui you were after, was it not?"

"Yes. Your child has a powerful spirit. I've spent many years with you, and during that time we often spoke of the oneness of everything around us. Today I must tell you that there are spirits in this world powerful enough to keep an independent presence within that oneness."

"Kao Hui?"

"We knew of her existence the moment she was born. We also knew that her strength could help our beliefs take root in the new China. We communicated with Emperor Ming and he commanded us to travel to your farm."

"At last I know that what I have long suspected is true. You did not come for me that day. You came for my child. Then why did you take me? It cannot be that Kao Hui needed her mother or you would not have separated us."

"We knew you would resist us if we tried to take Kao Hui alone. We gambled that your husband was not so strong. We were right."

"What is it about Kao Hui's spirit that is powerful?"

"Her place in the oneness is so great that she can know the past of all spirits. Most of us must meditate for many years before we can hope to know of our own past, while Kao Hui can see everything with little effort. Her stories are amazing to hear."

"Does she know of *my* life?"

"Only what I've told her. Yet she knows of the many lives you lived before you were Kao Si. In some ways she knows you better than you know yourself."

"I understand."

"Perhaps you do, but you do not know of Emperor Ming's wishes."

"I understand the power of his desires," she said. "Does he want Kao Hui to bear him children? I have been unable to do that for him."

She Moteng shook his head. "This is a different type of craving. He wants her power."

"Oh?" Now it was Kao Si who was shaking her head. "Even an Emperor has limits. He must know that."

"I don't believe he does. Zhu Falan and I have trained Kao Hui to be his teacher and his spiritual guide. She is excellent at that already in simple matters. But now that she is turning fifteen Emperor Ming will expect more from her."

"Emperor Ming is a good man. He will not hurt Kao Hui. I am certain of that."

"My impression is the same as yours. She has nothing to fear from the Emperor. But there are ambitious men around him who will do anything they can to win his favor. If Kao Hui's path takes an unexpected turn, those men could be dangerous."

"What should I do?"

"There are people in the palace who have been watching Kao Hui for years. They are part of a troupe of performers. She has a fondness for the shadow plays they put on and they have written a few stories in her honor. I trust two of them completely, Yin Ji and Wei Lihua."

"I have seen their shows, but I have never spoken with either of those women."

"Come with me now. I will bring you to them."

Kao Si stood to follow. The skirt of her tunic was long, making it difficult for her to move quickly, but She Moteng did not appear to be in a hurry. Kao Si was nervous. Although Kao Hui was not the only child to be raised by people other than her mother, the distance felt unnatural to Kao Si. She had always experienced a feeling of emptiness when she thought about her daughter.

They had to walk to the other side of the palace, which meant going down three long hallways then crossing a courtyard. It was early spring, so the garden was filled with pink from the flowering peach trees. Kao Si loved the color and smell in the courtyard at this time of year. This time, however, Kao Si followed She Moteng through the garden without taking time to appreciate the blossoms.

Over the years she had spent many hours in this garden when she had permission to be there. Her access was carefully monitored so she would never be in the same place at the same time as Kao Hui. The emperor's guards were invisible to her, but they were diligent. She had never tried to sneak to where she might see her daughter.

The troupe performed the shadow plays in a room that could fit about twenty people sitting on mats. The plays were a form of puppet theater with flat, leather puppets controlled by sticks held by performers who stood behind a raised, white screen. A bright light was positioned in back of the screen so the shadows of the puppets appeared on the opposite side. The puppets were transparent enough to show color in their shadows. Yin Ji was one of the puppeteers. Wei Lihua was a singer who accompanied the story with her voice.

The plays were all scenes from the lives of women of the court who had died. The emperor believed the puppets captured their spirits, so he would watch the performances as part of the mourning process. Kao Si had also seen many of the shows. She knew that as one of Emperor Ming's consorts there would someday be a number of plays based on her own life. In preparation she had spent many hours dictating her story to She Moteng so he could help write the work.

Kao Si had never spoken with either Yin Ji or Wei Lihua. She would have if she had known they were tasked with some of the responsibilities of raising Kao Hui. She had asked She Moteng many times for the names of her daughter's teachers, but he had been specifically instructed not to reveal them and had never gone against that command until now.

She Moteng left her alone with Yin Ji. There was much to ask. She Moteng had relayed facts to her with great detail, but it would be different speaking with a woman.

"I have enjoyed your performances," Kao Si told the puppeteer. "The shadows on the screen pull me to another world. I have discussed that feeling with She Moteng and he assured me it is proper. But it seems wrong because it feels so good. Has anyone ever told you that before?"

"Many women have. Men are different. They are more accepting of experiences that feel good."

Kao Si laughed. "That is right, but I have never heard it said so clearly before."

"Your daughter has your laugh."

"Ahh. That is good to hear. Are there other qualities we share as well?"

"I cannot say. I know Kao Hui very well, but you have only been to a few of our performances and we have never talked before this day. I will have to learn your traits as well as I know hers."

"Forget about me. My daughter is the one I am interested in. She Moteng tells me she is bright and does well with her schooling. I want to know other things."

"What things? Kao Hui loves animals, especially the palace dogs. One in particular follows her around."

"It is good she shows respect for all life. But I have heard similar stories from She Moteng. You and Wei Lihua are the mothers I was not allowed to be. Tell me a story of how she bonded with you."

"No one ever lied to Kao Hui about you. She understood you would be with her if it was permitted. And she knew neither of us could ever be her mother. She missed you."

"I am not jealous, but I must know."

Yin Ji nodded. "I will tell you this," she said. "Kao Hui is here because She Moteng and Zhu Falan sensed her gift and could tell that her spirit was in your home. An infant when she arrived, as she grew she needed teachers. That is when Wei Lihua and I became part of her life. It was Zhu Falan's idea that we should learn the art of shadow plays and use the stories to teach her."

"Is that why the Emperor allows women to be performers?"

"We are the only two," Yin Ji said with pride in her voice. "But let me continue."

Kao Si nodded without speaking.

"Her own story was one of the first shows we put on for her. We often use parts of older puppets to make new ones, but we still have the one that represented Kao Hui. Let me show you."

Yin Ji led Kao Si behind the screen where there were some puppets from the most recent play. But she did not pick up any of those. Instead she went to a wooden chest of drawers and pulled out the bottom drawer. She pulled out two puppets and carefully set them on the floor, then she pulled out one that she held up for Kao Si to see.

"This one represents Kao Hui," she said, holding the puppet up. It was leather, but almost as thin as a paper doll. The puppet's face was yellow, her tunic red, and her hair black.

"Finally, after all these years, I meet my child again and this is how it is to be."

Yin Ji looked up with a start, but Kao Si was smiling.

Yin Ji said, "Let me show you how it works." She took a step toward one of the oil lamps behind the screen and lit it from a burning candle in a table lamp. When Kao Si heard the woman's words and saw her start to set up the puppet theater, she was assured that her attempt at humor had not been ill received.

"What are you doing?" someone shouted. It was a man's voice, heavy and dark. Kao Si turned to see Chen Jiang entering the room.

"Forgive me, master. I was simply showing Kao Si how I work my craft."

"You know better. You should not be revealing our secrets."

"My work is not such a secret and this is Kao Hui's mother."

"Are you arguing with me?"

"I meant no disrespect."

"The show is over. Kao Si must return to her quarters."

"They had my approval," She Moteng said. Kao Si had not noticed when the monk had come back into the room. As much as she hated Chen Jiang telling her she could not speak with Yin Ji, she was more uncomfortable with the knowledge that She Moteng had been secretly watching them.

"You have no authority in this room," Chen Jiang told She Moteng.

Kao Si was worried there would be a confrontation, but the monk merely bowed and said, "Perhaps I do not have the Emperor's authority in this theater, but there are other forces in the universe. Emperor Ming would be the first to tell you so."

Chen Jiang looked angry and Kao Si was certain he would take out his frustrations on Yin Ji. "We will do as you wish," Yin Ji told the master, defusing the situation.

"It would be good if you left us alone," Chen Jiang said to Kao Si. "Take your spiritual leader with you. There is no need for either of you to be with us as we explore different worlds."

Different is right, Kao Si thought as she turned to leave the room. Chen Jiang seemed to be a self-important, ruthless man, and she was not sorry to leave his presence.

***

"Wake up, slowly," Glen called in as gentle a voice as Hannah had ever heard. "Come back to your current life."

Hannah rolled her shoulders after she sat up. It had been a long session and she was tired from it. She was also disappointed. She had been close to learning about the life of Kao Hui and believed that she could help them discover the reasons behind the crimes that had cost

Paige and Jamie their lives.

"There was ugliness in Chen Jiang," she told Glen, "and it wasn't only from his irritation with finding Kao Si there. I wish we hadn't been forced to leave. If I'd been able to watch him for a while longer I think I'd have discovered if what I sensed about him was something powerful enough to perservere over all these years."

"We'll get back to him in your next regression," Glen told her. "But we're not done for today. It's my turn. I've been thinking about something else that's shared by your lives in England, in China, and in the present. There's always some performance going on: community theater in modern times, a circus in that of Molly and Rose, and shadow plays during the Han dynasty. Maybe it's a coincidence, but it seems like something we need to look at further."

She would have preferred going back under and searching through her memories for more contact with Chen Jiang, but she knew he'd never agree to regress her again that quickly.

"I want you to help me bring back Molly's memories of her life in the circus so we can look for more reasons why she's there."

"You were Molly, and you have no other connection to any performances I know of in this life. And you weren't even in the life I had as Kao Si. So I'm not sure your theory makes sense."

"I understand what you're saying. I may *not* be the connecting thread. But when there are show people in every life you've led, something has to be going on."

CHAPTER FIFTY

Molly's circus had experienced a tragedy. Hiram Foster, the snake charmer and wild animal trainer, died while performing. Since Hiram's career had put him in cages with potentially violent animals, he'd been at risk more than most of the others. But the chance of death was always there for everyone in Molly's circus.

It was the bear that got him, a toothless, declawed animal who turned out to still be dangerous. Hiram was hugged to death.

Some of the performers demanded to cancel the show out of respect, but the owner didn't agree. It wasn't the first death, and once again he said, "The show must go on."

Molly was dressed in a red tutu over red, wool tights, with a leotard that was half red and half white. Her black shoes were a soft material, custom made to allow her to grip while standing on Baraka. Riding boots made more sense when staying in the saddle, but that would be dull for a performance. The soft, slipper like shoes allowed her to feel Baraka's back.

Molly's routine was not the riskiest of the performances, but it was still difficult. She knew she couldn't let what happened to Hiram affect her own work or she might suffer a similar fate. She delivered a flawless performance. Baraka rolled over, shook hands, allowed Molly to ride while standing up, and crossed a small bridge while Molly was sitting on her backwards.

Although Molly had to concentrate to complete her show, she was aware enough of her surroundings to particularly notice two people in the stands. The first person she saw was Rose. She was thrilled the woman had come. It had been a few weeks since they had talked and she was eager to learn if Rose had had any more contact with Mr. Moss. The second person she saw in the stands was Mr. Moss himself. The shock caused her to lose balance and almost fall.

He was sitting a few rows behind Rose and seemed to be studying her. Rose did not appear to know that he was there, although Molly realized that her friend could be pretending for some purpose she wasn't aware of. When Molly's act was done, Mr. Moss moved as far away from Rose as he could before descending the stands and leaving the tent.

Molly wanted to follow him, but she had to take her bows and then she had to lead Baraka back to the stable tent. While she was brushing her horse down, Rose came to talk to her.

"Did you know Moss was behind you?" Molly asked after they had said their hellos and Rose had complemented the performance.

"By God, no. I wonder if he was following me."

"Has he been in touch with you recently?"

"No. He might have been spying on me and I didn't know about it."

"I don't think a man like that would come out here just to see the show."

Molly looked up when she heard shouting and the sound of someone running. It turned out to be one of the trapeze men.

"Have you heard about Hiram?" the man yelled at Molly as he passed.

"Yes, of course."

"I don't mean his dying. His body's gone. Someone took it."

"Come on, Rose," Molly said. "Let's see what's going on."

They hurried toward the train cars where the performers had their bunks. Molly had a bed in one, but she generally spent her London nights in the house where she had the artifacts.

Hiram's body had been laid out on his bed waiting for the police and the undertaker to arrive. Everyone in the circus knew that. They also knew it had taken the owners a while to notify the authorities about the death, being more concerned with the show than with the body.

"You don't suppose Mr. Moss had something to do with this, do you?" Rose asked Molly.

"I don't think his being here was a coincidence."

There was a crowd gathered outside the railroad car. Most of the people were performers, but a few from the circus audience had joined them. They were getting quite a show for the price of their tickets.

A constable stood up to speak. "There's nothing to see here. If any of you think you can help us identify who did this, please stay here until one of us has had a chance to interview you. But as for the rest of you, please go about your business. We'll do the best we can to solve this."

The trapeze man was standing near Molly. He turned to her and said, "Hiram would have enjoyed the idea of his body floating off to somewhere unknown."

Molly shrugged, quite certain Hiram would have taken back this awful day if it was within his power.

"Let's go," Molly said to Rose. "I need to change."

Rose spoke as they walked. "When bodies are stolen they generally end up on the east side of town and never intact."

"Never?"

"That's what I've heard. Most of them are used by the bloody teaching hospitals. I'm wondering if this one might be connected with Annie somehow, since Moss was here."

"I had the same thought."

Molly's area provided as little privacy as the rest of the train. There were other women walking about, some changing their costumes. Molly grabbed her clothes and spread them out on the bed. She turned her back to Rose while she pulled off her leotard and tights to put on a light cotton union suit with frills on the leg hems and shoulder straps. Over that she donned a riding skirt with a matching jacket, not taking the time to struggle with the corset she normally wore. She added stockings, riding boots, and a hat.

"I'm done for the day. Will you come back to the house? You can spend the night."

"I'd like that."

"I don't have a carriage, so you'll have to ride behind me on Baraka's back."

Molly put her costume away in a chest and locked it. She and Rose walked out of the sleeper car and back to the tent where the horse was kept.

"We've never talked about your session with Ratinam," Molly said.

"No, we haven't."

"I'd like to hear about it."

Rose nodded. "I don't think Ratinam was responsible for Annie's death, but I think he feels guilty. Maybe he suspects Mr. Moss like we do, so he makes excuses for being involved with him. He told me death isn't the end."

"He proved it, didn't he?"

"Her death was still the end of her life as Annie, no matter where she is now."

"I see your point."

"I don't believe I was looking at heaven, but the soul I met was Annie. I think she was in some sort of waiting area."

"Purgatory?"

"Call it what you want, but she was there. Maybe she's going to go on to heaven or maybe to hell. We both lived lives of sin and she doesn't have any time left to ask for forgiveness. I do, though, and I suppose I should after what I saw."

"Maybe Annie will have another chance."

"You mean another life?"

"Isn't that what Ratinam thinks? He's a Hindu, isn't he?"

"I don't know what he thinks and I don't know what Annie thought, either. All I'm know is she was there and she was waiting. Maybe she was waiting for justice."

"If that's true, then you and I have to find out if there was a connection between her death, the disappearance of Hiram's body, and Mr. Moss."

CHAPTER FIFTY-ONE

Stuart met with Victor Wood again at nine in the morning after spending the night in the trailer. Troy had also been in the double wide all night long, but, unlike Stuart, he'd had the freedom to move about. Stuart had been locked in his room until Troy let him out for breakfast.

When Victor walked in he had the box Stuart had brought back from Canada.

"How is Starr?"

"She's fine."

"You said you'd bring proof."

Victor handed Stuart a photograph of Star being held by Allison, who was stroking the young girl's hair. On a table beside them there was a copy of yesterday's *Rutland Herald*.

"How do I know this picture wasn't Photoshopped?" Stuart asked.

"Your daughter is smiling," he said, ignoring the accusation. "If you want her to stay happy, you need to keep working with me. You made good progress yesterday. The man I work for can remember parts of his past lives, just as you can. He wants to build on his skill and that's where you come in. People who can remember other lives are not simply reaching into the backs of their minds. They don't have ancient memories that have somehow been reestablished in the brains of their current bodies. Perhaps that's how instinct works in animals, but the theory falls flat if a person's soul was in the body of someone with whom he had no genetic connection. And that happens all the time. We have to look further to understand the reality."

Stuart ran his hands along the edge of the table. "I'm not sure how real the memories are. They felt real to me yesterday, but couldn't they be placed in my head through hypnotic suggestion?"

"We confirmed enough of what you told us yesterday."

"Then what do you want from me?"

"When your soul was in Ratinam, extra measures had to be taken to get basic cooperation just like today."

"I'm cooperating." Stuart's frustration came out in the tone of his voice. "I proved it yesterday and when I moved the boxes around for you." He stopped before he added, "before you murdered my wife and stole my daughter."

Victor looked at him. "You turned on us after those boxes."

"I was exhausted and scared I'd get caught." And Jamie had paid the price for his fear. "I'll do whatever you ask. Just don't hurt Starr."

"The Buddhists have a concept of oneness at the core of their beliefs. Past lives fit into that concept more than they do with the idea of inherited memories. Every life that's been led is a part of the whole. You have a connection that allows you to tap into that pool of memories. When you were Ratinam, you came very close to the goal."

"Which is?"

"Plenty of people can recall the memories of the individuals who once shared their souls. The true gift is recalling the memories of everyone else, both living and dead."

Stuart struggled with the concept of that much power. "That's what you're after," he exclaimed.

"We've been chasing this ability over many lifetimes. We've been close before and we're close again. Think of it as a database, Stuart, the largest database possible, one that contains every thought anyone has ever had. The information has always been there. The key is learning how to get the specifics."

Stuart was reeling from the concept. "Knowing how to do that would make you the most powerful man in the world," he said.

"Not me—at least, not me alone."

"And if someone can remember his own past lives then this ability would last forever?"

"If you do this you'll be able to know everything Paige and Jamie ever thought. You'll also know the connections to their next physical existences, if that's important to you."

"You had them killed so I'd work with you?" Stuart was horrified.

Ignoring the question, Victor said, "You came very near to success when you were Ratinam and now that you can recall that life, you can pick up where you left off." Placing it within reach, he added, "Open the box you brought back from Canada. It should help."

Stuart pulled at the cardboard flaps that were glued in place. Inside was a strange flat doll, a female character made of a leather as thin as paper with sticks attached. He carefully lifted it out. The leather was dyed in multiple colors: red, yellow, and green.

"It's a shadow puppet. Do you recognize it?"

Stuart shook his head.

"Feel the leather. It's soft, very thin, and in excellent condition considering its age."

Stuart touched the figure, but all he could say was, "I don't understand."

"I was hoping this would trigger memories the way the pictures did yesterday. It was an important part of the ritual Ratinam used. Puppet icons can guide you the way a spirit doll might. Ratinam positioned this one near each person he regressed. It was part of the ritual, like the stones."

"I didn't see anything like this when Glen sent me back. I would have remembered."

"When this puppet was made, Ratinam's abilities increased a hundredfold. The same will be true for you. There are two new puppets, specifically made with you in mind. I can promise you they will be very powerful."

Stuart examined the figure closer. His idea of a puppet was a glove with a head and arms. He'd had his share of those when he was a child and he had been able to handle them as well as any of his friends. This one, though, would take a master to operate. It had multiple hinged parts, each with its own stick. It was as complicated as a string puppet, only controlled from underneath rather than above.

"Think of it as an icon."

"There's something wrong," Stuart said.

"Wrong?"

"Yesterday, when the memories came back of my life as Ratinam, I felt some comfort in the knowledge that death really isn't the end. But when I look at this, I don't feel anything but fear. There's something about this strange leather puppet my soul wants to forget."

"We'll work on your attitude."

"I'm not sure we can."

"Remember, even though death isn't the end, we still want Starr's present life to be as pleasant as possible."

Stuart understood the threat. "I'll do whatever you want me to do."

Victor smiled thinly, then began to instruct Stuart in a new exercise. "Imagine the scene in *Miss Julie* when Julie is trying to convince Jean to run off with her to someplace where no one will know them. Can you do that?"

"I saw Jamie in that play so often I almost have it memorized."

"Good. But now we need to trick your memory. Try not to think of Jamie in the role of Julie. Instead, visualize this leather figure saying the same lines."

"Jamie and that role are one in my mind. I thought that was clear with the success we experienced yesterday."

"It was. But it is important that you move beyond that."

"I'll try," Stuart said, knowing what would happen to Starr if he didn't.

CHAPTER FIFTY-TWO

"I should go back first today," Glen said to Hannah. "There had to be a reason Moss was at the circus. Molly's got him in her scope now, and we need to find out what's going on. I have a feeling there's a connection somehow."

Hannah disagreed. "That guy in the circus was squeezed to death by a bear, not murdered like Paige and Jamie. Looking into Chen Jiang makes more sense to me. If his soul is traveling through time with the rest of ours, he has to be connected to the murders somehow. I say regress me first."

"I still think we have the most to gain from Molly's era. It makes more sense to step back to the time when people were searching for what we're after."

"How about we flip a coin?"

Glen was surprised. "Not exactly scientific, but I suppose we might as well since we can't come to a conclusion any other way. I'll flip. You call."

He reached in his pocket and found a quarter. He tossed it in the air and let it fall to the floor while Hannah said, "Tails."

The coin landed head up. Hannah sighed her surrender.

"Go back to the day when Hiram died and his body was lost," she said once Glen was positioned on the floor. "You and Rose are riding Baraka. You are looking for Mr. Moss. Go back. Tell me if you found him. Tell me what happened next."

***

Rose came out of the Old Bull Tavern shaking her head. Molly, who had stayed outside with Baraka said, "Nobody knows where he is, right?"

"If they do, they won't tell."

"Ratinam might. Let me give you a hand up. We can look for him in the abandoned building where he regressed you."

"What now?" Rose asked when they arrived at their destination.

"You hold Baraka while I try the doors."

"There should be other doors," Molly said, when the first entrance proved locked. She found two others, but they were both secure as well, and she was unable to force them open. There were windows that were low enough to reach, but they didn't open. If she broke the glass she'd still be unable to squeeze through the mullions. She returned to tell Rose what she'd found.

"All locked and dark. Let's try the building that's on the other side of The Pavilion."

"Ratinam warned us to stay away from there."

"True," Molly agreed, "but that was to avoid encountering Mr. Moss, and he's the one we're looking for."

Molly decided it would be dangerous to split up the way they'd just done, so they would both have to wait in the shadows a bit away from the building and hope that Mr. Moss would come out. Instead, Ratinam appeared.

"Where's Moss?" Molly asked when they reached him.

"He'll find you," Ratinam said. "Two women riding on a white horse—everyone in the city can see you."

"One of the circus performers died and his body is missing. We think Moss had something to do with it."

"So you ride in here like this because you think he's committed a murder?"

"There was no murder this time, but we think Mr. Moss had someone steal the body."

"You need to leave now. Go back to the circus. I'll meet you there in a couple of hours."

That would be past one o'clock in the morning, but Molly was eager to talk to Ratinam. "Where do you want to meet?"

"Outside, by the *Punch and Judy* show."

Molly was surprised by his choice, but she knew where the small show was located. She'd never spoken with the man who worked the *Punch and Judy* puppets.

CHAPTER FIFTY-THREE

Hannah knew the *Punch and Judy* show was puppet theater. Hopefully, she could find out if there was a connection to what she'd experienced in her China regressions. She didn't want to follow Molly and Rose on their long ride back to the circus, so she carefully brought Glen into his memories two hours in the future. There was a risk that Glen would come too far out of his trance, but he responded perfectly.

***

"There was a time when more of the world's people understood the power of images," Ratinam told the two women. He'd arrived on time, but Molly was irritated because she and Rose had been early and had been waiting for nearly twenty minutes.

Ratinam continued, "The belief in images is still in our nature. Why else would we be drawn to puppets during childhood?"

"Is that why you wanted to meet here?" Molly probed. "To talk about puppets?"

"Give him a chance."

"I'm sorry." Molly looked at the *Punch and Judy* stage as she spoke. It was not clear to whom she was apologizing.

"You want to know about Mr. Moss, correct?"

"Do you have any idea why he was here earlier today?"

"I'm not included in discussions between Mr. Moss and his employees. But I have been told certain things so that I can be productive in my work, and, with a little conjecture, I believe I understand more of what is going on than Mr. Moss realizes."

"What do you know?" Rose asked.

"That the man who works this *Punch and Judy* show also works for Mr. Moss."

"Do you mean Hu Kang?" Molly asked.

"That's right."

"He's from China, isn't he? Between you and Kang, Mr. Moss seems to have quite an international group."

"He finds the people he needs and then finds ways to force them to do whatever he wants."

"And what is Kang's specialty?"

"Puppets."

Although Molly didn't know the shy Hu Kang personally, she had seen portions of his show and appreciated how talented he was. His art form seemed innocent. His association with Mr. Moss—and with the missing body — surprised her.

Rose said, "I understand what Moss gets from you. The session I had was powerful. How can anything about a puppet show compare with sending me to a place where I could talk with the souls of people who have died?"

"It isn't his show that's important. He makes all the puppets he uses; some of them can be powerful additions to my rituals. I'm not talking about the hand puppets he uses or even the marionettes he works with on special occasions. He also makes very elaborate Chinese shadow puppets that are connected to the world of spirits in ways that have surprised me. He's performed with those puppets in his homeland, but I don't believe he's ever put on a shadow puppet show in England. Instead he passes his work on to me so I can use them as icons."

"The connection to Moss is interesting," Molly said, "but does it have anything to do with the missing body?"

"Shadow puppets have a long history in Asia. They were originally used by religious shamans. That was a time before any written history, but scholars believe that those puppets were made from the skin of people. If Hu Kang has followed that ancient tradition it would explain the power in the images and also why Mr. Moss would want a dead body."

"To make a puppet?" Rose asked.

"Think of it as a religious icon. What is important is that if Mr. Moss wanted to get a dead body away from this area, he would need the help of someone who understood what he wanted and," Ratinam turned to indicate the puppet theater, "had access to a space where the body could be stored."

Molly studied the large wooden box. It wasn't much bigger than an outhouse, but it was large enough to store a half dozen bodies.

"Should we take a look?" Rose asked.

Molly nodded.

Circus performers were traditionally night people, so, although it was late, there was a constant flow of people walking by. They needed to be cautious.

The moon was almost full, but a number of clouds kept drifting in front to block the only light, which would help in maintaining secrecy.

The theater for Hu Kang's show was a square slightly larger than three foot by three foot and about six and a half feet tall, taller because of the large, decorative molding at the top. The box was painted bright red on the front, and the sides were blue. The back, painted the same shade of blue as the sides, had a small door in it with a cast iron lock. The opening on the front was closed with wooden shutters that were hooked from the inside. Molly bent down to look at the bottom. She'd been hoping it was open underneath, but there appeared to be a floor.

She stood up and nodded as two clowns passed by. When they were gone, she started examining the puppet theater much closer. Ratinam and Rose followed her example, and it was Rose who discovered that the hooked shutters covering the performance window could be pulled open a small bit. When Rose pushed her face against that slight crack, she immediately gasped and pulled back.

"What is it?" Molly asked.

"It's a rotten smell mixed with something repulsively sweet."

"Like a body that's been in that box all afternoon?"

"All I know is it's bloody foul."

"We have to look inside."

"Here comes someone," Ratinam warned.

The women backed away from the little stage and joined Ratinam in a loose circle, trying to look as if they were just innocently loitering.

The wife of the man who had a trained dog act in the show was walking a pair of bull terriers. Molly didn't know either the woman or her husband, but nodded as she passed.

"Do you think we should come back in an hour or two?" Rose asked Molly.

"These are night people. The traffic won't let up."

"I'll try to open the lock," Ratinam said. "You stay here and keep watch for Mr. Moss. He's the one I'm most concerned about."

Molly and Rose kept their eyes fixed on the path in opposite directions while Ratinam tried to get inside the puppet theater. Each time anyone walked toward them, the women would turn to each other and pretended to be gossiping. Molly would nod to the performers when they passed even if she didn't know them well.

"Do you think Hiram's in that box?" Rose asked.

"You were the one who had a whiff. What do you think?"

"I've seen people die, but those bodies were all fresh. If he's in that box, he's been in it for a while. It wasn't very hot today, but it was warm enough to spoil meat. I've been around that smell enough to know this smelled the same."

"You've seen people die?"

"I've spent enough time in pubs. Sometimes, fights get out of hand. I also had a couple of men fight over me one time a few years back. That was bloody bad. I had to lift my skirt for the one who didn't die, right there in full view of the body. He wanted to celebrate."

"Listen," Molly held up her hand to stop Rose's story. "It's a cart."

"You think Moss has come back for the body?"

"Turn your back. Don't let him see you."

The cart drove by with the driver and three other men in it. Mr. Moss wasn't one of them, but the cart stopped beside the puppet theater and all the men got off.

Molly and Rose hid behind a cluster of trees to watch.

It was clear the men were after the puppet theater. It would have been too large for a single person to move, but four strong men could do it.

"Where's Ratinam?" Molly asked.

"I haven't seen him for a little while. We didn't warn him like we said we would. I shouldn't have been talking so much."

As soon as the cart was out of sight, they ran to where the puppet theater had been, but there was no sign of Ratinam. If the men had discovered him, he would have resisted, but there had been no sign of a fight.

Rose bent over to pick up something off the ground, holding it up for Molly to see. It was the lock from the door to the puppet theater.

"Is he in the box?" Rose asked.

"Lord, I hope not. If he is, they'll kill him when they find him. Look around. Maybe Ratinam is still hiding. I'll go get Baraka and try to catch up to the cart on the road. If I hurry, I can follow it."

"What'll you do if you catch them?"

Molly was turning to run as she answered, "Whatever I can."

CHAPTER FIFTY-FOUR

"Why did you pull me back?" Glen asked, shaking his head to try to get his focus. "What if something happens to Molly?"

"You're telling me you're so caught up in what's going on you've forgotten that these are just memories? Whatever happened to Molly has been history for more than a hundred and twenty years. I shouldn't have to tell *you* that."

"I know I can't change that outcome, but what we learn from Molly could tell us something about what Stuart's going through. I could have handled some more time."

"You made up the rules, and according to what you've told me, the time had long passed when I should have brought you back. You'll find out what happens to Molly tomorrow, after you've had time to rest. Meanwhile, I need to know what happened to Kao Si."

***

She Moteng arrived for Kao Si late in the afternoon. They were to go together to the White Horse Temple, a temple that Emperor Ming had built to give Buddhism a home in China. She Moteng and Zhu Falan spent most of their days in this sanctuary, praying and meditating. Kao Si had visited the temple previously, but this time would be different. Yin Ji and Chen Jiang were to present a sacred shadow play. She Moteng had invited Kao Si because he hoped that Yin Ji might have more time to speak to her about her daughter, Kao Hui, if they were away from the palace.

"But you say Chen Jiang will be there as well?" Kao Si had asked her friend.

"Yes. But he will act properly. He will worry that rude behavior in a temple will mean bad luck for many days."

"And you think that is enough?"

"He is Taoist. It should be."

There was derision in She Moteng's words. Sometimes the human side of the great Indian monk came through in ways that he didn't realize. Yet there was no one in Kao Si's life she admired more. Perhaps her respect was intensified by the fact that she had once been a believer in the old ways. Religious converts have the strongest faith, she thought.

The temple was a short distance outside the city limits, so the trip was easily done. Kao Si rode in a litter carried by two servants, while She Moteng walked along beside, close enough to talk.

"When I travel I am most aware of the differences you and Zhu Falan brought to my life. If you had not come by my home I would have spent the rest of my life toiling in our field. Now I am carried as an object of great value. Yet I would never have lost Kao Hui if I had stayed with my husband. There is great grief in that realization."

"You may be closer to your daughter than you have been in many years."

"You believe what you are saying?"

"Yes. Yin Ji is the key you are looking for. I am sure of that."

The litter rocked unexpectedly, forcing Kao Si to hold on to the bamboo edge. She Moteng raised his hand to protect her from falling.

She Moteng said, "Allowing a little happiness in your heart will not hurt you or your chance to be with your child."

"I cannot feel what is not there."

"Perhaps you can. Sometimes happiness is the reason for a smile, but sometimes a smile can be the reason for happiness."

"So you have said many times, but I will wait until Kao Hui is in my arms again before I smile from my heart."

The path they were on narrowed for a short ways, forcing She Moteng to walk behind the litter.

"What do you know of Chen Jiang?" Kao Si asked when he was again close enough to talk. She Moteng looked at the eunuchs carrying her litter and Kao Si understood he was thinking they could be spies.

"They have been with me for years," Kao Si told him. "I trust them."

He nodded, then said, "When the possibility of realizing an ambition presents itself to Jiang, he loses all sensitivity to others. It is a trait that has helped him gain what he has wanted at a high cost to the people around him. Within the palace walls he has accrued a great deal of power and would like even more. That makes him dangerous. But in the temple he will be less so."

Kao Si wondered how She Moteng could be certain. If anyone else had told her there was no need to fear Chen Jiang while in the temple, she would not have believed it. But she had never known She Moteng to be wrong about anything important in all the years she'd known him.

He had spoken about the unity of everyone's soul and had told her that she was with Kao Hui in spirit even though they couldn't be together physically. At first she thought he was saying anything he could to help her accept the separation from her child, his words like honey in wild bitter tea. But eventually she began to see that She Moteng had faith in the message he offered and, through the strength of his belief, she began to understand his meaning. There was a center to all of life, and, although she was in it, it was not in her.

"I often wondered why Zhu Falan hardly speaks to me. You both came to my farm and you both brought me here. Why did you become my friend while he did not?"

"People take different roads. Just because they are not on your road does not mean they are lost."

"That is true, I suppose," Kao Si said, "but I still wonder about Falan's reasons." She paused for a moment, then added, "And yours."

"You are a wise woman. Zhu Falan did what was right for the greatest good and now has moved on to other deeds and to further meditation. The deeper question is why I was unable to do the same."

"You believe bringing Kao Hui here was an action for the greatest good?"

"Yes, and I believe her unique relationship with the spirit of all life might have been inhibited if she had kept her connection with you. I also saw the harm in keeping you away from her. The difference between Falan's response and mine is that I felt the negative of our action more than he did. I kept in touch with you as a response to those feelings, and gradually developed respect for your strength and for the beauty of your soul. After that, I always wanted to be a part of your life. You have helped my spiritual growth as much or more than I have helped yours."

Kao Si had heard She Moteng's excuses for Zhu Falan many times. She'd spent hours dwelling on the actions of one monk verses the lack of action of another. She wasn't sure she should judge one man based on what another one offered her, yet she still believed there was more to the story than the simple explanation She Moteng gave her.

When they reached the temple, Kao Si and She Moteng went through the main entrance together, while the eunuchs carried her litter away. She Moteng stopped at the fish pool to pray. He signaled with a nod that she should step into the temple alone.

Inside, Kao Si found a room lit with a multitude of candles and decorated with carvings of lotus flowers and too many figures of Buddha for her to count. She also found Yin Ji sitting on the floor at the front of the temple. Yin Ji was meditating. Her eyes were closed. Kao Si did not believe Yin Ji knew she was in the room. Kao Si stepped to the side and stood watching.

Time passed, but neither woman made a move to acknowledge the presence of the other. Kao Si was willing to stand there as long as it took.

Kao Si's feelings toward Yin Ji were mixed. She knew the woman was kind and wise, but she was jealous because Yin Ji had been able to watch Kao Hui grow. Kao Si was there because she hoped that Yin Ji would be able to tell her what Kao Hui was like, but, even more than that, she wanted to know what Kao Hui would have been like if they had never moved to the palace.

Yin Ji began to stir. She took hold of her right foot and moved it away from her left thigh then her left foot also slipped from her right leg. She had unraveled the yoga position. Kao Si wasn't certain *unraveled* was the right word, but it described the impression she had of the way the puppeteer stood up.

"I am glad to see you again," Yin Ji said to Kao Si when she had walked to the back of the room. She made the traditional greeting sign by interlocking the fingers of her left hand with the fingers of her right and waving them in front of her chest. Kao Si returned the polite gesture.

"You must be eager to hear more about your child."

"Officially, I am here to see your sacred shadow play, but Kao Hui is always in my heart. This time, however, I would like you to tell me about yourself."

"Why do you want to know about me?"

"When Kao Hui had questions, you were the one she took them to. I want to know how you answered. I want the assurance your words were not far from the ones I would have chosen."

"Kao Hui is a brilliant young woman, more aware of life's answers than either of us. She was a young girl when I was charged with caring for her. She asked me many things. Sometimes I answered and sometimes my puppets answered."

"I am sure that was fun for her."

"It was."

"Who answered if she asked something important?"

"What do you mean?"

"For example, what happened when she asked where she came from? Children always want to know that."

"Most children, but not Kao Hui. That is the perfect question for us to ask her. I do not know how much She Moteng explained about Kao Hui, but she has an awareness that is far beyond anything anyone else possesses.

"She asked me many things over the years, things such as *what is above the sky?* But her questions were about reaching out to me, not about getting answers. Kao Hui can look into our hearts and know the answers. The puppets were a game for her."

"I do not understand."

"It is your turn now to listen as Kao Hui did over the years. I will be presenting *The Sacred Shadow Play* by the fish pond this evening when it is dark enough. Some of the answers you seek will be in that work."

***

"Move forward," Glen told Hannah. "Go to that evening in the courtyard."

***

Kao Si sat on a cushion under the dark night sky, in the position of an honored guest. Behind her were people on benches and even more people standing behind them. Some were monks from the temple, but most were townspeople from Luoyang and the surrounding area. The event had attracted many more people than Kao Si had imagined.

There was a white cloth screen hung up in front of a table and behind the table were a number of oil lamps. The audience grew quiet as the lights were turned on and the play began. Kao Si knew what the leather puppets were like: flat and thin enough for the light to shine through them so that when held up to the screen, their shapes and colors were clear. Kao Si also understood that Yin Ji was one of the people giving life to the animated characters who began to appear on the screen. But even with her understanding, there was still magic in the performance. She was enthralled as the story of Buddhism in China began to unfold.

Emperor Ming was the first hero of the tale. He was the one who had studied Buddhism and realized that the ways of the Tao were outdated and the religion from the south could breathe new life into their culture. He sent messengers to India to bring information back about Buddhism, so he could spread the seeds in the Han dynasty.

After the story of the emperor concluded, the figures of Zhu Falan and She Moteng came onto the screen. These were the dedicated monks who brought the sutras into China tied to the back of two white horses. But Falan and Moteng were more than simple messengers. They were adept at meditation and had the skill to allow their souls to step into the oneness of life. While in this state they could feel the presence of all life.

"A child exists with a great presence," the puppet of She Moteng told his Zhu Falan counterpart.

"I know. I can feel her power. We must find her."

"Yes, and we must train her to use her abilities wisely. Emperor Ming would want us to bring her to the palace so that she can spread the teachings of the Buddha when she is ready."

"Perhaps she will be the first woman to be a Buddha. I do not know if that is possible, but I can feel her strength."

As Kao Si heard the words of the shadow play she began to understand the role of Kao Hui. She was the child the monks were speaking of. She had been taken away so her training could be controlled. They wanted to raise her in an environment of discipline, away from the individual love that might inhibit the greater love they wanted her to feel for all of life.

Kao Si shook her head. She was jumping to conclusions that were unfair. She Moteng had been her friend for all her years in the palace.

Surely that friendship wasn't simply a means to keep her isolated from her daughter. If isolation was all they wanted, they could have just as easily killed her. She was never allowed to see Kao Hui, so her daughter wouldn't have known if she was dead.

The story went on, telling of the journey She Moteng and Zhu Falan made over the mountains and across sandy and swampy lands. Finally, they made it to the farm where Kao Hui was living with her parents Kao Jin and Kao Si.

It had been many years since Kao Si had heard the name of her husband spoken out loud. A selfish man who had not cared enough for his family, he was at least honest and a hard worker.

"This is the farm," the puppet of Zhu Falan said, as the images of two horses and the monks bounced across the screen.

"I can see they are working the land," She Moteng said. "And even from this distance I can see the child's mother is a great beauty."

Kao Si was surprised by their words. She knew she had become more attractive after she had reached the palace and was allowed to live a life of leisure. But when she was on the farm she spent too much time outside in hard physical labor. Her hands had been calloused and her ragged clothes always drenched with sweat. The description of her as a great beauty made her doubt the rest of the story.

"This is wonderful," Zhu Falan told She Moteng. "If we need to bring Kao Hui's mother to the palace we can offer her a position as consort to the emperor. I am certain Emperor Ming will be pleased with our decision."

"Excellent idea."

Kao Si did not want to hear her friend agree to treat her as a gift, even for a man as powerful as the emperor. She reminded herself that this was a play. These words were written and delivered by people participating in this show, people who were also part of the emperor's court. They had changed the story.

Then the puppet of Kao Jin offered to sell his wife and daughter for gold statues. This part of the story was true.

The play went on to tell the story of Kao Hui at the palace, the section of the plot Kao Si had been waiting for. There were stories of her lessons with the two monks and stories of long talks with Emperor Ming. Yin Ji was also a character, as the play told of her efforts to help raise Kao Hui. It was unclear if Yin Ji was working the puppet of herself or if another puppeteer was manipulating her character; another way in which the role of the truth was blurred.

When the play was done, Kao Si remained, waiting to speak with Yin Ji. Instead, Chen Jiang came to her.

"Did you enjoy our show?" he asked.

"I already knew the story."

"You were there, of course. But did you like our telling?"

"Some parts were untrue, but those did not hurt the play."

"I am happy to hear you say so. It is always good to see a mother finally take interest in the life of her daughter."

Kao Si was stung by Chen Jiang's thinly veiled accusation of her indifference, and felt the need to defend herself. "I only learned recently that you and Yin Ji were Kao Hui's teachers."

"Yin Ji and Wei Lihua have spent the most time with her, but I have always been near."

"I wish I could have been there," Kao Si said. Her tears began to flow although she struggled to control them. She was opening her heart to Chen Jiang despite her belief that he was the last person she should confide in. "I miss her so much."

"I am sure you do."

Kao Si saw Yin Ji crossing the courtyard in their direction. Chen Jiang also noticed. He leaned close to Kao Si and spoke low so she alone could hear. "Come visit me when we are back at the palace. Choose a time when we can be alone. There are ways I can arrange for you to have time with Kao Hui. But Yin Ji might be jealous, so you should not mention this to her."

Chen Jiang stepped away from Kao Si as Yin Ji came near.

"Was Jiang threatening you?" Yin Ji asked.

"No. Why would you ask such a thing?"

"He can be aggressive at times, especially around people he believes he can control."

"Are you saying I am one of those?"

Yin Ji lowered her eyes. "I don't know you well enough to know and neither does Chen Jiang. What worries me is that he might test you."

Kao Si wasn't sure how to respond. Her first impression of Yin Ji had been that she was a loving and nurturing woman, and Kao Si had been glad that the woman was chosen to teach her child. But Chen Jiang had just warned her that Yin Ji could be jealous. She did not know them any better than they knew her, and didn't know which she should believe.

"I have a secret," Yin Ji said. "But I could get into a great amount of trouble if anyone discovered that I revealed it to you. I will tell only if you promise not to let anyone know where you have heard it."

A secret?

"Tell me."

"You promise you will never say you heard it from me?"

"I do."

"Chen Jiang has the ear of Emperor Ming. He is the one who convinced the emperor that Kao Hui would be better off if she was guided by tutors rather than her own mother."

"Jiang was the one?" This was a question that had wracked her brain since the day she was separated from her child. Her mouth went dry and every muscle in her body froze. She could feel her heart beating.

"She Moteng argued against Chen Jiang. Most of the time when that happens the emperor listens to She Moteng, but this time Jiang accused the monk of getting too close to you on the journey from your farm to the palace. Emperor Ming believed him and declared that you and Kao Hui should be kept apart. Chen Jiang suggested that you be banned from the palace, but She Moteng was able to win that argument. He reminded the emperor that you were beautiful and willing to be his consort."

"He spent many nights with me. How could he lie down with me after taking my child?"

"Sometimes beauty is a blessing, and sometimes it is a curse."

"I was lonely and wanted another baby. But now that I have heard this I believe I was blessed to be barren after Kao Hui was born. I would not want a child with such a man."

"People are complicated and Emperor Ming is no exception. He is a good man who did something evil. It is unfortunate that you had to pay the price for his bad decision. That will certainly change your luck."

Kao Si noticed that Yin Ji said *luck* rather than *karma*. Like Chen Jiang, she was Taoist. It was very odd that Emperor Ming would have put Kao Hui in the care of two people who did not follow the Buddhist faith. Kao Si saw their religion as a reason to trust one no more than the other.

"Thank you for confiding in me," she told Yin Ji, although she wasn't certain that her confidence had led her to the cautious path Yin Ji had suggested.

If what Yin Ji said was true and Chen Jiang had been the force keeping her child away, then it was in his power to change that decision. She would visit him at the palace as he suggested.

"Tell me stories about Kao Hui that were not in the play," Kao Si said. "I want to know the little things."

***

"Go forward again," Glen called out to Hannah from thousands of years after Kao Si's life reached its ultimate conclusion. "Go to your memories of the palace, to the time when you met Chen Jiang. Tell me what happened.

***

There were leather puppets everywhere, hanging on the walls and lying on the work tables. A few were in pieces, but most were complete. There were also other thin leather objects shaped like trees, stones, and small buildings, the set pieces for the shadow plays.

Chen Jiang was not present, although she expected him to arrive soon. They had arranged this meeting to be held in secret, during the day, when it would not seem odd for her to be walking through the palace.

"Did anyone see you?" Kao Si looked up to find Chen Jiang standing in the doorway.

"No one knows where I am."

"That is good."

"Tell me about Kao Hui. How soon can I see her?"

"We need to work."

"I do not understand. Where is my daughter?"

"Step over here. Now," Chen Jiang commanded. He sounded irritated. Jiang was standing by the table where his tools were stored, holding an awl. As Kao Si approached, he turned to the table and shuffled some tools. When he turned back, he was holding a knife, a serrated blade that was intended for sawing through leather.

Kao Si's immediate reaction was fear until she realized that Chen Jiang was holding a tool, not a weapon. She swallowed the phlegm that had risen in her throat and took another step, one last step that took her close enough to touch him. She was not going to allow fear to keep her from Kao Hui.

Chen Jiang grabbed Kao Si's hair with his left hand and pulled her to him, forcing her to spin around halfway. He raised the knife to her neck. She writhed, trying to free herself, but Jiang was stronger than she was.

"Do not fight me," Chen Jiang commanded. "You will be with your child forever."

***

"Come back to me," Glen shouted. He didn't want her to experience the death.

Hannah rubbed her eyes and tried to speak, but her words were slurred.

"Take it easy," Glen told her. "You've been through a lot."

"He was going to kill me." This time her words were clear.

"It was more than that. He *did* kill Kao Si. I didn't want you to experience that, so I pulled you back as quickly as I could. Are you okay?"

"I feel a little woozy, but I think I'll be all right."

"Good."

"We were in a workshop where they made the puppets for the

shadow plays. The place was filled with leather and tools to work the leather. I'm thinking that's like the factory where Stuart works, but maybe not."

"What is that?"

"Milwood Leather."

CHAPTER FIFTY-FIVE

Victor pulled his cell phone from the holster he wore on his belt, tapped a few times on the screen, and spoke into it. "He's ready. Come as soon as you can." He nodded goodbye, then left the house by the back door. Stuart watched him through a window, but knew he couldn't follow. He had to wait for the next person and probably additional tests. *God, how many people in this gang are people I know?*

He spent the next half hour pacing around the living room. Troy was outside, he knew, watching to be certain he didn't try to leave. But it was Starr who was keeping him there, not the amateur thug assigned the task of guarding him.

Stuart wasn't certain what he was "ready" for, but he had a good guess. He'd been pulling past life memories and visualizing scenes from nineteenth century plays for a reason. The next step had to be accessing the oneness Victor had spoken of.

Victor had asked him to replay a memory of his life as Ratinam with the weird, thin puppet substituted for Annie Chapman. There was no way Victor could have known what was replaying in his head, but Stuart recounted it honestly; Starr's life hung in the balance. After a couple of tries, he had described a scene that seemed to satisfy his captor.

Victor Wood had then taken the strange puppet interaction a step further. He had Stuart follow the Annie Chapman stand-in away from Ratinam.

It felt almost natural. He hadn't even realized what they'd done until they were finished and he'd had time to think. He'd stepped back into memories from the eighteen hundreds, memories that weren't his.

The puppet was the key.

Jamie, who'd been in a couple of plays that had had puppets in them, had done some research into the subject. "Puppets have a mystical side to them," she'd told him once. "They're images of people, like dolls, but with the ability to move."

Stuart hadn't been interested at the time; he wished now he'd paid more attention.

His thoughts turned to wondering about the person on the other end of the phone call Victor Wood had made. *It might have been Paul.* Paul, who had "discovered" Paige's body.

But when the door finally opened, it was Dr. Saffell who walked in.

"So you're the one behind this," Stuart said, standing up.

Dr. Saffell shrugged but didn't reply.

"Can you bring me to Starr?"

"If your cooperation continues, I can do whatever you want."

"And you won't hurt her?"
"She's in good hands."
"Both Victor and Troy told me the same thing."
Dr. Saffell nodded as if to say, "Of course they did."
"Victor worked with me to get the important memories back," Stuart said. "I believe I can pick up where Ratinam left off."
"Excellent."
"The stones are the key," Stuart said, then added sarcastically, "I suppose you already know that, since you're the one who's been smuggling them into this country."

Dr. Saffell reacted to Stuart's tone with a slight start. "You're the one who carried the box across the border." His smile caused a chill to run across Stuart's back. "In any case, you're wrong. The stones are an important part of the ritual, but we can reach our goal without them. If we merge my knowledge with your talent we can accomplish what mankind has always wanted to achieve. We can beat death."

"My wife was murdered and you talk about beating death?" Stuart's temper was fraying.
"Death is not the end."
"But Jamie's still gone."
"If what you two had was worth anything, it has the strength to return. Bringing Jamie back is another reason for you to work with me."
"My daughter is the reason I'm cooperating."
"As I said, Starr's in good hands. She'll be fine as long as you stick with us."
"I'm listening. Tell me what you want me to do."

Dr. Saffell touched his temple as if he were concentrating. "I need you to regress me. But I don't want to go back to a past life. I can do that on my own. I need to go much deeper, into the force within all life."
"You think I can send you there?"
"I *know* you can."
"Then take off your clothes and lie on your stomach. I'll place the artifacts and we'll see what happens."

Dr. Saffell nodded. "Good." He walked over to the table where Victor had been sitting, where the puppet Stuart had smuggled into the country was lying. "This one is in excellent shape," Dr. Saffell muttered, picking the leather icon up and turning it about. "Very good."

Dr. Saffell placed the puppet on the carpet in the living room area then went into the small kitchen and opened a pantry to reveal two more puppets. Stuart assumed they were the ones Victor had mentioned. Their colors were brighter than the first one, so they had to be newer, he reasoned. Dr. Saffell placed them on the floor near the first one, then went to the couch and began to remove his clothes.

Dr. Saffell's boxers were the next to last item to come off, leaving him wearing only a T-shirt. After the doctor folded his boxers and placed them on top of his pants he finally removed the shirt, and Stuart understood why he'd kept his top half covered as long as possible. The man had a half dozen square scars on his back, evenly spaced, three on each side.

If the scars had been random, Stuart would have assumed they were the result of some accident. But these cuts had clearly been done for a reason. They looked more like brands than scars.

The marks triggered a memory that Stuart knew was from his time as Ratinam, but he wasn't certain when or where. For some reason he associated them with Mr. Moss, but he didn't have a recollection of regressing Moss.

"I take it these body decorations are a requirement of your cult?" Stuart asked.

"You can answer that."

Ratinam must have known about the scars, then.

"If I need to know, you should tell me."

"It's not necessary."

When Dr. Saffell positioned himself face down on the carpet with one puppet on each side and one above his head, Stuart understood why they had taken his daughter. He could have picked up a lamp and smashed the doctor's head in.

Although in good shape for a man in his sixties, Stuart decided that Dr. Saffell looked better with his clothes on, and not just because of the scars on his back. He had fat rolls around his midsection that he wasn't able to hide when not wearing a shirt, and his buttocks were pale, soft and wrinkled.

Stuart took the stones from the boxes by the table and placed them on the critical places on Dr. Saffell's body: Mooladhara, Swadhisthana, Manipura, Anahata, Vishuddhi and Ajna. The ritual he'd performed as Ratinam was in his head, but he didn't have a clear connection with the man who'd held his soul in the nineteenth century. He took one of the chairs from the kitchen table and placed it beside Dr. Saffell. Before he could do anything else, he had to establish that link.

"I have to go back into my head. This may take some time, but it's the only way."

"I understand," Dr. Saffell said, loud enough to make himself clear despite being face down on the floor.

Stuart closed his eyes and tried to pull back the feeling he had when Glen had first regressed him. He pictured himself floating through a giant cloud. Although it was tempting to hold the image of Ratinam in his mind, he didn't succumb. Instead he allowed his self-regression to direct him, confident that the chance that he would go back to the wrong life was slight.

When he opened his eyes he saw Albert Moss lying in front of him; when he looked at his own hands he saw the dark skin of Ratinam. The regression had worked. He was in the memories of his former life.

But this was only the first step. He understood he had come close to performing the type of regression Mr. Moss was seeking because Victor Wood had told him. But close wasn't good enough. Stuart had to learn from what Ratinam had accomplished so he could use the skills to send Dr. Saffell where he wanted to go.

Ratinam was experiencing a great amount of pain, which affected his ability to accomplish his task. Stuart reached back into the old soul to understand and found more similarities with his own life. Ratinam had left a child behind in Asia. The men who worked for Albert Moss were holding that child. It was the boy's safety that was forcing Ratinam to work for this man, just as it was Starr's safety that was forcing Stuart to work with Dr. Saffell. They hadn't changed their method of control.

Ratinam spoke to Mr. Moss. He sent him into the cloud, but he didn't push him through it toward a single destination. Instead he kept floating him deeper into the mist. Each time they seemed to reach the edge of the whiteness, Ratinam pulled Moss back.

"The mist is thought. Each drop, each molecule, is an idea, an inspiration. To understand them you have to absorb them. You have to become one with the cloud."

"I see," Moss said.

"Don't speak. Just float. It will take time, but you are almost there."

"Oh, God, it hurts!"

"Every thought is there and many of them are painful. Whatever human existence is in a single life, this is multiplied by millions times millions."

"Pull me back! Pull me back!"

As Ratinam complied, Stuart also left the memories. He had the knowledge he needed to attempt the type of regression Dr. Saffell was demanding. It was time to return to the present.

Stuart opened his eyes and looked down at the naked man lying on the floor. It was hard to believe that such a picture of weakness could be on the verge of becoming the world's most powerful person.

Stuart understood that by putting his love for his child above everything else, he was committing a horrible act of treason. He was betraying his parents. He was betraying Hannah. He was betraying everyone he'd ever known. But Jamie was gone and Starr was all he had left. He would do anything to save her, no matter the consequences.

"Do you remember how painful it was?" Stuart asked.

Dr. Saffell said, "I'm prepared." He reached to the side, touched one of the leather puppets, then pulled his arm back under his body. "Do it."

Stuart understood that the puppets were powerful, that he had worked with them as Ratinam, but he still did not understand *why* they held such power. He contemplated going back into the memories of Ratinam to attempt to gain that understanding, but knew Dr. Saffell wasn't going to wait much longer.

Stuart realized that the regression into the oneness that is the center of all life had failed for Moss and Ratinam because there had been no control, just a plucking of random thoughts and emotions that had belonged to other souls, both human and other. Ratinam might have sent Moss into the feelings of a fox caught in a steel jaw trap or a starving child in central Africa. The pain had been clear, but not the reason behind it.

Stuart believed that even though Glenn didn't follow his subjects into their regressions, instead relying on them to recount the experience, Ratinam had been able— and right—to keep the connection with his subject when he regressed him into the universal, shared consciousness instead of into individual life memories, but thought he should have been more of a guide. He decided that he would try to reach forward to see what emotions they were accessing before bringing Dr. Saffell into them.

"I'm thinking of water, of a peaceful lake scene. Jamie and I went to Lake Willoughby one summer. I'm back there in my head. There was a bench near the lake's edge where we would sit and watch boats. It's a quiet lake, so there weren't many. But a few times we got lucky and saw a sailboat or a canoe. There are few things more pleasant than that view." Stuart wasn't trying to take Dr. Saffell into his experience with Jamie. He couldn't control stepping into a specific memory at this point. He was just starting to understand the concept of a universal consciousness. But Dr. Saffell wanted specifics and eventually he would need to provide them.

"Reach out and touch one of the puppets," Stuart directed as he got off the chair and down on his knees. He touched the other side of the puppet Dr. Saffell had put his hand on, completing the connection. Stuart could feel his body swelling. He was ready to lead.

"Feel the power. We're floating up now. We're heading into the cloud."

They swirled down into the specifics of the universal consciousness. Stuart was leading, but not entirely. The leather puppet, which had come alive with a presence that felt familiar and warm, was also guiding them forward.

They touched the consciousness at a point where there was a great heat that Stuart felt was purging him of all his problems, like the feeling he got when lying in the sun that it was pulling all the tenseness from his body.

The specific feel of the sun became stronger and Stuart realized that this wasn't like sunbathing—this *was* sunbathing. He was accessing an event from the collection of experiences. It hadn't belonged to him prior to this moment, but now it did. He tried to understand where and to whom this event had occurred, but it was more difficult than he had expected.

There are many more experiences in our world than the ones that happen to us. Two ideas came to him from that thought. The first was that the experience he'd touched was not a human one. That would explain the lack of defined word-names; the animal's thought process was sensory rather than cerebral. Wherever the memory was from—perhaps a lion near a pond in Africa or a sea lion on a rock somewhere along the Pacific shore—Stuart was experiencing greater contentment than he had ever thought possible.

He pushed his spirit back toward the puppet guide to seek help in identifying what he was going through and was given a name: Paige Stackman. That realization jolted his control, nearly forcing him out of the consciousness.

He wanted to know more, but Dr. Saffell's spirit was pulling him away from Paige. He couldn't stay with either, and swirled back to his spot beside Dr. Saffell on the floor of the double wide.

Stuart looked down at the puppet they both were touching. "What is this?" he asked, breathing hard. "Or should I say *who*?"

Dr. Saffell sat up. "You've already exceeded what you were able to do in London. But what we touched wasn't human. We can't simply separate the experiences into pleasant and unpleasant. We need to filter into specific thoughts. I need to be able to pick someone important, perhaps a scientist or a politician, and look into the ideas he had at some definite time in the past. Anything less than that is useless."

"Tell me about the puppet," Stuart insisted.

The doctor smiled. The look was back, the one that had earlier told Stuart he was in trouble. "My thoughts are in the universal consciousness just as yours are. Find them."

CHAPTER FIFTY-SIX

"We can't afford to wait until tomorrow," Glen said to Hannah.

"You always tell me that multiple regressions in a single day put too much strain on a person's heart."

"But this is too important to wait. I'll be fine."

"I know you'll be fine, because I'm not going to regress you."

"Stuart is powerless against the people who took his daughter," he said sharply, sucking in a breath before continuing. "There are two goals here. We've got to get Starr back to her father, but we also have to prevent this situation from reoccurring. We have to find answers and we have to find them quickly."

"I'm not arguing with you," Hannah said. "But you're the experienced hypnotherapist. It's safer for you to guide me than the other way around. You can bring me back if I'm going through too much, but I might not recognize the signs if you're the one in the trance."

"All right, then," Glen said. "I'll send you back to Victorian London. But if you give me any reason to worry, I'm bringing you out and we're switching places."

***

Ratinam was standing beside Rose, not curled up in the box with Hiram's body. He explained how he had dropped the lock and hid in the entrance to a tent when he had heard the sound of an approaching cart.

Ratinam had brought her to an East London building on Whitechapel High Street, saying he was confident the puppet theater—and the body—was inside.

"Do you think Molly was here?" Rose asked.

"Probably." Ratinam tried the door on the street side and found it unlocked. He touched his finger to his lips to indicate that they should be as quiet as possible then led Rose inside.

"They couldn't have brought a box of that size through the front, so it's probably in the backyard. They could have opened it there and carried the body downstairs to the basement kitchen." He was whispering, barely loud enough for Rose to understand. "We can go outside and circle around back or we can make our way through the house."

"Where do you think Molly is?"

"She doesn't know this building the way I do, so if she went in, she may still be here."

"Let's look for her," Rose said.

There were stairs to the second floor in the front lobby, but they walked to the side of them, staying on the first, stealthily walking toward the back of the house. They knew they'd made the right choice when they heard voices coming from the open door to what they presumed was the cellar.

Ratinam crouched and started to approach the doorway, but Rose tugged on his sleeve and signed that she wanted to go back toward the front of the house. If Molly wasn't in the house—and now she didn't think she was—it made no sense to stay. They quietly made their way to the door through which they'd come in.

There was an alley between that building and the next, not wide enough for a carriage, but the men could have carried the puppet theater through. Ratinam and Rose approached, watching and listening for any signs of someone guarding the back.

Behind the house was a tall, wooden fence with a wide gate that opened toward the alley. While Ratinam tried to look through cracks in the fence, Rose examined the surrounding area. There were a few trees that had branches overhanging the fence. Rose was pleased to discover Molly peeking out from behind a moderately tall maple, silently signaling to them. She had gathered the riding skirt she was wearing in front of her body so the material wouldn't poke around the trunk.

"I see her," Rose whispered to Ratinam.

"Where?"

"Over there. She wants us to go back to the street, I think. We should do it."

Rose and Ratinam crossed Whitechapel, one of the filthiest streets in London. People dumped their chamber pots—or just relieved themselves without bothering with the pot—and tossed their garbage in the gutter, including kitchen waste. The stench was nearly overpowering.

"I was glad to see you weren't in the puppet box," Molly said to Ratinam when she slipped across the street to join them.

"Not as glad as I."

"If they'd found you with the body I don't know what I could have done to help."

"What did you see?" Rose asked her.

"Mr. Moss went in the house with three men and the body. Do you have any idea why they would need a corpse?"

"They might be skinning it."

"Why would they do that?" Rose asked.

"To make leather," Ratinam said, coughing quietly before swallowing.

"From bloody human flesh?" Rose was shocked, her eyes wide.

"I said *might*. I don't know for sure."

"You've got some explaining to do," Molly said to Ratinam, "but first I need to see for myself if you're right."

Rose and Ratinam followed Molly as she slowly opened the front door and went in.

"Where?" she whispered. Ratinam pointed.

They slowly worked their way to the back of the house, stopping at the top of the stairs to peer down, counting on sheer luck to keep whoever was down there from looking up and seeing them.

There were a couple of bright gas lamps in the room below them, so they could see clearly. Moss and his men had placed Hiram's body on a table and had made some cuts into the lower part of his neck. They were using a small, cylindrical pump to fill him with a liquid that had a strong, biting smell. Molly turned to Ratinam and saw that he understood what was going on. He signaled her that they should leave.

"What were they doing?" Molly asked when they were outside again.

"They weren't skinning him," Ratinam told the women. "They were embalming him. It will preserve his body for a good length of time. That smell was formaldehyde. It's a substitute for arsenic that was just developed in Germany. They pump it into his circulatory system to replace all his blood."

"Why?"

"Only Mr. Moss can tell you that."

"So they're preserving him. That's exactly the opposite of what skinning him would do. Why do you think they want to do that?"

"It's not the opposite, exactly. They would make leather from his skin. The leather would be around for a long time."

Molly grabbed his arm with her right hand and Rose's with her left.

She said, "I left Baraka tied up over by The Pavilion. Walk with me while I get him." She added to Ratinam, "And talk while we walk."

Ratinam began his story. "In addition to the stones I use during the regression sessions, there are a number of religious icons, puppets made of leather. Mr. Moss brings those. I didn't object because I didn't think they would do any harm, but I soon found there was power in them that I didn't understand."

"Power?" Molly asked.

"They make the sessions easier by steering the subject toward the important elements in the universal consciousness. To put it another way, they appear to hold the hands of the people I'm regressing."

"Is that why they're puppets?"

"I don't know, but religious icons are often in the shape of people. Puppets go a step beyond that because they can move. This is where Hu Kang probably comes into the picture. I don't know his history, but I would bet he's more than a performer. Someone is making these shadow puppets in the ancient Asian tradition. Puppets date back before written history. Shamans would make puppets to keep the souls of powerful people alive."

"Why didn't you say something about this before now?" Rose asked.

"These are ancient traditions. I never put much stock in them before working with Mr. Moss. But there are aspects to all traditions that are powerful. I have a greater appreciation for that reality than I used to."

"So he's harvesting skin to make these icons?" Molly asked.

"The skin has to come from specific sources. Moss has scars on his back from where he harvested some of his own."

"And Annie?" Rose asked.

"I don't know about her or about Mary Ann Nichols, who seems to have been one of the other victims. But I suspect they were important."

"Enough to kill?"

"I think so. It would fit with the fact that both those women were not only murdered, but also cut up after they were dead. Some of the puppets Moss brought to our sessions had been made recently. But one seemed as old as the stones."

Baraka was where Molly said she had left him, tied to a rail outside a building on St. Peter's.

"You and Rose get on the horse," Ratinam said. "I'll be fine. I'm used to walking."

"Why don't we all walk," Molly suggested. "Baraka deserves a break and I want to hear more about the power of these shadow puppets."

"I've told you most of what I know."

"Where does Hiram fit in all this?"

"I don't know. Perhaps he has a strong spirit. That's just a thought, of course."

"What about Mr. Moss?"

"What about him?"

"How did he know to contact you?"

"I suppose I have a reputation. I was guiding regressions for years before I met him."

"Still, he was in London and you were in India, yet he found you—the perfect person to accomplish what he needs."

"I can't explain that, but it is true that Mr. Moss has a great deal of knowledge. It gives him power over people like us."

"I wonder if his knowledge is somehow connected to the souls in those puppets."

Rose wasn't sure why that possibility was any stranger than the other things they'd been discussing, but it seemed to surprise Ratinam. He paused before responding to Molly's suggestion.

"That would explain a lot," he said.

"How?" Molly asked.

"If those souls can somehow contact him in each of his incarnations, he'd be born with knowledge. But those souls would have to be special."

***

"Come back to me, Hannah," Glen instructed. "Are you all right?"

"I'm a little tired, but I'll be fine."

She sat up, shaking slightly. The session had been hard on her, but she was young and strong. He'd regressed people in the past who were less capable of handling the stress. Still, he didn't like taking chances.

"Can I get you a glass of water? Or something stronger?"

"I'm okay. Why did you bring me back?"

"I was worried I'd left you under too long. And we need to talk about what you learned."

"What about it?"

"The leather shadow puppets seem to be the connecting point between your incarnations.

"I remember the picture of a shadow puppet performance hung on the wall of the sets of *Miss Julie* and *A Doll's House*. And the puppets have been in all three of my existences: China, London, and here. So what does that mean?"

"I don't know," Glenn told her honestly. "The concepts Ratinam was explaining are in an area I've never experienced."

Hannah held her breath for a moment.

He continued, "Ratinam said there were old puppets and new ones. If there was contact between Moss's soul and those icons, it had to be through the old ones. New puppets would be needed to contact future incarnations. That *seems* to be the process, the way this soul goes on from one lifetime to another while maintaining knowledge of the past. It could explain how he finds the stones as well as the shadow puppets each time, too."

"Are you saying skin from Paige and Jamie could have been made into those puppets?" Hannah asked. Her own skin had turned the color of milk.

"I don't know if that's what happened," Glen said, "but I know their bodies were mutilated after they were killed. That could have been why."

Hannah shivered and said, "Maybe Stuart has the answer buried in one of Ratinam's memories."

CHAPTER FIFTY-SEVEN

The pantry wasn't a walk-in closet; the double-wide didn't have enough space to dedicate a small room to pots, pans, and canned goods. It was more like a wardrobe that had been painted white. About thirty inches deep, there was plenty of room to store stuff, and Stuart wondered what else Dr. Saffell might be keeping in the oversized cabinet.

He tried the door a couple of times. It was locked, but the lock was small and wouldn't be hard to break. Under the circumstances, with Starr still being held hostage, he decided that he probably shouldn't.

He walked to the door and looked for Troy. His guard didn't appear to be present. There were certainly some odd things about the way he was being kept prisoner, Stuart mused.

He went back to the pantry and tried the door again, achieving almost a half an inch gap at the bottom. But he could feel the strain he was putting on the door, so he let it slip back.

He looked around for something he might use to pick the lock. He opened a drawer and found a couple of paper clips under a handful of old pens and some scrap paper. He pulled one out and started to bend it to the shape he needed.

Stuart wondered why the leather puppets were stored in a pantry with a flimsy door and a lock that wasn't very secure. He turned slowly, surveying the room, thinking again about how Troy wasn't within sight of the building.

He concluded that there had to be a camera somewhere inside, since he couldn't imagine they'd leave him completely unsupervised. But, since cameras could be hidden in just about anything, if there was one, it would take him a long time to find it. And there might be more than one.

His next other theory was that Dr. Saffell had intentionally left the puppets accessible to him. If that was so, then they wanted him to study the icons on his own. More training.

Stuart bent a small hook into the end of the paper clip.

It took him just under three minutes to get the pantry door opened. The puppets were the only objects inside. He carefully removed them, one at a time, and laid them on the table. They looked so fragile, made of the thinnest leather he'd ever seen.

Stuart began his study of the icons with one of the two new puppets, although he used the term *new* in a loose way. The one he considered *old* had signs of decay in the leather. The other two, which could have been made a week or ten years ago, did not. Leather was durable, although not forever.

The puppet was the figure of an Asian woman, probably Chinese, dressed in a yellow one-piece outfit that had loose pants rather than a long skirt. The head, arms, and legs all attached to the body with joints that allowed them to be moved by the puppet master.

In addition to the yellow dye that colored the majority of the body, the creator had used pink, green, purple, and black inks to cover the figure with bows and flowers. She wore a large, flowered headdress that struck him as being more like something worn by a resident of a Caribbean island than of China.

The leather was made of a patchwork of squares glued and sewn together, giving it a quilt like appearance when examined closely. The squares reminded Stuart of Dr. Saffell's back; he was certain he knew the source of some of those leather pieces.

Stuart moved on to the next, the one that appeared older than the others. There were cracks throughout the entire puppet and a layer with a different consistency seemed to be poking out from underneath the surface. This deterioration made it fragile, especially since the leather was so thin. Stuart tried to be very gentle, as Victor Wood and Dr. Saffell both had.

Thinking of Wood and Saffell again reminded him that he was probably being watched. He tried to put himself in the minds of his captors and was sure he was doing exactly what they were expecting him to do. They wanted him to be curious about these icons. They needed him to understand as much as possible about their power.

This puppet was a warrior with a red blouse, a green helmet, and green pants covered with yellow chaps. He had a black sword at his side. The sword could be removed from the warrior's belt and attached to his hand if the script called for him to attack. But the leather was so old that Stuart doubted it had been manipulated in that way for many years for fear of damage. Like the first, the puppet was decorated with images of flowers, larger and more abstract, giving them a masculine feel.

The third puppet was made of young, fresh leather like the first. It was an asexual figure dressed in a long, flowing robe with a web-like pattern that matched its headgear. The outfit gave it a royal appearance that could have belonged to either an emperor or a princess.

He ran his fingers over the patchwork leather. It was soft, almost like suede. He studied the pattern of the robe very carefully and discovered something surprising. In the center of the puppet was a blue 8. The pattern of the robe had been inked over the small image, but Stuart was certain it was an eight.

But why was it there? Stuart turned the puppet sideways and looked at it again. That's when it clicked. It wasn't an eight. It was the symbol for infinity, the same symbol once tattooed on Paige's body.

Stuart had slept with Paige on a few summer afternoons, mostly out of mutual boredom. The first time, after the sex was over, Paige stood up and started to look around for her clothes, but Stuart took her hand and turned her to face him. He suspected she was feeling guilty about Hannah, ashamed of what they'd just done. Her eyes were downcast as she stood before him for a long moment. The picture was clear in his mind: the infinity tattoo was on her lower abdomen, slightly offset toward her left side.

The symbol on the puppet explained why Paige was one of his guides during the regression of Dr. Saffell.

And since Paige's flesh was part of this puppet, then some of the other squares of leather on this or the other new one could be — had to be — Jamie. Stuart felt as if he was going to choke on his heart.

Both the women had been cut up and now defiled in yet another way. Their flesh was mixed with Dr. Saffell's flesh and, if these icons were as powerful as Saffell and Wood claimed they were, their souls were mixed with his as well.

Their souls are trapped. Would destroying these icons free them? Or would their souls be destroyed along with the leather from their bodies?

Now he understood why they'd put the puppets in a pantry that was so easy to break into. They wanted him to discover the meaning of the icons. They needed him to know both Jamie and Paige were in the puppets, so that he could call on their souls to help bring power to the next regression.

He got down on his knees and kissed both of the puppets before carefully putting them away.

CHAPTER FIFTY-EIGHT

Hannah and Glen were disappointed to find that Stuart wasn't home. Hannah was fairly certain he was trying to help his daughter and hadn't gone in to work. She had lost her own job that morning when she had called in to say she was taking another sick day.

"We should see if Stuart picked up his mail today," Hannah said.

They walked over to the small shelter where the apartment mailboxes were kept. Just as she had suspected, Stuart's was full. They didn't have the key, so they couldn't go through what was there, but the quantity was enough to tell them he hadn't picked it up in at least a few days.

As they walked back to her car, she explained a thought she'd had. "In every memory from my past lives—and in my current life, as well—there has always been a group of performers in the center of everything. Jamie and Paige were both actresses, Molly was a circus performer, and Yin Ji worked with puppets. The same is true of my enemies. In Victorian England, Mr. Moss had a working relationship with Hu Kang, the puppet master, and, in ancient China, Chen Jiang worked with Yin Ji and the shadow puppets."

"I think you're on to something. I've always had my doubts about Dr. Saffell, and he's on the theater board."

"I know. And what about Allison? She was in *Miss Julie*. And Paul Trepanier and Troy Allen. They're both theater people and they discovered Paige and Jamie's bodies."

When they reached Hannah's Versa she opened the door to the driver's seat while Glen walked around to the passenger side. "We should look for Stuart," she said, when they were both in the car. "But where?"

"We could try Dr. Saffell's home," Glen suggested.

"He's our best choice," Hannah said. She backed out of her parking spot and left the apartment complex.

"What are you thinking about?" Hannah asked after they'd been driving in silence for a few minutes.

"Your relationship with Stuart."

Hannah had been waiting for this conversation for a while, but she was surprised by Glen's timing. "He's a good friend," she told him. She expected him to follow up by asking if that was all Stuart was to her. Instead Glen's conversation took an unexpected turn.

"Stuart has been very important to you in this life. In some ways he's been as important to you as Kao Hui was to Kao Si. There must be a reason for that. Stuart was Ratinam and his abilities seem to connect with Kao Hui's. Souls often travel through time together, like a spiritual family. I'm sure you and I were together in time periods besides the one Rose and Molly shared and I'm confident we'll be together again. That's how it works. It also works that way with you and Stuart."

Hannah tapped nervously on the steering wheel. "What if you're right and Kao Hui had Stuart's soul? How would that help us find him?"

"We could try to think like she would think," Glen suggested.

"They took her from Kao Si at such an early age. I have no idea what she thought about. Even if he shares her soul, he isn't a young woman. Young women have a unique way of thinking."

"Everybody is influenced by who they are physically and what they experience. But there are also qualities that are a part of their core. That's what I'm talking about."

They were a quarter of a mile from Dr. Saffell's home when a gray Volvo passed them, heading in the opposite direction. Although Hannah didn't get a good look, she was certain the driver was a dark haired man.

"I think that was Troy," she told Glen.

"Does he live out here?"

"No, but maybe he was visiting Saffell. Maybe we should follow him."

Hannah pulled into the driveway of the next house on her left then backed out to turn her car around. At the rate Troy was traveling she could catch him without any problems, but she'd never tailed anyone before. For the first time, she wished her car was a color other than bright red.

"Slow down," Glen told her. Her foot was already on the brake. Troy was stopped at a light; she didn't want to pull up right behind him. The light turned green, allowing Hannah to stay back about fifty yards.

"Do you know where he lives?" Glen asked.

"Not off hand. Why?"

"It would give us a place to look, if we lose him."

"If that happens we can swing back to Dr. Saffell's."

Troy's car slowed down as he turned into a shopping center, giving Hannah ample time to follow without having to make a sudden stop to maintain her distance. He drove toward the parking area in front of the Shaw's supermarket. She kept close enough to watch him, but stopped a few parking lanes over. Troy got out of his car and walked to the store.

"What do we do now?" Hannah asked.

"I guess we wait. He'll see us if we follow him inside."

Hannah turned the key to shut off her engine and shifted her position in the driver's seat to turn toward Glen.

"There are reasons Troy might have been at Dr. Saffell's that have nothing to do with Stuart and Starr. They could be working on a fund raiser for the theater or Troy could be lobbying to add a show to next year's schedule. I've heard he can be pushy."

"You're right. He could have been doing most anything. We don't even know if he *was* at Saffell's house. All we know is he was driving from that direction. But following Troy makes about as much sense as anything else we've come up with."

"It's weird to think how we were tailing people back when we were Rose and Molly. Maybe this kind of thing comes naturally to our souls."

"There are aspects to the core of people's souls that don't change from lifetime to lifetime. I have a feeling there's something inside the two of us that makes us want to figure things out. And I also think there's something that makes us want to work together while we're doing our figuring."

Hannah reached over and touched Glen's arm, giving it a little squeeze. "We do work well together," she agreed, smiling.

Glen put his hand on hers. "You said something after your last regression as Kao Si that may be a good lead. You said that the place where Yin Ji and Chen Jiang made their puppets reminded you of Milwood Leather."

"Right, the place where Stuart works."

"I imagine that factory has tanning equipment and also machines that can sew leather, thick or thin. Making leather from human flesh isn't something you want your neighbors to know you're doing. Having access to a leather company could solve that problem."

Hannah was taken aback by Glen's implication. Her first response was to defend her friend. "Stuart loved Jamie. He couldn't have been involved in something like that."

"I'm not saying it was him, but it makes sense that somebody from that company is. The thing I don't understand is what they get from those human icons."

"Ratinam used them for his ritual. If Dr. Saffell is behind all this, then he's got to be using them, too."

"Still, it seems as if there would be something more. Human flesh and religious rituals—the combination has to be powerful to someone who knows what he's doing."

"There he is," Hannah told Glen. Troy was wheeling a well-laden cart out of the store.

They were too far away to tell what he'd bought as he unloaded the brown paper bags into his trunk, but she could see he had a gallon of milk.

Hannah waited for Troy to get in his car and start to drive off before she turned her ignition key. She moved out of her spot, but kept her distance in case he had trouble pulling out on to River Road. She didn't want to come up on his tail and have him recognize them. As soon as he left the parking lot, she followed.

"You're good at this," Glen said.

Hannah smiled, glad he'd noticed. "You can call me good after we've followed Troy the entire way without being noticed."

In less than ten minutes, Troy pulled into a driveway next to a gray, two story house on Valley Street. She'd seen this house many times in the past, but had never associated Troy with it.

Glen and Hannah drove past, found a place a short distance up the road, and parked the car. They crossed the street to walk on the sidewalk, walking slowly, two people out for nothing more sinister than a stroll.

They watched Troy take his groceries out of his car and bring them into the back of the house.

"We better go back to the car before he notices us," Glen told Hannah.

"We can't just drive off. We can't afford to lose him."

"The only way that will happen is if he sees us. We need to make a plan before we do anything."

Hannah agreed and they walked back to her car. They didn't want to drive past Troy, so they went the long way around to get to a little restaurant on Main where they could sit and talk.

Glen said as they sipped their drinks and waited for their food to arrive, "I doubt Stuart is being held by brute force. They're using Starr to manipulate him. He'll do anything they say as long as they've got her. That's his pattern. He gives in rather than fighting. Even if we could get a message to him he wouldn't pay any attention."

"I don't think Stuart is in that house," Hannah said.

"You don't?"

"They have more control over Stuart if they keep him in the dark about where his daughter is. I think maybe we've stumbled on the place where they're keeping Allison and Starr."

"What makes you think that?"

Hannah explained about a package she thought she'd seen poking out of Troy's grocery bag. "We were a good distance from his car, but I've bought enough of that brand of pad to be fairly certain. I think he's got a woman in there with him and if it's Allison—with Starr—then I'm betting Stuart's somewhere else."

"That makes sense."

Hannah sucked in a breath and decided to go all the way with her theory. "Stuart was Ratinam. We know that. I think Kao Hui might have also shared that soul. So, to me, that says that Stuart is the one they've been after this entire time. I think those boxes he was smuggling might have had some important things inside them, but they were also a test. They wanted to see how they could best manipulate him, and they discovered his weakness is his family."

Glen nodded, then added, "Now that Jamie is gone, Starr is the only one they have. They wouldn't keep her where Stuart could snatch her and run off. They'd lose everything if he did that."

"Yes, I think that, too."

"There's another piece to this puzzle that I think we aren't giving as much importance as it deserves, though."

"What's that?"

"When Troy passed us earlier he was coming from the direction of Dr. Saffell's."

"You think Stuart's there?

"It's a possibility."

"So do we go for Stuart first or do we wait for Troy to leave and try to get Starr?"

"We should wait a while," Glen said, "then check to see if Troy's car is still in front of his house. Once he's gone we can risk looking closer. I think we need to make sure that Starr and Allison are in there first. Then we need to find Stuart."

CHAPTER FIFTY-NINE

"Are you ready for another regression?" Dr. Saffell asked upon his return.

"That's a question you'll have to answer."

"All right, then, let's do it."

Dr. Saffell unlocked the pantry and took the puppets out, one at a time, and placed them on the carpet in the same positions he'd had them earlier that day. When he was done he stood up straight and looked at Stuart.

"This morning we were able to filter the memories somewhat. Allowing only pleasant thoughts to make their way through is one step toward the level of specificity we need, one move in the right direction. I expect to keep moving that way, understand?"

Stuart nodded.

Dr. Saffell took off his clothes and placed everything on the couch, neatly folded as he had done that morning. He got down on the floor between the icons, but sat up to make one more point. "Try to keep the thoughts human," he said, with no obvious criticism in his tone.

Stuart determined he'd *try* as best he could.

He brought the stones from the table and placed them on Dr. Saffell's body. He glanced at the puppets lying on the carpet beside the man and thought of the way the skins of Jamie and Paige were intermingled with patches of Saffell's.

He fought to control his emotions.

"Here we go," Stuart said, closing his eyes. He drifted up into the cloud where he could feel more of the presence of Ratinam. It was his own soul, so the presence was always inside him, but in the atmosphere of the cloud it was easier to feel it clearly. He felt the pain caused by Ratinam's concern about his son and it matched his own worries about Starr. He took in a deep breath and exhaled slowly as he tried to understand what to do next.

Dr. Saffell's soul was drifting with him. Stuart took the position of guide once more, allowing his physical body to get down on its knees and to move close enough to one of the puppets to touch it. This time, he felt the souls of Jamie and Paige fill him.

What surprised him was the awareness that Jamie and Paige had a shared history. They hadn't been particularly close in this life. He didn't understand what he was sensing, but it seemed as if their souls depended on an enormous root system. They had been like two apples on a tree, appearing independent but thriving on the same background. Perhaps that's why they were both actresses.

Both women conveyed wordlessly that it was important to them for him to understand their relationship, and that there had been a specific reason Dr. Saffell wanted their skin for his icons. Stuart decided to find out what the doctor knew about the souls of Jamie and Paige.

Dr. Saffell's request had been that the memory they accessed should be human. He would judge the success of the regression by how well Stuart could achieve that goal. At the same time, Stuart needed to keep away from the painful memories. He had to access a pleasure that was uniquely human. How would he do that?

"Stick with me," Stuart said. "Feel what I feel."

The souls of Jamie and Paige also heard his words.

"I'm sitting in front of a campfire. The sky is clear and the stars are as bright as I have ever seen them. The night is like an enormous planetarium. I am aware of the sound of insects in the trees, the smell of a nearby brook, and the feel of a slight breeze. Outdoors is much more beautiful than that planetarium could ever be and it is the fire that drives the point home most of all.

"I can feel the heat of the flames. I watch them dance and enjoy their colors: shades of yellow, orange, and even some red and blue. This fire was built for me, to bring me pleasure. I can feel the joy expanding within me as I sit by my friend and watch his father toss another log on the pile. I am not scared of fire. I am in awe."

Stuart's spirit flew into the cloud. Dr. Saffell followed, as did the souls of Jamie and Paige.

What they experienced was not at all what Stuart had anticipated. They were in the memory of something that was not human. He had failed. There was pleasure at first in the memory they were experiencing, although pleasure was the wrong word. What he felt was more a sense of relief. They were lost and trying to hide. They were drawn to the light with an instinctual hope that they would find the right way to go when they reached it. Instead they found intense heat and, before they could turn away, they died.

Stuart woke, shaking with fear. Dr. Saffell also was shaking as he turned to his side and pressed his hand on the ground to sit up.

"I told you to make it human."

"I tried. I don't understand what happened. Animals are afraid of fire. Only people are drawn to it."

"Those were the memories of a moth, damn it! You brought us the thoughts of an insect. How could you screw up so badly?"

"I tried."

"Next time, try harder."

CHAPTER SIXTY

"Here's my plan," Glen said. "We drive by the house to be certain he's still there. When we've passed it, I let you off and you start walking. I'll go back a ways and park the car. If I see him pass, I'll call you on your cell. You can do the same for me. Then I'll pick you up and one of us will sneak around to the back of the building. With luck we'll see some activity, and with a little extra luck we'll find Allison and Starr."

"You don't think you'll look suspicious just sitting in your car?"

"That's why I won't be where he can see me. There's a beauty salon at that intersection. I noticed it when we drove by the first time and was going to use it as a landmark. I'll look like someone waiting for his wife. I could also pretend to read something. Do you have a book in your car?"

"Just the owner's manual."

"That'll do. I just need something to hold in my hands. I'll actually be concentrating on the cars that pass, looking for the gray Volvo."

They finished their meal and paid the bill, then left. When they passed the house, Troy's car was still in the driveway. After Glen let Hannah out, circled, and came back through, Troy was pulling out and turning right. Fortunately, he was aggressive enough to pull out quickly, so Glen ended up following Troy rather than the other way around. When they reached the intersection, Troy turned right and Glen made a left then turned around in the parking lot of some abandoned shops before swinging back to pick Hannah up.

He opened his door and started to step out to allow her to take the driver's seat.

"He's gone?"

"Yes. He drove up River Street like we thought he would. What are you doing?"

She was walking to the passenger side of the car and reaching for that door instead of the driver's.

"You're going to drop me off so I can be the one who sneaks around back."

"It's too risky. You drive. I sneak."

"You're a man. You get caught wandering around someone's back yard and you'll be arrested for peeping. If I get caught, I'll just say I'm selling Avon door to door."

"That's the dumbest thing you've said since I met you." But he got back in on the driver's side and drove to the next driveway to turn the car around.

Glen moved to the side of the road when he reached the house, rather than pulling into the driveway, hoping there'd be less chance someone might hear the car if he stayed out by the street.

"Wait here," Hannah told him as she got out.

He turned off the key as she walked toward the back of the house. He reached in the glove compartment and found the owner's manual. If someone asked him what he was doing he could say they were having car trouble and Hannah was at the house looking for help. But if a police officer stopped to find out what was going on he'd ask Glen to try to start the car, and his excuse would fall flat.

After a few minutes, Hannah returned.

"We're good," Hannah said as she got in. "Allison's there. I had to get close to the window to be certain, but I'm sure she didn't notice me."

Glen started the car and drove down the road toward town.

"I didn't see Starr, but they had some kid's things in the back, a wagon and a set of big plastic blocks. They must be keeping her in that house, but it looks as if they're treating her well."

"Considering they murdered her mother."

"Yeah," Hannah agreed. "Considering that."

They continued on in the direction Troy had gone, toward Dr. Saffell's home.

"Hope our luck holds," Glen said.

"I wish you hadn't said that. You'll jinx us."

Glen smiled and Hannah smiled back, but she wasn't kidding. "Luck has a momentum of its own and a few wrong words can change everything. I suppose it's got something to do with the mindset of the people who listen to the words, but that doesn't matter. What's important is that our luck can turn if we aren't careful."

Glen thought she was overreacting to what he considered an innocent comment, but he decided not to argue. "You're right," he told her. "I'll watch what I say."

By the time they reached the street where Dr. Saffell's house was, it was after five o'clock. The sun was low in the sky and the shadows were long. They had only a couple of hours of daylight left. The plan was for him to watch the house from the woods then to call Hannah on her cell if someone left the house, someone who needed to be followed. If that happened, Glen would then look for signs of Stuart while Hannah tailed the car.

Glen began to worry about Hannah after he had been staring at the empty house for close to a half hour. He pulled out his cell and called her.

"Are you all right? I can wait back here all night if I have to, but somebody in a passing car might stop to see what you're up to. We've been lucky no one's stopped yet."

"You call this lucky?"

"I forgot. You think I jinxed us. Sometimes I can't tell if you're kidding or not."

"What do you want me to do?"

"Drive a ways toward town and pick a new spot to park. You do that every half hour or so and I think you'll be okay. Anyone leaving Saffell's house is probably going to go that way, so you'll be able to pick up and tail them. I'll call you when anyone leaves. Just don't count on getting that call anytime soon."

After another half hour of hanging in the woods, Glen was getting restless. He decided to circle the building in hope of seeing something useful through one of the back windows.

He left the shelter of the trees then crouched down as he hurried to the near end of the house. About halfway to his destination, he slowed his pace and stood upright, having realized that bending over and moving quickly did nothing other than make him appear suspicious. He drew in a breath then continued walking around the house.

Glen counted twelve windows facing away from the road. Seven were on the second story, but he could get to the others. He went to the first window and peered into the den where Allison had played the piano on the night of the cast party. Nobody was in the room.

The next window also looked in on the den. The third was a kitchen window. That room was empty as well.

Glen tried the back door when he came to it. Locked. But getting inside wasn't part of his plan.

He had a feeling the next window might be in a bathroom, but when he tried to peer in he found his view blocked. Sure that since the shade was drawn tight anyone inside would have turned the light on, he moved on again.

The next two windows looked in on a bedroom. He'd seen this room on the night of the party; nothing appeared to have changed. The bed was large, with tall posts. There was a low, wide bureau and a tall, narrow one. There was a sizeable mirror over the wide bureau. He could see his reflection in its surface.

The last window also looked into the bedroom. He started toward the front of the building.

Looking in the front windows was more dangerous, he knew, because a car could arrive at any time. Still, he wanted to be sure there wasn't anything he'd missed. He passed all the windows, looking in quickly. No sign of Stuart.

He called Hannah. "I'm not finding anything here. Can you drive back to the end of the street to pick me up? I'll walk out."

"I might as well drive down to meet you," she said. "People are noticing me out here."

"Did anyone talk to you?"

"Nobody stopped, but I've been getting some strange looks."

"Don't be disappointed," she told him as she drove out of the neighborhood. "Even if we didn't find Stuart, we did find Starr. Do you think we need to concentrate on that house?"

"I still think Dr. Saffell's involved. I'm certain Troy was coming from Saffell's house when we saw him. I just think we picked the wrong day."

"We can try again tomorrow, but you can't park and wait. You'll have to keep moving after you drop me off."

"But that will make it almost impossible for me to follow anyone leaving the house."

"Let's go home. We'll see if we can come up with a better plan."

"You just called my apartment home. Did you mean that?"

CHAPTER SIXTY-ONE

"This time, pay more attention to your spirit guides," Dr. Saffell ordered Stuart. "I have no desire to be led again into the awareness of a moth."

"You sure you don't need rest?"

"I'll be fine, if you can find a memory that is human. The spirit guides know how important that is. Their souls go back for thousands of years and they've always been together. Put your trust in them."

He got down on his knees again and touched the closest icon, feeling the leather and the power.

He closed his eyes and swirled up into the cloud once again. Paige and Jaime waited. When he reached them, their joint thought came to him: he was to steer Dr. Saffell toward something painful. They wanted him to do it by dwelling on a memory of his own. Stuart was sure that was what Jamie and Paige wanted, however contrary it might be to Dr. Saffell's instructions.

He cast back in his this-life memories until he found what he was looking for: a memory, a possibility so unthinkable he'd walled it off, locked it away. There was a possibility Starr wasn't his child, that Jaime had been unfaithful.

Yes, he had hit on the place where his pain was most intense. He didn't have enough faith in his love for his daughter to believe he could get beyond learning that he wasn't her biological father.

That will do, Jaime's soul thought to him.

He had revealed his most painful secret to the soul of the woman whose actions had inflicted it on him.

Turn your force on Saffell, came from Paige. *Let him feel what you're feeling*.

Stuart spun around in the cloud and flung his spirit toward the soul of the doctor, forcing the pain on Saffell, knowing that it would cause the doctor's own feelings to swirl up inside his spirit.

While Dr. Saffell's soul held memories from countless lives, the strongest came from the life he had led thousands of years earlier in ancient China as Emperor Ming of Luoyang. It was during that time that he had first encountered the souls of Jamie and Paige. In that incarnation they had been two powerful monks named She Moteng and Zhu Falan. They had brought sacred Buddhist texts and icons to China from India. During their journey they were drawn to another powerful soul that resided in a girl child named Kao Hui. They had brought her with them to meet Emperor Ming.

Stuart recognized Kao Hui's soul as his own, which explained why

Dr. Saffell was so focused on him, both now and as Ratinam. Their souls had been together as far as Stuart could look back.

There were other souls he could recognize that had traveled with him through all the lives to the present one. In the time of Emperor Ming a man named Chen Jiang had been the soul of Stuart's boss at Milwood Leather, which proved, at least in Stuarts' mind, that the man was involved in everything that had happened to him. Kao Hui's father, Kao Jin, had been the soul of Victor Wood.

You don't have much time, came the next thought from Jamie. *Find what you need to know.*

Stuart went into Dr. Saffell's current life and studied what had happened in the last year. Had the doctor killed Paige and Jamie? If so, that would be a strong image. Nothing. Yet Saffell did have a memory of Stuart's boss reporting on each murder. So he was the one who had killed them and taken their flesh to Milwood, where he could clean and cure their skins quickly.

Stuart needed one more bit of information: where Starr was. He saw a gray, boxy building that he recognized as a house close to downtown Springfield, Troy's home.

Out of the cloud, Paige commanded, *now*!

He spun down on to the carpet of the trailer. He was still on his knees, touching the puppet. Dr. Saffell was lying in front of him. Stuart jumped back as Saffell began to stir. Would he know?

"There was too much pain," Dr. Saffell said as he struggled up into a sitting position, "just like what I went through when you were Ratinam."

"I guess I was concentrating too much on making the experience human."

"Was it? I couldn't tell."

***

Stuart got up shortly after midnight on the night following Dr. Saffell's regressions. He had a chance to save Starr—if he did everything perfectly.

Someone would be monitoring him, but that person wouldn't expect any resistance, since he'd been compliant until now. He had determined there was no guard watching from outside. There probably was a camera, or even more than one, but cameras need light. The outside doors might have alarms on them. The windows could as well, he supposed. All were chances he'd have to take.

Stuart slipped out of his bedroom and into the living room. The windows there would be easier to get out of, as there weren't any bushes blocking the way. He tried the first one, and it moved without resistance.

He went through head first, thankful that the drop wasn't far. He touched the ground with his hands as his feet were leaving the sill and he rolled to ease his landing.

There was a three-quarter moon and isolated few scattered clouds. He was able to see well enough to start walking, except when the clouds blocked the light. Fortunately, those moments were brief.

In about twenty minutes he came out on a road that had some traffic. He arbitrarily turned right. No cars stopped for him, despite his frantic waving, so he had to keep walking. After he had gone for another few minutes he came upon a long split rail fence. Stuart recognized the fence and the fields it bounded; he'd driven this road many times.

He was going in the right direction, but at his current pace it would be morning before he would reach Springfield. There was another option, one he had to take, he decided. He turned around. There were gas stations and diners in the little town of Chester. If he could find one that was open or one that still had an outside, public phone, he'd be able to call Hannah.

***

Hannah knew exactly where the Shell station Stuart had called her from was in Chester.

"I wonder how he escaped," Glen said as they sped along.

"Stuart must have found out something about Starr or he wouldn't have even tried. I hope she's okay. Maybe we should have grabbed her when we had a chance."

"We didn't know and still don't know what Starr's situation is. Besides, you never saw her, just Allison and some toys meant for a child. She could have been dead for days."

"Dead? You think there's a chance of that?" Hannah let the car swerve slightly, but quickly got it back under control.

"You want me to drive?"

"I'll be all right. I know where the Shell station is and I drive faster than you. We have to get there as soon as we can."

"I'm sure she's fine."

"Tell that to Paige. And Jamie."

Neither of them said anything for a few minutes. Finally, Glen commented. "Paige and Jamie were different. Judging by what Moss did in that last regression, I believe he wanted their skins. There have been a lot of horrible things going on, but I don't think Starr is at risk. If she's alive, she's important to them, if only to control Stuart. If she's dead, they have nothing."

Hannah drove up to the gas station where Stuart was waiting. He opened the back door, got in, and gave them an address. "Take me there. That's where they're holding Starr."

"I know the house," Hannah said. "We followed Troy there and saw Allison through a window. But we never saw Starr."

"She's there. At least she is now. They'll move her as soon as they know I left the trailer and they may know already. I think they had the place bugged."

Glen turned in his seat to look at Stuart. "How did you find out where they have her?"

"Jamie guided me into Dr. Saffell's head."

"How could it be Jamie?" Glen asked, before Hannah could say anything.

"Saffell has these thin stick puppets that look like large paper dolls. They're made out of leather from human skin. He's mixed patches of his own flesh with skin he took from Paige and Jamie. Somehow I can feel the spirits of both Paige and Jamie through those puppets. Saffell called them my guides and forced me to communicate with them."

"We know the puppets," Hannah said. "We discovered them during our regressions to Victorian London. They were also in a regression to ancient China. Those spiritual icons have been following our souls through lifetime after lifetime."

"China?"

"Yes, China."

"The Han dynasty," Glen added.

"When Jamie led me into Dr. Saffell's thoughts I learned that the souls of the people who were behind the murders and the kidnapping have been traveling with him for thousands of years, along with the souls of Jamie and Paige. All this seemed to start during an incarnation in China. I don't know what dynasty it was, but the emperor's name was Ming."

Glen nodded knowingly. "Ming was an emperor during the Han dynasty."

"Whose souls are you talking about?" Hannah asked.

"Dr. Saffell has the soul of Emperor Ming. That one was easy to remember. The others I'm not so sure about. The names are foreign to me and that makes them hard to remember. I know this though, my boss was one. He's always been a part of this. That's why he pushed me into it. All the things that have happened are part of the plan and I'm at the center of it all."

"What was his name when he was in China?" she asked.

"It was something that began with a C-h, like Chin, maybe?" Stuart told her.

"Could it have been Chen? As in Chen Jiang?"

"That sounds right. Why does it matter?"

"Hannah was part of that life, until Chen Jiang killed her," Glen answered.

"The soul of a murderer, which means he's most likely the one who killed Jamie. I should have known," Stuart said.

"Does the name Kao Hui mean anything?" Hannah asked.

"I couldn't forget that one. I was Kao Hui."

"I thought so. You were my daughter."

Only the sound of the tires against the pavement filled the silence after Hannah told Stuart about their relationship in that past life.

***

"We're going to be there in a few minutes and we don't have a plan." Glen said.

Hannah said, "There are windows in the back that look into the kitchen. That's where Allison was when I saw her. There's also a door. I don't know what's on the other side of the house, but I did see a patio door. I didn't dare go any further because I was worried Allison would notice me."

Stuart frowned as he spoke. "I think we're going to have to improvise, since we don't know what doors or windows might be unlocked. Worst case I smash the glass on the patio door. There's got to be a tire iron in the trunk of this car. That will be noisy, but maybe that won't matter. It will be the three of us against the two of them."

"Troy could have a gun," Glen said.

"If we have to break in I'll go in alone," Stuart said. "He won't shoot me. I'm too important to them."

"But he might threaten to shoot Starr."

"He might, but he knows how I'd react."

"Does he?" Hannah asked, thinking how submissive Stuart had been whenever Starr had been threatened in the past.

"The bedrooms are on the second floor," Stuart continued. "When I was in Saffell's head I saw Starr in a room that looked over the backyard. There are only two of those."

"If we can go in quietly, we all go in. If we can't, you go alone. Other than that, we just hope for the best. That's the entire plan?" Glen didn't sound convinced.

"That's it."

***

The first thing Hannah noticed when they arrived at the house was

Troy's Volvo parked in the driveway. She pulled in behind it. The circumstances would have been best if Allison had been alone with Starr, but Hannah hadn't honestly expected such good fortune. At least they knew what they were dealing with.

"First, let's take care of his car," Glen said as he slipped out of the passenger side.

"What?" Hannah asked.

"If it's unlocked, I'll pop the hood and start pulling any cables and hoses I can find. If I can't do that, letting the air out of one or two of his tires will slow him down."

"We'll check the back of the house," Stuart said. "You do what you can with the car. Just don't attract attention from anyone driving by."

Stuart led Hannah around the house where she saw that the wagon and large plastic blocks were still there.

Stuart tested the back door then moved on toward the patio door. Hannah also tried the knob of the back door, even though she knew from Stuart's attempt that it was locked.

Then she glanced at the windows Stuart seemed to be skipping in favor of fussing with the patio door.

"Is it locked?"

Stuart held his finger up to his mouth in a keep quiet gesture. He was wiggling the door, rocking it in its track while repeatedly pulling it to the left and pushing it back to the right. It was locked, but it was an old aluminum door. Perhaps it wasn't secure.

It took him nearly a minute, but the lock finally released. He pushed the door open and went inside. Hannah followed.

Toys were scattered around the room, on the furniture—a brown couch and two matching chairs—and in front of a three story doll house that was taller than Starr. Hannah was amazed. The child had more toys here than she had at home.

Stuart walked out of the room into the hall. Hannah started after him, but stopped as Glen came through the patio door. He glanced around the room quickly before they left together to find Stuart.

There were stairs by the front door. Hannah nudged Glen to draw his attention to Stuart, who had begun to quietly creep up the stairs. Glen grabbed her arm, keeping her from following. He shook his head for emphasis, and she realized he was right. More people increased the risk of discovery.

They waited for what felt like much longer than the few minutes it actually was, and then, when they heard a woman shout, "Troy!" they dashed up the stairs, taking them two at a time.

Hannah made it to the top just in time to see Glen tackle Troy as he came out of his bedroom. Before he could recover, Glen sat on his back.

Allison stood in another open doorway, trying to block Stuart from entering.

"Get out of my way or I'm coming through you," he said.

Hannah copied Glen and ran straight at Allison. She closed her eyes and ducked her head, managing to grab a handful of Allison's hair as she fell to the floor. Allison screamed and fell on top of Hannah.

Hannah kept fighting, slapping, punching, pulling Allison's hair, and ripping her pajamas. She wrestled her way on top of Allison, who wasn't fighting back, just trying to protect her face with her arms. Hannah punched her as hard as she could. She aimed for the face, but hit her in the neck.

Hannah scrambled off Allison and jumped to her feet, delivering a few well-placed kicks before she ran back to the hall to find that Glen had managed to truss Troy with his belt, making it so he was unable to do anything other than lie on the floor. They ran down the stairs and out the door. Stuart was waiting for them in the driver's seat of Hannah's car, with Starr in the front passenger seat. The back door was open for them, and they dove in.

"No need to speed," Glen said after he squirmed to get Hannah out from under him and they both worked their way to sitting positions. "I pulled wires *and* deflated the tires. There's no way they can drive. And after what Hannah did to Allison, that girl won't be following anyone for a long time."

The car was quiet for a few moments until Hannah asked the question everyone was wondering. "What now?"

"I don't know," Stuart said.

"The first few days I was in Vermont I stayed at the Holiday Inn," Glen said. "Go there. It's a public place. We'll be safe. It'll give us a chance to rest and think."

"We need clothes for all of us, including Starr," Hannah said. "Can we make a couple of stops at our homes?"

"Troy can't follow us, but he can call Dr. Saffell," Glen said.

"Or my boss, John Glodek," Stuart added. "He not only killed Jamie and Paige in this life, but in the London life he was the one who killed Mary Ann Nichols and Annie Chapman."

"He was Jack the Ripper?" Hannah was surprised.

"He did anything he was asked to do by Saffell—or Moss, as the man was called back then. He murdered. He cut up bodies. He harvested skin."

Glen interrupted to say, "I think we can pick up some supplies if we hurry. We've got two phones: Hannah's and mine. One of us can stay outside and call in if someone shows up."

They wasted no time in either apartment, going in pairs—Stuart and

Hannah into Stuart's, Glen and Hannah into Hannah's—while the third stayed on lookout. Throwing what they needed into garbage bags they grabbed clothes and bathroom supplies at both places. From Stuart's, Hannah made sure they also took stuffed animals and toys. She thought about all the playthings the little girl had been given at Troy's and wanted to be sure Starr didn't regret being saved.

Stuart also took his own car.

They took two adjacent rooms: one for Hannah and Glen and another for Stuart and Starr. They felt relatively secure, but they parked their cars as far away as they could, just in case.

On the third day of their motel stay, Hannah turned on the TV to watch the morning news and was shocked by the headline story: Murder-Suicide in Springfield.

The news anchor rehashed the murders of Paige Stackman and Jamie Tilley as a prelude to playing up the connection three of the newest victims had with the community theater—all but one. Canadian native Victor Wood had no association at all with the theater.

"Local arts patron James Saffell apparently committed suicide after shooting three people," the news anchor, whom Hannah watched regularly, stated.

"Doctor Saffell was found dead in the home of Troy Allen, one of the murder victims. Mr. Allen, Allison Simpson, and Victor Wood all died of gunshot wounds to their heads. Police believe Saffell turned the gun on himself after killing the others. Troy Allen and Allison Simpson had recently appeared in a local production of August Strindberg's *Miss Julie* along with Jamie Tilley, the victim of another recent murder. Authorities are investigating possible connections."

Hannah was giddy. The man who had murdered Paige and Jamie had a bullet in his head; the people who had kidnapped Starr couldn't try to take her again. They were all dead. Every person who had threatened them was gone.

Except Stuart had just told them there *was* one more person involved: his boss.

She reached for the motel phone to call the next room. She wanted to be sure Stuart had his TV on, picturing his joy at the news.

But Glen touched her hand, stopping her attempt to dial. "This isn't over. Saffell's retreated, but he hasn't surrendered."

CHAPTER SIXTY-TWO

"We're okay, right?" Stuart asked. There was hope in his voice. "I mean for now. Starr can live without looking over her shoulder, can't she?"

"She can live out her life without fear, and so can you, but only this life. Saffell will be back with a different name and a different face, but with the same purpose."

"What about Allison and Troy?" Hannah asked.

"They'll be back as well, to work with whoever Saffell is. That's how this will continue, life after life after life, until either Saffell gets what he's after or we put a stop to it."

"There has to be something we can do or you wouldn't be telling us this, not now and here." Stuart glanced over at his daughter.

Glen said, "Saffell is born to each life with memories of his past existences. Without those memories, not only would he not be able to find the souls he needs, he wouldn't even have a reason to look. The secret is in the leather puppets. They are powerful, spiritual icons and the connection between his lives. He's found a way to mix his own soul with two ancient souls that were once the monks Zhu Falan and She Moteng, the ones you saw in your regression. Each time he's born those souls cry out to him. They reawaken his memories. They do what he needs most. They helped him find the soul of Kao Hui in Ratinam and again in Stuart."

Stuart nodded; the look on his face one of understanding rather than surprise.

"I think you know this part," Glen said to him. "You're his connection to the center of life. In each incarnation he can take advantage of the fact that he knows how powerful you are while you are completely in the dark. He depends on your ignorance to control you. Once you understand who you are, he loses the upper hand."

"There's one flaw in all of this," Stuart said. "Jamie was the one who told me how to use pain to get into Saffell's thoughts without his knowledge. If her soul and Paige's soul are always there, won't they always protect me?"

"They'll always try. Saffell's hope is that in one of the incarnations you won't trust Jamie's soul enough to follow her."

"But he told me to follow her. He was very specific. He said, 'depend on your guides.' And he didn't have to. Jamie was my wife. I always trusted her."

"Excuse me for saying so, but your marriage had some issues. Dr. Saffell hoped to exploit those. When that didn't work, he retreated. Like I said, he will be back in another life, ready to try again."

"How do we stop him?" Hannah asked.

"We have to destroy the puppets."

"First we drop Hannah and Starr off at my place."

"Why me? I proved my worth at the last house we broke into," Hannah protested.

"You did," Glen told her. "But Stuart has to come. He's the only one who knows where the trailer is. Someone has to stay with Starr."

"What about you?"

"Starr doesn't know me as well as she knows you."

"She knows you well enough, but I'll do whatever you need me to do."

***

After dropping Starr and Hannah off, Glen drove while Stuart rode shotgun and gave directions. Glen was impressed with how well Stuart remembered the way, given that he had walked in the opposite direction after his escape.

When they arrived at the trailer Stuart said, "The first time I was here I was too worried about Starr to pay much attention. And the last time I was here the sky was dark. Things are different from the way I remember. The trailer is brown, but for some reason I remembered it as a lighter color. And I didn't notice the shrubs under the living room window."

"You're sure this is the right place?"

"I spent a lot of time looking out the window and this is what I saw." Stuart gestured at the trees across the road. "Besides, this is the only mobile home in the area."

"My gut feeling is we won't find Glodek," Glen said. "But we need to be careful. The only reason Saffell would have for leaving him alive is to protect the icons."

"Nobody in there," Stuart said. He picked up a stone that was about the size of his fist, walked to the front door, and smashed one of the window panes.

"Not the careful type, are you?"

"I've been careful way too long."

Stuart reached through the pane and turned the inside knob. Glen followed Stuart to the kitchen and watched him open the pantry. It was empty.

"The puppets are gone."

"I thought they would be," Glen said. "Do you see anything unusual, anything that might give us an idea where they've been hidden?"

Stuart began opening drawers and cabinets. He even looked in the oven. Meanwhile Glen went into one of the bedrooms and began to go through the bureau drawers. After a minute or so, Stuart came into the room.

"It doesn't appear that anything was taken other than the puppets. Have you got any idea what kind of clues we're looking for?"

"No. They have to reach out to Saffell when he's reborn. That could be hundreds of years from now. They'd have to be put in a place where they can be safe for a long time."

"Hundreds of years, you say?" Stuart said. "This state's good at preserving our history, but that's a long time. Most of the homes around here will be gone by then. There's a national park in Woodstock that might still be around, though. It's the home of a conservationist who was related to the Rockefeller family somehow. Someone could sneak into the woods up there and bury them. They'd have to be preserved somehow, vacuum packed in plastic maybe, like a wedding gown."

"Preserving the icons makes sense," Glen responded, "but Saffell had money. I can't see him sneaking onto public land to dig a hole when he could buy land and set up a trust to take care of it. And he could use one of those steel time capsules the school kids use to hang on to letters they've written to their adult selves, the ones they plan to read thirty years in the future. A capsule would be more secure than a plastic bag."

"But wouldn't there be a paper trail if Saffell set up a trust?"

"Maybe there is."

"We're going to have to search his house, then. I don't think he'd leave anything that important here," Stuart said.

"Let's look anyway, and then we'll see."

Stuart and Glen explored the trailer, but didn't find as much as a receipt from a gas station, much less important papers. They needed to move on.

"You were right," Glen told Stuart.

"About this place being a dead end or about needing to go to Saffell's home?"

"Both, I suppose. Let's give the place a quick once over, just to be sure we haven't left any signs we were here." Glen paused for a moment then added, "other than the broken window."

CHAPTER SIXTY-THREE

"You must be glad to be home," Hannah told Starr. "Those toys you had at Dr. Saffell's were nice, but these are special. Why don't you introduce me to some?"

They were in Starr's bedroom, looking in her toy box, a pine chest with a flip top that was light enough for Starr to open on her own. She pulled out a stuffed turtle. It was similar to one Hannah remembered from her own childhood.

"This is Shell," Starr said, holding the turtle above her head.

"He's a pretty one."

"Shell's a girl."

"Sorry. I should have known. Does her nose squeak?"

"No."

Hannah reached over and pinched the soft, long head that stuck out of Shell's pillow like body. It had a squeaker in it, just as she'd thought it would. Starr didn't seem to mind that Hannah had just proven her wrong. Hannah smiled, thinking that when Starr said *No,* she actually meant *Let's look at the next toy.*

"This is Monkey," Starr told Hannah, holding up a soft toy about the size of Starr's forearm. Monkey had a brown body with white hands and feet. He also had a feather on the top of his head made from red yarn.

"Pleased to meet you, Monkey."

"He likes you."

"I like him, too."

"This is Cow," Starr said, holding up an Asian baby doll dressed in pink pajamas with green trim. The doll had jet black hair with a pink ribbon in it.

Shell was a turtle and Monkey was clearly named for what he was, so Hannah was surprised that Cow was a little girl rather than a barnyard animal.

"Does Cow say Moo?"

"No."

"Does Cow give milk?"

"No, silly, Cow is a girl."

"I see that and a very pretty girl."

"Cow is my friend. She makes puppets."

"Puppets?" Hannah asked, catching her breath slightly. *Cow or Kao?* She'd heard children were closer to their past lives than adults were, but she didn't want to jump to conclusions. "What kind of puppets?"

"They have shadows," Starr told her.

Shadows? Could we have overlooked Starr's connection to all of this because of her age? Maybe, but it's also possible she could have heard something Stuart was discussing and she's just parroting it.

"Tell me more," Hannah said.

"Sometimes Cow is mean."

"Is that so? What does she do?"

"She doesn't let me play with her friends."

"Oh. That *is* wrong. I hate it when my friends don't include me in what they're doing. It makes me feel lonely and that makes me mad. Are you mad?"

"It's okay. These are Cow's make-believe friends."

"I see. I guess that's different, isn't it? Imaginary friends are sometimes hard to share."

"She tells me all about them, but I never met them."

"What are their names?"

"Zoo is one of them. He's quiet. The other is Mountain. He talks *all* the time."

"Those are funny names," Hannah said, thinking as she spoke that Zoo could be Zhu and Starr *could* have gotten Mountain from Moteng, although that was a bit of a stretch.

"You shouldn't say funny," Starr told Hannah. "You could hurt their feelings."

"I'm sorry. Tell me more. What does Mountain talk about?"

"He says he's the leader and Cow has to follow him. I think he's bossy."

"Mountain is a boy?"

"Yes, silly. Zoo and Mountain are both boys."

"Maybe Mountain's bossy because he's a boy. You think so?"

"Yes. Boys can be that way."

"I'd like to play a game with you sometime, Starr," Hannah said. "Would you like that?"

"Maybe."

"It's a game called hypnotism. I think you'll like it."

CHAPTER SIXTY-FOUR

"Be careful this time," Glen told Stuart as he pulled Hannah's car up to the front of Saffell's home. The house was as isolated as the double wide. It seemed Saffell had liked his privacy, which made sense given the activities he had been involved with.

Glen was pleased that the house wasn't cordoned off with police tape. That was, he supposed, because it wasn't the crime scene—just the home of the criminal. The fact that there was no tape nor any police vehicles parked outside didn't assure him that the police wouldn't show up. The amount of publicity the murder/suicide had garnered guaranteed that the authorities were investigating Saffell, and sooner or later, they'd get to his house.

"Let's go around back," Stuart said as he started to circle the house. Glen followed.

They climbed through the first window they tried, which led to the den. It was a noisy entry, but they weren't too concerned, since the house appeared to be empty. Stuart knocked a bi-fold picture frame off a table as he half crawled-half rolled into the house. Neither glass broke, so he was able to put it back in place. Glen glanced at it after he was through the window and saw that the right side was a scene from *Miss Julie*, with Jamie center stage. Paige Stackman was on the left in a scene he thought was from *A Doll's House*.

This was the room where Allison had played the piano during the cast party and the same room Glen had studied from outside just a few days earlier.

"I'll look for an office. You see if there's anything in this room that can help us."

Glen found no information, nothing to tell him where the shadow puppets were hidden. There were books—an interesting collection of history texts, play collections, and mystery novels. There were also two books on Buddhist Meditation: *Transform Your Life* and *Mindfulness in Plain English*. Both had worn covers indicating they'd been read multiple times. He thought they could be a good place to keep a slip of paper that was supposed to be kept secret, so Glen leafed through them, with no result.

When he'd searched the den thoroughly, Glen went to find Stuart in an upstairs office that held a desk, a file cabinet and a couch bracketed by two end tables.

"Have you found anything?" he asked.

"I think the police have been here. I can't even find a checkbook."

"Maybe Saffell didn't keep his records here."

"Or he could have taken the paperwork and hid it before …."

"I suppose that's possible," Glen said. "But I think it's more likely he kept his records someplace less obvious. I assume he made his money by selling artifacts. In each life, he'd recover some of the most valuable pieces he'd hidden in the past and probably replace them with other items he thought would be worth something in a few hundred years. Technically, the items he was selling weren't stolen, but it would seem they were, so he'd have to work through the black market. He wouldn't leave records about those transactions just lying around."

"Then where would he keep them?"

"I don't know, maybe under a floorboard or in a tin he has buried out in the backyard? Where would a spy hide things?"

"He'd choose a place we wouldn't think about," Stuart said. "Which means we could be here for months, randomly searching."

"Let's go back to the den and start over."

They went back to the bookcase Glen had examined earlier. He started to pull a few books out, but changed his mind. He was doing exactly what Stuart had warned against, a random search. There had to be a way to put some sense into their hunt.

The piano was a baby grand. Glen bent over to look underneath. Nothing was taped there. He examined the top, which was up, the small lid prop supporting it. He lifted it but saw nothing except the harp-like guts of a piano. He braced the top with the long prop then played a few notes while watching the mechanism move inside. If there was anything hidden inside he would definitely hear a change in the sound.

Stuart sat on the couch across the room from the piano as Glen moved to examine the rest of the room. "Saffell killed himself and all his associates except for Glodek," he said. "I think we can assume Glodek is alive because it's his responsibility to hide the puppets. So why would Saffell leave a paper trail in this house?"

"I agree," Glen told Stuart. "We're wasting our time here. We need to take another approach."

"Got any ideas?"

"No, but I know someone who probably does. Or maybe I should say I *was* someone who probably does."

"Molly?"

"Saffell's pattern was the same when he was Moss. We can't find anything in our time. We need to hope Ratinam, Molly and Rose were more successful in theirs."

CHAPTER SIXTY-FIVE

"We're not involving her in this," Stuart told Hannah firmly. "Can you imagine how scary a past life regression would be to a five-year-old? It would be like a nightmare, only she'd know it was real. Sometimes this stuff makes *me* feel screwed up."

Glen quickly concurred. "I've never regressed a child for the same reasons. It's true that children are supposed to be closer to their past lives than adults, and I imagine a session with Starr would be extremely productive, but I agree with you. We need to find another way."

"What way?" Hannah asked.

"Regress me again," Stuart suggested. "We haven't begun to discover what Kao Hui knew."

Glen shook his head. "I still believe Molly has more to teach us. Hannah should regress me first. I'll do a session with you when I'm done."

"It's your call," Stuart told him. "Just keep Starr out of this."

***

"I don't believe Moss embalmed Hiram just because it was convenient to do so," Molly told Ratinam and Rose. "He has plenty of money, enough to easily pay a grave robber if all he needed was a body. There has to be a reason Hiram's important."

Ratinam pointed out that the recent murders could have been done by another killer or killers. "We don't know if the other deaths were Mr. Moss's work. The only wound Liz Stride had was a cut on her throat."

"True, but Catherine Eddowes was killed that same night and her body was mutilated. Maybe the murderers were interrupted and had to go on to a second victim."

"You can imagine all sorts of scenarios, but they're meaningless. Nobody knows who was involved."

Molly hated sounding so pessimistic. She fidgeted with her lower lip between her teeth before she spoke again. "We know Hiram's body was stolen. If we can figure out why, we'll be a step closer to understanding Moss."

They were in Molly's stone cottage. Since Ratinam had been staying in a room at Moss's warehouse and Rose lived day to day in lodging houses, it seemed the best choice. There were two beds in separate rooms; both had mattresses filled with horse hair. Ratinam tried them and decided that they were much more comfortable than the hard surface he was used to sleeping on, but he insisted that Rose and Molly have the beds. "I'm used to the floor. I'll sleep in the main room."

Molly had a good supply of potatoes and some bacon, so there was enough food. They talked while they ate. There was only water to drink, but it was cold and clean.

"Do you think it's strange that Hiram was killed by a bear?" Rose asked.

Molly responded first. "He was an animal trainer. His job was dangerous."

"I've been to the bear baitings and I've heard that some of the baiters get killed, but the way Hiram died still makes me wonder."

"A connection is not out of the question," Ratinam said. "There are native tribes in America who believe in animal spirit guides."

Molly knew that Hiram had been an animal trainer for years. Maybe he'd simply become careless. But she recognized that behind Ratinam's suggestion was the idea that religious beliefs from any source could impact the reality of their situation. The puppets made from human skin confirmed his belief to a degree. According to him, they sprang from ancient traditions of China and Turkey.

"It seems more likely that the bear was angry," Molly said. "He'd been abused for years."

"Perhaps you're right."

Rose's frustration was obvious. "Moss is the man who killed Annie to get her skin. I don't see how sitting around a bloody table talking about animal spirits is going to make him pay for what he did."

Molly set down her cup of water. "I wouldn't be surprised if Moss is open to the concept of animal spirit guides only because he appears to be open to everything else. My problem with this is that we seem to be grasping at straws. Hiram died in a bizarre accident, but things like that happen all the time without having anything to do with spirits."

"The puppets are guides," Ratinam said.

"If Moss already has access to a deeper level of life through the puppets, why would he need spirit guides?"

"Maybe he doesn't. Maybe they're fighting him, protecting someone or something," Rose suggested.

"Killing Hiram didn't protect Moss," Molly argued.

Rose turned to Ratinam. "Can't you figure this out? You're the one who has experience with these things."

"It's possible Mr. Moss thinks keeping Hiram around will appease the spirits, or perhaps intimidate them. I can look into that possibility through a session with one of you, but I need to tell you something important. I can't stay in England much longer. My son is being held by Moss's people in India. It won't take long for him to figure out I've betrayed him, so I have to get home to do what I can to free my boy."

"I'm sorry," Molly said.

"My son and I are as caught up in this as you are. When I came here from India I was convinced that I could do whatever it took to protect my child. Now my only hope is my knowledge that this life we're living is not the only one we'll have."

"Then stay here and work with us."

"You could come to India and help me there, but I can't remain here."

Molly's first thought when she heard Ratinam's plan was that India wouldn't work because Moss was in England. But the reasons he needed to be in London — Annie Chapman and the other Ripper victims — were dead. Under these new circumstances there was some logic to the idea that Moss might follow Ratinam.

"I intend to stay here if Moss does and trail after him if he leaves," Molly said.

"Not me," Rose said. "If he leaves I'll just say good riddance and get back to living my life."

"Let's contact Hiram's spirit," Molly said.

"We don't have the stones," Ratinam told her.

"Then try without them."

Ratinam shook his head. "I have no experience working without icons."

"This can be your first time," Molly said.

"Sit in a circle," Ratinam said, giving in, "and we'll see what happens."

They sat on the floor facing each other and they held hands. Séances were popular in London, so Molly knew what was supposed to be done. One of the things she knew was that three people was a good number.

The words Ratinam spoke were what she had expected he would say. "Hiram, we are reaching out to you. We care what happened to you. We welcome you to our lives to offer you comfort. Come among us and let us know you are here."

Nothing.

"Come among us," Ratinam repeated. "Come among us and let us know you are here."

Still nothing.

"Perhaps we should meditate quietly first," Rose suggested.

"All right. Think about Hiram for a while. Reach out to him with your minds."

They continued to hold hands. Ratinam began gently rocking back and forth and soon the two women were mimicking his actions. He made a soft humming sound which Rose started to imitate. Molly, however, remained quiet.

Nothing.

Finally, Ratinam released their hands and stood. "I have spent my life studying ways to tap into the energy of souls. I've brought out the past lives of hundreds and I've served as a spiritual guide to help others feel the force that is beyond our physical presence. But I cannot work this way."

Molly quickly realized what was happening. There had been a successful communication, but between the two of them, her and Ratinam, not with Hiram's spirit. Their time together was over.

CHAPTER SIXTY-SIX

Glen shook his head and sat up. Stuart, who had been standing during the regression, stepped forward.

"Not much there," Glen told him. He turned to include Hannah and added, "I'm not sure what drew me to that point in my history. I suppose it was important because it was the moment when we went our separate ways."

Stuart grimaced.

Hannah said, "Discovering who shared Starr's soul could be the key that leads us to the puppets."

"Or not," Glen said.

Starr had gone to her bedroom, bored with the actions of the adults. Stuart looked toward her room then turned back to Hannah and Glen. "Send me back if you think I can help, but you can't regress her. I won't permit it. She's too young."

***

Kao Hui was wearing a silk-lined robe, by far the most expensive article of clothing the emperor had ever given her. He had been pleased when she told him she intended to wear it to her lessons with Yin Ji.

When Kao Hui arrived Yin Ji said, "You are dressed so beautifully. How does it feel to wear such a robe?"

"It is smooth against my legs and the sleeves are so wide I feel as if I could fly, like a falcon."

Kao Hui was a grown woman who still wanted to hold on to her childhood. She longed to imagine herself as a bird, but couldn't let her mind wander. She had to maintain her dignity. She might have been married by this time, if the emperor hadn't opposed any arrangement.

Yin Ji seemed to understand her thoughts. "The shadow plays are magical because we all can pretend, no matter how old we are. Sometimes what we pretend is closer to the truth than a life without imagination."

Kao Hui was sitting in front of the white cotton screen. The room where Yin Ji was to put on the presentation was lit from a single window, so that the light was cast on the screen. The shadows would be sharp and clean that day. The light was bright enough for the colors of the thin leather to show up with rich hues.

Yin Ji told her that this performance would be important.

"They all are." Kao Hui's words made her sound as if she were disputing what Yin Ji said. That was not her intention. She hoped Yin Ji did not misunderstand. She watched as Yin Ji went behind the screen before either of them could speak again.

As Yin Ji started to sing, Stuart's modern-day consciousness had a different reaction to the shrill sound that Kao Hui found to be beautiful, reinforcing his knowledge that music did not evoke the same response in different eras. He knew, however, that the words were more important than the melody that accompanied them.

Kao Hui wondered what could be so special about this particular presentation. She had been to hundreds of shadow puppet shows. It was the main method Yin Ji used to teach. Kao Hui listened closely as a puppet appeared on the screen. She was impressed with the beauty of its bright colors. She knew Yin Ji held it by its guide sticks, but it seemed to move on its own.

"My spirit will always be with you. I will call out to you through life after life. I will reach for you through emperors and through monks and also through poor and oppressed people. Our souls will always be one."

The words went on, sometimes repeating concepts that Kao Hui had already heard, but bringing new thoughts or emotions. When she was born, Kao Hui left her mother's womb to begin her life in this world. This play made her feel as if she were going back, becoming a part of Kao Si once again. She felt her mother's lips on her forehead and heard the beating of her mother's heart.

Kao Hui's mother's words came to her, exploding in her mind, as Yin Ji continued to sing.

You were born with a connection to the life force. Your strength is why Emperor Ming needs you and why Zhu Falan and She Moteng sought you out when you were a baby. You have no idea how powerful you are, but you will learn. Keep me in your thoughts and I will try to guide you.

There will always be great pressure on you because you are so gifted, but you must learn to resist what is wrong.

From her earliest years, Kao Hui had met with Zhu Falan and She Moteng to study meditation techniques. They had taught her meditation as a method to reach into the essence of life. This was the area of her lessons Emperor Ming took the most interest in.

Yin Ji did not have to sing Kao Si's thoughts on meditation. Those thoughts swirled into Kao Hui's mind like clouds blown by the wind.

You are to offer what you know to the emperor, but never give him everything he asks for. In this game of cat and mouse, you, Kao Hui, will always be the mouse. And the mouse can win if the mouse is careful.

When the performance was over, Yin Ji came out from behind the screen and sat beside her.

Kao Hui eyes filled with tears. "When did my mother die?"

"Less than half a year ago. How did you know?"

"I always knew that my mother would speak with me if it was within her power to do so. Now she speaks to me from a world apart. Could there be any other answer?"

"She speaks, but only you can hear," Yin Ji said. "You were born with a connection to the spirit world that is greater than the skills the most lauded monks have developed after years of meditation."

"I heard what you sang and I listened to my mother's voice in my head, but how do I know what the truth is?"

"Come with me."

Yin Ji took Kao Hui's hand and led her around the screen. The puppet that had been used in the shadow play was lying on a table at the far end of the room.

"This is not simply a part of the shadow plays we perform. This is an icon that is rich with spiritual strength," Yin Ji told Kao Hui. "Do you sense the spirit in this image?"

"My mother?"

"Chen Jiang built this with elements of your mother. Although I could sing her song, only Kao Si could reach out to you and only you could hear. Go on. Touch it. Do you sense the spirit?"

Kao Hui reached out to the leather puppet as Yin Ji continued to speak. "It feels smooth, like a strong silk. Run your fingers across the dyed portions to see if you can feel where the color has been added. Allow your emotions to swell inside of you."

"I know my mother is dead and I feel her presence, but I don't understand how or why."

"Let the rushing thoughts become images. Allow your hand to rest on the puppet. Feel those images surge through your arm, your shoulder, your neck, and finally into your mind. It is a spiritual experience, but it will come to you through your physical body. Remember your lessons with She Moteng. He told you that your spirit was contained in your body and would grow when your body was strengthened. He gave you exercises and explained their benefits."

Kao Hui could see the knife in Chen Jiang's hand as he brought it to her mother's throat. She could feel the sharp, helpless pain of Kao Si's death.

***

"Are you all right?" Hannah asked Stuart. Glen's expression showed the same concern.

"I'm okay."

She was surprised at his lack of emotion.

"I'm going to check on Starr."

"Do *you* think Yin Ji was in on the conspiracy that led to Kao Si's death?" Hannah whispered to Glen after Stuart was out of the room.

"I don't think so," Glen said. "She was Kao Hui's teacher for many years and every indication was that she cared about her."

"Do you think Yin Ji had Starr's soul?"

"Perhaps. We may never know, since, unfortunately, we aren't going to regress her."

"What do we do next?"

"There's a chance we can find out more about Hiram through Molly. Regress me again."

After Glen positioned himself on the blanket, Hannah sat in the chair and repeated the low, chanting words she always used to send him into Molly's memories.

***

Molly was performing in the circus. She was standing on Baraka, who was loping around the ring. Molly hopped off to take a bow while still hanging on to the reins. After acknowledging the applause, Molly remounted and rode out of the tent.

This session had a slightly different feel than the other times Glen had regressed into Molly's memories. Although he understood that he and Molly were the same within their core, during this regression he was getting the sense that he was eavesdropping on Molly's thoughts rather than owning them.

Molly rode Baraka to the stable tent where there were temporary stalls set up to keep the animals separate. She got off Baraka and walked him to his assigned place, then began the process of un-tacking and brushing him down. As she worked, her thoughts wandered back to the embalming of Hiram's body. Her understanding of the process was that it slowed down the degeneration of the body rather than stopping it, even using the newly invented preservative, formaldehyde. So why did Moss risk so much for a little extra time? Hiram had been an animal trainer in life. His soul must have been powerful to control the animals. Could his body still have enough of his soul present to protect others?

Baraka raised his head and perked up his ears. Molly glanced over her shoulder to see who was in the tent with them. There was a boy hoof picking another horse, but he wasn't a stranger.

Her thoughts turned to the last time Molly had talked to Hiram. She'd been discussing her need to ride Baraka more. He'd suggested a jaunt up to Norwich, which was a long distance from London. He had said there was a new cemetery up that way he thought was quite beautiful.

Molly thought it was odd that Hiram had talked about a cemetery such a short time before he died. She wondered if he had some idea of what was about to happen to him. It might not be a bad idea to visit the place called Rosary Cemetery.

***

"Come back. Come out of your memories, Glen."
Hannah's voice brought him up into what seemed like a cloud of dry mist. Then she set him down again.
Glen was still Molly and still in England, five days later.

***

Molly was walking among the graves while Baraka grazed. She had brought a rope along and had tied her horse to a tree with its long length. She'd considered riding the train, but the chance to spend some days alone with her horse was more than she could resist. Lately, Baraka felt like her only friend.

Rose had resumed spending her days at the Old Bull, her evenings walking the streets, and her nights in lodging houses. Ratinam was back in India. Molly hadn't seen either one of them in more than a month.

Through Ratinam, Molly had recovered enough of the artifacts to satisfy her New York boss, at least temporarily, which was important since Mr. Moss and his gang had disappeared. Life had become as peaceful as the Thames on a clear summer afternoon. Like the river, however, Molly's life had the potential for trouble. That potential was what was on her mind as she walked through the aisles of Rosary Cemetery.

Molly stopped at the head stone of an actor. As with many of the grave markers, there was an intricate carving at the top to indicate the deceased's occupation. For him it was the masks of tragedy and comedy. Comedy was facing forward and wore a malevolent grin while tragedy was in profile and had a shocked expression. Molly wondered what carving Hiram would have if he was ever granted a head stone. Animals? The last time Molly had spoken with Hiram was at a *Punch and Judy* show put on by Hu Kang. Ironically, they had stood in front of the same puppet theater that had later been used to carry Hiram's body.

Judy had left Punch with their new baby and, of course, the child started to cry. Punch tried to shush it a couple of times. When that didn't work he began to beat it viciously and finished by throwing the child out of a window. The audience thought this hysterically funny; Molly thought their response was strange.

"Why do people laugh at such brutal behavior?" she had asked Hiram.

"It's the way reality is twisted. The same response applies in my act to elephants standing on their hind legs or dogs riding tricycles. Things are wrong enough to be funny."

The way reality is twisted. If that was the standard for entertainment then Hiram's death was probably the most amusing aspect of his life.

Molly continued to walk through the cemetery until she had read the text on every grave marker in the yard. Hiram wasn't there. Perhaps Mr. Moss would bring his body to Rosary after he was through with it, but she thought it more likely he would dump it in one of the alleys where Rose brought her men.

Molly returned to Baraka and began her long ride back to London.

***

Hannah brought Glen back again, this time all the way to the blanket on the floor of Stuart's apartment. He was stretching his legs and rubbing his arms when Stuart spoke.

"That regression didn't seem to give us anything useful."

Glen felt a little defensive, but before he could say anything Hannah spoke. "It was worth a try," she said.

Glen sat up. "My subconscious led me to that memory. There may be something to it we don't see yet. She spent a long time thinking of Hiram as a performer rather than an animal trainer. She thought his grave should have the masks of comedy and tragedy. There's a message there."

"There could be a clue at the theater. I know Dr. Saffell spent a lot of time there. Maybe he left some personal items, things he didn't want to carry back and forth. You two go look; I'll stay with Starr."

"You never know," Hannah said, but she did not believe their task could ever be that simple.

***

Hannah saw the problem as soon as she pulled on to the street where the theater studio was located. There were about fifteen cars parked outside the building. There was a rehearsal taking place. It was nearly seven thirty, so the cast was probably just getting started.

"Any idea what show they're doing?" Glen asked.

"No. Does it matter?"

"Not really. Just if it's something like *Annie* or *The Sound of Music* the place will be filled with kid actors running everywhere."

"You mean we're going inside?"

"Yes."

"Wouldn't it make sense to come back when it's empty?"

"This way we don't have to break in. If someone asks, we just say we're looking for something that belonged to Jamie."

Glen and Hannah entered the theater through the front door, but turned away from the performance area to look for the office. They'd agreed that was the most likely place for Dr. Saffell to have left any personal items. If they found nothing there they'd check the costume area and the shop.

They could hear the cast working on a song. It was *Lily's Eyes* from *The Secret Garden*, a duet. It was possible the music director, pianist, and two male leads were the only people rehearsing at this time. It was also possible there were other actors in the theater who would be sitting around while that song was being worked. If so, they could soon be coming out of the theater to use the bathrooms or grab a drink from the refreshment area.

"Let's look in the costume room first," Hannah suggested. She was concerned they might be noticed if the actors came their way, since the office was open to the hall.

"Where is it?" Glen asked.

"Over here."

They searched through the narrow aisles of old men's suits and women's dresses. There seemed to be an abundance of clothing from the early twentieth century. She felt a little claustrophobic and could tell he did as well.

"If Saffell had a box of personal stuff, this room would probably be the place he'd keep it. The office is too small and the shop is too dusty."

"But he was on the theater board, not an actor. Would he spend much time up here?"

"He might have come here to meet with Allison or Troy. The costume room would be a quiet place to get together without attracting attention."

They looked through three racks of costumes before Hannah found something interesting tucked behind a bookshelf loaded with men's shoes. It was a box holding bottles of alcohol. There were a few half empty bottles of vodka, one Grey Goose and two with *McCormick* labels. Hannah sniffed them. The alcohol was real. Of course the Grey Goose might have been filled with the less expensive McCormick. Hannah couldn't tell the difference.

There were two other bottles in the box, a Johnnie Walker Red scotch and a bottle of wine with a label Hannah had never seen before, Chateau des Charmes Aligote. The wine was the only bottle that hadn't been opened. She pulled the box out and called Glen over to show him her find.

"I thought they might be props for a show with drinking, maybe *Who's Afraid of Virginia Wolfe?*, but it isn't water in those bottles."

Glen put the hard liquor back, but held on to the wine.

"You're taking that with you?"

"Yes. It's a Canadian wine. I want to show it to Stuart."

"There's no reason to think it belongs to Dr. Saffell," she said.

"It could have been Troy's. That doesn't matter."

Hannah thought it could have belonged to lots of people, but she didn't argue. Instead she suggested moving on to the shop.

"Good idea," Glen agreed. "We're not going to find anything else up here."

There were a couple of Styrofoam tombstones that attracted Glen's attention as soon as they stepped into the room where the sets were constructed. They reminded him of the grave markers Molly had been studying.

"They do a 'haunted theater' fund raiser every year around Halloween," Hannah told him. "Those props don't have anything to do with any of the shows either Paige or Jamie were in and they don't have anything to do with the deaths of Dr. Saffell and his friends."

"They're putting on *The Secret Garden*, aren't they? That has to do with death, if I remember right."

Hannah thought for a moment. "*The Secret Garden* is about *dealing* with death, which could have been the reason they chose it."

She started flipping through a stack of paintings leaning against a wall. "Look at this." She pulled a drawing out and held it up for Glen to see. "It's the picture that was hung on the sets of *A Doll's House* and *Miss Julie*. I couldn't recognize it before you brought out my China memories, but I do now. It's the shadow puppet show that Yin Ji put on for Kao Si."

She turned the painting so Glen could see it. "Paige said this art belonged to one of the board members. Yet here it is, in this dusty environment."

"After it was displayed, Saffell apparently didn't care what happened to it."

"Why?"

"He probably was using it to awaken memories, a process he no longer needed."

"Whose memories?"

"Paige's or Jamie's—or maybe Stuart's. Past life memories are spiritual rather than physical. They're not recorded in the folds and grooves of a person's brain the way current life memories are, but establishing a connection to physical memory can bring them out. It's what déjà vu is about and one of the reasons ritual can help the process. Saffell understood how the links work both ways, spurred on by the memories or as a stimulus for them. It's why white horses kept showing up in your dreams, but it's also why the theater group produced two plays set in Victorian times. I'm surprised they didn't do *Madame Butterfly* to establish the Asian connection."

"That's an opera, although there's a musical theater version called *Miss Saigon*."

Glen nodded then moved on to look through some stacked platforms. Hannah slipped the painting back in the pile and resumed her own search.

There were a number of boxes in the room, but they all contained things like ornamental molding or canvas for flats. It was looking as if the shop was going to be a dead end for them, until after Glen decided to take a closer look at the tombstones. They were papier-mâché on frames made from one-by-two lumber, so they were light enough to carry easily.

Glen turned away from the tombstones and stepped to a workbench. "Look at this. There's a stack of photos here." He started shuffling through the pictures.

"Of what?"

"They're all cemetery pictures. The top one has something scribbled on the back. It says *Fourth Concession*."

"They needed photos to make papier-mâché tombstones?"

"Maybe they wanted them to be authentic?"

Glen set the pictures back on the work bench where he had found them.

They left the shop and went back to the office. The file cabinet and the desk were both locked, but Glen was able to look through what was on the bookshelf. None of it seemed to have anything to do with Dr. Saffell.

They left the building without encountering anyone, Glen still carrying the bottle of wine.

When they were back in Hannah's car and driving away from the theater, Hannah asked him to explain the importance of what he had found.

"The wine's from Canada," he said. "I wonder if the cemetery pictures are, too."

Hannah mused that even if the Canadian connection was right, they still had to find the puppets somewhere in the world's second largest country.

CHAPTER SIXTY-SEVEN

After they returned to Stuart's apartment they used his computer to do a search on *Fourth Concession*. The results were so random they didn't give Glen anything he felt he could use. He added Canada to the key words and got back information about a section of Princeton, Ontario. The wine they'd found at the theater shared the Ontario connection since the Chateau des Charmes winery was near Niagara Falls. But the wine was sold all over Canada and Stuart had retrieved the box he'd smuggled at a home in Quebec. Glen changed the word 'Canada' to 'Quebec' and got the hit he thought was the most encouraging. *Fourth concession* was the name of a cemetery near Noyan, Quebec.

Glen discovered a website that listed the names of the people whose remains were interred in that cemetery. Most of the dates of death were from the nineteenth century, and a few of them were of members of the Trepanier family. They could have been Paul's ancestors.

"We've got to go there," Glen said.

"Paul?" Hannah asked.

"I thought his name would come up again, since he was the one who found Paige. His association with Dr. Saffell was apparently more important than we thought. Maybe Glodek wasn't the one left behind to hide the puppets."

"You think Paul intends to bury the puppets in a *cemetery*?"

"They have to be protected until the time when they can call out to Dr. Saffell's soul or the cycle will be broken. If you were Paul and you were looking for a place that would be secure for a hundred years or more …."

"They're leather," Stuart said. "If he just buries them in the ground they'll deteriorate."

"Maybe he intends to protect them somehow, to shrink wrap them or to place them in an airtight casket."

Hannah said, "Yes, we need to go." She then turned to Stuart and asked, "Can somebody watch Starr?"

"My parents."

"Good," Glen said. "Make the arrangements. Hannah and I will go back to her place so we can pack and get a night's sleep. We'll pick you up tomorrow around noon. Don't forget your passports"

***

Glen lay on his back. Hannah was curled up, resting her head on his bare chest. She wiggled about a bit to pull her nightgown down over her legs, managing to do so without lifting her head.

The other times they'd had sex, she'd come to him and had left when they were done. He didn't know what was expected of him, so he squirmed a little to indicate he was getting up. Hannah squeezed him tighter, letting him know she didn't want him to leave.

"Could you pull the covers up?" He was naked and a little cold. She had to sit up to oblige, but she put her head back on his chest when the blanket was over them.

"I hope we're doing the right thing." Hannah was speaking in her softest voice.

Those weren't the words Glen wanted to hear. He thought again of how she was so much younger than he was and felt guilty.

"Do you want me to go back to my room?"

"That's not what I meant. I hope we're doing the right thing to go to Canada. I don't know if the clues we found in the theater are enough."

"It's all we've got."

"Then shouldn't we look more, before we leap?"

"That's why we're going to Canada, to look for more clues."

"I see," Hannah said. "And to answer your question, no, I don't want you to go back to your room. I'll sleep better if I know you're beside me."

Glen thought he'd also sleep better if he was beside her, rather than under her, but he didn't say that. He tried not to think about sleeping and to enjoy the feel of her warm body. Some of Hannah's hair was touching his mouth. He brushed the strand away.

"Things happen in life that aren't easy to explain. That's why there are so many fatalists in the world. I can't accept their belief because I've been in many circumstances I've had to work my way out of. Instead, I think spirit guides, like the souls of Jamie and Paige, lead us in the direction we need to go. I know we can be guided by the souls that care about us and I believe those souls can also cause others to leave signs when it's important for us to know what to do. That's very close to what you did for me during the last regression."

"So you're saying there's more to these clues than what they appear to be on the surface?"

"Yes."

"And we need to go up to Noyan to see what's there?"

"That's right."

"That makes sense," Hannah said. She lifted her head up, kissed Glen one more time, then rolled away into a position better for sleeping.

Glen got up. He grabbed the pajama bottoms and T-shirt he had tossed to the side, pulled them on and got back into Hannah's bed.

"I love you," Hannah whispered as Glen settled in beside her.

His stared at the dark ceiling. He hadn't expected such a jump in their relationship. They were good together, but *love*? Yes, *love*. He seemed to feel the same way. He just hadn't put the word to it yet. He sat up and reached out to Hannah, turning her toward him. Then he kissed her and said, "I love you, too."

***

This trip to Canada had an entirely different feel for Stuart than his last, when he'd been forced to do Dr. Saffell's bidding. This time he was working with Glen and Hannah to keep that man's soul from ever again terrorizing another of his lives. He didn't know if they'd succeed, but it felt good to be trying.

The border guard was the same stocky woman in a black uniform who'd checked his papers on the last trip. She still had the gun on her right hip. If they robbed a grave while they were up in the great white north she might have a reason to use it, but so far they were just three more tourists passing through. The officer checked their passports and signaled them to drive on.

Noyan was ten minutes away from the border and, once there, they had no trouble finding the cemetery. The name, *Fourth Concession*, came from the original designation of the town section the cemetery served, although in this case nothing around the graveyard maintained the old name.

The *Fourth Concession* graveyard turned out to be approximately forty headstones, mostly rectangular slabs. There was no fence surrounding it. Most of the markers were leaning, some of them radically. The grass was overgrown and patchy. There were three thin, scraggly trees growing among the graves. It was cloudy and cool with a slight wind and felt more like autumn than the middle of May.

"What do we look for?" Stuart asked.

Glen studied the grounds. "Signs that one of these graves has been dug recently."

Stuart glanced around the yard then leaned over to examine the closest headstone. "Nobody's been buried here for close to a hundred years, remember?"

"Look at the grass around each grave. Maybe one of them has been dug up and reburied."

There weren't many graves, so it didn't take long. Stuart started at the far end, Hannah at the near, and Glen in the middle. They all came to the same conclusion: nothing had been disturbed for a long while.

"The puppets can't be here," Stuart said.

"They have to be."

Hannah shook her head. "You're putting way too much faith in that stack of pictures back in the theater. Somebody else might have taken those photos. Maybe some volunteer has an ancestor buried here."

Glen knelt by the nearest stone and pointed at the inscription. "Someone else named Trepanier?"

"There's nothing newly buried," Stuart said knowing his frustration was apparent in his voice. "No icons and no John Glodek or Paul Trepanier born within the last hundred years."

Glen stood and looked around. There was a farmhouse at the base of the hill where the cemetery was. That home, the barn, and a shed were the only buildings in the immediate area they could see. There was a road on the other side of that house and a road that intersected it to Glen's right. Behind him and to his left there was nothing other than a pine forest.

"This is an odd cemetery," Hannah said. "It dates back more than a hundred years, but it isn't near a church. I thought all the cemeteries from that era were in churchyards."

Glen frowned. "Maybe there was a church here at one time or maybe this place broke the rules."

"What do we do next? Go back to Vermont?" Stuart asked.

Glen shook his head. "I still believe we're looking in the right place. We should find a place to spend the night."

"Why? We found the cemetery you were after."

"I'd like Hannah to regress me again. Maybe Molly had some thoughts about the cemetery she visited that will help us with this one."

***

They found a hotel on the south side of Noyan with a French name that had the words "4 Saisons" in it. It was a plain, two story building with a canopy over the entrance that looked out of place. Fortunately, there was a bilingual clerk at the front desk, so they had no trouble getting a room with a roll-out cot for Stuart. Hannah was a little anxious about the idea of sleeping with Glen with Stuart in the same room, but she didn't have a choice.

They went out to eat dinner in a small restaurant they had passed when driving from the cemetery to the hotel. Glen checked the wine list, but they didn't carry a *Chateau des Charmes Aligote* like the one they had found in the theater. He bought a cabernet sauvignon from California. It was good, but less symbolic.

Stuart finished a glass of wine before he again brought up the question of what they were doing in Canada. That was still bothering Hannah, as well. There had been three clues that had led them there: the fact that Stuart had been sent up this way to smuggle a package, the bottle of Canadian wine, and the stack of photos. The family name Trepanier on a few of the head stones had made them think they were on the right track, but nobody had dug up the graveyard to bury anyone—or anything—recently.

Glen was still convinced. "I can't give you a clear answer, but I can say there's more. It's a feeling that some of this has happened before."

"Déjà vu?" Hannah asked.

"Not exactly. We know Saffell has hidden the icons many times in preparation for other lives. The process has become a routine, but it's not déjà vu just because we know it's happened before. That would be like saying folding laundry is a déjà vu experience. What I have is the knowledge that this event has happened before and a feeling about the *Fourth Concession Cemetery*. I just haven't been able to put the two together."

"So we're up here trying to chase down your feelings?" Stuart asked.

"If we had a better idea of where to search I wouldn't insist on being here, but we don't. This is the best place we've got."

"This and the places in our heads," Hannah said.

"That's why I need you to send me back into Molly's memories. She saw something and I need to find out what it was."

***

Glen chose the cot for the regression because it was firmer than the bed. Stuart sat and watched as Hannah, also sitting on the double bed, guided Glen back to nineteenth century London.

Glen had instructed Hannah to send him back to Molly's life, but not to try to guide him to a specific time. Instead she was to lead him through questions into a part of Molly that hopefully had some understanding of—or even just a hint of knowledge about—the hiding of the puppets.

Hannah asked, using her soft, chanting voice. "The icons made from the flesh of Annie Chapman and Mary Ann Nichols are hidden. Do you know where they could be? Carry us back into your thoughts. Tell us what you saw. Tell us what you know."

Glen felt himself spinning back into that life. He felt Molly's strength, but he also felt her fear. He was back in the house where Moss and his men were embalming Hiram. Molly, Rose, and Ratinam were watching from the top of the stairway that led down to the basement kitchen.

Glen believed this was the when and where that would tell him what he needed to know. He had to concentrate on everything Molly could see and on her thoughts.

Molly was crouching down so that Ratinam and Rose could see around her. There were a couple of lights on in the basement, gas lights, exactly as Glen remembered it from the last time he was regressed to this event.

He concentrated on what he could see through Molly's peripheral vision, something that hadn't registered with her yet.

The men with Mr. Moss ran through an opening in a corner of the wall that seemed too close to the side of the house to have even a closet on the other side.

It had to be a hidden room.

The three observers walked back to get Baraka from the place in front of The Pavilion where Molly had tied him. Molly was listening to Ratinam explain why Mr. Moss had an interest in harvesting skin from his victims and didn't notice that the lot besides Moss's house was a cemetery. It was small, only ten headstones, so it was hardly noticeable, but it was there and Glen knew how important it was.

"Another cemetery?" Hannah asked after she ended his regression. "Could the one up in Norwich have been a red herring?"

"If so, then Hiram was working with Moss," Stuart said. "Molly's ride to Rosary occurred after this, but their conversation at the *Punch and Judy* show occurred before it."

"Maybe he was forced to work with Moss," Hannah said, "the way you were forced to deliver the boxes. If Moss thought Hiram provided protection from animal spirits, he could have been using Hiram the way he used Ratinam."

Glen swung his legs around and sat on the edge of the cot. "Animal spirits are guides, so I can see the conflict with Moss's desire to use the icons role in the same way. And if Moss believed he needed Hiram to resolve that conflict it would explain why he embalmed him. He must have thought the process would preserve his soul for a time, but didn't want him to become a part of the puppets."

Hannah seemed to like this possibility. "Maybe Hiram was trying to help. Maybe he got the cemetery part right, but the place wrong."

"Maybe, but what's important now is the cemetery we have," Glen told her.

"You're thinking we might have the wrong one."

"I'm thinking the farmhouse next to the cemetery might have a similar setup to the house where Hiram's body was taken."

Glen didn't want to say more than that because he was still suggesting they act on his intuition rather than fact.

CHAPTER SIXTY-EIGHT

Hannah woke just before two in the morning and lay in the hotel bed with her eyes open. Stuart was on the cot a few feet away and Glen was in the bed with her. It was a comforting feeling to be so close to them.

Her regression to her past life as Kao Si and the discovery that Stuart had been her daughter during that incarnation left her with the belief that her relationship with Stuart would always be platonic. With that realization, committing to Glen became simple.

Hannah was a little surprised and disappointed by how easily Stuart had accepted her relationship with Glen, and adapted to the role of the third wheel. She wondered if he had also been affected by what they had been in their former life.

Hannah rolled over to try to get back to sleep. Glen had said he wanted to take a closer look at the farmhouse near the *Fourth Concession Cemetery*. Given what they'd learned from his regression, the next day could be an important one.

***

They parked Hannah's car in the graveyard; to a casual observer, they'd appear to be there to see the historic headstones or possibly to visit the grave of an ancestor. They'd been wandering around the stones for less than an hour when someone arrived at the farm.

The person appeared to be a man, although from their distance even that detail was difficult to ascertain. He arrived on horseback, so he headed toward the barn to stable his horse. Hannah was about to comment on her observation that she didn't see any car or truck on the property when she noticed the color of the man's mount.

"The horse is white." She tried to keep her emotions out of her voice. "What does it mean?" she asked Glen.

"I have no idea."

"It could be a trap," Stuart said, not sounding scared, just cautious.

"Other explanations are possible. Maybe a white horse is part of the ritual to protect the icons."

"Or maybe the man has nothing to do with Saffell's people," Hannah suggested. "Maybe he just likes white horses."

Glen shook his head. "We need to get into that house."

The farm was fenced into multiple fields. Hannah counted five, plus the green area around the farmhouse. A wooded area was behind the property, two roads bordered the front and the right, and the hill they were descending was on the farm's left. There was a retention pond near the barn on the opposite side from a long, narrow shed. The buildings were all freshly painted and the fields were recently mowed.

"There could be somebody else in that house," Hannah told Glen as they walked down the cemetery hill.

"We'll find out soon enough."

"We need to be careful *how* we find out."

"We'll approach him, not attack him."

The man came out of the barn when they were about halfway down the hill. Stuart stopped suddenly.

"What is it?" Hannah asked, reaching out to touch his shoulder.

"It's Glodek."

"I guess we're at the right place," Glen said.

The man looked up at them then ran into the barn.

Stuart and Glen ran after him immediately. Damn it, Hannah thought. They're going to get themselves killed. She ran after them as fast as she could.

Stuart scrambled over the split-rail fence without pausing. Glen slowed down a little, but he also made it over. When Hannah reached the barrier she squeezed through instead of trying to go over.

She was almost to the barn when she heard the first gunshot.

Her first reaction was to rush away from the danger as fast as she could. But she wasn't about to leave her friends.

She could see two entrances to the barn, one opening that was big enough to drive a tractor through and a side door.

The men had all gone in through the large entrance. Hannah decided to try the side door, which opened into a small room filled with odds and ends of tack, two long coils of rope, a couple of feed barrels, a few different types of shovels, a pickax, and three pitchforks. Hannah wanted a weapon. She reached for the pickax, but switched to one of the pitchforks because it was too heavy. She knew a pitchfork wouldn't do much good against a gun, but having it made her feel better.

There was a door on the far side of the room that had to lead into the main part of the barn. She cracked it and carefully peered through. Stuart was lying motionless in the middle of the center aisle that ran the length of the building.

CHAPTER SIXTY-NINE

Hannah took a step back and struggled to catch her breath. Once again her first impulse was to go to her friend, but she could hear Glodek shouting. She went back to the door and looked out again. Glen had gotten the white horse and was holding it by its halter in a way that kept the body of the horse between him and Glodek. Glodek couldn't get a clear shot at Glen without risking the horse, and Glen kept moving.

Glodek was close to Hannah, but she could tell he didn't know she was behind him. He seemed to be fully concentrating on his attempt to shoot Glen without hurting the horse. This was the man who had killed Paige. Hannah knew what she had to do.

She ran through the door and straight at the gunman with all the force of her grief and rage. She pierced his body with the pitchfork as he turned halfway toward her, stabbing him with all four prongs at once. He slumped to the ground, dropping the gun before he could fire it.

Hannah ignored the man she had just killed and ran to Stuart. She fell on her knees by his body and put her ear to his chest. He wasn't breathing and she couldn't hear a heartbeat.

"He's dead," Glen shouted. He sounded excited and relieved.

Hannah's first thought was that Glen was talking about Stuart. But when she looked in his direction she saw him kneeling by Glodek's bleeding body.

So is Stuart, Hannah thought, her mind whirling. She turned back to Stuart and hugged him. Hannah had put her arms around her friend countless times over the years, but this time he was limp. He would never again hug her back.

She felt Glen's arm on her shoulder. "I'm sorry," he said.

"Oh, God," she cried as she buried her face in Stuart's lifeless chest. "You're sorry?" She knew it wasn't Glen's fault, but her emotions were too raw to hold in check.

"I *am* sorry Stuart's gone, but we can still save his future lives. This is almost over. We have to see it through to the end."

She looked up at Glen. He had picked up the gun Glodek had dropped. John Glodek had murdered Paige, Jamie, and now Stuart.

"We've got to get to the house," Glen told her.

Hannah shook her head. "We have to take care of Stuart's body first. He deserves some respect."

"What Stuart deserves is a chance for a better life the next time. He won't get that if the puppets call out to Saffell's soul."

"So we just leave him here, lying next to that monster?" She looked back at Glodek's body.

"We've got to get to the house," Glen repeated.

"Paul could be in there."

"I'll bring the gun."

Hannah thought about Paul as they crossed the yard to enter the farmhouse. If he was in the building, he'd surely have heard the gunshots. Was he waiting for them or had he left while they were in the barn?

They found the front door unlocked. Glen went in and Hannah followed him, surprised and concerned by his lack of caution.

"We need to find the cellar," Glen said.

"We don't even know if this house has one."

"Molly saw one in Moss's house."

"That doesn't make any sense."

"Find it."

They opened every door on the first floor, stepped into each room and peered into every closet, but they couldn't find what Glen was after.

"Maybe there's an outside entrance."

"Be careful," Hannah said, but once again she followed him.

They found the entrance, but it wasn't what Hannah had expected. She thought that in a farmhouse there would be one of those low, angled doors that led straight down. Instead there was a stairway that ran between a concrete wall and the back of the house. At the foot of the stairs, on the right side, was a door. Glen ran down the steps and tried it, but it was locked with a hasp and an old key lock.

"The key might be upstairs in the kitchen," Glen said.

"While you look there I'll go back to the barn. Lots of tools were in that side room; maybe there's a bolt cutter."

She ran around the barn to the outside entrance. It wasn't much longer that way and she didn't want to pass Stuart's body again.

When she was inside she found a workbench near the larger hand tools. She'd been so concerned with grabbing a weapon before that she hadn't noticed the bench. There were cabinet doors on it, so she opened them and found smaller tools. No bolt cutter, but there was a hacksaw. That would take a little longer, but it would do the job.

Hannah grabbed the saw, circled the barn, and ran to the house. When she reached the cellar entrance, she discovered that the door was open and the lock was on the ground with a key hanging in it. Glen was inside. Hannah went in after him.

There was one large room with a concrete floor, an eight foot high ceiling, and panel walls that had been painted recently. There was no furniture and no carpet.

Glen was at the side of the house that was to the left of the door. He had a kitchen knife in his hand that he was using like a crowbar to tear down the wall panels.

"What are you doing?" Hannah yelled.

"These walls are new. I need to find out what's behind them."

He had loosened an end of a panel enough to slip his fingers under it and pulled until it gave way. He ripped the panel off and, just as he had expected, there was something underneath. More accurately, there was a space.

"What's that?"

"A tunnel to the cemetery."

Of course, Hannah thought. Glen saw something similar in Molly's memories during the last regression. But in that life the cemetery was next to the building where they were embalming Hiram. Here, the graves are more than two hundred yards away and all uphill.

Glen continued, "They buried the puppets in a cemetery that hasn't been dug up in a hundred years. Nobody could find them there."

"Unless someone followed this tunnel."

"We knew what to look for because of Molly's memories. The chance of anyone else finding the tunnel would be slim. Even if the house was destroyed, the tunnel would collapse, but the cemetery will still be here. It's worked before. It's the way Moss hid the icons in his lifetime."

Hannah stared at the hole in the wall. The passage was reinforced with plywood, making it seem like a long wooden box. It was sized to accommodate sheets of plywood without them having been cut, so it was large enough to crawl through easily, but nothing like Mr. Moss's walk-in tunnel.

"I saw a flashlight in the kitchen when I was looking for the key. I'll get it."

"See if there are two. I'm going with you."

Glen was about to argue, but he must have seen the determination in her expression because he said, "If that's what you want."

She didn't exactly *want* to crawl through hundreds of yards of an underground tunnel like a garden mole. However, the alternative of pacing around while she waited for Glen to come back would be much worse.

CHAPTER SEVENTY

There were four flashlights in the kitchen so they picked out the best two. Hannah searched until she found a rubber band to tie her hair back, then they went back downstairs to start. They took off their jackets, leaving both of them dressed in jeans with sweatshirts over T-shirts and sneakers, good clothes for the task. The long sleeves would protect their arms and their jeans were thick enough to protect their knees.

Glen went into the floor-level hole first. Hannah followed as soon as he was far enough in to allow her room.

The plywood floor made the crawl easier than Hannah had expected, but it still felt to her as if she was in the passage for hours. She picked up a splinter in her left index finger when she brushed it against one of the small plywood squares that were used to join the large sheets. It hurt, but was more of an annoyance than an injury.

At first she found that Glen's pace was not as quick as what she would have set, but after her arms started to ache and she had trouble keeping up, she was glad he wasn't trying to rush too fast.

Hannah wondered about the tunnel as she crawled through it. Since Dr. Saffell's goal had been to hide the puppets where they wouldn't be found, secrecy was important, so she was sure they hadn't hired a crew to dig it. It must have been a project they were working on for years, telling her that there was always a plan to retreat and try again in another incarnation. Saffell's murder/suicide had taken her and Glen by surprise, but this tunnel offered some explanation of why it had happened so quickly.

Her knees were hurt and her back was sore. It was also getting warm in the confined space. She wished she'd left her sweatshirt back with her jacket.

"How far have we gone?" Hannah asked, speaking loudly because she was talking to the bottom of his feet. As soon as the words had left her mouth she regretted them. It sounded as if she were whining. She didn't want to leave him with that impression. If he could do this, she could, too.

"I don't know," Glen answered, pausing a bit as he turned his head back to speak to her, but turning back as he finished the thought. "This is the furthest I've crawled since before I learned to walk."

They went on for another few minutes without speaking. Hannah reminded herself of the massive set of steps up the slope of Mount Royal leading to St. Joseph's Oratory in Montreal. Sick and injured people of all ages climbed those stairs almost every day, stopping on each step to pray for God's blessing. If they could drag themselves up a mountain, she could crawl through a tunnel, she decided.

"It looks like it's opening up just ahead of me," Glen shouted.

If that was true, it had taken them less time than she had thought it would. It was much easier to keep going now that the end was in sight.

She watched Glen climb out of the tunnel and stand, then she followed him to discover that they were in a small room. There was plywood on the floor and the ceiling, with posts holding that plywood up, but, unlike the tunnel, the walls were dirt.

There were metal racks along two sides of the room with stones stacked on the shelves. Hannah knew those stones were artifacts, selected because Dr. Saffell believed they would either grow in value before his next incarnation or because they were already priceless. The valuable objects were fascinating, but they weren't the reason she and Glen were there.

The only other item in the room was a casket. Glen was staring at it.

Hannah turned her flashlight on it. The casket was oak, neither the most expensive nor the least expensive material. About thirty inches wide and a little less than that in height, it was on casters and had probably rolled through the tunnel without much trouble. She was surprised it wasn't just a plywood box, but maybe there was some advantage to keeping the puppets in something a bit nicer. Maybe the souls knew the difference. Or maybe the wood helped preserve the leather.

"Do we open it?" Hannah asked.

"That's next." Glen walked toward it.

Hannah hoped that all they would find in the casket would be a stack of shadow puppets. But even if her heart told her the possibility existed that the icons were alone, she didn't believe it. When Glen lifted the casket cover she knew she was right. Paul Trepanier lay inside, the puppets spread out over his body.

Glen reached into the casket. "I count six. Two of them seem to be in good shape, but the others are partially deteriorated. I have no idea how old those four are. The newer two must be Paige and Jamie, so we know how recently they were made."

"Paige would have been twenty-two in June."

"That's not what I meant."

"I'm just saying it's a tragedy how young she was. I miss her so much."

Glen never seemed to be jealous of Paige and Hannah was glad about that. She wanted to keep her memories of Paige and was glad Glen wasn't the type to try to compete with a dead lover.

Hannah shined her light on Paul's face, and started at the spooky sight the light created. A corpse was enough to frighten her, anyway, even if this particular dead man deserved his current condition. She wondered if they had embalmed him, the way Moss did with Hiram. Saffell would have wanted him near the icons for as long as possible, to protect the souls; Moss must have wanted the same from Hiram. Of course, Paul couldn't protect these icons from two living people. He was on the wrong side of death to do that.

"Do we destroy the puppets here or take them back with us?" Hannah asked.

"I want to burn them."

They couldn't light a fire in the confined space unless they were prepared to die from smoke inhalation.

"So how do we carry them back? The older ones look as if they'll disintegrate if we touch them."

"I think they're tougher than they look, but we need to be as gentle as possible. We should lift the puppets out of the casket carefully and set them to the side. Then we can dump Paul out on the ground. We'll put the puppets back in the casket to carry them to the farmhouse. The casket is on casters, so it should roll through the tunnel without too much trouble. I'm glad they built a floor."

"Wouldn't it make more sense just to carry the icons?"

"They're fragile—and there are two dead bodies in the barn."

Hannah was horrified. "You plan to use the casket to bring Stuart into this hole and dump him here?"

"I'm sorry. If there was a way I'd take him back to Vermont, but we can't cross the border with a body in our trunk."

"Stuart deserves better."

"We're going to destroy the puppets. That means a better life in the next incarnation. Think of Paige and Jamie as well as Stuart and Star. We're doing this for all of them."

"My God. Starr," Hannah exclaimed. "What's going to happen to her?"

"She's with Stuart's parents. I imagine she'll stay there."

"I should be the one to take care of her."

Glen didn't want to have that conversation. "We can talk this out later. Right now we've got to get Paul out of the casket and the casket out of this tomb."

Paul was hard to lift. Hannah moved to his head, expecting to hold his arms. She was surprised when they wouldn't budge from their carefully folded position across his mid section. After she told Glen, he took the head and she shifted to the feet. He picked Paul up from under his shoulders while she lifted his lower half.

Hannah was happy they'd switched. She wanted to stay as far away from Paul's head as possible. She still believed the head, and the eyes in particular, were the closest body parts to a person's soul, even though the puppets had proven that souls can be in places as unexpected as a person's skin.

Glen counted as they swung the body. On three, they both let go, tossing it face down in the corner furthest away from the tunnel.

"Now we put the icons back in the casket and wheel it through. When we reach the other side we'll look for a good place to start a fire."

CHAPTER SEVENTY-ONE

Finding a place to burn the puppets wasn't difficult. There was a trash barrel near the pond that had been used for burning. Hannah thought it might have been a place to have a fire to warm ice skaters when they were taking breaks. All they needed to do was collect branches from the woods and light them.

The process of burning the puppets was no different from burning any other trash. Glen and Hannah left the casket in the basement of the farmhouse and carried the shadow puppet icons up to the fire where they tossed them in without ceremony. The emotional side of the process was much more complex.

Paige's soul had been in one of those puppets. Hannah stared at the fire, hoping she could see her girlfriend's soul rise. There was a lot of smoke, but it looked like nothing more than the smoke of burning wood. If any of it was spiritual, Hannah couldn't tell.

Over the years Paige's soul had been shared by people of all races and genders and physical abilities. She'd been a Buddhist monk, a Victorian prostitute, the best damn karaoke singer in Vermont, and the love of Hannah's life. Now Paige was free to rest, or perhaps to come back for another go 'round, one that wouldn't be stopped midway by a monster wanting to harvest her flesh. Paige's life had been a gift to Hannah and now she felt she'd repaid the gift the best she could.

Of course, Paige wasn't alone in the fire. Jamie's soul had been in the other new puppet. Mixed in was the skin of Dr. Saffell and perhaps some of the old flesh of his former self, Mr. Moss. That soul was free just as the souls of Jamie and Paige were. The person that soul would be born into would probably conduct him or herself in an evil manner, she knew. But without the power a clear view into the center of life could bring, the destructive capacity of that person's deeds should be limited.

"We're not done yet," Glen said, drawing Hannah out of her thoughts. "We still have two bodies to deal with."

They went into the house to look for something to wrap around the bodies. There was still enough daylight for someone driving by to see them carrying a corpse, so they wanted to make it look like something else. Hannah searched for a throw rug but didn't find one. Glen took down the shower curtain from the upstairs bathroom. That would do.

They split up as they passed Stuart lying on the dirt floor of the barn. Glen gave a wide berth to his body, but Hannah walked right beside him, staring down as she passed. When she looked up she was crying. She tried to stop before Glen noticed, but reminded herself that she had a right and a reason to be crying over Stuart. He had been a good friend.

After Glodek was wrapped in the shower curtain, they raked the area. Some of the bloody dirt could be turned into the ground, but most of it they picked up in a wheel barrow and hauled to a compost pile in back of the barn. When they were done, the area looked clean. Hannah knew that an examination by a forensic team would reveal plenty of evidence, but she hoped that no one would look that closely. Glodek, Stuart, and even Paul would all be missing from the States. There'd be no reason to look for them in Canada.

After they carried Glodek inside and put him in the casket, Hannah expected they'd wheel it back. She was surprised when she saw Glen walking toward the door.

"Where are you going?"

Glen stopped and turned toward her. "We've got to get Stuart's body."

"Can't we wait until after we've taken this one?" When they were carrying Glodek's body in from the barn it had felt inanimate, like a sack of stones. She didn't want Stuart to feel lifeless, even if lifeless is what he was.

"It doesn't make sense to move the bodies one at a time. It's too hard to wheel the casket through the tunnel."

She knew he was right.

"Once we've got them moved, we can toss Glodek anywhere you want. We can position Stuart in the casket and we can have a ceremony, if you think that will help. I'm sorry if my decision feels disrespectful. I'm just trying to be practical. We've got more to do here and the longer we stay the greater the chance someone will see us."

"More?"

"We've got to repair the wall panels, and, before we do that, I think we should mask the tunnel with new cinderblocks. What if someone decides to tear down the facade?"

Hannah nodded to acknowledge her acceptance.

The process of cleaning where Stuart was shot was exactly like what they'd done with the first body, except Hannah cried as they carried her friend. She wanted to drop him and fall on top of him and hug him forever. Instead she kept helping Glen until both corpses were through the tunnel.

Glen dragged John Glodek's body out of the casket and arranged Stuart the way he'd seen them at funerals. He closed the part of the casket top that covered Stuart's legs, but left the other half open so Hannah could speak to him. She sat on the ground, sorting out the words she needed to say.

When Glen was done, Hannah approached the casket and looked down on her friend. Glen shone his flashlight on Stuart's face so she could see him as she leaned over to kiss his lips. Tears were pouring down her cheeks, but she knew she had to say the words that were in her heart. And she had to say them straight to Stuart, as if Glen wasn't there with them.

"It has only been since we discovered our past lives that I have come to understand our relationship. Maybe I was drawn to you because in one of our other lives you were my child. It's impossible to know if that affected us before we were aware of its truth. I only know that I loved you in a way that was unique and beautiful. Now you're gone and I miss you so much it's hard to breathe.

"I have the realization that we will share another life some day and that knowledge is my sole consolation. Yet there are still many years in this incarnation and those years will have an empty place where you should be.

"I don't know where you are or if you can hear what I'm saying. There is something important that I now know with my heart as well as my mind. I know that our souls are forever and that we will see each other again. If there's a lesson from the horror we've been through, this is it: our souls are everlasting."

EPILOGUE

Hannah leaned against the split rail fence, watching Glen move the horse around the riding ring. He was the first person she'd known since Paige who seemed to be able to accomplish everything he set out to do. The clearest evidence that his positive attitude was infectious was the fact that she had finally signed up for a class at the University of Vermont: European History. She hoped to study traveling shows in Victorian London: menageries, maybe freak shows, but definitely circuses.

Glen was standing on the horse's back, another goal he had set for himself. He said if he could do it when he was Molly, he could do it today. He'd ordered a trick saddle as well as the best helmet he could find. Then he returned to Fowler Farm, signed a paper releasing the owner from any legal responsibility, and started to practice. Today he was showing Hannah what he'd accomplished.

Hannah glanced down at the little girl next to her. Starr was the reason Hannah had only signed up for a single course. She planned to take it slow so she could spend as much time as possible with Stuart's daughter. Starr's grandparents didn't mind; in fact, they appreciated the breaks. She could be a little whirlwind.

The police had asked Hannah about Stuart after he was missing for a couple of weeks. She told them Glen and she had been on vacation up in Canada during that time. There was no reason for the officers to think Stuart was with them, since he hadn't told anyone where he was going. They went on looking for him elsewhere.

It was harder keeping her secret from Stuart's parents, who were upset not only with the loss of their son but also with the lack of closure. Perhaps she could have trusted them if the truth had been less emotional and easier to explain.

Glen circled around the ring, passing Starr and Hannah again. Hannah thought how wonderful their relationship had been, but it was time for him to move on.

Glen had been contacted by a man from New Jersey whose daughter believed she had multiple past life experiences having to do with the Lady of the Lake from the King Arthur legend. When Hannah pointed out to Glen that the girl was claiming a connection to a fictional character, he had said, "That's exactly what makes her story interesting."

It was the oddest reason for a break up Hannah could have imagined, but she accepted that Glen needed to get back to his work, and this was an excuse he could use without making her—or himself—feel too bad.

They spent their last evening alone, dropping Starr off with Stuart's parents, before going out to dinner. They enjoyed the meal but decided to skip dessert. Their conversation was of necessity restricted when they were in public and there were many private things Hannah wanted to reminisce about. She had bought a Cabernet Sauvignon that she knew he liked along with some crackers and cheese to add to the party atmosphere. She wanted to make love one last time and was hoping he would feel the same. She wasn't disappointed.

***

Glen flew out the next morning.

"Write me," she said before they separated at the security checkpoint. She wanted to tell him she loved him, but she knew that word could complicate everything, especially as part of a goodbye. She had said it to him once before. He would remember and so would she.

"I won't just write," he told her, his voice cracking as he hugged her close. "I'll call and I'll be back when my next job is over."

Hannah knew not to count on his return, although his words made her feel warm inside. She'd miss him. Her life was better because he had come into it and she knew her future lives would be better as well. But other people were in need of Glen's talents, even if their stories sounded as odd as the woman from New Jersey.

Hannah waited in the airport until she saw Glen's plane on the runway. As she watched him leave, she thought of the most important lesson he'd taught her: there are no permanent goodbyes. The human soul is eternal.

Source Material

The following is a list of the source material I used while writing White Horse Regressions:

- Buddhism and Buddhists in China by Lewis Hodous, D. D. published by Hard Press, 2006
- Ancient China Simplified by Edward Harper Parker, M.A. published by Forgotten Books, 2012
- Portrait of a Killer - Jack the Ripper Case Closed by Patricia Cornwell, published by Berkley Books, 2002
- If You Lived in the Han Dynasty by Cheryl Kirk Noll published in Appleseeds, Oct 2002, Vol. 5 Issue 2
- Vedanta: Death and the art of dying by Pravrajika Brahmaprana (website) http://www.thefreelibrary.com/Vedanta%3a+Death+and+the+Art+of+Dying.-a079589757
- White Horse Temple (Baima Si), Lyong (website) http://www.sacred-destinations.com/china/white-horse-temple.htm
- Buddha Statues in White Horse Temple (website/video) http://www.chinaassistor.com/video.php?f=videoInfo&videoId=76
- London in the Nineteenth Century (website) http://www.uncp.edu/home/rwb/london_19c.html
- Theatres in Victorian London (website) http://www.victorianweb.org/mt/theaters/pva234.html
- Casebook Jack The Ripper (website) http://www.casebook.org/press_reports/woodford_times/880914.html
- Victorian Slang Glossary (website) http://www.tlucretius.net/Sophie/Castle/victorian_slang.html
- Victorian Social History (website) http://www.victorianweb.org/history/sochistov.html
- Birth Control in Nineteenth- Century England (website) - http://www.questia.com/read/104557950/birth-control-in-nineteenth-century-england
- Travelling Menageries (website) http://www.nfa.dept.shef.ac.uk/history/shows/menageries.html
- Cathy's Wee Victorian Fashion page (website) – http://locutus.ucr.edu/~cathy/weev2.html
- Chinese Shadow Puppetry (website) - http://www.travelchinaguide.com/intro/focus/shadow-puppetry.htm
- Shadow Play (website) http://en.wikipedia.org/wiki/Shadow_play

About the Author

White Horse Regressions is the second novel in Steve Lindahl's past life mysteries series. The first, Motherless Soul, is also published by All Things That Matter Press. Steve has published short fiction in Space and Time, The Alaska Quarterly, The Wisconsin Review, Eclipse, Ellipsis and Red Wheelbarrow. He served for five years as an associate editor on the staff of The Crescent Review, a literary magazine he co-founded.

His Theater Arts background has helped nurture a love for intricate characters in complex situations which is evident in his writing. Steve and his wife Toni live and work together outside of Greensboro, North Carolina. They have two adult children, Nicole and Erik.

MOTHERLESS SOUL

Emily Vinson's entire life was impacted by the loss of her mother when she was two years old. At eighty-two, Emily contacts a hypnotist, hoping to draw out hidden memories to discover as much as possible about the short time she spent with the woman who gave her life.

But Glen Wiley teaches her more than she had expected to learn by helping bring out memories of many past lives, including an experience that took place on a smoke-filled battlefield.

All of Emily's lives have had the same tragic outcome: the loss of her mother at a young age. Her soul is caught in what Glen calls "circularity"; the tragedy will occur again and again unless she can break the pattern. To do that, they must revisit her past lives and use what they learn to find the other souls who are part of the circle, using the past to change the future.

The people in Emily's world are as influenced by who they were and what happened to them as they are by the present, making for complicated and fascinating relationships.

Emily's desire to know her mother is realized in intricate and unsettling ways no one could have imagined possible.

***

Lindahl has a remarkable way of exploring many different ideas... layering his work with rich texture that pulls the reader in and keeps the pages turning.
    -Joni Carter, freelance columnist for the *News and Record*

ALL THINGS THAT MATTER PRESS, INC.

FOR MORE INFORMATION ON TITLES AVAILABLE FROM
ALL THINGS THAT MATTER PRESS, GO TO
http://allthingsthatmatterpress.com
or contact us at
allthingsthatmatterpress@gmail.com